YEAR OF THE TIGER

Lisa Brackman has worked as an executive at a major motion picture studio, an issues researcher in a presidential campaign, and as the singer-songwriter & bassist in an LA rock band. She's lived and travelled extensively in China. Brackman is a southern California native and lives in Venice, CA. *Year of the Tiger* is her first novel.

Praise for *Year of the Tiger*:

'Lisa Brackman's novel gets off to a fast start and never lets up . . . Ellie is a perfect spunky heroine . . . Be prepared for a wild ride'

New York Times Book Review

'Takes you deep into the dangerous, complicated heart of modern China, with a tough and appealing heroine'

Jeff Abbott, author of *Fear*

'An electrifying debut . . . The China scenes are fast paced and strikingly atmospheric, and Ellie's backstory is tough, sad, and endearing . . . The book's exotic setting and tough heroine will definitely appeal to fans of John Burdett and Stieg Larsson'

Publisher's Weekly, Starred Review

'A splendid debut novel by a gifted new writer. Her Chinese setting is exotic and chilling, and the characters live and breathe. The story is smart and fast as a sports car. Keep an eye on Brackman'

Jefferson Parker, author of *Black Water*

'A timely and hip debut novel is a thriller with a plucky heroine . . . Brackman sure can write'

Boston Globe

'A remarkable debut'

Seattle Times

'A highly original expat thriller. It's a wild ride – but don't turn the pages too fast. Brackman's evocation of China, funny, frustrating, frightening, sometimes tender, and always real, is worth savoring'

Nicole Mones, author of *Lost in Translation* and *The Last Chinese Chief*

YEAR
OF THE
TIGER

Lisa Brackman

HARPER

Harper
An imprint of HarperCollins*Publishers*
77–85 Fulham Palace Road,
Hammersmith, London W6 8JB

www.harpercollins.co.uk

A Paperback Original 2012
1

First published in the USA in 2010 by Soho Press as *Rock Paper Tiger*

Copyright © Lisa Brackmann 2010

Lisa Brackmann asserts the moral right to
be identified as the author of this work

A catalogue record for this book
is available from the British Library

ISBN: 978-0-00-745319-1

Set in Sabon by Palimpsest Book Production Limited,
Falkirk, Stirlingshire

Printed and bound in Great Britain by
Clays Ltd, St Ives plc

MIX
Paper from
responsible sources

FSC
www.fsc.org

FSC™ C007454

FSC™ is a non-profit international organisation established to promote
the responsible management of the world's forests. Products carrying the
FSC label are independently certified to assure consumers that they come
from forests that are managed to meet the social, economic and
ecological needs of present and future generations,
and other controlled sources.

Find out more about HarperCollins and the environment at
www.harpercollins.co.uk/green

YEAR
OF THE
TIGER

CHAPTER ONE

I'm living in this dump in Haidian Qu, close to Wudaokou, on the twenty-first floor of a decaying high-rise. The grounds are bare; the trees have died; the rubber tiles on the walkways, in their garish pink and yellow, are cracked and curling. The lights have been out in the lobby since I moved in; they never finished the interior walls in the foyers outside the elevator, and the windows are boarded up, so every time I step outside the apartment door I'm in a weird twilight world of bare cement and blue fluorescent light.

The worst thing about the foyer is that I might run into Mrs Hua, who lives next door with her fat spoiled-brat kid. She hates that I'm crashing here, thinks I'm some slutty American who is corrupting China's morals. She's always muttering under her breath, threatening to report me to the Public Security Bureau for all kinds of made-up shit. It's not like I ever did anything to her, and it's not like I'm doing anything wrong, but the last thing I need is the PSB on my ass.

I've got enough problems.

Outside, the afternoon sun filters through a yellow haze. My leg hurts, but I should walk, I tell myself. Get some PT in. The deal I make with myself is, if it gets too bad, I'll take a Percocet; but I only have about a dozen left, so it has to be really bad before I can take one. Today the pain is just a dull throb, like a toothache in my thigh.

I pass the gas tanks off Chengfu Road, these four-story-high giant globes, and I think: one of these days, some guy will get pissed off at his girlfriend, light a couple sticks of dynamite underneath them (since they don't have many guns here, the truly pissed-off tend to vent with explosives and rat poison), a few city blocks and a couple thousand people will get incinerated, and everyone will shrug – oh, well, too bad, but this is China, and shit happens. Department store roofs collapse; chemicals poison rivers; miners suffocate in illegal mines. I walk down this one block nearly every day on my way to work, and there are five sex businesses practically next door to each other, 'teahouses' and 'foot massage parlors,' with girls from the countryside sitting on pink leatherette couches, waiting for some horny migrant worker to come in with enough *renminbi* to fuck his brains out for a while and forget about the shack he's living in and the family he's left behind and the shitty wages he's earning. Hey, why not?

I still like it here, overall.

I guess.

I'm just in this bad mood lately.

So I call Lao Zhang. That's what I do these days when I'm feeling sorry for myself.

'*Wei*?' Lao Zhang has a growly voice, like he's talking himself out of a grunt half the time.

'It's me. Yili.'

That's my Chinese name, Yili. It means 'progressive ideas' or something. Mainly it sounds kind of like Ellie.

'Yili, *ni hao*.'

He sounds distracted, which isn't like him. He's probably working; he almost always is. He's been painting a lot lately. Before that, he mostly did performance pieces, stuff like stripping naked and painting himself red on top of the Drum Tower or steering a reed boat around the Houhai lakes with a life-size statue of Chairman Mao in the prow.

But usually when I call, he sounds like he's glad to hear my voice, no matter what he's doing. Which is one of the reasons I call him when I'm having a bad day.

'Okay, I guess,' I answer. 'I'm not working. Thought I'd see what you were up to.'

'Ah. The usual,' he says.

'Want some company?'

Lao Zhang hesitates.

It's a little weird. I can't think of a time when I've called that he hasn't invited me over. Even times when I don't want to leave my apartment, when I just want to hear a friendly voice, he'll always try and talk me into coming out; and sometimes when I won't, he'll show up at my door a couple hours later with takeout and cold Yanjing beer. He's that kind of person. He works hard, but he likes hanging out too, as long as you don't mind him working part of the time. And I don't. A lot of times I'll sit on the sagging couch in his studio while he paints, listening to my iPhone, drinking beer, surfing on his computer. I like watching him paint too, the way he moves, relaxed but in control. It feels comfortable, him painting, me sitting there.

'Sure,' he finally says. 'Why don't you come over?'

'You sure you're not too busy?'

'No, come over. There's a performance tonight at the Warehouse. Should be fun. Call me when you're close.'

Maybe I shouldn't go, I think, as I swipe my *yikatong* card at the Wudaokou light rail station. Maybe he's seeing somebody else. It's not like we're a couple. Even if it feels like we are one sometimes.

Sure, we hang out. Occasionally fuck. But he could do a lot better than me.

'Lao' means 'old,' but Lao Zhang's not really old. He's maybe thirteen, fourteen years older than I am, around forty. They call him 'Lao' Zhang to distinguish him from the other Zhang, who's barely out of his teens and is therefore 'Xiao' Zhang, also an artist at Mati Village, the northern suburb of Beijing where Lao Zhang lives.

Before I came to China, I'd hear 'suburb' and think tract homes and Wal-Marts. Well, they have Wal-Marts in Beijing and housing tracts – Western-style, split-level, three bedroom, two bath houses with lawns and everything, surrounded by gates and walls. Places with names like 'Orange County' and 'Yosemite Falls,' plus my personal favorite, 'Merlin Champagne Town.'

But Mati Village isn't like that.

Getting to Mati Village is kind of a pain. It's out past the 6th Ring Road, and you can't get all the way there by subway or light rail, even with all the lines they built for the '08 Olympics. From Haidian, I have to take the light rail and transfer to a bus.

4

It's not too crazy a day. The yellow loess dust has been drowning Beijing like some sort of pneumonia in the city's lungs, typical for spring in spite of all those trees the government's planted in Inner Mongolia the last dozen years. The dust storms died down last night, but people still aren't venturing out much. So I score a seat on the bench by the car door, let the train's rhythms rattle my head. I close my eyes and listen to the recorded announcement of the stations, plus that warning to 'watch your belongings and prepare well' if you are planning to exit. All around me, cell phones chime and sing, extra-loud so the people plugged into iPods can still hear them.

The *nongmin* don't have iPods. The migrants from the countryside are easy to spot: tanned, burned faces; bulging nylon net bags with faded stripes; patched cast-off clothes; strange, stiff shoes. But it's the look on their faces that really gives them away. They are so lost. I fit in better here than they do.

Sometimes I want to say to these kids, what are you doing here? You're going to end up living in a shantytown in a refrigerator box, and for what? So you can pick through junked computer parts for gold and copper wire? Do 'foot massage' at some chicken girl joint? Really, you're better off staying home.

Like I'm one to talk. I didn't stay home either.

When I'm about fifteen minutes away from Mati, I try to call Lao Zhang, thinking, maybe I'll see if we can meet at the *jiaozi* place, because I haven't had anything to eat today but a leftover slice of bad Mr Pizza for breakfast.

Instead of a dial tone, I get that stupid China Mobile jingle and the message that I'm out of minutes.

Oh, well. It's not that hard to find Lao Zhang in Mati Village.

First I stop at the *jiaozi* place. It's Lao Zhang's favorite restaurant in Mati. Mine too. The dumplings are excellent, it's cheap as hell, and I've never gotten sick after eating there.

By now it's after six P.M., and the restaurant is packed. I don't even know what it's called, this *jiaozi* place. It's pretty typical: a cement block faced with white tile. For some reason, China went through a couple of decades when just about every small public building was covered in white tile, like it's all a giant bathroom.

The restaurant is a small square room with plastic tables and chairs. There's a fly-specked Beijing Olympics poster on one wall and a little shrine against another – red paper with gold characters stuck on the wall, a gilded Buddha, some incense sticks, and a couple pieces of dusty plastic fruit on a little table. The place reeks of fried dough, boiled meat, and garlic.

Seeing how this is Mati Village, most of the customers are artists, though you also get a few farmers and some of the local business-owners, like the couple who run the gas station. But mostly it's people like 'Sloppy' Song. Sloppy is a tall woman who looks like she's constructed out of wires, with thick black hair that trails down her back in a braid with plaits the size of king snakes. Who knows why she's called 'Sloppy'? Sometimes Chinese people pick the weirdest English names for themselves. I met this one guy who went by 'Motor.' It said something about his essential nature, he told me.

Sloppy's here tonight, sitting at a table, slurping the juice out of her dumpling and waving her Zhonghua cigarette at the woman sitting across from her. I don't know this woman. She looks a little rich for this place – sleek hair and makeup, nice clothes. Must be a collector. Sloppy does assemblage sculpture and collage pieces, and they sell pretty well, even with the economy sucking as much as it does.

'Yili, *ni hao*,' Sloppy calls out, seeing me enter. 'You eating here?'

'No, just looking for Lao Zhang.'

'Haven't seen him. This is Lucy Wu.'

'*Ni hao*, pleased to meet you,' I say, trying to be polite.

Lucy Wu regards me coolly. She's one of these Prada babes – all done up in designer gear, perfectly polished.

'Likewise,' she says. 'You speak Chinese?'

I shrug. 'A little.'

This is halfway between a lie and the truth. After two years, I'm not exactly fluent, but I get around. 'You speak Mandarin like some Beijing street kid,' Lao Zhang told me once, maybe because I've got that Beijing accent, where you stick Rs on the end of everything like a pirate.

'Your Chinese sounds very nice,' she says with that smug, phony courtesy.

She has a southern accent; her consonants are soft, slightly sibilant. Dainty, almost.

'You're too polite.'

'Lucy speaks good English,' Sloppy informs me. 'Not like me.'

'Now *you're* too polite,' says Lucy Wu. 'My English is very poor.'

I kind of doubt that.

'Are you an art collector?' I ask in English.

'Art dealer.' She smiles mischievously. 'Collecting is for wealthier people than I.'

Her English is excellent.

'She has Shanghai gallery,' Sloppy adds.

'Wow, cool,' I say. 'Hey, I'd better go. If you see Lao Zhang, can you tell him I'm looking for him? My phone's dead.'

Lucy Wu sits up a little straighter, then reclines in a perfect, posed angle. 'Lao Zhang? Is that Zhang Jianli?'

Sloppy nods. 'Right.'

Lucy smiles at me, revealing tiny white teeth as perfect as a doll's. 'Jianli and I are old friends.'

'Really?' I say.

'Yes.' She looks me up and down, and I can feel myself blushing, because I know how I must look. 'It's been a while since we've seen each other. I was hoping to catch up with him while I'm here. I've heard wonderful things about his recent work. You know, Jianli hasn't gotten nearly enough recognition as an artist.'

'Maybe that's not so important to Lao Zhang,' Sloppy mutters.

Lucy giggles. 'Impossible! All Chinese artists want fame. Otherwise, how can they get rich?'

She reaches into her tiny beaded bag, pulls out a lacquer card case, and hands me a card in polite fashion, holding it out with both hands. 'When you see him, perhaps you could give him this.'

'Sure.'

What a bitch, I think. Then I tell myself that's not fair. Just because she's tiny, pretty, and perfectly put together, it doesn't mean she's a bitch.

It just means I hate her on principle.

I order some takeout and head to Lao Zhang's place.

Lao Zhang's probably working, I figure, walking down

8

Xingfu Lu, one of the two main streets in Mati Village. When he gets into it, he paints for hours, all day, fueled by countless espressos – he's got his own machine. He forgets to eat sometimes, and I'm kind of proud of myself for thinking of bringing dinner, for doing something nice for him, like a normal person would do. It's been hard for me the last few years, remembering to do stuff like that.

Maybe I'm finally getting better.

As I'm thinking this, I stumble on a pothole in the rutted road. Pain shoots up my leg.

'Fuck!'

I can barely see, it's so dark.

There aren't exactly streetlights in Mati Village, only electric lanterns here and there that swing in any good wind and only work about half the time, strung up on storefronts and power poles. Right now they dim and flicker. There's problems with electricity sometimes. Not so much in central Beijing or Shanghai, but in those 'little' cities you've never heard of, places with a few million people out in the provinces somewhere. And in villages like this, on the fringes of the grid.

But the little market on the corner of Lao Zhang's alley is decorated with tiny Christmas lights.

I buy a couple cold bottles of Yanjing beer (my favorite) and Wahaha water (the label features this year's perky winner of the Mongolian Cow Yogurt Happy Girl contest) and turn down the alley.

Lao Zhang lives in one of the old commune buildings, red brick, covered in some places with red wash, surrounded by a red wall. The entrance to Lao Zhang's compound has two sculptures on either side, so there's no mistaking it. One is a giant fish painted in Day-Glo colors. The other is a big empty Mao jacket. No Mao, just the jacket.

Inside the compound are four houses in a row. Sculptures and art supplies litter the narrow courtyards in between. Lao Zhang shares this place with the sculptor, a novelist who also paints, and a musician/Web designer who's mixing something now, a trance track from the sound of it, all beats and *erhu*. Not too loud. That's good. Some loud noises really get to me.

The front door is locked. Maybe Lao Zhang isn't home. Maybe he's already over at the Warehouse for the show. I use my key and go inside. I'll have a few *jiaozi*, I figure, leave the rest here, and try the Warehouse.

The house is basically a rectangle. You go in the entrance, turn, and there's the main room, with white-washed walls and added skylights, remodeled to give Lao Zhang better light for painting.

The lights are off in the studio, but the computer's on, booted up to the login screen of this online game Lao Zhang likes to play, *The Sword of Ill Repute*. A snatch of music plays, repeats.

'Lao Zhang, *ni zai ma*?' I call out. Are you there? No answer.

To the right is the bedroom, which is mostly taken up by a *kang*, the traditional brick bed you can heat from underneath. Lao Zhang has a futon on top of his. On the left side of the house there's a tiny kitchen, a toilet, and a little utility room with a spare futon where Lao Zhang's friends frequently crash.

Which is where the Uighur is.

'Shit!' I almost drop the takeout on the kitchen floor.

10

Here's this guy stumbling out of the spare room, blinking uncertainly, rubbing his eyes, which suddenly go wide with fear.

'*Ni hao*,' I say uncertainly.

He stands there, one leg twitching, like he could bolt at any moment. He's in his forties, not Chinese, not Han Chinese anyway; his hair is brown, his eyes a light hazel, his face dark and broad with high cheeks – I'm guessing Uighur.

'*Ni hao*,' he finally says.

'I'm Yili,' I stutter, 'a friend of Lao Zhang's. Is he . . .?'

His eyes dart around the room. 'Oh, yes, I am also friend of Lao Zhang's. Hashim.'

'Happy to meet you,' I reply automatically.

I put the food and beer down on the little table by the sink, slowly because I get the feeling this guy startles easily. I can't decide whether I should make small talk or run.

Since I suck at both of these activities, it's a real relief to hear the front door bang and Lao Zhang yell from the living room: 'It's me. I'm back.'

'We're in the kitchen,' I call out.

Lao Zhang is frowning when he comes in. He's a northerner, part Manchu, big for a Chinese guy, and right now his thick shoulders are tense like he's expecting a fight. 'I thought you were going to phone,' he says to me.

'I was – I tried – My phone ran out of minutes, so I just . . .' I point at the table. 'I brought dinner.'

'Thanks.' He gives me a quick one-armed hug, and then everything's normal again.

Almost.

'You met Hashim?'

11

I nod and turn to the Uighur. 'Maybe you'd like some dinner? I brought plenty.'

'Anything without pork?' Lao Zhang asks, grabbing chipped bowls from the metal locker he salvaged from the old commune factory.

'I got mutton, beef, and vegetable.'

'Thank you,' Hashim says, bobbing his head. He's got a lot of gray hair. He starts to reach into his pocket for money.

I wave him off. 'Please don't be so polite.'

Lao Zhang dishes out food, and we all sit around the tiny kitchen table. Lao Zhang shovels *jiaozi* into his mouth in silence. The Uighur stares at his bowl. I try to make small talk.

'So, Hashim. Do you live in Beijing?'

'No, not in Beijing,' he mumbles. 'Just for a visit.'

'Oh. Is this your first time here?'

'Maybe . . . third time?' He smiles weakly and falls silent.

I don't know what to say after that.

'We're going to have to eat fast,' Lao Zhang says. 'I want to get to the Warehouse early. Okay with you?'

'Sure,' I say. I have a few *jiaozi* and some spicy tofu, and then it's time to go.

'Make yourself at home,' Lao Zhang tells Hashim. 'Anything you need, call me. TV's in there if you want to watch.'

'Oh. Thank you, but . . .' Hashim gestures helplessly toward the utility room. 'I think I'm still very tired.'

He looks tired. His hazel eyes are bloodshot, and the flesh around them is sagging and so dark it looks bruised.

'Thank you,' he says to me, bowing his head and

backing toward the utility room. 'Very nice to meet you.'

Chinese is a second language to him. Just like it is to me.

'So, who's the Uighur?' I finally ask Lao Zhang, as we approach the Warehouse.

'Friend of a friend.'

'He's an artist?'

'Writer or something. Needed a place to stay.'

He's not telling me everything, I'm pretty sure. His face is tense; we're walking next to each other, but he feels so separate that we might as well be on different blocks.

A lot of Chinese people don't trust Uighurs, even though they're Chinese citizens. As for the Uighurs, a lot of them aren't crazy about the Chinese.

You're supposed to say 'Han,' not 'Chinese,' when you're talking about the ninety percent of the population that's, well, Chinese; but hardly anyone does.

The Uighur homeland used to be called East Turkestan. China took it over a couple hundred years ago, and now it's 'Xinjiang.' For the last thirty years or so, the Chinese government's been encouraging Han people to 'go west' and settle there.

The government takes a hard line if the Uighurs try to do anything about it.

Since the riots in Urumqi last year, things have only gotten worse. Gangs of Uighurs burned down shops and buses and went after Han Chinese with hammers and pickaxes. So much for the 'Harmonious Society.'

This guy Hashim, though, I can't picture him setting things on fire. He looks like a professor on a bender. A writer or something, like Lao Zhang said. Maybe he's an activist, some intellectual who got in trouble. It doesn't take much for a Uighur to get into trouble in China.

'You should be careful,' I say.

Lao Zhang grins and squeezes my arm. 'I know – those Uighurs, they're all terrorists.'

'Ha ha.'

The other thing that's screwed the Uighurs is that they're Muslims, and you know how that goes in a lot of people's heads.

The Warehouse is at the east end of Mati Village, close to the *jiaozi* place. It's called that because it used to be a warehouse. The building is partitioned into several galleries and one big space, with a café in the corner. The main room has paintings, some sculpture, and, tonight, a band put together by Lao Zhang's courtyard neighbor. The highlight of the evening is the end of a performance piece where this guy has been sealed up in what looks like a concrete block for forty-eight hours. Tonight's the night he's scheduled to break out, and a couple hundred people have gathered to watch.

'I don't get it.'

'Well, you could say it's about self-imprisonment and breaking free from that,' Lao Zhang explains. 'Or breaking free from irrational authority of any kind.'

'I guess.'

'Hey, Lao Zhang, *ni zenmeyang*?' someone asks.

'*Hao, hao*. Painting a lot. You?'

Everyone here seems to know Lao Zhang, which isn't surprising. He's been in the Beijing art scene since it started, when he was a teenager and hung out at the Old Summer

14

Palace, the first artists' village in Communist China. After a couple of years, the cops came in and arrested a lot of the artists, and the village got razed. That happened to a lot of the places where Lao Zhang used to hang out. 'Government doesn't like it when too many people get together,' he told me once.

Finally, Lao Zhang gave up on Beijing proper. '*Tai dade mafan*,' he'd say. Too much hassle. Too expensive. So he led an exodus to Mati Village, a collective farm that had been practically abandoned after the communes broke up. A place where artists who hadn't made it big could live for cheap.

'You think they'll bust you here?' I asked once.

Lao Zhang shrugged. 'Who knows? It lasts as long as it lasts.'

I have to wonder. Because even though Mati Village is pretty far away from Beijing proper, far from the villas and townhouses on Beijing's outer fringes, people still find their way here. Foreigners, art-lovers, journalists.

Me.

And that Prada chick from the *jiaozi* place tonight. Lucy Wu.

'Jianli, it's been a long time.' Lucy Wu smiles and extends her hand coyly in Lao Zhang's general direction, having spotted us hanging out by the café, behind the PA speakers where it's not quite so loud.

'Luxi,' Lao Zhang replies. He takes her hand for a moment; it's dwarfed in his. He stares at her with a look that I can't quite figure out. 'You're well?'

'Very.' She takes a step back, like she's measuring him up. 'I met your friend Yili earlier this evening. Did she tell you?'

15

'Sorry,' I say. 'I forgot.'

Lucy giggles. 'Not to worry. I knew we'd find each other.'

I watch them watching each other, like a couple of circling cats.

'I'm going to get a beer,' I say.

Back in the main room, muffled thuds come from inside the 'concrete' block (I'm pretty sure it's plaster). Cracks appear, then a little chunk falls out, then more pieces, and all of a sudden there's a hole, and you can see this skinny, shirtless man covered in sweat, swinging a sledgehammer against the walls of his prison. The room is flooded with a rank smell, which makes sense, considering the guy's been in the box for a couple of days.

Everybody cheers.

I drink my beer. Grab another. The crowd starts to thin out around me. Show's over, I guess. It's been almost an hour since I've seen Lao Zhang.

I think about looking for him, but something holds me back. Someone, more accurately.

She's got to be an old girlfriend. Except I couldn't tell if he was really happy to see her.

'Sorry.'

It's Lao Zhang, who has appeared next to me, without Lucy Wu.

'How was it?' he asks.

'Okay.'

He rests his hand on my shoulder. But it's not a friendly gesture. I can feel the tension in his hand.

I look behind him and see Lucy Wu, standing over by the entrance to the video gallery, too far away for me to

16

make out her expression, except I can tell she's watching us.

'Let's go,' he says.

We go outside. I start to turn down Heping Street in the direction of Xingfu Road, toward Lao Zhang's house.

'Wait.'

I turn to look at him. The frown from earlier tonight is back. 'It's better if you don't come over tonight,' he says.

I shrug. 'Fine.'

I should've figured. No way I can compete with a Lucy Wu.

'Here.' He digs through his pockets and pulls out some cash. 'Some money. For a taxi.'

I don't take it. 'Why didn't you just tell me not to come?'

'I didn't think . . .' He grimaces, shakes his head. 'I should have. I'm sorry.'

I don't know what to say. I zip up my jacket and wonder where I'm going to find a taxi this time of night in Mati Village. Down by the bus station, I guess.

'Yili . . .' Lao Zhang reaches out his hand, rests it gently but urgently on my arm. 'Don't go home tonight. It's better you go someplace else. Visit some friends or something. Just for tonight.'

That's when everything shifts. I'm not mad any more.

'What's going on?'

'It's complicated.'

'Are you in trouble?'

He hesitates. 'You know how things are here,' he says. 'Anyway, it's not the first time.'

'Can I help?'

17

I don't know why I say it. I'm not even sure that I mean it.

I still can't see his face very well in the dark, but I think I see him smile.

'Maybe later. If you want.'

CHAPTER TWO

There aren't a lot of places I can think of to go in Beijing at one in the morning.

I tell the taxi driver to take me to Says Hu.

It's eleven thirty now, and it'll be dead by the time I get there in an hour and a half; I figure I can hang out, while British John closes up, and decide what to do next.

I forgot it was Karaoke Night.

People come out of the woodwork for this: expats from the Zhongguancun Electronics District, students and teachers from the Haidian universities, ready to get loaded and give us their best rendition of 'You Light Up My Life' or 'Hotel California.'

When I walk through the door, the place is packed, and a rangy Chinese girl with dyed blonde hair is singing 'My Heart Will Go On.'

I almost turn around and leave, but British John has already spotted me. He tops off a pitcher of Qingdao and comes out from behind the bar, beer belly leading his narrow shoulders, face permanently red from too much sun and alcohol.

'Ellie! Good, you're here. Rose didn't show up. Boyfriend crisis. Stupid bint.'

'I'm not here to work.'

'When are you ever?'

'Fuck you,' I mutter. Maybe I'm late sometimes, but I do a good job for British John.

Some days it's hard to leave the apartment, that's all.

I pick up a rag and start wiping down tables.

Says Hu is an expat bar on the second floor of a corner mall next to an apartment complex, above a mobile phone store. It's dark, furnished in cheap plastic-coated wood, with dartboards, British soccer posters, and jerseys on the walls. Old beer funk mixes with that bizarre cleaner they use here in China, the one that smells like acrid, perfumed kerosene.

I work here a few shifts a week. That's plenty.

I don't mean British John's a bad guy. He's not. He's hinted about hiring me to run this place so he can start another business, making me legal and getting me a work visa, which god knows I need.

But doing this?

'And my heart will go on and on!'

I duck behind the bar, pour myself a beer, and swallow a Percocet.

Between pouring drafts and mixing drinks, I think about what happened in Mati Village.

Lao Zhang has to be in some kind of trouble, but what? The central government doesn't care much about what anybody does, as long as they don't challenge the government's authority. Lao Zhang's not political, so far as I know. He doesn't talk about overthrowing the CCP or democracy or freedom of speech. Nothing like that. He talks about living a creative life, about building communities to support

20

that, places that encourage each individual's expression and value their labors – the opposite of the factories and malls and McJobs that treat people like trash and throw them away whenever they feel like it.

Maybe that's close enough to freedom of speech to get him in trouble.

But why am *I* in trouble?

You're a foreigner, you cause problems, usually they just kick you out of China. Which, if I don't get my act together, is going to happen anyway.

He told me not to go home tonight.

Maybe it's not the government, I think. Maybe it's gangsters. Or some local official Lao Zhang pissed off. A back-door deal gone wrong.

And then there's Lucy Wu. Ex-girlfriend? Undercover Public Security Officer?

He should have told me what was going on.

My leg hurts like a motherfucker, even with the Percocet, so I start drinking Guinness, and I end up hanging out in the bar after we close, drinking more Guinness with British John, his Chinese wife Xiaowei, an Australian named Hank, and two Norwegian girls. One of them, the taller of the two who looks like a supermodel, is a bitch. She keeps going on about the evils of American imperialism. 'It was American imperial aggression that created the desire for a Caliphate,' and 'The Taliban was a predictable response to American imperial aggression.'

British John keeps giving me looks, like he thinks I'm going to lose it.

'Hey, we need more music,' Xiaowei pipes up. 'What should I play?'

'You choose, luv,' says British John. 'As long as it's none of that fucking awful Korean pop.'

Xiaowei pouts. She loves Korean pop, which as British John points out, really is fucking awful.

'Reggae!' shouts Hank the Australian.

'It was America's criminal invasion of Iraq,' the Norwegian chick drones on. She's kind of drunk by now, too. 'Everyone involved is a criminal. You know, Falluja, Haditha, Abu Ghraib, these are war crimes . . .'

Hank and the other Norwegian girl, meanwhile, have gone over to the jukebox, draped over each other like partners in a three-legged race. 'Redemption Song' booms over the speakers.

'These soldiers, they killed innocents, and you Americans call them heroes.'

'Why don't you just shut the fuck up?' I finally say. I'm not mad. I'm just tired. 'You Norwegians are sitting on top of all that North Sea oil or you'd be making deals and screwing people like everyone else. Plus, you kill whales.'

Supermodel straightens up. Actually, she looks more like a Viking. All she needs is a spear. 'Norway contributes more percentage of its income to foreign aid than any other country. While you Americans –'

'Oh, it's wrong to kill whales,' Xiaowei says, her eyes filling with tears. 'And dolphins. They are so smart! I think they are smarter than we are.'

'Darts, anyone?' British John asks.

I end up crashing at British John and Xiaowei's place, finally dragging myself off their couch the next day around noon to make my way home.

Of course, I run into Mrs Hua, who is hustling her kid

into their apartment, him clutching an overstuffed, greasy bag of Mickey D's.

'Somebody looking for you,' she hisses, her little raisin eyes glittering in triumph. 'You in some kind of trouble!'

I roll my eyes. 'Yeah, right.'

'Foreigners,' she continues. 'In suits! You in trouble.'

I freeze, but only for a moment.

'Whatever.'

I unlock the door and make my way through the living room, which is cluttered with all kinds of random stuff: books, magazines, dirty clothes, a guitar amp, and a cardboard standup figure of Yao Ming draped with a plastic lei. My roommate Chuckie has the blackout curtains drawn, and I can hardly see a thing, just Yao Ming, the red of his jersey blanched gray by the dark.

Foreigners in suits. It doesn't make sense. How can Lao Zhang be in trouble with foreigners in suits?

Then I think: maybe it's not Lao Zhang they're looking for.

I'm not in trouble, I tell myself. I'm not. All that shit happened a long time ago, and nobody cares about it any more.

'*Cao dan! Zhen ta ma de!*'

'Chuckie? What?'

Chuckie bursts out of his bedroom, greasy hair bristling up in spikes, glasses askew, Bill Gates T-shirt about three sizes too big, knobby knees sticking out beneath dirty gym shorts.

'That fucking bastard stole my seventh-level Qi sword!'

'I'm sorry to hear it,' I say. 'Who stole your sword?'

'Ming Lu, the little shits! I should go bust his damn balls!'

23

I try to picture Chuckie busting much of anything and fail. The reason I have such a good deal renting this apartment is that Chuckie gives me a break in exchange for tutoring him in English conversation. Sometimes I listen to him and think that I'm not really doing my job.

'So . . . Chuckie . . . I don't understand. This sword, I mean, it's not a real sword, is it? It's like . . . it's part of the game, right?'

Chuckie stares at me like I've suddenly grown horns.

'Of *course* it's part of the game!'

'So, um . . . if it's not real, how did Ming Lu steal it?'

Chuckie paces around the dim, dank apartment, which I notice smells like some weird combination of sour beer and cement dust. 'I lend it to him,' he mutters. 'I *trust* him!' He slaps the cardboard Yao Ming for emphasis. 'And that turtle's egg, *jiba* son of a slave girl go and *sell* it!'

I had a lot to drink last night and I'm pretty sleep-deprived, so maybe if I had some coffee I could follow him a little better. Still, he's talking about a virtual sword in an online game. How can I take it seriously?

Chuckie's game is *The Sword of Ill Repute*, the same game Lao Zhang plays. That's how I met Lao Zhang, actually, through Chuckie. Lao Zhang was throwing a party at this space off the 4th Ring Road, and he'd invited his online friends to attend. Chuckie hadn't really wanted to go. He didn't approve of Lao Zhang's gaming style. 'Too peaceful!' he complained. 'He don't like to go on quest, just sit in teahouse and wine shop and drink and chat all the time.'

Me, I was tired of virtual reality and thought an actual party might be fun. I'd thought maybe I was going crazy, sitting in that apartment all the time. I was having a lot of nightmares, not sleeping well, and I needed to get out.

So we went to the party, which was at this place called the Airplane Factory (because it used to be an airplane factory). When we got there, a couple of the artists were doing a piece, throwing dyed red mud at each other and chanting slogans every time they got hit. A DJ was spinning tunes while another artist projected images on the blank white wall: chickens being decapitated and buildings falling down and Mickey Mouse cartoons. At some point, this fairly lame Beijing punk band played, though I had to give them points for attitude.

I wandered around on my own, not talking to anybody, because even though I'd wanted to come, once I got there I felt awkward and nervous, like I couldn't have been more out of place. Eventually I saw Chuckie standing over by this installation piece, a ping-pong table that lit up and made different noises depending on where the ball hit. That's where the beer was, iced for once, in plastic tubs.

Chuckie was talking to this big, stocky guy with a goatee and thick eyebrows, wearing paint-splattered cargo shorts, an ancient Cui Jian T-shirt, and a knit beanie. The guy had just opened a bottle of Yanjing, and instead of drinking from it, he gave it to me, eyebrow half-cocked, grinning. There was something about his smile I liked, something about how it included me, like we were already sharing a joke. 'You're Chuckie's roommate,' he said. 'Chuckie says you're crazy.'

That was Lao Zhang.

Now I'm thinking: talk about a pot/kettle scenario, 'cause here's Chuckie, pacing around the living room, muttering about how some *jiba* ex-friend of his has ripped off his virtual sword.

Chuckie grabs his backpack and heads for the door.

'Hey. Where are you going?'

'Matrix,' Chuckie mumbles.

'Why?'

'Because that's where Ming Lu is.'

'So, what are you going to do?'

'Make him pay.'

'Hey, Chuckie, wait a minute. Just . . . wait.'

He pauses at the door. 'What?'

'You're not going to do anything stupid, are you?'

Chuckie swings his backpack over his shoulder. 'That Qi sword is worth 10,000 *kuai*! I'm going to make him pay me for it!'

'You're kidding.'

Ten thousand yuan is no small sum of money. It's over fourteen hundred dollars. More money than I make in a month. More money than Chuckie makes a month doing his freelance geek gigs, I'm pretty sure. He's a genius with computers, but he's always getting canned for spending too much time online doing things he shouldn't.

'I don't kid about this!' Chuckie yells, wild-eyed. 'I'm going!'

'Hey, Chuckie, wait a minute. *Deng yihuir*,' I repeat in Chinese for emphasis. 'Was there anybody looking for me this morning? Some foreigners? In suits?'

Chuckie pauses by the door and frowns. 'Oh. Some guys came by a couple hours ago. I said you weren't around.'

'What did they want?'

'They didn't say.' He shrugs his backpack onto his other shoulder and opens the door.

'Wait a minute,' I say again. 'What *kind* of guys?'

'I don't know,' Chuckie replies, clearly frustrated. 'Foreigners in suits, like you said.' And he starts to leave.

'Wait, I'll come with you.'

I throw on some fresh clothes, replenish my backpack with clean underwear, which I always do in case I end up crashing somewhere else, which, objectively, happens kind of a lot. Then I grab my passport and retrieve the roll of cash that I've hidden in a balled-up T-shirt tossed in the corner of my tiny closet.

When I come out of my room, Chuckie is pacing in a little circle by the door, looking like he's ready to bolt.

So am I. I don't want to stay in this apartment. Not for another minute.

Matrix is a couple miles away, so we hop on a bus that's so packed, I hardly move when it jerks and squeals and halts – it's like I'm surrounded by human airbags.

Our destination is a couple of blocks from the bus stop, just east of Beida, short for Beijing University. Chuckie's pissed off and walking so fast that I can barely keep up.

'He'll be there,' Chuckie mutters, 'that little penis shit. He's always there right now.'

'You don't say "penis."'

Chuckie looks confused. 'Penis means *jiba*, right?'

'Yeah, but you should say, like, "fucking," or "dickhead." It sounds better.'

We pass the new Tech center covered with LED billboards and the latest weird-shaped mirror glass high-rise that resembles some gargantuan star cruiser squatting on a landing pad; practically everything they've built in Beijing the last ten years looks like part of a set in the latest big-budget science fiction movie.

27

Matrix Game Parlor takes up most of the ground floor of a six-story white-tile storefront that's probably slated for demolition in the near future, since it must have been built way back in the eighties. It's a maze of navy blue walls, computer terminals, and arcade games, and though most of the serious gamers are wearing headsets, a lot of the casual players aren't, so there's this cacophony of cartoon explosions and thumping bass lines and corny synthesized orchestras. Plus everybody's cells are going off all the time with these loud polyphonic ringtones, and nobody talks quietly into their cells; they yell, like they don't trust that the person on the other end will hear them otherwise, and I'm already thinking I want out of here. And even though they've passed laws in China against smoking in public places, *everyone* smokes in this place, so I'm following Chuckie through the maze and this blue smoke haze that's lit up by neon screens and intermittent strobe lights, and I'm starting to cough. I always have a little bronchitis from the pollution here, and I just can't handle the smoke any more.

I used to smoke. Everyone around me did back then. That's what we'd do, me and my buddies, we'd smoke cigarettes and crack jokes to keep each other loose, just laugh at shit, you know? You had to laugh at all the shit sometimes.

Embrace the Suck, we used to say.

'There he is!' Chuckie hisses.

I recognize Ming Lu. He's this short, fat guy shaped more or less like a dumpling with limbs and a head. Right now he's sitting in front of a terminal littered with junk food, using a fancy joystick, probably his own, to manipulate his avatar. I figure he's probably either killing or fucking someone, from the exultant expression on his face.

28

Chuckie grabs Ming Lu's T-shirt by the collar and slaps him upside the head.

Ming Lu whirls around blindly, glasses askew, scattering his shrimp chips.

'What –? Who –?'

'You mother fucking dog's bastard!' Chuckie screams.

As I start to form a mental picture of that scenario, I lose track of the argument entirely. For one thing, the two of them are talking way too fast for me to follow, and Ming Lu has this Sichuan accent that gets pretty thick when he's excited and being slapped around by somebody. For another, I glance over my shoulder and see, dimly through the smoke haze, two guys heading in our direction. Foreign guys in suits.

'I'm sorry, I'm sorry,' Ming Lu is babbling, 'but I *had* to!'

I don't think. I run.

I duck down an aisle, bumping into a couple of giggling teen girls with Go Gaiyuko backpacks. I turn a corner, slipping and sliding past a cluster of Dance Dance Revolution games, and I don't even know why I'm running; I just don't want to get caught.

Up ahead there's a little hall where the bathrooms are. At the end of that, what looks like an exit. I run as fast as I can, praying under my breath that this isn't one of those places where the emergency exits are locked so we would all die horribly if there were a fire, and hit the release bar on the door.

I'm blinded by daylight. I blink a few times. I'm in a little courtyard that serves mostly as a trash dump and a place to park bicycles and mopeds off the street. A few sad trees in crumbling concrete planters. An old-style

29

six-story apartment building across the way. Laundry hangs from the cramped balconies; random wires crisscross limply from roof to roof. It's oddly silent, except for a couple of chittering sparrows.

Then I hear a burst of dialog and music from one of the apartments; a guy bellowing about revenge against the Emperor, some cheesy historical soap on TV. 'I'll drink to his death!' echoes in the courtyard.

That unfreezes me. I plunge into the apartment building, down the narrow corridor that leads past the stairwell, and out the other side.

I'm on a little street with no real sidewalks, a few small cars shoved up against the buildings amidst a tangle of bikes. An old man sits on a tiny folding stool by the nonexistent curb, mending a pair of pants, a few odds and ends for sale spread out on a blanket next to him: a fake Cultural Revolution clock, a couple DVDs, a blender. 'You want?' he says to me, holding up the clock, winding it up to show me how the Red Guard waves her Little Red Book to count off the seconds. 'You want buy?'

'*Buyao*,' I say. I don't want. I run down the street.

I don't run that well because of my leg, but for once I'm hardly feeling it. I keep running. I pass more highrises, Tsinghua University's new science center, billboards, animated LED ads: giant stomachs, pills, and cars. Here's the Xijiao Hotel. Okay. I know this place. I'm breathing hard and sweating. Now my leg really hurts, and my shoulders feel bruised from my bouncing backpack, which I should've cinched up, but I've gotten out of the habit. I slow down, wipe my forehead. I don't see any foreigners in suits.

I'm by this little street leading into the Beijing Language & Culture University campus from the Xijiao Binguan that has small shops, restaurants, and stalls that live off business from students – places where you can buy cheap electronics, pirated DVDs, school supplies, tours to Tibet. And phone cards.

I stop and buy a hundred-yuan card for my phone, dial the number, scratch off the silver, and punch in the voucher code. I've got a string of messages waiting for me.

I'm still feeling exposed out here on the street. I decide to go onto the BLCU campus. I'm almost young enough to be a student. Besides, I dress like one: I'm wearing high-top sneakers, a long-sleeved snowboarding T-shirt decorated with flowers and snowflakes, and jeans, and I'm carrying a backpack. I blend in here, unlike foreigners in suits. I could be just another foreign student trying to better myself by learning Chinese. That's what I was doing, not so long ago.

I head over to the Sauce, a coffeehouse that's been on campus forever. It's not bad. I stand in line behind a skinny white boy chatting up a cute Chinese girl, order myself a regular cup of coffee, and take a seat by the window. I stare down at the street, at the egg-shaped orange phone booths, at the newly green trees, and I check my messages.

British John, asking me if I can cover Rose's shift for Karaoke Night. A bunch of text-message spam in Chinese, which I can't read. Delete, delete, delete.

Then a message from Lao Zhang. '*Yili, ni hao*. I'm leaving Beijing for a few days . . .' A pause. 'I wanted to let you know.' Another pause. 'Anyway, see you later. *Man zou*.'

31

Go slowly. Be careful.

I start to delete the message, but my finger hovers over the key for a moment, and then I hit save instead.

Next message.

'Hey, babe. It's me.'

My heart starts to thud, and the bottom falls out of my gut.

'Listen, I need to see you,' he continues. 'Right away. It's important. Call me as soon as you get this. Okay?'

I stare at the phone. Fucking Trey. Why does he do this to me?

CHAPTER THREE

I call him, of course. I know I shouldn't, but I do it anyway.
I'm pretty sure I know what he wants, and I'm not going
to give it to him. But I still call.

I hear that rich caramel voice in my ear. 'Hey, babe.'

'Hey,' I say, trying to keep my voice flat. 'What's up?'

'Listen, I need to talk to you. Can we meet someplace?'

I shrug. Like I don't care. Like he can see me. 'Talk to
me now.'

'Don't be like that. Look, we need to get together.' He
sounds so sincere. 'It's important.'

'I'm not signing anything, Trey –'

'I know. It's not about that.'

I let out a breath and stare out the window, look at
the knots of students walking below me, talking, laughing.
A couple arm in arm, the boy with spiked green hair, the
girl carrying a stuffed toy backpack. They're so cute. The
little shits.

'Okay,' I finally say.

I'm making a mistake, I'm pretty sure.

We arrange to meet in a couple hours at a pub in Henderson Center on Jianguomen Dajie, in the heart of Beijing. I take the train, transfer to the Ring subway line, and get off at Jianguomen by the Ancient Observatory, this lopped-off pyramid of gray brick from the Ming Dynasty, now dwarfed by all the big buildings on Chang 'An Boulevard. 'Vegas, with Chinese characteristics,' British John calls it – glassy high-rises with green Chinese-style roofs perched on top, like somebody put tiny party hats on the heads of awkward giants.

Fucking Trey, I think, as I walk to Henderson Center. He's probably lying to me. I'll meet him, and he'll try to talk me into signing.

He keeps threatening to file without me. Go ahead, I tell him. You do that, and it's all coming out. Every bit of it.

You wouldn't do that, he says. It'll hurt you as much as it'll hurt me.

At this point in the conversation, I generally laugh. Yeah, like I have as much to lose as you do.

But I know he's right. I'll never tell.

I would sign, though. I'd sign if he'd get me what I keep asking him for. But he won't, and I don't really get why.

Let it go, Lao Zhang keeps telling me. You don't need him. You can figure something else out. You already crossed the river; why carry the boat up the mountain? Let it go.

But I can't.

You could do it, I always say to Trey. Talk to your friends, the ones who can pull some strings. He just looks at me with those green eyes of his that shine like some kind of gem and says: I've tried, babe. I'll keep trying, I promise. But we gotta get on with our lives, don't we?

On this one point, I guess I'd have to agree with him. We really do.

It's not like I want to be married to him any more.

Barton's is the kind of expat place that's pretty typical for Beijing, which is to say it looks like any chain place you'd find in the U.S.: a wooden bar with a selection of imported beer and liquor, red leatherette booths, high-def TVs playing sports. Today they've got a baseball game on, with promises of basketball to follow.

Trey sits in a booth by the window, taking in the view from the thirtieth floor, drinking a beer and eating fries.

I don't like the way I feel when I see him. After everything that's happened, I still feel it, and I can't decide who I hate more for it: him or me.

Trey smiles when he notices me and half-rises to be polite. 'Hey, Ellie,' he says. 'You look good.'

Bullshit, I want to say. I'm pretty sure I don't look good. I'm sticky with sweat from my run through Matrix and coated with the general grime of Beijing. I slip into the booth across the table from him. 'Hey, Trey.'

'You have lunch? I was gonna get a burger. They make good ones here.'

'Thought you were on a health kick,' I mutter.

Trey grins and pats his gut. He's got a bit of one, but it's not bad. The truth is, he's the one who looks good. His hair is buzzed close to his scalp, all the better to minimize his slowly receding hairline. He's tan; his muscles strain the sleeves of his T-shirt. 'Yeah, well, you gotta make exceptions sometimes, you know?'

I look away. I just can't meet his eyes. 'What do you want, Trey?'

'Some lunch, right now.' He raises his arm to flag down the waitress. '*Xiaojie*!' he shouts.

The waitress – a cute little thing who gives Trey the eye – comes over. Trey orders his burger. I'm in one of those moods where nothing sounds good and I don't know what I want, but I figure I'd better eat something. For one thing, Trey's paying, and I like making him pay.

'Spaghetti,' I finally decide. The Chinese invented it, right? 'And a Yanjing beer.'

'No Yanjing. Have Qingdao.'

'So how you been, Ellie?' Trey asks, after my beer arrives.

'Fine. You?'

'I'm good.' He stares at me with the utmost sincerity. 'I really am.'

'Glad to hear it.' And then, because I can't help myself, I say: 'So, how's . . . what's her name? Ping Li?'

'Li Ping,' he corrects me. In point of fact, I knew that. 'Or Lily, if you like. She's good, Ellie. Really good.'

I nod.

Trey leans forward, his green eyes glowing. 'She's come to Jesus,' he says huskily. 'I feel like a part of me's been reborn with her.'

I chug my beer. 'That's just swell, Trey.'

He shakes his head. He looks so sad. 'Look, I fucked up. I could keep apologizing forever, and that's not gonna make it up to you. You want to hate me; I get it. But don't hold what I did against Jesus. It's not His fault.'

While my loss of faith is not the last thing I feel like discussing, it makes the top-ten list for sure.

'Why are we talking about this? I mean, what's Jesus got to do with . . . with *anything* right now?'

'Because He can help you.' Trey reaches across the table, rests his hand on mine. 'I know you're hurting. You're in the desert, Ellie. But there's water for you. All you have to do is drink it.'

Oh, if I only could. If I could only sink back into that warm, comfortable place, back when I could feel that glow, that love, that connection and certainty.

And the thrill. That smell of his, the wedge of his triceps, the look in his eyes.

I can't help it. I still want him.

'You are so full of it.' I yank my hand away. 'What would Jesus say about you dumping me for her? About you *fucking* her when you're married to me!'

'We're all sinners,' he says intensely. 'That's the point. And I *told* you what the bottom line was for me. I need to be with somebody who wants to live a Christ-centered life. And you've left that, Ellie. You've left that, and nothing I can say makes a difference. So what am I supposed to do? I can't live without it. I just can't.'

For a moment we stare at each other.

'Okay,' I finally say. 'Okay. We've had this discussion how many times? You wanna live with little Miss Come to Jesus, that's fine. You wanna get divorced, that's fine with me too. But you *know* what I want, Trey. You know it. Give me what I want, and I'll sign anything you want me to sign.'

Trey leans back in his chair. 'That's why I wanted to see you. I think I got it figured out.'

At that moment, two things happen almost at once. Two foreign men in suits approach our table. 'Mr Cooper,

Mrs Cooper,' one of them says in an American accent. They sit. And the waitress brings us our food.

'Parma-san?' she chirps.

'Hey, guys.' Trey flashes his smile at them.

I just sit there, staring at the mass of coiled noodles, which suddenly don't look like something I much want to eat.

'Mrs Cooper, sorry if we startled you earlier,' Suit #1 says.

I don't say anything. I twirl a forkful of spaghetti, and I eat it. Not bad, actually. Good noodles. 'Yes,' I tell the waitress. 'Please bring parmesan.'

Suit #1 leans forward. He's the younger of the duo, a wiry guy with wide eyes and an earnest expression. 'We're not here to cause you any problems.'

I take another bite of spaghetti. It tastes okay, but it's going down like glue. 'So why are you here?' I ask.

'Ellie –' Trey begins, all concerned and placating, but Suit #2 cuts him off.

'The Uighur. Hashim Abdullaabduzehim.'

I have to think about this for a moment. 'Abdulla . . .?'

'Abdullaabduzehim,' Suit #2 repeats impatiently. He's a half dozen years older, a couple inches taller, and a whole lot bulkier than Suit #1, with heavy-rimmed glasses, a bristling mustache, and a scary edge. The bad cop, apparently.

I decide it's best not to say anything. I focus on twirling the perfect forkful of noodles and sauce, braced against my spoon.

'You met him, right?'

Why is it so hard to get the right amount of noodles on your fork? You either end up with a few pathetic strands or half the bowl.

'I meet a lot of people,' I finally say. 'So what?'

Suit #1 puts his elbows on the table and leans forward. 'Mrs Cooper, it's very important that you tell us anything you can about Mr Abdullaabduzehim.'

'Why?'

'Mr Abdullaabduzehim is a known associate of Islamic extremists who plan to carry out attacks against American interests.'

'Against people like your former comrades-in-arms,' Suit #2 says. He sounds pissed. 'If you still give a shit about them.'

I put down my fork. 'You know what? Fuck you.'

'Mrs Cooper . . .' Suit #1 sighs. 'I know you've had a rough time. We wouldn't intrude on your privacy if it weren't extremely important. Mr Carter here . . .' He stares at me, those wide eyes of his suddenly seeming like a cartoon of sympathy. 'Mr Carter gets impatient.'

'Parma-san.' The waitress has returned, with a little green can of cheese. 'More beer?'

'Yes, please,' says Trey.

'The Uighur,' Suit #1 continues. 'He was staying with a friend of yours, Zhang Jianli. An artist of some sort, right?'

I don't say a word.

'In Mati Village. You went to Mati Village yesterday. You spend a lot of time there.'

I drink some beer. I turn to Trey. 'What have you been telling them about me?'

'It's not him, Mrs Cooper,' Suit #1 says.

'Who is it, then?'

He smiles. 'We have an interest in Mati Village. A lot of interesting people go there.'

'Listen, Ellie.' Trey gives me a look, as warm as can be, like he really cares. 'You help these guys, they can help you.'

'Oh, yeah?'

'They'll set you up with a job – you won't even have to go to work if you don't want, but you'll get your visa. So you can stay here after I leave, if that's what you want.' He stares at me, and those green eyes turn hard. ''Cause I'm leaving. I'm divorcing you, and I'm gonna marry Lily, and I'm taking her home to the States with me.'

I have to blink a few times. Because for a moment – and it's the weirdest thing – I just want to cry. I know he doesn't love me, and I don't love him either. He's a shit. A total shit and a hypocrite. Why should I care what he does?

'Oh, I get it,' I say furiously. 'They promised you something, didn't they? Like a no-hassles green card for your girlfriend.'

Suit #2 slaps the table. 'This is a waste of time.'

'I don't think so,' Suit #1 says calmly. 'We just need to get things back on track. I'm sure that Mrs Cooper wants to help, and maybe we can help her with a few things.' He turns to me. 'You're receiving, what is it, a seventeen-percent disability?'

I don't bother to ask him how he knows that.

'Seems a little low.'

'That's what they rated me,' I say.

'Those leg injuries looked pretty severe. And I don't know why they turned you down on the PTSD. Obviously you've had significant adjustment problems. Working part-time in some dive bar in China – not exactly what I'd call a career choice.'

I really want to tell him to go fuck himself, but I don't like being repetitive.

'Look,' I say, 'I met a guy named Hashim, maybe for all of five minutes. The last thing I would have figured him for was a terrorist. He was just an ordinary guy. We said hello, we ate some dumplings, and that's all I know about him.'

'And your friend, Zhang, what's his association? Have you heard him express any anti-American sentiments, or –?'

'He's an *artist*,' I say with emphasis. 'He's not political. This Hashim guy was just a friend of a friend. That's all.'

'You've never heard him express any political opinions?'

'No. We don't talk about that kind of stuff.'

'What *do* you talk about?' Suit #2 interjects.

'I don't know . . . just . . . stuff. Movies. TV shows. Beijing traffic. He's not political,' I repeat. He just likes taking in strays, I want to say. But I don't say it, because these two already think I'm some kind of psychotic low-life.

'He's your lover, right?' Suit #1 asks casually.

I flinch. I hate that expression, 'lover.' Like this is some kind of fucking romance novel. 'I don't think that's any of your business.'

'I assume you know he sees other women,' Suit #1 says.

I feel like I've been slapped.

'So?' I manage.

'Well, I wasn't sure how close you two were.'

I don't say anything.

Suit #1 locks his eyes on mine.

'I'm sure Zhang is a great guy. But he's gotten himself involved with some questionable people. You'd be doing him a favor if you helped us with this.'

41

'So, what is it you want me to do?' I finally ask.

'Are you in touch with him?'

I shrug. 'No.'

'But there's a good chance he'll contact you, isn't there?'

'What if he does? You want me to ask him about the Uighur?'

'Well, it depends,' Suit #1 says. 'On what kind of relationship the two of you have. On the level of trust.'

Suit #2 snorts. 'If Zhang contacts you, the main thing is, you tell us. If you can find out where he is, that's a bonus.'

I lean back in my chair, push my fingers through my greasy hair. 'And what? You'll get me a Z visa? Up my disability? That's a promise?'

'We'll do what we can for you,' says Suit #1. 'The more you help us, the easier it is to make the case. Being a pair of eyes for us in places like Mati . . . that could be very helpful.'

I gulp down the rest of my beer and stand up. I turn to Trey. 'Tell Lily I said hi.'

'Ellie –' Trey begins.

Suit #2 stops him. 'Let her go. She doesn't want to help, it's her loss.'

'Mrs Cooper.' It's Suit #1. 'If you hear anything, anything at all . . .' He holds out a business card. 'Call us. It's very important.'

I stare at his hand, at the white card, the blue logo with the letters GSC.

Global Security Concepts. The company Trey works for.

I take the card and stick it in my pants pocket. I'm not going to give him the courtesy of reading it.

'Here,' Suit #2 says abruptly, thrusting his card at me.

Whatever. I take his too.

Then I leave. No way I'm paying for that lunch.

In the elevator, I lift up my hand to punch the button, and it's shaking.

CHAPTER FOUR

Outside, the dust has kicked up, filtering the sun through a yellow haze.

I walk down Jianguomen. There's a Starbucks around here someplace. I could get a cup of coffee. I fixate on that. A cup of coffee. I'll get a cup of coffee and try to think. But I can't remember where the fucking Starbucks is, exactly. It's around here. I keep walking down the street. I just need to get a cup of coffee, and I'll be able to sort all this out.

Tears run down my face. I'll just blame the dust. Because the other stuff, I can't think about that. Trey and his little ho' girlfriend. Loves Jesus, my ass. The stuff he did . . . How can he talk about love?

And Lao Zhang. It's not like I love him. What's love, right? I thought I loved Trey, and how stupid was that?

But I like him. Lao Zhang's a good guy. Maybe the Suits are telling the truth; maybe he's fucking around, but so what? I never asked him not to. All I ever asked was if I could come over, and he always said yes. I think: all

the time we've spent together, hanging out, it felt . . .
comfortable. Like belonging somewhere. And now . . .

What's he gotten himself into?

Then I think: it's not the Chinese government that's
after Lao Zhang. It's Global Security Concepts. Trey's
company. Not official. But they might as well be.

I know how those guys work.

How did the Suits find out about Lao Zhang?

I'm slick with sweat, like a fever's breaking. They've
been watching me, no matter what they said. They
followed me to Mati. To Lao Zhang.

How long have they been watching?

Finally, I spot the familiar green-and-white Starbucks
logo.

Inside, the air is perfectly conditioned, and they're
playing their latest retro Brazilian compilation; the baristas
are smiling, the espresso machine hisses, and it smells like
roasted coffee. They're advertising Fair Trade beans and
selling Starbucks Beijing coffee mugs. There's a couple of
tourists, a student or two, and a few local businessmen
with pocket PCs and laptops.

I feel better already.

'Yi bei benride kafei. Zhong.'

'Room for cream?' asks the barista. They all know the
English for coffee words.

They give me my coffee of the day, size medium. I put
the cup down on an empty table and go into the restroom
to wash my face. Under the fluorescent light above the
mirror, I can see where my tears have cut through the
dust and soot of a Beijing spring day.

I look like shit.

I used to be cute. It wasn't so weird that Trey wanted

me, back in the day. I used to be fresh-faced and smooth and round. Nice tits. Good hair. Standard American Attractiveness Template.

Now? I have circles under my eyes, black ones, as dark as the Uighur's. Crow's-feet. Lines running down from my nose to my mouth, deep as slashes. Blemishes and brown spots on my face from the sun. I'm seven years older. And I'm not sure I'm any wiser than I was.

Fucking Trey. It's his fault my life's turned out this way. I was young and dumb, and I would've done anything he wanted me to. And he knew that. He knew that, and he crooked his finger at me, and I followed him.

Then I think: but you went. You didn't have to. You should've known better.

But there's nothing I can do about any of that now.

I wash my hands, my face. Go out and sit at my table. Sip my coffee and try to think.

They watch Mati Village, Suit #1 said. Who's watching? Someone I know? One of the artists? A waitress at the *jiaozi* place?

I should call Lao Zhang, let him know these guys are looking for him. I get out my phone, and then I hesitate. The Suits never asked me for his phone number. I sip my coffee and think, they must have it already. And I think: how is that? I stare at my phone and wonder. They probably know my number. Fucking Trey probably gave it to them. Can they tap these things?

How did they find me earlier at Matrix Arcade? They didn't follow me from Chuckie's apartment, did they? So how did they find me?

Cell phones all have GPS built in. You can find people with GPS – that's what it's for, right?

46

I switch off my phone. This is crazy. They can't just do that, can they?

I laugh in spite of myself. Yeah, right. They can do whatever they want to do.

Besides, this is China.

I stare at the iPhone. It was a gift from Trey two years ago: top of the line then, out of date now. He bought it in Hong Kong, unlocked, which is technically illegal, but everyone does it here because you couldn't get iPhones legally in China until last year, and the legal ones cost a fortune.

How does this stuff work? If my phone is off, does that mean they can't find me?

I almost get up and throw my iPhone in the trash. I want to hurl it across the room. It's hard for me to stop myself, but the phone was expensive, and it's got all my numbers and photos and tunes on it.

I think: it's off. They can't find me if it's off.

Right about then a couple of students come in, two guys, Americans or Europeans. I can tell they're students by the backpacks, the counterfeit North Face jackets, the perfectly broken-in T-shirts, the vaguely ethnic bead necklaces.

I think for a minute while they get in line. Then I stand up and say, '*Duibuqi*.' Excuse me.

The two guys look at me. 'Hi,' I say. 'Do you speak English?'

'Sure,' one of them says. He's wearing a Bob Marley shirt and a crocheted cap.

'Great,' I say quickly, 'because I'm kind of in a bind. I really need to make a call and my phone died.' I hold up my switched-off iPhone, which I figure looks pretty convincingly dead. 'Do either of you have a phone? I'll buy your coffee if I can make a quick call.'

'You can use mine, no big,' says the second guy, the one in the Bruce Lee shirt. 'So long as you aren't calling Mongolia or something.'

'Nah, just Kazakhstan,' I joke back.

The kid hands me his phone (a new iPhone, way cooler than mine). I quickly punch in Lao Zhang's number.

'*Wei, ni hao*.' I talk in a low voice, as fast as I can. I'm hoping these guys are beginning Chinese students and won't be able to understand me if I Beijing it up. 'It's me, Yili. I met two foreigners today,' I continue in Chinese. 'Americans. They asked a lot of questions about you.'

Then I'm not sure what to say.

'Take care,' I finally add. 'Be careful.'

I hit the red button and hand the phone back.

'Your accent is really good,' Bob Marley T-shirt guy says.

They're students, like I thought, just finishing their first semester at Beijing Language and Culture University. Mark and Jayson. 'How long you been here?' they want to know. 'Where did you study Chinese?' Before I know it, they've invited me to their dorm for a party tonight. What the hell, I think. Maybe I'll go. It's close to home, and I don't know what else I'm going to do with myself.

We say our 'nice meeting you's' and 'later, dude's,' and I exit onto Jianguomen Road, heading toward the subway station. Maybe I'll go to the Ancient Observatory. Climb up to the flat roof, pretend I can't see the gaudy high-rises and ugly apart-ment blocks, and try to imagine what it was like when the Ancient Observatory was the tallest building around, looking out over a sea of peaked gray tile roofs. When you'd hear donkey bells and peddlers' cries instead of car horns and screeching brakes.

I try to imagine it, but I can't.

Jayson and Bob Marley T-Shirt guy's party is pretty standard for a party in a foreign students' dorm: loud music, tubs of Yanjing beer, people spilling out of one room into the hall and flowing into another. I catch the scent of hash, no doubt supplied by the local Kazak dealers, and over the din of the music make out English, Korean, German, and attempts at Chinese. I see a few people here close to my age, grad-student types, and I tell myself I don't look that out of place.

I'm bored the moment I arrive.

I grab a beer, open it, find a clear space along the wall, and lean against it, wondering if I could find some of that hash I'm smelling. Kids bump past me, laughing, stumbling. I don't even see Jayson or Marley T-shirt guy.

This is stupid, I think. Why did I come? No one's going to talk to me, and I don't feel like talking to anyone. It's like there are these black waves rolling out from me, warning everybody off. Stay away. Don't fucking talk to me.

'Hello!'

I look up. Standing in front of me is a Chinese guy, thirtyish, wearing a cheap leather jacket and a faded Beijing Olympics T-shirt, the one with the slogan 'One World, One Dream.'

'So sorry to bother,' he continues. 'You are American, right?'

'No. I'm Icelandic.'

'Ice . . . ?' he stammers.

For whatever reason, I suddenly feel sorry for the guy. He's not bad-looking; he's got that near-babyfaced handsomeness like Chow Yun Fat did when he was young, but he also has a slight stutter and this sort of clueless vibe, like he doesn't know what to make of me messing with him.

'Yes, I'm an American,' I allow. 'And you're . . . Chinese, maybe?'

He grins broadly, revealing slightly crooked but very clean teeth. 'Why do you say that?' he replies, joking back. Maybe he's not so clueless.

'Just guessing.'

'Yes,' he says. 'Yes, Chinese. I am even a Beijing native.'

I snort. Everyone claims to be a native Beijinger. 'Right. And you were probably born just next to the Temple of Heaven.'

He gives me his squinty-eyed, puzzled look again. 'No. Close to Da Zhong Si. You know Da Zhong Si? That Great Bell Temple?'

'Heard of it,' I say noncommittally. I've been there before, actually. It's no longer an active temple, but instead a bell museum, with bells from all around China and the entire world. Cool place, if you're into bells.

'That Great Bell was once biggest in the world,' the guy says, seeming enthused about playing Beijing tour guide. 'But now no longer. Now is Zhonghua Shiji Tan. Century Altar.' He speaks English carefully, laying peculiar stress on the first syllables of the words. 'Made in 1999, for the, the . . . the new . . .'

'Millennium?' I guess.

'Yes,' he says eagerly. 'Yes, millennium.'

He extends his hand. 'I am John.'

I can feel the tendons and muscles as his hand lightly

closes around mine. He gives my hand a quick, awkward shake and lets go.

'Yili,' I reply.

John beams. 'Oh, I think you speak Chinese. Am I right? Are you a student here, Yili?'

'Sometimes.'

'This is my, my . . . *alma mater*. I still come back at times. I enjoy to meet foreign students. So that I can practice. My English.'

'Your English is very good,' I say, because it's what you're supposed to say, and I'm sure his English is better than my Chinese.

'No, no, my English is very poor.' He stares at me for a moment. There's not a lot of light in the hall, and it's hard for me to make out his expression.

Then he blinks and ducks his head. 'Yili, can I fetch you another beer?'

I should say no. I should leave, go back to the apartment. Spend some time thinking about what I'm going to do with my life after Trey divorces me and leaves the country and my visa runs out.

I should think about going home.

'Sure,' I say. 'Thanks.'

Like I want to think about any of that.

In no time at all, John has returned with two cold Yanjings. He hands one to me with a small flourish, then holds up his bottle.

'*Ganbei*,' he says with a grin. Drink it dry.

We clink bottles and drink.

'So, Yili, are you married? Do you have children?'

I try not to roll my eyes. Just about every Chinese person I meet asks me these questions.

51

'Aren't you gonna ask how old I am?' I reply, as this is the inevitable third question in the 'Way Too Personal' trifecta.

John waves a hand. 'Oh, no. I can see you are still very young. Maybe . . . not thirty?'

Actually, I'm twenty-six. 'Just about.'

'But no husband or children?'

'No kids. Yes on the husband. But we're separated.'

John shakes his head sadly. 'This is the nature of the modern times, I think. The family life always suffers.'

'Are you married, John?'

'Me?' For a moment, John looks uncomfortable. 'No.'

'Are your parents upset?'

Because if there's one thing a Chinese son is supposed to do, it's get married and have kids.

'I just tell them to have patience,' John says dismissively. 'I am still the young man. I have . . . I have . . . *benchmarks.*'

'Benchmarks?'

'Of accomplishment. Before I am to have children. I have not achieved these yet, but I achieve them soon, I think.'

'Oh,' I say, and wipe my forehead. I'm already feeling a little buzzed. Not surprising, considering all I've had to eat today is a couple bites of spaghetti.

'You see, it is hard if you are a young man in China and you are not rich,' John continues, warming to his topic. 'Because the Chinese women, they want a successful man. And they can choose who they want, because we have more men than women.'

He leans in closer to me. 'Some Chinese women, they have second husband. Do you understand my meaning?'

'Ummm . . .' I think about it. Take another swallow of beer. 'More than one?'

'Not real husband,' John confides. 'More like . . . boyfriend. But these women, they have money. So they take care of boyfriend. Like concubine. You know that word?'

'Sure,' I say, finishing my beer. 'My husband has one of those.'

'Oh.' I can see comprehension slowly dawning. 'Your husband . . . he has . . .' And here John ducks his head and sneaks a little grin. 'The yellow fever, perhaps.'

'Yeah, he's fucking a Chinese girl,' I snap, my knuckles whitening around the beer bottle, 'if that's what you want to know.'

John flushes red. 'I am sorry. I just . . . I just made a bad joke. Please forgive me.'

His face is so open, so kind, that for a moment I'm flooded with guilt. And something else. Warmth, I guess. Just from having somebody be nice to me.

How pathetic is that?

I let out a big sigh. I feel like I've been holding my breath.

'That's okay.'

The weird thing is, suddenly it *is* okay. It's been over between me and Trey for a long time. And considering what it is that held us together, the thing we *really* shared, maybe I should start being glad that it's over.

Starting right now.

'I'm sorry too, John. It's just that I've had a rough –' A giggle starts bubbling up from my throat. 'A rough six years or so,' I manage.

I want to laugh, and keep laughing, and never stop.

John grins back. 'Yili, would you like another beer?'

Maybe I shouldn't, because I pounded this one, and I'm already kind of loaded. But it feels good. I feel lighter somehow.

'Sure,' I say. 'Thanks.'

I lean against the wall and close my eyes. What would it be like, really being free from Trey? Just not caring about him any more. Not ever seeing him again or having anything to do with him, and not having that feel like some hole in the place where my soul is supposed to be, like the part of me that's able to care about somebody else has gone missing.

Not ever thinking about those times again.

You'll always think about those times, I tell myself. Always. But maybe, maybe you can think about those times and, from now on, they won't hurt you so much. Those times, they'll just be things that happened in the past, and that's all.

'Yili?'

I open my eyes. Here's John standing in front of me, holding two bottles of beer. He's actually pretty handsome, not really baby-faced; he has a strong jaw, bright eyes, light stubble on his chin. And he's taller than I am. Solid, with some muscle. I think I can see the outline of his chest beneath the T-shirt.

One World, One Dream.

'Do you feel okay?'

'Sure. I'm just a little tired.'

John hands me a beer, already opened, like the last one. 'We could go sit down somewhere,' he says, 'if you are tired.'

'Okay,' I say. I'm tired of all the noise, anyway.

We make our way outside. 'I know a good place,' John says. I stifle a giggle. Does he want to make out or something? I might be up for that. It might be fun, messing around a little. He's cute, I've decided. I take another swallow of beer.

It's a nice night. I'm warm enough with just my light jacket. John leads me down a bricked path that leads to a garden of sorts. I've been here before. There's a fountain and a marble wall inscribed with calligraphy, the grooves highlighted by gold paint. Some fucking proverb about wisdom and self-cultivation, probably.

We sit on the stone bench by the fountain. I can hear the music from the party, but it's so faint that I feel like I could almost be imagining it, making up music from the gurgle and flow of the fountain's water.

'This where you used to take girls?'

John grins slyly. 'Sometimes.' He takes a pull of his beer and leans toward me a little. 'Do you have a boyfriend, Yili?'

'Maybe. Sort of. I don't know.'

'What does that mean?' John sounds curious. Like he honestly wants to understand.

I have to really think about it for a minute. I look up, through the haze of dust and city lights. Haloes surround the streetlights, the stars. It's all so beautiful, in an ugly kind of way.

'He's a good guy,' I finally say. 'A really good guy. I like him. And I know he likes me. He's nice.'

Then I can't help it: I start laughing. 'That sounds really lame.'

'No, Yili, it doesn't sound . . . lame.' John has to work a little to get that last word out, like it sticks somewhere on the middle of his tongue. 'But you say you don't know about him.'

'I mean, I don't know . . .'

My head feels funny. The sound of the fountain thrums in my ears, or maybe it's the music. I swallow some more beer. It goes down like it's something alien, cold and coppery. 'What he wants from me. I mean . . . we spend a lot of time together. But I'm not sure why.'

'You think he wants you to do something for him?'

'No. No, I . . .' I squeeze my eyes shut. Everything feels funny. My eyes are too big; they're sticking out, and I need to cover them up. 'He's nice,' I repeat. 'Maybe he just feels sorry for me.'

'Yili?' John says. 'Yili?'

It's too loud. I put my hands over my ears. 'I feel kind of weird,' I manage.

'Are you ill?' John asks anxiously. 'Should we go to the doctor?'

'No. No . . . I just . . .' There's a beer bottle in my hand. I'm holding it. It's solid and cold, and I can feel the damp from the condensation. Like, the beer that's inside the bottle wants to get out, and it's squeezing through tiny holes in the glass. I take another sip. Free the beer!

'Feel weird.'

'I think maybe you should go home, Yili.' He holds out his hand. 'Come. I'll take you.'

I stare at him. His eyes are bright, sparkling almost, even in the dark. I stare at his hand. It looks too big.

'I don't want to go home,' I say.

'Here.' His hand reaches down. Finds mine. Closes over it, dry and hot, like some trespasser from the desert.

'Stand up,' he says.

I do what he tells me to. I don't even think to argue about it. I stand up, and my bad leg buckles, and I pitch forward.

John catches me. I see his face as I fall; he looks surprised and almost embarrassed.

'Sorry,' I mumble. 'My leg's messed up.'

'I'll help you,' John says. 'Here, I take your arm.'

He has me drape my arm around his shoulders, and he threads his arm across my back and under my armpit. He won't quite look at me, I notice. That's funny, I think. Why should he be embarrassed? I'm the one who's somehow gotten so fucked up that I can't walk.

How'd that happen, I wonder?

It finally occurs to me, as we mutually stagger down the path that leads out of the garden and into the campus proper, that I've been dosed with something.

'Wait,' I say. 'Wait. I don't wanna go with you.'

'What, Yili?'

'Let me go,' I say. 'Let me go. I just wanna . . . Let go of me.'

'Yili, I think maybe you are a little sick,' John says, sounding very sympathetic. 'I help you to get home. That is all. You don't need to worry about me.'

I don't believe him. I try to pull away. The arm encircling me holds me tighter against him. We stumble down the walkway, through the quad of dormitories, past the take-out window of the Xinjiang restaurant where students line up for lamb skewers and sesame bread.

I should yell. I should scream. I should kick him in the nuts and run. But I don't. I can't. We keep walking, his fingers pressing hard against my ribs, until we've reached the campus gate, where teenage security guards in stiff gray polyester jackets stand nominal sentry.

'Come on, Yili,' John says. 'This way.'

A shiny silver car waits for us on the other side.

CHAPTER FIVE

I picture the finger-shaped bruises John's hand is making on my ribcage as he guides me toward the silver car. There's a guy leaning against it, smoking a cigarette. John gestures angrily at him. 'Off my car!' he snaps.

'Fuck your mother,' the guy mutters. But he lifts himself off the car, takes one last drag on his cigarette, and flicks it into the gutter before ambling away.

'Hey,' I say. 'Wait.'

'Now, Ellie, you don't want to talk to that guy,' John chides me. 'He is just some rascal.'

'It's all a show,' I say, 'isn't it? That guy drove the car here.'

John does his best puzzled squint, but I'm not buying it any more. 'Of course not. He is just some local rascal.'

'But there's no parking here,' I say, and I'm feeling like this is maybe the most brilliant thing I've ever said.

John laughs as he opens the passenger door. 'Oh, Yili! You are very funny. Now, get into the car.'

I don't want to get in. I plant my feet, but I'm really

messed up, and my leg isn't that stable anyway, and John somehow knocks me off balance, and I fall across the seats, hitting my cheek against the gear-shift, and John swings my legs into the car and slams the door.

The car has an open moonroof. I stare up, trying to see through the haze to the stars.

The driver's door opens, and John gets in, putting the keys in the ignition before his butt hits the seat. My head's touching his thigh as the car pulls away from the curb.

'Where're we going?' I mumble. My mouth feels like it's full of stones.

'I told you, Yili. To your home.'

I can't even sit up. I just lie there, head pressed against John's thigh, feeling his muscles bunch and relax as he brakes and accelerates. Streetlights pass over us.

I don't know how long we drive.

Finally, it seems, we get somewhere. John rolls down his window, mutters something to another teenage security guard in a gray polyester jacket, I don't hear what. I stare up through the moonroof. I can see the tops of tall buildings, satellite dishes, a square of sky. But no stars.

'Here we are, Yili.'

He gets out and opens the passenger door. I lie there. I don't think I can move. John's face looms over me. 'Oh, Yili,' he says. 'I think maybe you are very sick.'

'I . . . I . . .'

'Here. Take my hand.'

I try, feebly grasping at it like my fingers have gone boneless; they're just these white worms, jellyfish fingers, waving around in a black sea.

John scoops me up, hands placed beneath my shoulder

blades and butt, lifting me out of the car. My feet touch the ground but don't want to stay there.

'Here,' John says. 'I carry you.'

And he does. My arms circle around his neck, because they don't know what else to do.

I rest my cheek against John's leather jacket and close my eyes, lost in the rock and sway of his steps as he carries me along like I'm some little kid in her daddy's arms. I catch his scent beneath the smell of cheap, tanned leather: sweat mixed with some bad cologne. I like the sweat better.

'Yili,' John says, his breath warm in my ear. 'What is your apartment number?'

'What?'

'Your apartment number. What is it?'

I open my eyes, and it's the weirdest thing: my apartment building looms above us.

Wait, I think. Wait. He doesn't know my apartment number, but he knows where I live. That doesn't make sense. How does he know where I live?

'You told me this, Yili. At the party. Don't you remember?'

Did I just say that out loud? I guess I did.

'Twenty-one oh-five,' I slur.

I just want to lie down.

I just want to go home.

We take the elevator upstairs. It's empty, the tall stool where the *fuwuyuan* sits when she's on duty unoccupied. I stare at it, the empty stool surrounded by mirror tile, fake wood paneling and fluorescent light, and try to conjure up some meaning to it, but I can't.

Here we are in the foyer.

61

As John fumbles at my door (Does he have my keys? Did I give them to him?), I see a sharp beam of white light, and fucking Mrs Hua pokes her head out from her apartment.

'What sort of things are going on now?' she hisses. 'This is really more than anyone should bear!'

John turns his head in her direction. 'Your business ends at your eaves, old Auntie.' The way he says it, so cold and matter-of-fact, would scare me – that is, if I could feel afraid right now.

Mrs Hua can. She pulls back behind her door. 'Show some respect,' she mutters as she slams it shut and locks it with both chain and bar.

John carries me inside.

He steps carefully through the maze of computer parts, the cardboard Yao Ming, the piles of clothes and books in the near-dark, the only light in the room what's leaking in through the windows from a Beijing sky that's never really dark any more.

'Which room, Yili?'

Now, suddenly, I do get scared. 'Chuckie?' I say. But my voice is weak, weak like in a dream where you can't cry out, where you can't make anyone hear you. 'Chuckie?' I try again.

'No one is here,' John tells me. 'Besides, you shouldn't worry.'

He takes me into my room and lays me down on my futon. He doesn't turn on the light, but the nightlight by the door has come on.

For a moment, he stands over me. His face is in shadow, but he's staring at me, I can tell.

'I am going to make you more comfortable,' he says softly.

He kneels down by the futon. First he takes off my sneakers and socks, balling up the socks and putting them in the shoes, placing the shoes in the closet, lined up neatly.

Then he hesitates before reaching for the top button of my jeans.

'Don't,' I say. 'Don't.'

'Now, Yili, you cannot be comfortable in these.'

I can't stop him. I can barely move. He unbuttons my jeans, lifts me up, and slides them over my butt and then off. He folds them up, looks around, and then puts the jeans on the room's one chair.

He kneels down next to me again. His eyes fall on my bad leg, and he reaches out and lightly touches a place where two long scars cross, then the hollow from the chunk of missing muscle. 'Oh,' he says, in a curious voice. 'You were badly hurt, I think.'

I bite my lip and nod. Tears stream from my eyes, and I can't control that either.

He gives my leg a final, gentle pat. Then he reaches under my back, beneath my shirt, and unhooks my bra. He rocks back on his heels. 'Yili, I have to take this off too,' he says, with a trace of apology. Then he peels my shirt up and over my head. For a moment, the shirt catches on my chin, collapses on my face like a death-mask, and as I breathe in, the cotton sealing my nostrils, I think maybe it will suffocate me, and that's what John wants to do to me. But no. He frees the shirt from my head. Turns it right side out, folds it, and lays it neatly on top of my jeans on the chair.

He turns back to me, smiling awkwardly. He pulls one bra strap down along my arm until it clears my hand.

Then the other. He holds my bra in his hand, and for a moment he stares at my tits. Then he looks away and drapes the bra over the back of the chair.

I'm lying there naked except for my panties. I'm shaking. The room seems to vibrate.

John's back is to me. He's rummaging through the little dresser next to my closet. 'Ah,' he says, satisfied. 'This is good.'

He has in his hands a large T-shirt. 'I think maybe this will be comfortable for you.'

He puts it over my head, lifts me up a little, and I can feel the dry heat radiating from his hand pressed flat between my shoulder-blades.

After he gets the T-shirt on me, he finds the light blanket I use most warm spring nights and covers me with it.

'Just a minute,' he says, and leaves.

I lie there. The room is still vibrating, but not so quickly.

When John returns, he carries a glass of water and something wrapped in a dishcloth. He sits cross-legged by my head. 'Here, Yili,' he says. 'Have some water.'

'I don't . . . You put something in it.'

'Don't be silly. You are sick. You need some water.'

He tilts up my head so I won't choke and pours a little water between my lips. I swallow. He pours some more. It tastes good. Like nectar. Like something I need.

'There. You see?'

When I finish, he smoothes the hair from my forehead. 'I have some ice,' he says, holding up the dishcloth. 'Your face, it's bruised. I think maybe when I help you in the car, I'm too careless.' He puts the dishcloth against my cheek. 'I'm sorry about this, Yili.'

I feel the cold seep through the cloth to my cheek, soaking into my skull and spreading through my head. Everything slows down.

'That's okay,' I say.

John sits there quietly, holding the ice against my cheek.

'Why you come to China, Yili?' he finally asks.

I chuckle. 'Trey. He got a job. I came with him.'

'What kind of work does he do?'

'Security consultant. For a big corporation.' I laugh again. 'Kind of like a really well-paid bodyguard.'

'Really?'

'Kind of.' Of course, it's more than that, really. Trey assesses threats. Looks for holes. Keeps people safe.

'I see.'

I must have spoken out loud again, without meaning to.

'And this pays well?'

'It pays okay.'

John brushes a stray hunk of my hair off my face.

'So, Trey, he does not work for American government.'

'Big corporation.' I laugh. 'What's the difference?'

John nods sagely. 'You know, here in China, PLA, Peoples' Liberation Army, owns many businesses. They hide this better now than before, but still it is this way. So maybe this is somewhat the same as America.'

This irritates me, and I'm not sure why. 'It's the other way around in America,' I tell him. 'Companies own the Army. They send us where they want us to go. To do their shit for them. So they can get rich.'

'Ah. I see. So you are in the Army, Yili?'

'I don't wanna talk about it.'

'Why not? It can be good to talk, I think.'

'No. It's not.'

But I can see it. That's the thing. I can fucking see it. I don't want to. I don't want to see this shit any more. 'Oh god,' I say. 'Oh, Jesus. Where the fuck were you? You fucking liar.'

John strokes my face, my hair. 'Yili, I am sorry. I don't want to upset you.'

I'm crying again. 'Fuck you,' I say. 'You're just another liar.'

He says nothing.

After a while, he gets up and leaves the room, closing the door behind him.

I lie there. I'm floating. I'm swaddled in clouds. I can't move.

'John?' I call out. 'John?'

He doesn't come. I'm alone.

'I'm sorry,' I whisper, 'I'm sorry. I didn't mean it. I didn't mean to. I hate myself. I want to die.'

'Yili, why do you talk like that?'

'John?'

Where did he come from? He crouches down next to me. Takes my hand. 'Have some water.'

I drink. I drink like it's somehow going to save my life. Like it will replenish everything I've lost.

I'm pretty fucked up right now.

John sighs. 'This boyfriend of yours. I don't understand. Why doesn't he take better care of you?'

'He's busy.'

'But this is not right,' John states. 'If you are together with him, he should take care of you. This is only proper.'

I stare up at the ceiling. Kaleidoscope patterns fold and

unfold on the peeling beige paint. Like flowers in one of those sped-up nature movies.

'I guess he's not really my boyfriend,' I say after a while. 'I guess we're just friends, that's all.'

'But friends take care of each other too,' John says gravely. 'Maybe this fellow, maybe he isn't really your friend.'

'He is,' I insist. 'He is.'

'But he left you.'

'He had to.'

'Why?'

'Because . . .' I squeeze my eyes shut. Then I open them, because little armies keep marching across my eyelids, and I don't want them there. 'Because he had to.'

John sighs. 'Yili, why are you so sure that this man is good guy? What do you really know about him?'

For a moment, I can't think of anything at all. I stare at the ceiling. The peeling paint curls and uncurls.

'Maybe he is okay guy like you say,' John continues. 'But maybe now he is mixed up in something that is bad.'

I turn my head to look at him. John stares at me intently, his eyes shining.

And it doesn't matter how fucked up I am, how much bad shit I'm seeing in my head, and how scared I was before. I know exactly what this is about. He can't hide it from me any more.

'This is about the Uighur guy, right? You know what, John? You're an asshole. You could've just asked me. You didn't have to do all this. You didn't have to . . .'

I can't finish. I'm feeling this sob coming up from my gut, choking me. I want to scream; I want to hit something; I want to run and run and never stop. But I still can't move. I lie there crying like a fucking five-year-old, and I hate myself for it.

John's eyes widen, look away then look back, like he isn't sure what to do now. 'Yili, I –'

'Shut the fuck up. I don't care any more. I really don't.'

I manage to lift my hand up to wipe my face. 'You could have just asked me,' I repeat. 'And I would have told you. I don't know anything. Nothing.'

Silently, John takes the damp dishcloth that held the ice and dabs my face with it, cleans off the tears and the snot.

'Lao Zhang's an artist. He's got a lot of friends. People crash with him all the time. It doesn't mean anything.'

I can't keep my eyes open any more. I feel like everything's dissolving into foam. 'Just leave me alone,' I mumble.

'Okay, Yili,' I hear John say from far away. 'I let you sleep now. You'll feel better when you wake up.'

Right, I think. Right. I'll feel better.

CHAPTER SIX

What I remember most, from that first day in the sandbox, is how fucking hot it was, and how I was so thirsty because there wasn't enough bottled water, and the donkey.

I was looking out the window of the Humvee, trying to make out the landscape through three inches of dirty glass, and it was almost like being under water. I saw desert: flat, endless scrub, different shades of dirt, an occasional clump of cinderblock buildings that blended into the gray dust.

We ground to a stop at the outskirts of some little town – just a crossroads and a couple of telephone poles stuck between mud-brick houses and a few painted cement storefronts. A truck was broken down in front of us.

Across from me, tied to one of those poles, was a donkey hooked up to a cart. Flanks crisscrossed by whip scars, ribs sticking out, head hanging down, like it'd had a lifetime of getting the shit kicked out of it.

'Heard Hajji's rigging donkey carts with explosives,' the soldier next to me said.

I must have looked scared. I *was* scared. I'd joined the National Guard, not the fucking Marines. I was nineteen years old. I'd enlisted in the Guard after high school and trained as a medic. I thought I'd learn a skill, get some money for college. I didn't think I'd be doing this.

'Hey, it's just a rumor.' He gave me an awkward pat and stared out the window. A little gaggle of kids hung out by the block wall surrounding one of the houses, laughing, shoving, daring each other to approach us. A couple of them waved. Behind them I saw two women, dressed head to toe in black abayas, looking like some kind of flightless crows.

'Most of these people are glad we're here,' the soldier told me. 'You'll see.'

I start to wake up, and I don't know where I am. Behind my eyes, everything's bright and yellow, and I'm filled with dread, because I don't want to be there again, in that place.

Except . . . except . . . I miss it too.

I open my eyes. I can't get oriented. The direction of my bed doesn't make any sense, the wall is on the wrong side of the room, my head's facing the wrong way, like I'm sleeping in the Bizarro universe. Then everything shifts into position, to where it belongs. I'm not over there. I'm lying on my futon in my little room in Chuckie's apartment off Wudaokou Dajie.

I lie there for a minute, rubbing my face, which feels kind of numb. My eyes feel swollen. I close them. Start sinking back into sleep.

I feel my heart thudding too fast in my chest before I actually remember what happened last night.

70

Was it really last night? Did that really happen? I have this sudden flash of myself lying in bed, John taking off my bra. I shudder. I think I'm going to throw up.

I struggle to stand up, rising first to my knees, grasping the back of the chair. My limbs feel like they're filled with sand.

As I brace myself against the chair and stagger to my feet, I see my jeans folded neatly on the seat, my shirt resting on top of that, my bra draped across the shirt like it's some kind of post-modern window display.

The bra was on the chair back, I think dimly. That's where John put it last night. He must have moved it.

I stumble into the bathroom, thinking I'm going to puke. But I don't. Instead, I splash some water on my face. Stare at myself in the mirror. My eyes look huge. Everything still glows around the edges.

What the fuck did he give me?

Okay, I think, okay. Whatever that was all about, he's gone, I'm here, and I'm okay now.

As I come out of the bathroom, I hear a lot of noise coming from Chuckie's bedroom.

For a minute I just stand there, my heart pounding in my throat. I'm thinking, what if John's still here?

But then I hear a crash that sounds like falling books, and Chuckie curses.

Okay.

I go back to my room and put on my pants – not the ones on the chair: I don't want to touch that pile of clothes just yet. I wander out into the kitchen. Slanting yellow light comes in through the window. It's past two in the afternoon.

I pour myself some water from the fridge. And notice

71

something weird: all the dirty dishes have been washed and are sitting neatly in the dish rack.

Not Chuckie, I think. In general, Chuckie doesn't do dishes. He lives on takeout. So do I. That's about two week's worth of dishes from both of us in that rack.

I shudder again and leave the kitchen.

Here's Chuckie coming out of his room, carrying an armload of clothes and a duffel bag.

He sees me and jerks back like he's stuck his finger in a light socket. Then he looks away.

'What's up?' I ask.

'Going home to see the family,' he mutters.

'Oh, yeah?'

Chuckie can't stand his family. At least that's what he always says to me. 'They are just idiots,' he complains. 'Hopeless.' And they live in Bumfuck Shanxi – nowhere Chuckie wants to hang.

'For a little while. My mother says she wants me to come.'

I see his face. Pale. Scared.

'You okay?' I ask.

His eyes dart around like he's being buzzed by gnats and can't figure out where they're coming from. He shakes his head, fractionally.

'You wanna go downstairs, get a cup of coffee?'

He nods.

There's this DVD store/coffeehouse in the collection of shops that make up the ground floor of the buildings facing Wudaokou Dajie. The coffee isn't great, but it doesn't totally suck either. I go there sometimes when there are no beans in the house.

Chuckie and I grab our coffees at the orange countertop

and sit at a little round table by the window with a scenic view of the parking lot and the lovely four-lane thoroughfare that is Wudaokou. Taxis and private cars whiz by while knots of pedestrians make their way across the street like avatars in some Nintendo game, risking all to gain the treasure on the other side.

Chuckie rips open two packs of sugar and dumps them in his coffee.

'So, what happened?' I finally ask. 'You get busted at the Matrix, or what?'

'Or what,' Chuckie says eventually.

I'm confused by this until I realize that he's attempting to play with the language. 'You got busted by somebody else?'

Chuckie doesn't exactly nod. He stirs his coffee, catching sugar grit between the spoon and the side of the ceramic cup.

'I am going to go home for a while,' he says, not looking at me. 'You should not stay here.'

It's not his fault; I know it isn't, but I'm still so angry it's hard for me to speak. 'Is this about Lao Zhang, Chuckie? Is it? 'Cause I haven't done anything wrong. You know that.'

'*Meiguanxi*.' Doesn't matter.

Neither of us says anything for a while. I stare out the window. Amid the taxis and cars and buses, a donkey cart piled high with bricks makes its way down the street, pausing for a minute so the donkey can crap in the gutter. The guy driving it, a peasant in patched clothes and a battered Mao cap, talks on his cell phone.

Huh. I thought Beijing outlawed donkey carts.

'They want me to tell them everything about you,'

73

Chuckie says rapidly. 'They want to know who your friends are, what you do, where you go. I tell them you, me, we just, we just . . .' He trails off. His hands are shaking. 'We just living, that's all. Just living.'

Them.

'Foreigners, in suits?'

'Foreigners? Why should I worry about foreigners?' he asks, regaining some of his typical bravado. 'What can foreigners do to me?'

'Nothing, I guess,' I say, hoping this isn't going to lead into one of Chuckie's rants about China's Hundred Years of Humiliation at the hands of foreign imperialists.

If it wasn't the Suits, who was it?

'This is China. Chinese people have stood up!'

'So they were Chinese?'

'Of *course* they were Chinese!'

Just like that, he deflates. When it comes down to it, Chuckie's too much of a fuckup free spirit to make a good foaming-at-the-mouth *fenqing*.

'Police, they say,' he whispers. 'But no IDs.'

He gets out a couple wrinkled ten-yuan notes and tosses them on the table. 'My train leaves from West Train station in a couple hours. I better go.' He looks away. 'You should be careful, Ellie,' he says. 'You should not stay here.'

And that's our big good-bye. I sit. Drink my coffee. Watch the passing scene outside the window. Wonder what the fuck I'm going to do now.

There's a surveillance camera in the ceiling above the DVDs, one of those domed things that you see everywhere you go these days. Not just in China, in the U.S. too. For security, right?

74

I stare at the thing, at its unblinking black eye. Wonder who's at the other end staring back.

They're making tapes, I tell myself, to catch shoplifters. It's not like there's somebody watching me right now. Is there?

I pay for the coffee and head back upstairs.

Chuckie hasn't taken a lot with him. The guitar amp, computer parts, books, and Yao Ming stand-up still clutter the living room.

I go into my little room. Stare at my narrow futon. Think I don't ever want to sleep there again. Like I ever *could* sleep there without thinking of John, of lying there waiting for him to do whatever he wanted to do.

All of a sudden, I really want to pack up my stuff and get out of here.

I think about the logistics of this. I've got some clothes. A couple cheap pieces of furniture. My laptop. I mean, what the fuck do I have, anyway?

I open up the little cupboard by my bed. That's where I keep my souvenirs. Things I thought I cared about.

Here's a little Beanie Baby. A neon orange-and-red squid. I always loved that stupid squid. It's just so funny. It makes me smile when I look at it. I throw it onto a pile of clothes to pack.

There's a little jewelry box from Trey. I don't have to open it; I know what's inside: a gold cross necklace studded with tiny diamonds. He gave it to me a long time ago, right after we were married. I don't wear it any more. I wonder why I've kept it.

I take the rest of the stuff out of the cupboard and dump it on the bed. A funny figurine Lao Zhang gave me, Mao as Buddha. A pennant from some soccer – oh, excuse me – *football* club called Arsenal from British John.

And here is that flat, hard box covered with dark blue flocking, about the size of a thin paperback. My service ribbons. My Purple Heart. I think: why did I bring this with me all the way to China? I don't even want to open it. Why does it mean anything at all?

I throw it on top of the clothes. Because I still can't bring myself to leave it behind.

I walk out of Chuckie's place with a duffel bag and a backpack. That's it.

By now, it's close to five o'clock. I'm supposed to start work at Says Hu in an hour. I stand at the curb for a while, watching the cars and the buses and the people passing by me in this blur of noise – shouting in Chinese, horns going off, phones with their stupid ringtones, a loudspeaker blasting bad Hong Kong pop – and I think: I just want to be someplace quiet for once.

But for now? I might as well go to work.

I spring for a cab to take me the couple of miles to Says Hu, thinking I'll get there early and have a beer.

The minute I walk inside, I can see that's not how things are going to go.

British John is trying to pick a table up off the ground. It's tilted on its side, one leg buckled under like it took a cheap cut block. A broken chair leans against the wall, beneath a dartboard.

'Hey,' I say. 'Crazy night?'

'Ellie.'

He crosses quickly to the door and locks it.

I stand there feeling the weight of the duffel bag on my shoulder.

'Let's have a drink,' British John says quickly, grabbing a bottle from the bar.

'Might as well.'

I pull up a barstool and throw the duffel on the floor and the backpack on top of that. British John pours us both shots of Jack and lifts his in a toast.

I don't even like Jack Daniels.

'What are we toasting?' I ask.

British John shrugs. We clink shot glasses in silence. And drink.

'So,' I finally say, 'you firing me, or what?'

British John shakes his head. 'Ellie, it's not like that.'

'So what's it like, then? Who came and talked to you? What did they tell you?'

I guess I'm pretty pissed off, because by the time I finish, I'm practically shaking.

'First I thought they were *Chengguan*. Just the usual shakedown.'

Urban Management officials. A police force found in every Chinese city, mostly demobbed soldiers and thugs, officially in charge of keeping order on the streets, cracking down on illegal vendors and the like. They like beating on migrants and extorting whatever 'fines' they can extract to supplement their crappy salaries.

British John pounds his shot and then pours himself another. I can see the tremor in his hand, and it's not from the booze. 'I don't know who they were. They asked a lot of questions. Gave me a number and told me to call them when you showed up. Told me I'd lose the business if I didn't cooperate.'

'I didn't do anything.' I hear myself saying it, and I have to admit, I sound like a sullen five-year-old.

'It has to be *something*.' British John sounds really frustrated. 'Look, I want to help, but you've got to tell me what's going on.'

I shrug helplessly. 'I don't know. I really don't. It's got something to do with Lao Zhang and some Uighur friend of his. But that's all I know.'

British John tops off our shot glasses. 'You can't keep on working here,' he finally says.

I toss down my drink. 'Okay. Fine. Whatever.'

'Ellie.'

I stand up. 'What?'

British John reaches into the cash register and pulls out a wad of bills. 'Here,' he says awkwardly, holding it out.

'I don't want it.'

'Don't be a fucking stupid cunt.' He slaps the money on the bar. 'Take it.'

He has a point. I pick up the cash and shove it in my pocket. 'Thanks,' I mumble.

'Look,' he finally says, 'just take it easy for a while. When this all settles down, you can come back.'

At that, I snort. 'Yeah, right. Like I want to come back to this shitty-ass job.'

I shoulder my backpack and my duffel. British John comes out from behind the bar, wraps his arms around my waist, and hugs me close. 'Try not to go to extremes,' he says. ''Cause you have a tendency to do that, you know.'

I hug him back. 'I'll see you,' I mutter into his shoulder. And then I turn and leave.

I start walking down the street, past a string of stores selling phones and MP3 players and cameras. I don't have a clue what to do. I've got two sets of spooks on my ass, no job, no place to live, no husband, no boyfriend, and this stupid fucking duffel bag is cutting into my shoulder and making my goddamn leg ache, and I've only got nine Percocets left.

Maybe I should just book myself a flight to the States. What's left for me here in China? Absolutely nothing.

But what do I have back there? My mom, and it's not like I don't miss her sometimes. She'd take me in, but how long would that work? Her life's still bound up in the church. In Sunrise. And that's pretty much the last place I want to be.

Sunrise, with its fake adobe buildings that make it look like an Indian casino minus the neon, which I guess works for Arizona, where I grew up. The auditorium, where the services are held with coffee and donuts and giant plasma TVs. At the bookstore you can get the latest Christian rock and hip-hop CDs, 'WWJD?' bracelets, T-shirts that say 'Stoned Like Paul' and 'Yes, I am a Princess – My Father is the King of Kings!' You can drop your kids off at the daycare center if you want while you go to an aerobics class. The minister, Reverend Jim, wears Hawaiian shirts and talks about joy and living in Christ and how to reach your professional goals, in a Christ-like way. Reverend Jim is big on reaching your professional goals.

There wasn't much else to do where I lived, so I went.

Mom started going too, when she wasn't working. She needed something – something that wasn't work and wasn't taking care of me in our shitty little townhouse down the street from the KFC. Christian parenting, Christian singles – all of a sudden she had this whole network supporting her. It was like she'd been falling and falling and had suddenly landed on this big, soft comforter held up by all these new friends, a place where she was finally safe.

How safe would I be in the U.S.? If the Suits are watching me . . . Would they really leave me alone if I went home?

Sometimes I miss having a weapon. Not my M16. What I want right now is a little M9. A nice reliable pistol. Because really, what's the point? My life's been a disaster ever since those times, and nothing's getting any better. It's just getting worse.

My steps have slowed down to a near shuffle.

Don't cry, you stupid bitch, I tell myself. Nobody cares, and it's not going to do you any good.

About the time I'm ready to stop walking, I find myself in front of a *wangba*, an Internet bar.

I guess I could check my e-mail before I go kill myself.

The girl behind the counter asks for my passport and then doesn't want to look at it, telling me to write the information down myself. So I say I'm 'Faith McConnell' (my sworn enemy from middle school) and claim to be living in 'Orange County,' this suburban development that's out by the Capital Airport, not the one in California. Being a foreigner, no one's going to question me about that.

This *wangba*'s okay, not too crazy with smoke and noise – it's just a long room with rows of computers, a counter up front where you sign in and buy drinks and snacks from a glass-front refrigerator if you want. The décor is mainly beige, with the obligatory 'New Beijing, Great Olympics' poster that no one's bothered to take down and a couple sad-looking potted plants here and there. Chinese and Korean students play games involving swords, explosions, and girls with big tits dressed in chain-mail bikinis; a middle-aged Westerner reads what he can access of *The New York Times* through the Great Firewall. Lately getting on news sites hasn't been too much of a problem, but things like Facebook and Twitter and Blogger are blocked.

Like Lao Zhang said, the government doesn't like it when too many people get together.

When I log in to my Web mail account, I've got over two hundred unread e-mails. Most of them are junk. Plus there's my mom's obligatory 'Send this message to Five Angels you know' e-mail and a couple of dirty jokes from her Christian friends. This is one of those things I've never understood. Why are Christians sending me dirty jokes about cowboys and nuns?

I delete all that, and I don't forward my mom's e-mail to five angels I know, because I don't know any, and I'm probably going to hell anyway.

Halfway down the page is an e-mail from Trey.

'Ellie, please turn on your phone. Call me. I know you're pissed off, and I get that, but let me know you're okay. Those are some heavy-duty guys – if you help them, they can help you. But don't fuck with them. Okay?'

Like he really cares if I'm okay.

My finger hovers over the keyboard. Reply or delete?

I do neither. I go back to my inbox.

Now, here's something weird.

'An Invitation To Tea.' The e-mail is heavy on the HTML, with graphics that look familiar.

'The Sword of Ill Repute,' it says on a banner at the top.

I scroll down, past a Flash animation of warriors

swinging swords, pectorals bulging or breasts heaving depending on their gender.

'Cinderfox, the Humble Servant of the Lord of the Boundless, requests the Swordswoman Little Mountain Tiger join him on a quest. We begin with a cup of tea at the Tears of Heaven's Pass Teahouse. I will be there after four o'clock. I await your response.'

It's Lao Zhang's game, the one he's so addicted to. Chuckie too. I'm Little Mountain Tiger. This is an invite for me to come and play.

I sit there for a moment. I haven't played this game in ages. In fact, I've hardly played it at all. Chuckie and Lao Zhang, they're serious players, high-level, not likely to pursue a lowly newbie with no points, no spells, no magic sword, and who doesn't give a shit about it. None of their friends would either.

Lao Zhang's screen name is Upright Boar of the Western Forest. Chuckie's is Eloquent Evergreen Monkey.

So who is Cinderfox? And why did he send me this invitation?

Here's the link to play, outlined in blue. I hesitate.

It's Lao Zhang's game.

I click on the link.

CHAPTER SEVEN

My first duty assignment was at one of the biggest forward operating bases in the Triangle. Life on the FOB was okay, in comparison to the alternatives. We had a PX, where you could buy toothpaste and iPods and tampons, a dining hall with a salad bar and a taco station, a little gym, air-conditioning some of the time, Internet connections. I could get a mochaccino in the morning if I wanted, before going out on patrol. That part sucked, though, and there was no getting around it. I was a medic, not some fobbit who never left the base. It was my job to ride along, in case somebody got shot or blown up.

You hear 'patrol,' and you're probably thinking 'combat'; we're out there fighting bad guys. It wasn't like that. I was part of a support company. Most of the time, we delivered supplies, guarded cheesecake for truck convoys run by private contractors like KBR, or escorted public affairs officers to some meeting with the locals.

The heat was like nothing I've ever felt before, like the sun and the wind were cooking me down to my bones, drying me out from the inside, and no amount of water was going to keep me from shriveling up into some girl-shaped piece of jerky. Everything was coated in greasy dust. I'd blow my nose and my snot would come out like it was just glue to hold the grit and dirt together. We were hacking this shit up all the time, always sweating, leaving stiff white salt stains on our T-shirts. With the women, sometimes you could see our tits outlined in white against the khaki. The guys loved that.

I fucked around a little. Not at first. At first it was like, 'Let's see who can freak out the good little Christian girl.'

Things like: 'Hey, Baby Doc, check it out.'

I was checking my e-mail, and Specialist Turner was sitting at the terminal next to me.

'What?'

'Got some pics from home.'

I leaned over to take a look. On his screen, this big dick was pumping in and out of some porn star's pussy, while another guy straddled her, his cock between her inflated tits, which she was squeezing together like she was playing an accordion.

I looked away. I wanted to say something funny or sarcastic or mean, like I didn't care, but I couldn't think of anything to say.

'Aw, come on, don't be such a bitch,' Turner said.

I went back to my e-mail. My mom had sent me one about what religion your bra is ('the Catholic type supports the masses, the Presbyterian type keeps them staunch and upright, and the Baptist makes mountains out of mole-hills') that said I should send it on to anyone who would appreciate it.

Turner and I hooked up a couple days later, out by the

laundry trailer, where there was a storeroom that was used for supplies. At night, nobody went there. At first, I felt pretty bad about it. Turner was married, had a kid, and I wasn't supposed to do things like that. But there I was, lying on a pile of dirty sheets, my T-shirt and bra in a heap over bottles of bleach and detergent, my fatigues tangled up around my ankles.

'It's TDY, Baby Doc,' he told me, sliding his finger in and out. 'TDY doesn't count.'

TDY means temporary duty assignment. It's all been TDY since then, you know?

The game takes a long time to load, but it's an elaborate game, and you never know what the Great Firewall is doing to your Internet connection here on any given day.

Finally, here's the log-in screen, a vaguely Chinese land-scape of misty, cloud-swaddled mountain peaks and pagodas. An animated warrior on horseback gallops across. Then the music comes on – a pseudo-traditional Chinese soundtrack with the mournful *erhu* and the twanging runs and staccato chords of the *pipa*, all with a heavy drum and bass backbeat.

It takes me three tries to remember my password, because it's been a while since I played this game. When I get it right, my avatar, Little Mountain Tiger, pops up, non-magical sword in hand.

The Sword of Ill Repute is based on Chinese myth and legend – the Hong Kong movie versions, anyway. A whole class of characters comes from the twelve birth animals of the Chinese horoscope. Most people play as a variation of the animal from their birth year. So if you're a Boar, like Lao Zhang, you have certain attributes based on your intrinsic Boar nature, plus others that have to do with the particular year you were born in, your elements, your rising sign, and so on.

I'm actually a Rat, but no matter how many times Lao Zhang told me that the Rat is a good sign –'Smart, clever, not like Boars. Boars too trusting. Too idealistic. Better in this world to be a Rat.' – I didn't want to be 'Little Sewer Rat' or what have you. 'Little Mountain Tiger' is based on the particular year, month, and day of my birthday, which happens to be a Tiger day. So that's how I play, with faint tiger stripes accenting my cheekbones.

The scene shifts. I'm in an unfamiliar setting, nothing like where I last left off playing. I'm walking up a steep mountain path, animated pebbles crunching under my feet. Crows caw in the pine trees overhead. A warrior steps onto the path, Shao Wu of the Wounded Mountain. An NPC – a non-player character.

'Halt and state your allegiance!' says the text in the main chat window. You can play this game in Chinese or English, thanks to Babblefish translators.

I try to walk on by, and the NPC pulls out his sword.

I hit auto-attack. The music turns martial. We fight. I kill him and gain a few experience points. Then I keep walking.

I continue on the path and see, off to the left, a wooden building with a steep pitched roof and a sign whose characters I recognize: *Cha Guan.*

A teahouse.

I go inside.

More *pipa* music plinks in the background. Animated figures sit in booths at wooden tables, sip tea, play cards, eat watermelon seeds. A female musician sings a song about lovers who drown themselves in a hidden lake. I'm not sure who's an avatar and who's an NPC. It's not that crowded. I walk slowly through the main room. Characters' names appear over their heads in shimmering text as I pass. There's some chatter about going to the market to purchase an Immutable Dagger and starting a quest on behalf of the Emperor for the Sacred Scroll of the Nine Immortals. No one engages me.

So where's Cinderfox?

Finally, at the back, I see a male figure, hair and beard a dark, deep red, slanted green eyes. He does have a sort of foxy look about him. I approach.

'Hail,' I type.

Nothing.

I take a few steps closer.

'Hail,' I try again.

His name appears over his russet head: 'Cinderfox, Son of the Boundless.'

'Greetings, Little Mountain Tiger. Glad you accept my invitation.'

I sit.

'Tea?'

'Thank you.'

After a moment or two, an animated serving girl appears, bearing a tray with a teapot and two cups.

Obviously, Cinderfox has way more pull in this game than I do.

'Jasmine? Dragon Well? Oolong?'

'Dragon Well,' I type.

Of course, the whole thing is ridiculous. I'm going to sit here and drink imaginary tea with a cartoon character?

The serving girl pours. We drink.

'Dragon Well is good choice,' Cinderfox types. 'You gain wisdom and stamina from this.'

I check out my character inventory. My wisdom and stamina have increased by five points each.

'Why did you invite me?' I type.

'I think we should keep our business private. Now that you found me.'

Just like that, a bamboo screen surrounds our little table.

The chat window has changed colors. The banner now reads 'Private Chat.'

'I make us anonymous,' Cinderfox types.

'Cool.'

'Have more tea.'

If I had the ability, Little Mountain Tiger would be squirming in her seat about now. I really don't feel like wasting more time drinking virtual tea, regardless of what it does to my wisdom score.

But I go along with it. This isn't my game.

'Okay, Cinderfox,' I type. 'What is this quest?'

'Maybe this up to you.'

'Don't know what you mean.'

'You Upright Boar friend?'

Upright Boar – Lao Zhang's avatar.

'Yes,' I type.

'Maybe you can help.'

I lean back in my chair. 'Who are you?' I ask.

'Upright Boar friend.'

'How do I know that?'

'You don't.'

I stare at Cinderfox, who sits on the bench, expression unchanging, green eyes unblinking.

'What do you want?' I type.

'I want nothing.'

Very helpful. I'm sweating. I swipe my hand across my forehead.

'Help what?' I type. 'Help in the game?'

A pause.

'Maybe not just game.'

I'm sitting there, my avatar on a bench in an animated teahouse, my butt on a crappy plastic chair in a Beijing Net bar, and I'm thinking about the Uighur and creepy John and the Suits and now this.

'What else?' I type.

'Help Upright Boar,' say the words about Cinderfox's pixellated head.

Okay, I think. Okay. I'm chatting with some guy I don't know, a guy who has my e-mail address, who invited me to go on a quest, and who says he's Lao Zhang's friend. I think of all those nights I used to watch Lao Zhang playing on his computer, and suddenly I wonder – what was he really doing? What game was he actually playing?

'Is he okay?'

'Right now, yes.'

'Can I talk to him?'

A pause.

'Right now, off-line.'

A long pause.

'Do you want to help?' Cinderfox finally asks.

Well, do I? That's a pretty good question. Whatever Lao Zhang's involved with, it's already cost me plenty.

But is that really his fault?

After all, the Suits probably know about Lao Zhang because of me. Because of what I did.

89

What did *you* do in the war, Daddy?

'Yes,' I type. 'I want to help.'

That's when a couple panels in the bamboo screen slide back, and three new avatars enter our booth.

I look at the names above their heads. 'Water Horse.' 'Monk of the Jade Forest.' 'Golden Snake.'

'Greetings, Little Mountain Tiger,' say the text boxes above their heads.

'Members of our Guild,' Cinderfox explains.

'Nice to meet you,' I type.

'Thank you for coming,' says Golden Snake, a female avatar with copper-colored scales that hug her body, merging into her flesh.

'Yes,' Water Horse (another female) chimes in.

Monk of the Jade Forest, a male avatar with jet-black hair and a green robe, sits down on the bench to Cinderfox's left.

'We appreciate that you've met us here,' he writes. 'And we are glad that you want to help. But you should know, we can't guarantee that there's no risk to you.'

Words appear over Cinderfox's head so quickly that he misspells a few. 'Not dangeros. We wont ask something like that. Just something you can do to hellp.'

'Cinderfox you shouldnt promise theres no risk,' says Golden Snake.

'If she wants to help, let her,' Water Horse objects. She's dressed in silver armor, with a long, thick ponytail that falls down her back, practically to her knees.

'It should not be dangerous,' Cinderfox types.

'So, which is it?' I ask. 'Dangerous or not?'

Another pause.

'Maybe we don't know for sure,' says Cinderfox. 'But shouldn't be *very* dangerous.'

'If the risk bothers you, then you should not help,' states Monk of the Jade Forest.

'I want to help,' I type. I'm not sure that I do, really, but I don't feel like backing down. The last few years, that's all I've done, caved; and look where it's gotten me.

Cinderfox stands up. 'I invite you join our Guild,' he types. 'Our name is the 'Great Community.' This is our sign.' He lifts his hand. Above the table, a shield materializes in mid-air, a golden, rough-edged crest with red characters in the middle: 大同

I know these characters. '*Da Tong*,' I mutter. The Big . . . Together?

Which I guess means the Great Community.

Cinderfox's hand stays raised. Little sparks fly off it. The shield pulses above the table.

'You acccpt, you can find us again, always. Log on, choose Yellow Mountain Monastery for location. Use anon/group command. Only we see you that way. You decline, that's okay. We go our separate ways.'

I hesitate for what feels like a long time.

You get yourself into some situations, you don't know exactly how you got there, and you have no fucking clue what shitstorm's going to hit you.

This time, I don't have that excuse. I already know that whatever this is about, I am in way over my head. I've been in over my head ever since I ate dumplings with the Uighur dude.

I should just quit this game, leave this country, and try

to figure out what to do with my increasingly fucked-up life.

But that's not what I do.

'Okay,' I type. 'Accept.'

'Welcome,' say my new circle of friends, their text boxes overlapping like a poker spread.

'So what do I do?' I ask.

A long pause.

'Go to where you eat *jiaozi*,' says Monk of the Jade Forest.

CHAPTER EIGHT

I keep thinking, if that medic hadn't been injured, I wouldn't have gotten the transfer. No transfer, and everything would've been different. I wouldn't be in this situation. Wouldn't have the Suits and god knows who else on my ass. I would've gone home at the end of my deployment, gone to school like I'd planned to do when I joined the Guard, gotten a degree, gotten on with my life.

Or maybe not. Maybe I would've been killed instead of just getting blown up.

Who knows? It's stupid to spend a lot of time thinking about what would have happened if things had been different. Things would have been *different*, that's all, and you can't change it anyway.

But sometimes I think there's another life I could have had. Should have had. And maybe some other version of me is having it, like in some Sci-Fi Channel movie.

Which probably means it's low-budget and lame.

The funny thing is, when I first got the transfer, I thought it might be good news, because the patrols were really starting to suck.

Like this one time, we were outside the wire on a cheesecake run, escorting a KBR truck that was transporting chow from our FOB to a small base about fifty clicks away, and we were almost there, the lead vehicle just rolling up to the gate.

'Creed's a bunch of pussies,' the soldier next to me was saying to me. 'You gotta check out System of a Down.'

That was when something exploded. It was so loud, it was like being on the inside of thunder. The left wheels of the Humvee lifted off the ground and fell back, bounced twice; metal spat against the hood and windshield like popcorn. Our gunner fired off one burst, two; somebody yelled into the radio; I smelled hot copper; and next to me, the soldier shouted, 'Oh, fuck!'

Standard operating procedure is, you move out of the kill zone, set up a 360, a secure field of fire, and request a quick reaction force, because a lot of times a bomb is followed by small-arms fire, hajji trying to pick you off in the confusion.

I waited for the gunfire, but it never came. Everything settled down, like a spent cloudburst.

It was a suicide bomber, not an IED. He'd blown himself up too soon, with most of the damage hitting a blast wall. The KBR truck got dinged and broke an axle. The trucker had a thigh laceration that was bleeding a lot, so they radioed back for me to come and help.

I trotted up the street thinking, oh God, I am going to die, trying to keep low, ears ringing, the heat and the smoke searing my lungs.

'Fucking shithole,' the soldier jogging next to me said.

They'd put the base at the edge of a town, securing the perimeter by clearing out the buildings on the surrounding block and throwing up some blast walls and razor wire. The KBR truck sat crooked and smoking, partially blocking the entrance.

I put a pressure bandage on the trucker (who was doing okay for an overweight fifty-two-year-old with high blood pressure and a pack-a-day habit), and we got him on a gurney to take him to the aid station inside the base.

About a half dozen soldiers had gathered by the blast wall closest to the gate.

One of them, a buddy of mine, said: 'Hey, Doc, check this out!' He pointed, grinning. 'Way to go, asshole!'

What was left of the bomber was lumps of gore, splinters of bone, shredded clothes, a leg flung up against the blast wall, sneaker still on the foot.

'Where's the other leg?' I asked.

'That's not the good part,' my buddy said.

I looked where he pointed. There was a face lying a couple feet from the torso, peeled off from the skull like a mask.

'Too bad it's not Halloween,' I said.

Even the trucker laughed at that.

Two weeks later, I got transferred to this new FOB because they were down a medic, who I later learned had gotten shrapnel in his head and throat from a mortar round. He didn't die, though, and I heard he only drools a little, so consider him Private Lucky Motherfucker. Because this FOB just sucked. No mochaccinos there. The place was about the size of a football field, if that. Let's call it Camp Falafel, which of course is not what it was called, because the U.S. Army prefers more serious names, like Camp Screaming Eagle, or Operation Enduring Kill the Stupid Rag-Heads. The base was built around an old Baathist government complex just outside of this provincial town that was a center of the insurgency, the insurgency that nobody wanted to admit existed back then.

In addition to what we called the Admin Core – offices, I thought at first – there were low, long barracks that used to house Iraqi soldiers. Republican Guards, I found out later. The existing buildings weren't enough for us plus the prisoners that ended up getting detained there, so Camp Falafel had rows of tents as well.

Though I still rode along on supply runs now and again, I was mostly tasked to assist the physician's assistant, Staff Sergeant Blanchard, at the aid station.

Blanchard was this tall, blocky guy with bad skin and birth-control glasses, those ugly-ass, Army-issue black-framed glasses that only look good on ironic alternative rock musicians, which he was not. The guy was a dick. He was always riding me, like I had no business hanging with the boys in a war zone. If I had been honest with him, I would have agreed. I didn't want to be there.

But I wouldn't admit that, because I wanted to do a good job. Instead, I just took all his insults, about how I couldn't lift the gurneys because I was too fucking weak, how I was too fucking stupid to know what to do. Mostly he was pissed off that I wouldn't sleep with him.

I hated being alone with Blanchard. I never knew exactly what he was going to pull, but I could always count on him to be a dick.

This was typical: One night when I was restocking the supply cupboard, he came up behind me and pressed himself against my back. I could feel his hard-on poking me. I really wasn't in the mood.

'Hey,' I said. 'Hey! What are you doing?'

'Nothing. I'm not doing anything. Just getting some Betadine.'

He had me pushed against the shelves, and his hand reached over my shoulder, toward the shelf that was right about level with my chest. I knew where it was heading.

I sidestepped and squirmed past him.

'Don't be such a bitch,' he called after me.

Mostly we dealt with everybody's owwies and boo-boos: sprained ankles, heat stroke, skin infections, dysentery, gastroenteritis, that kind of thing. Plus, given the age of some of the Guard, we had to treat high blood pressure, cardiac infarction, even a stroke. Then there was the soldier nobody knew, some specialist, who one day just blew his brains out. Who knows why? Nobody knew the guy. He arrived one day and, two weeks later, decided to kill himself. Pretty fucking inconsiderate of him.

Then there were the Iraqi prisoners. The PUCs. That's military-speak for 'Persons Under Control.'

The PUCs would come in all kinds of different ways.

CHAPTER NINE

I take the train and then the bus to Mati Village, duffel slung over my shoulder.

If this is about Lao Zhang, then the *jiaozi* place the Monk has in mind is the one in Mati Village where Lao Zhang and I always go. If not, well, at least I can eat some *jiaozi*.

But maybe this is a really bad idea. If the PSB or whoever the fuck that John guy works for are watching me, if they're looking for me, they must know this is a place I go.

If they find me, then what?

What do they want? What would they do?

Cattle prods, I'm thinking. They've got this thing for cattle prods, but that's not going to happen to me, right? I'm a foreigner. They don't do that shit to foreigners.

Don't think about it, I tell myself. Just go eat some *jiaozi*.

I get to the *jiaozi* place right before it closes. It's still pretty packed. I find myself a small table, stash my duffel on the chair opposite, and order up some *jiaozi* and a beer.

When the waitress brings me a tall, frosted bottle of premium Yanjing and a plastic tumbler, I stare at it for a moment. My mouth tastes like copper. I think about John handing me a bottle of Yanjing.

I fill up the tumbler and take a nice, foamy slug. It tastes good.

'Fuck you, John,' I mutter, lifting up the tumbler in a toast to the universe at large.

'Yili, *ni hao*.'

Standing in front of me is Sloppy Song, holding her thick braid in one hand, tugging on it absently like she's trying to remind herself of something.

'Hey, Sloppy.' I indicate the chair. 'You eat yet?'

'No, not yet. I work on new piece. No time to eat.'

'You want to join me?'

We shift the duffel onto another chair, and Sloppy sits down across from me. When my *jiaozi* come, I order another dozen and some side dishes too. The food's dirt-cheap here, I've got a wallet full of cash from British John, and maybe it's no coincidence, Sloppy's showing up like this.

Sloppy sips her beer, tugs on her braid, and doesn't say very much. We quickly eat the first bowl of *jiaozi*. Midway through the boiled peanuts and *yuxiang*-flavor pork, Sloppy lets go of her hair and asks: 'Have you heard from Lao Zhang?'

'Not for a couple of days.'

'Did he say where he is?'

I shake my head.

'Ah,' Sloppy says, and turns her focus to the fresh *jiaozi*.

'He said I could stay at his house a while,' I lie.

'His house is a little messy,' Sloppy says carefully. 'Some people come to visit.'

'I understand. I can do some cleaning while I'm there.'

We finish up our meal. Sloppy tries to force money on me, but I refuse. 'Next time, you invite me,' I say with a wave.

As I make my way to Lao Zhang's, I'm thinking about a number of things. I'm thinking: so, I went to the *jiaozi* place, and what did I learn? Sloppy Song turned up, and it would make sense if she was in on whatever it is that Lao Zhang is doing; they're friends, fellow artists and all. On the other hand, she's always eating at that *jiaozi* place, and it might not mean anything at all. Maybe somebody else in the restaurant's involved, the waitress, the cashier, the owner for all I know. Maybe there was another customer, someone I don't even know, or one of the regulars I tend to ignore, sitting there, watching me.

Maybe the Monk just wanted to see if I'd do what he asked me to.

Why a game? But then, why not? This is China. Bulletin boards and chat rooms are monitored. The government can read your e-mails whenever it wants. If you needed a way to meet people, to talk to them, and you didn't want the government to know, who'd think twice about a game? About avatars slinging swords and hurling spells at each other.

I stop at the corner market to buy more beer and water. There's a young guy hanging out by the door, a *liumang*, kind of a punk, with a dirty denim jacket, spiked hair, and sunglasses, one of those guys where you can't tell if he's an actual delinquent or just playing at being one. He leans against the power pole, beer in hand, lost in the tunes beamed into his head through his earbuds.

But I feel his eyes on me when I leave the store.

He's just a local rascal, I tell myself.

The courtyard of Lao Zhang's compound is dead quiet. No electronic *erhu* sounds from the composer across from him. No sounds of partying from the sculptor's, or the novelist/painter's. The empty Mao jacket seems to glow in the moonlight.

Did they split, I wonder? Take off for their own versions of Bumfuck Shanxi like Chuckie? Get arrested?

If it weren't for the moonlight, I wouldn't be able to see a thing. I fumble around and finally manage to slip the key in the lock of Lao Zhang's apartment door.

The lamp in the entryway has a red shade, making it look like you're going into a club. 'Hides the dirt,' Lao Zhang used to say. The place smells stale, dusty, like it's been closed up a few days.

Inside, everything looks the same. Not particularly messy. Not really neat either. Paintings stacked against the walls. Here's the couch, here's the TV. There's the computer.

Do I hear something? Something in the kitchen?

'Anyone here?' I call out, mouth dry.

It's just the wind, I tell myself. There's no one home. No one but me.

Still, when I go into the kitchen, I check the utility room to make sure.

No Uighur in the closet. Now what?

I grab a beer and some water and put the rest in the fridge. There's no way I'm going to risk using Lao Zhang's computer, so I turn on the TV. It's the usual stuff. Some variety show that alternates between comedians with animated sound-effect balloons blossoming above their heads and children dancing around, twirling banners. A news program about old people playing traditional Chinese instruments. A commercial for a 'tonic' that increases 'man's stamina' with a middle-aged guy in glasses who gives us a thumbs-up as he and some babe in a red dress clink champagne flutes.

I finally settle on a *wuxia* movie. It looks pretty dumb, but I like watching all those Shaolin monks flying through the air. I drink one beer, and then I drink another, and then I think: hey, why not, let's have a Percocet. I only get a little ways into the third bottle before I can't keep my eyes open any more. I'm too tired to go all the way into the bedroom. I pull the ratty quilt Lao Zhang keeps on the couch over me and rest my head on the arm of the couch. On the TV, an old blind monk with a wispy gray beard that reaches down to his crotch is hurling some mystical weapon that resembles a salad spinner at the bad guys.

I switch off the TV and close my eyes.

Sometimes when I drink too much, I'll pass out for a few hours, and then I'll wake up, and I won't sleep well after that, just kind of toss and sweat and doze. It doesn't take much to wake me up the rest of the way.

Little things, like the rattle of a doorknob. A creaky hinge. A light step across the threshold.

And I'm wide awake. My heart pounds like it's going to choke me. I freeze on the couch for a moment. Then I scramble off it, quietly as I can. Where to go? I grab the heavy flashlight Lao Zhang keeps by the TV in case of power outages, and I duck behind the couch.

A slight female figure, dressed head to toe in black, steps into the room, not exactly crouching, but doing a pretty good impression of stealthy.

I jump up from behind the couch, shine the flashlight in her face. 'Hey!' I yell. '*Ni shi shei*?'

Who the hell are you?

She's a pretty cool customer. She straightens up. 'Oh,' she says in English. 'Oh, please excuse me. I'm so sorry. I didn't realize anyone . . .'

It takes me a minute to place her.

'You're . . . you're that art dealer from Shanghai,' I manage.

She smiles at me. 'Yes. Lucy Wu. So sorry to disturb you.'

'Disturb . . . ? What are you doing here?'

'Oh,' she exclaims, smiling furiously. 'Jianli invited me here. To see his paintings.'

I look around. It's some time after dawn, but I'm pretty sure it's awfully early for an appointment.

'So, what's with the ninja outfit?' I ask, holding the flashlight like a club.

Lucy Wu draws herself up to her full, diminutive height. 'It's Vivienne Tam,' she says, mightily offended.

'Whatever.' I thump the flashlight against my palm. 'Anyway, Lao Zhang's not here.'

'Oh,' she says, recovering her smile. 'I know. That's why I've come so early. He told me I should just drop by. At my convenience.' She holds up a key. 'He left this for me.'

On the one hand, there's no way I believe this. On the other, there's Lao Zhang's habit of taking in strays.

But Lucy Wu? She's no stray. She's a fucking thoroughbred.

How did she get Lao Zhang's key?

I stand there with the flashlight, and I don't know what to do.

'You want a coffee?' I ask.

In order to make espressos with Lao Zhang's fancy machine, I have to put the flashlight down and briefly turn my back on Lucy Wu. She couldn't actually be dangerous, could she? It's not like you could hide a pair of numchuks in that catsuit.

'I'm so sorry to have disturbed you,' she says, as I tap down the grounds. 'It's only that I did not know anyone would be staying here.'

'Well, you know how Lao Zhang is. The door's always open.'

'Oh, yes,' she says, sitting down at the kitchen table. 'He's been like that as long as I've known him.'

I bring the espressos and sit across from Lucy Wu, who thanks me and stirs a little sugar into her tiny cup.

'You've known him a while?'

'Since Suojiacun International Art Camp. Are you familiar with it?'

'A little,' I say – meaning I've heard the name, and I know it was one of the places Lao Zhang used to hang out.

Lucy Wu smiles, and it's something different from the smug little grin I've seen on her face before.

'That was quite a time. People from all over the world came there to live and do art. Of course, after a few years, the government said Suojiacun lacked the proper permits, and they tore most of it down.'

For a moment, Lucy Wu stares down at her espresso. 'It seems trouble always follows Jianli.'

I feel like I'm two steps behind here, like if I were only a little faster, I might know what to ask, how to respond.

'You think he's in trouble now?'

'Well, I couldn't say. It's been a while since I've seen him. I don't really know what he's been up to.' She looks concerned. Almost eager. 'Is he having some problems?'

'I, uh . . . He just had to go out of town.'

'Of course things are different now,' Lucy Wu says with a tiny shrug. 'No one cares what artists do these days. As long as they are only doing art.'

How can you tell if someone's lying or not, when everything they do seems like an act?

'So, you were an artist?' I ask. I have a feeling I'm sounding a little desperate, but I'm not cut out for this spy stuff. I don't even know how to make small talk for real.

She giggles. 'A bad one. Jianli was kind to me, but it's the truth. Finally I realized I was better at appreciating good art than creating it myself.'

I study her face. I almost think she's telling the truth. And that little blush in her cheeks when she mentions Lao Zhang . . . Well, if I didn't know before what kind of 'old friends' they were, I'm pretty sure I know now.

Except, except . . . the way Lao Zhang acted that night at the Warehouse. Is that how a guy acts when he's happy to see an old girlfriend?

Maybe she dumped him.

'I'm so excited to see his paintings,' Lucy Wu continues. 'Because you know, his performance pieces and installations are very exciting, of course, but such things are difficult to exhibit at times, and to sell. While paintings, on the other hand . . .'

'You can make some money off of them,' I offer.

Lucy Wu frowns, her forehead creasing fractionally. 'Oh, I don't mean to suggest that I'm only interested in profit. My primary consideration is the artistic merit. And to help an old friend.'

'Right.'

We finish our espressos.

Or maybe he dumped her, and she's the psycho ex. A bunny-boiler. With Chinese characteristics.

'So,' she says, the tip of her tongue licking the last bit of sugar and coffee off her spoon, 'might it be possible for me to see some of Jianli's recent work? If it's convenient for you?'

'I guess.'

There are canvases stacked all around the house, leaning against the bedroom wall, stuck behind the couch, like they're part of the furniture. I hardly notice them any more.

'I think some of these are pretty recent.'

Lucy Wu crouches behind the couch and separates one painting from another. She arranges them in a row against

106

the front of the couch where the light from the skylight and courtyard windows filters in.

'Ah,' she breathes. 'These are very special.'

I squint at the paintings. I really haven't paid that much attention to what he's been doing lately. For a minute, I feel bad about that. Like, maybe that's why he left without an explanation. Because I didn't even care enough about him to take in what his work is about.

The paintings are kind of strange. It's like he's taken bits and pieces of things that look familiar but don't really go together. Fish in the middle of forests. Boats floating down broad Beijing avenues. Here's one that looks like a landscape painting – except instead of temples or pagodas, the buildings are Vegas-style casinos perched among steep jade mountains. I can see the symbols on a slot machine in the closest pavilion – two Mao faces, a BMW, a cell phone, and a cabbage.

Some of the other paintings, I can almost understand them, but not quite. Like somebody's whispering an explanation in my ear and I can't quite hear it.

This one, it's colors and shapes, and then I see there's a person, crouched by what maybe is a lake, and it makes me feel peaceful, but I'm not sure why.

And this one, gray streaked with red. A kneeling, huddled figure surrounded by large, dark men.

I don't like the way that one makes me feel.

Then I get a shock.

'Oh, that's you, isn't it?' Lucy Wu says brightly.

I guess it is. She looks like me, the woman in the painting – the lines in her face are more exaggerated, the features slightly elongated, but still. She stands in front of rolling sand dunes. One hand holds the scruff of a snarling dog; it's big, like a German shepherd or a Rottweiler, but it's missing one of its front legs. There's a cat cradled in her other arm, small with big eyes, fur puffed out like it's scared. Behind her, a helicopter spins out of control, spitting flame, and an explosion scatters sand and rock.

The funny thing is her expression. It's – I don't know. Calm. Strong, almost.

That part doesn't look like me at all.

Lucy Wu chuckles. 'Very amusing. Of course these themes have been explored by others, but still . . .' Her dainty tongue darts out and licks her lips. Her expression is avid. 'This work is very significant. I had no idea he'd done all this.' She gestures at a stack of canvases. 'Some of these paintings are ten, fifteen years old, and he's never shown them.'

'Lao Zhang's not here,' I say. 'It's not like I can tell you anything about what he wants to do with them.'

'Oh, of course. But perhaps, the next time you speak to him, you might mention our conversation.'

'Okay. I'll do that.'

'Well, I don't wish to disturb you any further,' Lucy Wu says. 'I'll let you get on with your day.' She turns to go. Then pauses. 'You know, some friends of mine are throwing a party. At Simatai Great Wall. Perhaps you would like to attend.'

'Thanks . . . I . . .'

Lucy Wu reacts fast, before any awkward silences, before I can say no. 'Tell me your e-mail address,' she says. 'I'll send you an invitation.'

Do I want to do this? Even if she's not the psycho ex-girlfriend, how do I know she isn't working for some Chinese security agency? Or even the Suits?

'I appreciate the invitation,' I say. 'I'm not sure if I can come.'

'I won't take no for an answer,' she says, wagging her finger at me. She giggles. 'Don't think you can get away from me so easily!'

CHAPTER TEN

After Lucy Wu leaves, I make myself another espresso. I'm stiff and sore and have a pounding headache from my night on the couch and all those beers, so I take a Percocet as well.

After that, I pace around the living room and stare at Lao Zhang's paintings, propped against the walls, against the TV, against the couch. Is Lucy Wu for real? Are these paintings brilliant? How can I be sure? What do I know about art?

Okay, I think. Okay. I need to do something. I don't know what.

Breakfast, maybe.

Mati Village has a cool coffeehouse that serves Western and Chinese pastries along with passable mochas. They've got Internet too. Not that I expect their Internet connection to be safe, exactly, but maybe it's slightly safer than Lao Zhang's.

This place is called Comrade Lei Feng's, which is pretty funny, Lei Feng being this low-ranking Peoples' Liberation

Army soldier who fell off a truck or something and died in the early 1960s and became a Cultural Revolution icon because he left this diary praising Chairman Mao and serving the people and helping little old ladies across the commune. The coffeehouse has a nice side business selling coffee mugs and T-shirts with the famous picture of Lei Feng looking resolute in his PLA Snoopy hat on them, except he's holding up a steaming mug of coffee.

I order up a large redeye and a limp croissant, and I park myself in front of a computer.

My inbox is full of the usual stuff. Here's an e-mail from my mom – animated kittens and puppies chasing each other, interspersed with the following text:

'Happiness keeps you sweet, Trials keep you strong, Sorrows keep you human, Failures keep you humble, Success keeps you glowing, But only God keeps you going!'

'One good thing about taking the bus to work,' my mom adds in a P.S.: 'I'm doing so much walking that I've lost seven pounds! You never know what might turn out to be a blessing.'

Here's Trey again. 'Ellie, you and I have got to talk. It's wrong for you to just keep running away this way. It's not going to help you. Call me on my cell. Love, Trey.'

Asshole.

And here's an Evite from Ms Lucy Wu – A Great Occasion – inviting me to a party at Simatai Great Wall.

That was fast.

There's nothing from Cinderfox or the Great Community.

I log on to the game and go to the Yellow Mountain Monastery.

My avatar looks different now. She – I – carries a shield that looks like a giant tortoise shell with the characters for 'Great Community' blazoned upon it and a sturdy walking staff taller than she is. I check my character inventory, and I've gotten stronger than I was the last time I played; smarter too; and the staff and shield have some major kill-and-protect power. Thank you, Cinderfox. Poor Chuckie. If only he knew what he missed out on by running back to Shanxi.

I'm walking up that steep mountain path again, bootheels crunching on round stones. I look up, and in one of the twisted pines there's a dragon twined around the branches, holding a black pearl between its front claws.

Then I remember I'm supposed to be anonymous. I type in the command.

The dragon opens its alligator snout and spits flame. Another non-player character, I think. Or, in any case, not one of my new buddies from the Great Community. The pearl is probably worth something, some big prize, but I don't care about that. I'm on a different quest.

I continue up the path, which twists and turns, disappearing into fog as it crawls up the mountain.

Here's a monk, sitting cross-legged on a huge boulder, eyes closed, hands resting on his thighs, palms up, thumb and index finger forming a circle. Meditating, I guess.

Monk of the Jade Forest.

I take a few steps closer. A couple of big black crows fly past, cawing like Edgar Allen Poe refugees.

The monk lifts up his head and opens his eyes.

'I went and ate jiaozi,' I type. 'Now what?'

Monk of the Jade Forest doesn't reply. He just sits cross-legged on his rock, blinking occasionally. I'm pretty sure my avatar can't blink. He probably paid extra for that.

I'm starting to get impatient. 'I have to go,' I type. 'What do you want me to do?'

Finally, Monk of the Jade Forest rises from his granite meditation seat. 'If someone invites you on a quest, you should accept,' he says.

'I already accepted this quest,' I type. 'What's it about? Can you tell me?'

'You'll see. If you go further.'

With that, he makes a sudden pass with his hands and disappears in a swirl of green mist.

I stand there for a moment, and then I log out.

I'm pretty close to thinking this whole game is bullshit: some weird, twisted joke, like one of those performance-art pieces I never understand.

How do I know Cinderfox and Monk of the Jade Forest aren't yanking my chain, having me run around for nothing? How do I know they aren't the same person using different avatars?

And, if I'm going to indulge in paranoia, how do I know that they're not steering me someplace I don't want to go at all?

A quest. Great. The only invitation I've gotten lately is to Lucy Wu's party at the Great Wall. I'm just supposed to go to her party and see what happens?

I track down Sloppy Song at the *jiaozi* place around dinnertime.

'So, Sloppy,' I say, filling up her plastic mug with Yanjing's finest, 'what do you know about Lucy Wu?'

Sloppy shrugs and spears a *jiaozi*. 'Art dealer in Shanghai. Has a nice place near Xintiandi.'

'Do you know that for sure? I mean, have you seen it?'

'I haven't been there. But I hear of her before.'

113

'Who told you about her?'

Sloppy frowns a little. 'I forget. You know, everybody around here always talking about something.'

'She says she's a friend of Lao Zhang's from Suojiacun Art Camp.'

'Could be. Maybe *he* told me about her.'

We sit in silence and eat *jiaozi*.

'Did you hear about the party at Simatai Great Wall?' Sloppy asks suddenly.

'She invited me.'

'Me too.' Sloppy refills my beer. 'Maybe we should share taxi,' she says casually.

I have no idea how to dress for 'A Great Occasion' at the Simatai Great Wall. It sounds fancy, but Simatai is pretty rugged in places. I settle for basic black – black jeans, black shirt, black leather jacket, and my best counterfeit Pumas – and hope I'm not going to look too stupid among the 'patrons of the arts' that Lucy Wu must run with.

I feel a little better when I meet Sloppy outside Comrade Lei Feng's, as she's wearing an outfit similar to mine.

It takes us about an hour by off-meter taxi to get to Simatai. We don't say much during the ride, but then Sloppy's never been the chatty type and, as mentioned, I suck at small talk.

I steal a glance at Sloppy now and then as we bounce along in our beater Jetta cab. Her attention seems to be focused on the landscape outside the car window. She's always been friendly to me, in her sort of spacy way, and I assumed she and Lao Zhang were pretty tight.

Now I wonder. She was having dinner with Lucy Wu that night I met the Uighur. Lucy Wu, who shows up at

Lao Zhang's place at the crack of dawn with her very own key, who might be his old girlfriend but isn't necessarily somebody he likes. Or trusts.

I know *I* don't trust her.

And now, here's Sloppy and me, both invited guests to Lucy Wu's 'Great Occasion.'

The taxi drops us off at the parking lot below the Wall. When I came here before, I humped it up the path to the Wall because I was too cheap to pay for the tram or a horse to carry me – and, also, I wanted to show that I could do it. That I could still walk up a hill if I wanted.

This time there's no need to prove anything, because they've got it handled. There are actual horse-drawn *coaches* to take us up to the Wall, Mongolian-style ponies and carts.

Servers in black tie circulate with champagne and hors d'oeuvres while we wait for our coach.

Eventually it's our turn, and we climb in and head on up to the Wall.

There's a really funny sign along the way, one of those Chinglish efforts that totally cracks me up, telling you to 'observe social morality, respect the olders, take good care of the children and be self-possessed.' When I was here before, there was a pack of local women hanging out by it, watching to see who was going up to the Wall, who might be likely targets for their souvenir books and postcards and lines about how poor they are and how they have no work and how they're trying to educate their children, so won't you buy a crappy book at an inflated price already?

But there are no local women sitting on the low wall by the signboard now.

Well, it's after dark. Maybe they've all gone home to tend to their unemployed husbands and uneducated kids.

Glowing white tents are set up here and there atop the Wall. A band plays a mix of standards, rock, and jazz. Guests cluster around portable heaters outside the tents – a cold breeze blows from the north, from Mongolia maybe.

Sloppy and I climb out of our coach.

'I'm going to the bar,' I say. 'You want anything?'

Sloppy's attention is already fixed somewhere else, on a couple standing by one of the heaters, an elegant Chinese guy in a black jacket and a white, collarless shirt and a European woman wearing an ethnic Tibetan coat over a faded, frayed T-shirt.

'Oh, my god,' Sloppy says. 'That's Harrison Wang and Francesca Barrows.'

'So go talk to them,' I reply, having no clue who either of these people might be. 'We'll catch up later.'

Sloppy goes off to network, and I reconnoiter in search of the nearest bar.

I find it close to where the band is playing. To my untrained ear, they sound pretty good. The tune is some old standard, something out of one of those black-and-white movies where the actors are always calling each other 'darling' and sipping champagne and martinis.

I stick to my usual Yanjing beer, tip the bartender, and go back outside to listen to the band.

'Oh, Ellie. I'm so glad to see you here!'

I pivot around, and there's Lucy Wu, posed by one of the heaters, one foot pointed out like she's waiting to have her picture taken.

'Hi, Lucy. Nice party.'

116

The two of us stand there for a moment, neither saying a word.

'Well,' she says, 'I was just saying to some friends of mine that it's past time for Zhang Jianli's work to receive a serious public showing. It really is a pity that the art market in China is either too conservative or too busy chasing after trends to recognize quality.'

I don't know if this is true or not, so I just sip my beer and nod. 'Yeah,' I say. 'Jianli's really talented.'

She leans closer to me, puts a hand on my shoulder. 'Ellie, I would be honored to show Jianli's work at my gallery in Shanghai. I can promise him that I will be respectful of his artistic intentions and that, at the same time, I can give his work the exposure it deserves.'

'That sounds great, Lucy,' I begin, 'but –'

'I know he's out of town,' she continues urgently. 'But perhaps, when you talk to him next, you might mention our conversation? I have a window in September. But I would need to book this fairly quickly.'

'Okay. If I talk to him, I'll let him know.'

'I hope you will.' She clasps my hand. 'I hope you'll let Jianli know that I support him and his efforts.'

Is this some kind of code? Is she telling me that she's part of the Game?

She leans forward, hand cupped around her mouth, like she's about to share a secret. I think: maybe, finally, somebody's going to tell me what's going on.

'The Chinese art market is crazy,' she says. 'For a few years, people paid far too much for mediocre work. Now, with the economic crisis, the bubble has deflated. But smart investors know this is the time to buy work of real quality.' Then she actually does whisper: 'I couldn't believe it when I found out Jianli has no representation. Other artists of his caliber are millionaires! We could all profit.'

She gives me a quick hug. 'I'd better mingle. Lunch next week?'

'Sure. Uh. Fine.'

After that, the only thing I can think to do is grab another beer. Okay, so Lucy Wu's just an art dealer. Maybe. Who knows? I chug my beer and get another one.

I go back out onto the Wall. Push past a knot of partiers dressed in high-fashion skateboard gear. It's getting loud. They've got a DJ and some light show on top of that, and gradually the whole party is morphing into some kind of Great Wall rave. I drink my beer. I'm wondering if I should find Sloppy and tell her that I'm bailing. I hate this repetitive music with its robotic drums, and I hate the strobing lights and all the couples laughing and stumbling and dancing, some twenty-year-old girl already puking on the historic pavement, and what did I find out from coming all the way up here? That Lucy Wu is *really* into Lao Zhang, which I already knew, and it's either about his art or about something else.

Lucy Wu: Undercover Art Babe.

On the other hand, maybe she's the best thing that could happen to Lao Zhang, somebody who appreciates his work and could help him profit from it.

Maybe that's the help Cinderfox and the Great Society had in mind, getting Lao Zhang some money to get him out of whatever mess he's in.

I start climbing along the Wall, away from the party and up the hill, looking for a quieter spot. My leg hurts. It's a cool night, but I'm sweating. It's really steep. It's also not completely restored. There are places where the paving stones jut out, where the bricks have crumbled. You have to be careful. There are lights from the party that shine up this way, but it's dark ahead. Security guards stand at what seems to be the party's official perimeter. Beyond that is one of the watchtowers. I'm thinking that might be a good place to hang out for a while.

I'm not the only one who had this idea; a few other people from the party have drifted up this way. I stop for a moment and rest my hand against the weathered stone of the Wall. I can feel grooves in its surface, Ming Dynasty graffiti maybe. The last time I came up here, one of the village ladies pointed some out to me, before she started going on about how foreign friends are so generous, not like Chinese, and could I please buy her postcard book so she could feed her children?

'Be careful, Miss,' one of the security guards says as I pass. 'Dangerous up here.'

I nod and keep going.

Inside the watchtower are a couple of local people, a man and a woman. She sits on a cooler; he squats next to her. They're watching a battery-operated TV that's playing a Chinese sitcom: I can tell by the frenetic yelling and the laughter. They look older than me in the flickering TV light: in their forties, I figure. But who can tell with people who have lived as hard as they have?

'Hey, Miss,' the woman calls out. 'Have water? Beer? Postcards?'

'No, thanks.'

'Come on, Miss, postcards sell you cheap.'

What do I look like, an ATM?

I keep climbing. Maybe I can make it to the next watchtower. Maybe I'll just turn around and find a cab.

About halfway to the next watchtower, I stop and lean against the Wall. I watch a flock of sparrows suddenly stir and rise up in a dark cloud over the valley below, twittering like some distant choir trying to get in key.

With the ambient light from the party and the light from the nearly full moon, I can vaguely make out the series of hills to the north that once formed the natural boundary between China and the rest of the world, the Big Outside, where the foreign hordes waited for their chance to conquer.

What happened was, the Mongolians and then the Manchurians who invaded eventually adopted Chinese ways and founded dynasties pretty much like the ones that had come before.

Funny, I think.

And then I hear: 'Yili. Is that you?'

Guess who?

CHAPTER ELEVEN

In the military, it's always mostly guys, but Camp Falafel was like that to the extreme, because the majority of personnel there were combat infantry. There were maybe seven hundred, seven hundred fifty soldiers, and out of those, six women, including li'l ol' 91-Whiskey, Health Specialist me.

I'd decided I wasn't going to fuck around any more. I didn't want to get the reputation of being a slut, as I was pretty sure Jesus would not approve, and I was really feeling the need for my best buddy Jesus by this point. I thought maybe I'd try hanging out with the girls for a change.

We bunked in two tiny cement slab rooms in the old Baathist barracks. My roomies were Pulagang, the laundry specialist, and Greif, the HUMINT linguist. HUMINT stands for 'Human Intelligence.' One time I made a joke about how we should requisition more of that for Camp Falafel. She didn't think it was funny.

In the other room were Torres, the admin specialist,

Unit Supply Specialist Madrid, and Humvee mechanic Palaver. At times this got a little awkward for Torres, because Madrid and Palaver were big dykes and really into each other. They were nice about it, and discreet, which you had to be in our Army of One. None of us were of a mind to report it, though Pulagang bitched to me about them once, figuring that, as another good Christian, I'd support her in her certainty that they were both going straight to hell. 'Yeah, I guess,' I said. I just couldn't get that worked up about it, since my own salvation was probably in question too, given all the fucking around I'd done.

'There's a prayer group meeting after chow,' Pulagang said to me and Greif when we were sitting on our bunks one night before dinner. 'Why don't you guys come with me?'

Greif hardly looked up from her laptop. 'No thanks,' she said. Greif was a strange bird, even looked a little like one; she was small, spare, and brown, brown hair, skin tanned nut-brown to match. An E-4 Specialist, she acted like she wasn't one of us. Which she wasn't. The rest of us all came from the same support company, TDY'ed to fill in some holes for guys who got rotated out. Greif came from a different company and was 'attached in direct support of' the combat unit to help out with the PUCs, speakers of even half-assed Arabic being in short supply. She spent her spare time studying her Arabic books and typing on her computer.

'Are you blogging?' I'd asked her once. I knew some guys who blogged back at my first FOB, in between crackdowns by HQ.

'Blogging?' She'd looked up at me, eyes magnified but

still distant behind her non-regulation, wire-framed specs. 'No. I wouldn't do that.'

She'd turned back to her laptop without another word.

'How about you, Ellie?' Pulagang asked me now.

I hesitated, tossed my Beanie squid up and down a few times, watched the trickle of water from the marginal air conditioner run down the stained concrete wall. I didn't really want to go. But I was thinking I should. Maybe just being around guys who were Spirit-filled would somehow get some Spirit back inside me.

'Okay,' I said. 'Sure.'

The meeting was held in the MWR center – meaning 'morale, welfare, and recreation' – which in our case was a sagging tent that smelled like cat piss and dust just past the hajji mart they'd let a couple of the locals set up. About a dozen guys, Pulagang, and me sat on folding chairs at the back of the tent, next to the sad collection of paperbacks and out-of-date magazines that some smart-ass had christened 'The Library of Alexandria.' (I finally looked that up one day, because for months I'd had no clue what it meant.)

Anyway, Pulagang and me pulled up chairs in this circle of guys, and things got really quiet all of the sudden, and I felt like I used to feel whenever I was trying to pretend that I fit in someplace: like I didn't belong, and this was the last place I wanted to be.

'Why don't we get started?' one of the guys said.

I focused my attention on him. Big guy, nice body, a sort of light behind his eyes.

'It's great to see y'all here,' he continued. "Cause you know, when Thomas Paine said 'These are the times that try men's souls,' I'm pretty sure it was times like these he had in mind.'

He smiled. His voice was like chocolate. 'I'm Trey Cooper. Why don't the rest of you introduce yourselves?'

I felt filled with something, but I was pretty sure it wasn't Spirit.

At first, Trey and me just hung out together and talked. We talked about all kinds of stuff. About Christ. About our lives.

Or maybe he talked, and I mostly listened.

I remember one time, we were sitting up on a berm by the southwest perimeter, watching the sun set, chucking rocks at a storage shed.

'It's tough, you know?' Trey said. He picked up a rock, considered its shape, and then hurled it at the shed, barely missing our designated target zone, the door. Still, the rock made a cool noise when it hit the corrugated metal. 'It's like, there's my life in Christ, and there's my life as a soldier. And they should be the same thing. But sometimes they're just not.'

I nodded. I wasn't sure what to say. I would have felt kind of stupid asking something like 'You mean the part where you have to kill people?' Because that's not particularly Christlike, in my understanding; but it's what soldiers do, by definition.

I focused on my rock. It was a nice smooth one. 'Okay, watch this,' I said. I wound up and let it fly. I nailed the door.

'Good one!'

Trey picked up a rock from our pile, tossed it up and down in his hand. 'It's just the circumstances, sometimes,' he said. He stared at me, with that intensity that made me feel like he was reaching deep down inside me, like he could devour me whole, and I couldn't do a thing about it. I wouldn't have wanted to. 'I know what we're doing is the right thing. Protecting our country, helping these people . . .'

He gave the rock a final toss, then he hurled it at the shed.

'Hey, I think you got the doorknob.' Hitting the doorknob was worth extra points.

''Cause they should get to live in a normal country, you know? Have decent lives.' Then he shook his head. 'But the circumstances . . . sometimes the circumstances just suck.'

If by 'the circumstances' he meant that the people around there were dirt-poor and lived in shitholes with intermittent electricity and contaminated water, and that a large percentage of them hated us and kept trying to kill us, well, I guess I'd have to agree.

Trey was a Sergeant First Class in MI ('Military Intelligence,' for the acronym-impaired). He wasn't an interpreter, but he'd picked up some Arabic, and he was always trying to teach me phrases, 'to be polite and show your respect for the locals.' I didn't really want to get to know the locals, to be honest, but I went along with him. I would have pretty much done anything he'd ask me to. That's how stupid-crazy I was about the guy.

Which is why, late one night when I was manning the aid station on my own (Blanchard being off-duty and the other medic out with Saddam's Revenge), I didn't ask too many questions when Trey and his OGA buddy Kyle brought in the PUC.

OGA means 'Other Government Agency.' Sometimes that means CIA, sometimes DIA, sometimes a private contractor like Blackwater. You don't ask.

'Hey, Ellie. Give us a hand here?'

Trey and Kyle carried this hajji between them, a middle-aged man with a gut who was dressed in U.S. Army fatigues that didn't fit him. His arms were flopping around, and he muttered something which, naturally, I didn't understand.

'Put him over there.' I pointed to a bed and went into my routine.

They laid him out on the bed and stepped away, like this wasn't something they were supposed to see.

Hajji looked shocky. Sweat poured off him, and his skin had a grayish tone to it. Pulse shallow, fast, and thready, respiration rapid.

'Hand me those pillows,' I ordered without thinking. Before I even tried to get a BP on this guy, I wanted to elevate his legs and treat him for shock.

Trey and Kyle stood there for a minute, frozen in place.

'Jesus,' I muttered and grabbed the pillows myself, lifted up the dude's legs with one hand, and stuffed the pillows under his knees and calves and feet.

Hajji screamed.

'Okay. It's gonna be okay,' I told the guy, taking hold of his hand. 'It's gonna be okay.'

He opened his eyes. Stared at me.

I got out the BP cuff. His pressure was 90 over 40. Not good. Not dying, but not right either.

'Okay,' I said. 'Let's see what's going on here.' I patted his hand and started to unbutton his fatigue jacket.

His eyes opened wider. His head shook back and forth, and he started babbling about something.

126

'They don't like women seeing them,' Kyle said.

'Trey,' I said, 'can you tell this guy I'm trying to help?'

Trey snapped out something in Arabic. The PUC didn't calm down. So Trey said something else. It didn't sound nice, but maybe that's just the language.

The guy stared at Trey, at me, and then he closed his eyes.

I unbuttoned the jacket.

Purpling bruises on his abdomen and point tenderness in at least five places along his ribs. Belly a little rigid.

Okay, I thought. Okay. Before I do anything else, I'm gonna get some oxygen and some fluids into this guy, both of which come under the 'do no harm' heading.

So I did that. But he still didn't look good.

'How is he?' Trey asked.

'I dunno.' I was thinking I should do the rest of my secondary survey, check out what was going on with his legs, for one thing. But whatever was wrong, it wasn't anything I'd be able to fix.

'You need to get him to a hospital,' I said.

'Fuck,' said Kyle, pounding his fist on his thigh.

'He's going into shock,' I explained. 'There's a lot of things that can cause that. Pipes, pump, or pressure.' I repeated the mantra I'd learned in EMT training, because I couldn't think of anything else to say. Then I thought to add, 'Like there might be some underlying cardiac insufficiency, especially if there was some respiratory compromise, but I'm guessing he's got some internal bleeding going on, from the look of those rib contusions.'

It was Trey's turn to stare, probably because he'd never heard me do my medic routine before.

'Look, he needs a doctor,' I said. 'I'm just a medic.

127

There's only so much I can do.' I was thinking we could transport him to the hospital in town, or maybe copter him to Camp Screaming Eagle Whatever where they had a full-on combat support hospital that could actually help him.

'What about Blanchard?' Trey asked.

'I mean, we could call him, I guess. But he's a physician's assistant. It's not like he can remove this guy's spleen or something.'

Kyle shook his head. 'I dunno,' he said. 'I dunno.'

For whatever reason, I wanted to tell him to go fuck himself. Maybe because all of a sudden I realized that I didn't like OGA Kyle very much. Which was weird, because Kyle had always struck me as this totally normal guy before. Like I couldn't even really describe him: just some dude around thirty, nondescript, even a little dumpy, nobody I ever would have noticed unless I had to.

I'd never thought about who he might work for. What his job might be.

Because I was frustrated, and because I didn't want to think about why I didn't like Kyle, I decided to do my job. I grabbed a pair of scissors and started to cut off the PUC's pants.

Hajji was pretty out of it, but this got a rise out of him. His head lifted off the pillow; his arms waved around ineffectually, and the oxygen mask muffled whatever he was trying to say.

'Sorry,' I said. 'Uh, *afwan*. Jesus, Trey, would you talk to this guy?'

Trey said something. Yelled it, almost. The PUC's eyes widened for a moment, and then his head thumped against the pillow.

128

He wasn't wearing any underwear. Was this normal for Iraqis? I realized that I had no idea. He moaned beneath the oxygen mask.

I finished cutting off the pants.

'Shit.'

His legs. His legs were a fucking mess. Purple with bruises, hematomas – blood-filled, egg-sized lumps on his shins.

'Shit,' I said again. 'What happened to this guy?'

Neither Trey or Kyle said anything for a moment.

'It happened during capture,' Kyle said carefully. 'He was a high-value target. He resisted, and things got a little rough.'

'Rough. Like, you ran over him with a Stryker?' The words came out of my mouth before I could stop myself.

'Ellie, this is a really bad guy,' Trey said, a pleading note in his voice. 'We think he's one of the ringleaders in the gang that's been dropping mortars on us the past three months.'

I shrugged. 'Whatever.' It wasn't like I particularly cared about Mr Ali Baba here. But I still had this notion that I should do my job, which meant helping people if possible. 'All I'm saying is that he's busted up pretty bad, and I can't fix him. He needs to get to a doctor.'

'Fuck,' Kyle repeated, sounding more irritated than anything else. 'Okay.' He turned to Trey. 'Let's make the call.'

'Someone's gotta stay here with her,' Trey objected.

'What, you think he's going anywhere? Just cuff him to the bed.'

So that's what they did. Meanwhile, I grabbed some blankets, covered the guy up, tried to get him warm. I was thinking MAST trousers, the anti-shock suit that you can also use for a legs-and-pelvis splint. Maybe that would help.

'I'll be back as soon as I can,' Trey said, resting his hand on my shoulder.

I didn't want to look at him. 'Okay.'

After they left, I put on the MAST, and I tried to be gentle, tried not to hurt him, but with every little movement of his legs he moaned or screamed and thrashed around, wrists straining against the cuffs, and I kept saying, 'Sorry, I'm sorry. *Afwan*,' but I was still hurting him.

When that was done, I checked Ali Baba's vitals again. About the same. I wanted to take a smoke break, but I was afraid to leave. Of course, if he started circling the drain, there wasn't a lot I could do about it.

'Hey, Doc.'

It was a soldier I'd seen before, National Guard like me, Private Abrams.

'What's up?'

'I got the runs like you wouldn't believe. Can you hook me up with something?'

'I can get you Imodium. Fluids if you're dehydrated.'

The disappointment showed on his face. 'Poole came in with the same thing,' he said, 'and the doc hooked him up with some serious meds. Stopped the shit right there.'

I almost laughed, because I had a pretty good idea what the guy had come here for. Nothing like a good dose of morphine to cure the trots. Or whatever else it is that ails you. 'Sorry. I can only get you Imodium. Come back and talk to the P.A. tomorrow if you need something else.'

'Shit,' he muttered. 'Well, I guess I'll take the Imodium, then.'

I sat down at the computer to take his info. Abrams peered around me and took a look at my other patient.

'Who's that?'

'Some PUC.'

'What happened to him?'

I shrugged. 'Got messed up.'

Abrams wandered over to the bed. 'Man, they fucked him good,' he said admiringly. I turned my head and saw that Abrams had lifted up the blanket for a better look.

'Hey, hands off the patient.'

Abrams dropped the blanket, raised his hands. 'No harm, Doc.' He laughed. 'Somebody beat me to it.'

It took almost an hour for the copter to come. Ali Baba's level of consciousness took a downturn while we waited; he was really out of it and started flailing around, and even with his wrists cuffed he almost pulled out the IV. But he was still breathing when they bundled him off, and that's all I know about what happened to him.

When it was all over, I sat on the stoop and smoked a cigarette. Trey sat down next to me.

'You okay?' he asked.

'Sure. Fine.'

My hand was shaking a little, though, and I had that hollowed-out feeling, like I'd been stretched tight and thin, and there wasn't enough of a wall between me and the world.

I hadn't had to treat anything really serious before, not like that. The patrol a couple weeks ago that got nailed by the IED, the two badly wounded soldiers were coptered out. I just had some minor shrapnel and burns to deal with. The heart attack, okay, that was serious, but it wasn't messy. The guy who blew his brains out was messy, but dead.

Sure, I'd been trained; I'd done well in my training, but I hadn't had all that much practice.

I stubbed out the cigarette and lit another. 'So, that guy, they really whaled on him.'

'Things got a little out of control,' Trey said uncomfortably. 'But you know, there's a lot of emotion, adrenaline gets going . . . He put up a fight, Ellie. That's what happens to bad guys out here when they don't do what they're told.'

I didn't reply. I was trying to imagine the fight that would produce those kinds of injuries, particularly the shin contusions, and I couldn't quite picture it. Repeated kicks, maybe? Blows with a rifle butt?

And why was he wearing Army fatigues?

'You did great in there, Ellie,' Trey said, giving me that look of his, like he's taking me in, like he sees everything about me. 'I know it wasn't easy.'

I shrugged. 'I just did my job.'

Trey put his arm around me, gave my shoulder a little squeeze, and all I wanted to do was melt into him, let go of all my doubts and fears, and trust him absolutely.

Who cares about Mr Ali Baba, anyway? I thought.

It was just that I kept seeing his purpling legs, how swollen they were in places.

So the next afternoon, after I woke up – I was still working night shifts then – I made myself a mocha and sat on my bunk in our hooch and regarded Greif, sitting on the bunk next to me, drinking a cup of green tea and tapping away on her laptop. She was working nights too.

132

Pulagang worked a normal day shift, making sure everyone got their clothes back from the Iraqi contractors.

'Hey, Greif,' I said hesitantly, because Greif never had gotten friendly with any of us. 'So, you work with the PUCs, right?'

She gave me one of her blank stares. 'I'm an Arabic interpreter.'

Meaning 'What the fuck else would I be doing, and why are you asking me such a dumb-ass question?'

'Yeah . . . I was just wondering . . .' I studied my mocha. I wasn't even sure what I wanted to ask. 'Well, there was this hajji that came in to the aid station last night, and he was pretty messed up. This OGA, Kyle, said he was high value.'

Maybe it was my imagination, but Greif suddenly seemed more alert. 'Sometimes the PUCs resist capture,' she said, staring at me through her wire-framed specs.

'Yeah, I know, but this guy . . . I mean, he was really fucked up.'

Greif shrugged, like she had no idea what I was talking about and she didn't really care.

'Stuff happens.'

She turned back to her laptop, but I got the feeling she was still watching me, somehow.

CHAPTER TWELVE

'Yili,' John says. 'I think you are feeling better now?'

I have two equally strong reactions: I want to run like hell away from this freak, and I want to claw his eyes out, punch him in the jaw, kick him in the nuts. Which isn't really realistic. But neither is running, because I don't run that well, and this section of the Great Wall is so steep I'd probably break my neck trying.

So I don't do anything. I just stand there.

'You look much better now,' John continues. 'I was worried about you that night.'

I have to give the guy credit for his brass balls, because he's wearing his most innocent expression, and I'm sure if I accuse him of anything, he'll do that squinty-eyed, puzzled look he has down to a Kabuki act.

'Hello, John,' I say. 'What brings you to the Great Wall?'

He smiles broadly. 'I am afraid maybe you are still mad at me,' he says. 'Because you were not in your right head that night.'

'So you came up here . . . to see if I was okay?'

That prompts the squinty look. 'Oh, Yili. I do not know that you will be here tonight. This is just . . . some kind of coincidence.'

'Right. A coincidence.'

John takes one step toward me, his hands half-raised to show how friendly he is.

'You know, in China we have this idea, *hong xian*. Have you heard of this?'

Hong xian means 'red thread.'

'No, I haven't.'

'It is about fate,' John continues, seeming to warm to the subject. 'It is the red thread that tangles but does not break. It is the thing that connects some people to each other. Because they are meant to be connected.' He takes a step closer. 'I think, maybe, you and I have this red thread between us, Yili. Don't you think so?'

I take a deep breath. 'Actually, John, I think I'm just gonna turn around and go back to the party. Okay? Because you really make me nervous.'

As John takes another step in my direction, I say: 'And seriously, if you come any closer, I'm gonna scream.'

'Okay, Yili,' John says, surprisingly calm about the whole thing. 'But I just want you to know something. If you have some trouble, some problem, you can call me.' He stares at me, and there's just enough illumination from the spots they put up for the party that I can see his dark eyes, staring at me. But his eyes, there's no light in them now; they're some dense, black metal, and they suck up all the light, and suddenly I'm really scared again.

'I'm going now,' I say. 'Please don't follow me.'

It feels like I'm fighting gravity, like the air has turned to syrup, and I can hardly move. I walk as fast as I can down the Wall, drenched in sweat, thinking: I can't turn around; I'll turn into salt; I just have to keep walking and not look back.

'Yili, wait –'

I run.

Half the party's moved up here. Knots of people; couples laughing, drinking, making out; they surround me. The beat of the music thrums in my ears. I stumble a little, bump somebody with my elbow. 'Sorry,' I say. '*Duibuqi*.' A bottle shatters, and I keep walking down the Wall. The lights strobe on and off, and John is following me, I know he is, and I've got to get out of here.

Then I hear gunfire. Full auto, in rapid staccato. I almost drop and roll. No, I tell myself. Don't be stupid. This is China.

It's firecrackers, dumbshit.

I hear drums. Like it's a Peking Opera, or that crazy Olympics opening show. The techno music stops. The drums get louder, and there's chanting. 'Hah hah HAH hah HAH!'

The crowd around me parts, and a girl standing next to me giggles and points. I look down the Wall.

Marching in tight formation are ranks of . . . what? Soldiers? They're Chinese, wearing uniforms, but the colors are wrong: they're wearing red vests and striped shirts, black ballcaps. Some of them carry drums, the drums that beat out the marching cadence. The others have . . . buckets. Paper buckets.

Around me, the crowd erupts in laughter, and then I get why: it's an army of KFC workers.

The KFC Army stops in unison. The drums pound. They chant and raise their buckets high.

Great, just what I need right now. Fucking performance art.

Okay, I think. Okay. I can squeeze past them on the right. They're doing their piece, whatever it means; they're not going to care about me.

I make my move.

And see a rival army climbing up the Wall.

McDonald's workers.

All at once, the KFC Army changes formation. The drummers fall back, still beating out their cadence. The personnel carrying the buckets surge forward to meet the encroaching cadres from Mickey D's.

What happens next is, the KFC people reach into their buckets and start throwing shit at the McDonald's people. Something wings me in the ear.

A drumstick. The KFC Army's packing drumsticks.

The McDonald's invaders drop to their knees, like good infantry. The front line pulls out slingshots loaded with something. McNuggets, I figure out when one lands by my foot.

'Hah hah HAH hah HAH!'

KFC versus McDonald's? On the Great Wall? Whatever. I push past the first line of Mickey D workers.

'Yili. Yili, wait –'

Something – someone – catches my sleeve, tugs it close, grabs my wrist. I try to pull away, but I can't.

'Yili –'

I turn. It's John, of course.

He doesn't look so scary now. He looks like the guy I met at the party: cute and kind of clueless.

I know that last part's a lie.

I don't fight him. Like I'm hypnotized.

'I just want to give you my . . . my *card*,' John says, with that peculiar stress on the last word. 'So if you have any problems, you can call me.'

In his free hand, in fact, is a business card.

I hesitate. I take the card and put it in my jeans pocket. 'Thanks, John,' I say.

I swing up my good leg, hinged at the knee like it's been held back by a coiled spring, and kick him in the balls.

He collapses like a deflated balloon, and I run like hell down the Wall.

I stumble through the ranks of McDonald's invaders, bumping shoulders with a cluster of art tourists dressed in groovy tees taking photos and videos of the performance. 'KFC is by far the most popular fast-food chain in China,' one of them says. 'McDonald's market penetration doesn't even come close.'

Good to know.

Ahead of me is a watchtower. I enter it. Here is the Chinese couple, watching bad sitcoms on their battery-operated TV, just like they were doing when I left them.

'Miss,' the woman says, in desultory fashion, hardly looking up from her little screen, 'you want postcards? Great Wall book?'

'No!' I practically shout. And then I get an idea. 'No,' I repeat, somewhat more calmly. 'But I'll tell you what. I'd like to see your village. No, really. Because I want to better understand the life of the common Chinese people.'

The woman stares at me. I repeat the whole thing in

Chinese. 'I want very much to see your village,' I say again. 'Tonight. And I am happy to pay you for it.'

The woman turns to her husband, whispers something behind her hand. The husband looks up at me. Frowns. Because maybe this is trouble, and nobody can afford that.

'You pay how much?' the woman asks.

I end up in an enclosed cart pulled by a motorcycle that looks like it's vintage PLA, sitting next to the postcard lady. Her husband drives. My feet rest on top of a case of beer, my elbow's leaning on a stack of Great Wall books, we're careening along this crazy winding road, hurtling through the dark, and I'm pretty sure we're all going to die, but that prospect isn't bothering me much at the moment, for some reason. Maybe because of the Percocet I took.

'Are you married?' the lady asks. 'Do you have children?'

I take a chance and turn on my iPhone for a minute – John found me even with the phone off, so who knows if it makes any difference? – and text Sloppy, telling her I found a ride and I'll catch up with her later.

Finally we get to their village.

This is the weird thing about China: you can be in a city like Beijing, with every modern convenience, with skyscrapers and Starbucks and bizarre underground performance spaces, and then you can go a couple hours away and end up in some village that's a throwback to the Qing Dynasty, except with satellite dishes and Internet connections and white-tile disease.

Tongren Village is a pretty shabby old place overall, tucked away a few valleys over from the Simatai Great

139

Wall. God knows what they do up here, aside from selling postcards to tourists, because the land looks hard, barren, like scratching out millet and winter cabbage would exhaust whatever life is left in it.

My hosts, Mr and Mrs Liang, put me up in their tiny house, in their kid's bedroom, which is sort of an alcove off the kitchen, and I guess their kid really is away at school, because she's not around, and the parents are using the space as a storeroom for their books and beers and bottled water. One bare bulb lights the smudged, white-washed room, which is decorated with a poster for some Korean pop star and an out-of-date calendar. The bed is a *kang*, but there's no coal burning underneath to heat it up, so I sleep in the T-shirt, sweatshirt, and sweatpants Postcard Lady rounds up for me to wear, with every available quilt piled on top because it's still cold up here in the late spring.

For a couple of postcard hawkers, my hosts are hospitable folks. In the morning, they serve me tea and congee and a bag of shrimp chips for breakfast.

I sit and eat, and Postcard Lady sits across from me and watches.

'So, you aren't married?' she asks.

I can't even get irritated, for some reason.

'I'm getting a divorce,' I say.

Postcard Lady shakes her head. 'This modern life, it's not well suited for family. So hard, to keep family together. Don't you think so?'

I stare across the little table at Mrs Liang, at her weathered face and her stained-tooth smile and her counterfeit UCLA sweatshirt, and think about her kid, off at some boarding school, in pursuit of a life that doesn't involve selling shit to tourists at the Great Wall.

'I think you've managed it,' I say awkwardly.

She giggles a little, pats me on the shoulder, and pours me more tea.

After breakfast, Mr and Mrs Liang leave for the Simatai Great Wall. They won't get back till after dark. I check out the village, walking along the one paved road that forms the center of town. Tongren Village has a market, a white-tiled municipal headquarters, a few vendors, elderly men and women selling baskets of candies and snacks. There's a *jiaozi* place for lunch and a teahouse for after that. I sit in the teahouse and read this trashy suspense novel that somehow ended up at the Liangs', try to lose myself in a world of terrorists and super-germs for a while.

A couple of the locals come up and start conversations. They ask me the usual questions: how did I learn Chinese, how do I like China, what do I think of their village, am I married? I answer some, dodge the rest, smile, and drink tea.

After that, I take a walk. There isn't much to see, though I find a crumbling temple that seems almost abandoned, the washed-out red paint of its walls peeling off in chunks. On the gray wall beneath are faded characters, Cultural Revolution slogans, something about 'smashing the Four Olds!' Flayed tires and cracked roof tiles are piled in a corner of the courtyard, and inside, the statue of Guanyin is missing an arm, its once-gaudy colors bleached to gray wood.

It's not a bad place, this little village in the shadow of the northern hills. It's relaxing here. Quiet. I wonder if I could find some place to stay long-term. Hang out. Just live.

I walk past an old house, its tiled roof peeking above

a gray stone wall, chipped stone lions on either side of the wall's red door. A scholar's home once, or an official's, it looks like. Maybe I could live there. Rent a room. My disability money would probably cover it. I could, I don't know, read books. Take walks. Eat *jiaozi*.

What would it be like, being someplace peaceful?

I realize I have no idea.

By now I'm really sleepy. No surprise, considering what the last couple days have been like. I decide to go back to the Liangs' place for a nap.

I walk up the dirt road that leads to the Liangs', past a few silent farmhouses tucked among barren fields that back into the hills, the late afternoon shade spilling over the road like a veil.

As the little house comes into view, I figure I'd better use the toilet before I go in.

The Liangs' bathroom is an outhouse above the pigpen – a squat shitter, two blocks straddling a trench, with a gap between the wall and the floor on the down-hill side. For me, with my leg, it's a little tough, even with the iron bar protruding from the bricks to grasp, especially because I've got my backpack, and the additional weight of that makes balancing harder.

As I squat there, clutching the iron bar, trying to breathe through my mouth, one of the hogs comes snuffling up to the gap below the wall, nosing at the run-off from the trench.

Pigs eat shit. Who knew?

I'm thinking maybe I don't want to live in a peaceful rural Chinese village.

As I'm thinking this and exiting the outhouse, I hear a car coming up the drive.

Not a motorcycle cart, not a farmer's blue truck. Something with a smooth, low-pitched engine and some horsepower.

I duck back into the outhouse.

Tires crunch gravel. The engine stops. A car door slams.

Standing on the block above the latrine, I can just see out the ventilation windows that run along the upper wall of the outhouse. A black car – maybe a Lexus.

A man approaches the Liangs' door. Knocks. He's stocky, broad across the shoulders, wearing a white polo shirt. Chinese, I think, but I can only see his back, his black, bristling hair.

He jiggles the doorknob. Locked. Walks around to the side of the house.

I duck down.

I think about running, but how far could I get?

The space between the outhouse wall and the latrine, where the trench runs down to meet the pig-pen. I scramble into it, then squeeze myself as far as I can beneath the floorboards next to the trench. The stench coats my nose and throat like liquid.

One of the pigs sticks its snout under the wall and stares at me. Snorts.

I stare back. Hold my breath. My stomach roils.

Footsteps. The outhouse door creaks open.

Bangs shut.

The pig snuffles.

A minute later, I hear the car start and then head back down the drive.

I wait until I can't hear the car any more, count to ten, and climb out, shaking so badly that I stumble at the outhouse door.

I tell myself, maybe he had nothing to do with me. Maybe he was, I don't know, the Liangs' postcard supplier. In a black Lexus. Right.

Inside the Liangs' house, I change out of the muddy sweatpants and sweatshirt that the Liangs lent me, clean myself and my fake Pumas as best I can, and put on my party clothes. I don't have anything else to wear.

I leave the house key and three hundred yuan on the table and lock the door behind me.

There's no way of knowing which way the Lexus guy went, so the only thing I can think of to do is head toward the bus stop at the end of town. And here I catch a break: a *mianbao*, one of those little white vans shaped like bread loaves, idles roughly at the bus stop, letting off passengers.

I approach the driver's window.

'*Shifu, ni hao*. I need to get to Beijing. Can you take me?'

I'm not going to Mati tonight. They know where to find me there.

The driver, round-faced and reeking of tobacco, shakes his head and taps out a last cigarette from his crumpled pack of Horse & Camels.

'Can't. They don't let us drive *mianbao* in Beijing City.'

'To Shunyi District; can you do that?' Shunyi's just outside of Beijing proper. I can catch a cab or a bus from there.

He takes a long drag on his cigarette and considers. '*Keyi*,' he says with a nod.

We agree on a price and set off.

I don't know where I'm going to go from Shunyi. I'll figure it out when I get there.

I power up my iPhone and check for messages.

144

A couple from Trey, which I ignore. Chinese text spam. And finally, a reply from Sloppy: 'Hi Yili, Harrison Wang invite us two for dinner tonight. Can you come?'

Harrison Wang. I don't know who this is. Then I remember: some art guy Sloppy was all excited about meeting last night at Simatai.

The dinner is at seven thirty, in Chaoyang District, which is northeast Beijing. It's about four o'clock now. I'm wearing the same clothes I've been in and out of since the party, and my fake Pumas smell like shit. I don't know what this guy actually does or why he might want to talk to me. I don't know anything about anybody, when it comes right down to it. I think Lucy Wu wants to make money off of Lao Zhang's art, but how can I be sure? I thought Sloppy was my friend, but how do I know that?

Harrison Wang? No clue.

I think I should just keep running. Go somewhere. Hide someplace.

That didn't work too well in Tongren Village, though.

If they can find me no matter where I go, what difference does it make if Sloppy or Lucy or Harrison Wang is part of it? They're going to catch up with me eventually. Whoever they are.

It comes down to this: I don't know what else to do.

Besides, I'm hungry.

'Okay,' I type back. 'I might be late.'

CHAPTER THIRTEEN

We met after our shifts like we usually did, on the berm by the guard tower. It wasn't yet dawn, and the air was shirtsleeve-cool, with a slight scent of rain. Trey was hyper, pacing back and forth, smoking cigarettes, jamming his hands in his pockets, then waving them around, like he was high on something, except I don't think he was.

'Ellie. I think we got the guy,' he said. 'The one who's been dumping mortars on us the last three months. I think we finally got him.'

'That's great, Trey.' I meant it. The mortars were why I was at this shithole in the first place, one of them having wounded my predecessor. Plus, the week before, a round had landed on our rec tent, taking out an exercise bike and the rowing machine, which seriously sucked.

Trey flopped down on the berm next to me. 'Yeah.' He tapped a cigarette out of the package and offered it to me, then tapped out another one for himself. 'I feel like we're finally getting somewhere,' he said. 'You know? We take out this guy, he's the leader – maybe we cut the guts out of this whole bullshit resistance around here. If that happens, we can finally get things running the way they should. Fix the sewers and the power plant, show the locals it's all been worth it.'

He flicked his Zippo to light my cigarette, but the wind came up, so he cupped his hand around mine to form a break, and I felt his palm on the back of my hand, and all of a sudden, neither of us gave a shit about the cigarette any more. We were kissing, sitting there on the berm, his hand on my back, on my tit, the beard coming in on his chin scraping against my lips, and I'm thinking, Hallelujah, fuck me now.

Then he stopped.

'We can't do this,' he said.

'We can't?'

'Not here.'

I almost asked why, and then I realized that he was actually making sense.

'Yeah.' I sat up, pulled down my T-shirt, and picked my cigarette out of the dirt.

Trey stared at me. 'We could go someplace,' he said. 'If you want to.'

'Yeah,' I said, staring back. 'Yeah. I want to.'

The thing about Camp Fucking Falafel was that, unlike my first FOB, there weren't a lot of places to go for privacy. My first thought was the laundry facility (seeing as how that had served me well back at the old FOB), but Trey had another idea.

'People'll be showing up at Laundry any time now. But there's some rooms in the Admin Core nobody's using.'

I'd hardly ever been in the Admin Core: once when I

147

got here for processing, and a couple times for mission briefings when I was subbing for Menendez or Hilliard, the medics who usually pulled the off-campus patrols. Otherwise, I didn't have any reason to go there. My bunk was in an outbuilding, part of the old barracks, and so was the aid station.

Trey took me to a wing I'd never been to, through an entrance guarded by a soldier I'd met a few times.

'Hey, Morris,' he said casually. 'You know Doc McEnroe, right?'

'Sure,' he said, trying not very hard not to stare at my tits.

'I got a PUC problem she's gonna help me out with. Off the books.'

The soldier gave a half-shrug, like this was the last thing he cared about. And we went inside.

You ever been in a place you know is wrong?

I'm not going to claim I figured that out right away. That night, that early morning, it was just another Iraqi dump as far as I was concerned: a concrete-block maze that had been painted this sort of baby-food puke yellow, now scabbing over the walls like an infection, revealing the plaster and cement underneath. The lights were bare bulbs, sometimes encased in rusting metal cages.

Trey and I walked down the hall, passing a couple of closed doors, then an open door into a room containing a bunch of battered file cabinets, where another soldier sorted papers. We crossed a wider hall. At the very end I could see a couple soldiers loitering by a door, laughing, giving each other shit. Then we turned down a smaller corridor. At the end of that was a staircase. At the top of that, another hall, this one with a wooden floor and baseboards and molding.

Trey stopped at one of the doors and jiggled the knob. Unlocked. He opened the door, and we went inside.

There was a desk and a couple chairs, like this had been somebody's office. At the back of it was a narrow door.

'It's not much,' Trey said, in a hushed voice. 'I wish I could give you something better.'

It was practically a closet, with a cot stuck inside that took up almost all the room. I guessed whoever had worked here used to take naps or even spend the night. An old wool blanket was spread on top of whatever thin, lumpy mattress covered the springs.

'It's fine,' I said. 'It really is.'

We didn't talk. He didn't whisper how much he cared about me; we didn't fall asleep and wake up in each other's arms. We fucked until Trey came and I felt like my butt was bruised from the busted springs in the bedframe. I didn't come, and neither one of us did anything about that.

But it felt like what I needed right then.

Afterward we lay there for maybe fifteen minutes, a half hour at most, smoking cigarettes and not saying very much.

'We'd better go,' Trey finally said.

'Yeah.'

We got dressed and walked out of there. I went to my bunk, and he went to his.

The next day – night – after our shifts, we met up on the berm as usual. We didn't talk about what we'd done. We just sat there, smoked cigarettes, and chucked rocks at the storage shed. We didn't get around to doing it again for about a week. It started with us sitting up on the berm, me talking about some shit, Master Sergeant Dickhead Blanchard, I think, when Trey suddenly leaned over and kissed me and mumbled, 'Do you wanna go to the room?' and I of course nodded and said 'Sure.'

So that became our pattern. We'd hang out; we wouldn't talk about what we were doing; we'd go and fuck; we'd wait a couple days and then do it all again.

And that was fine by me. I was crazy about the guy. So what if we didn't talk about it? I didn't want to talk any more than he did. I just wanted to be with him, to hang out on the berm, to fuck as much as we could. To just get through all of it somehow.

I think I figured that if we talked about us, maybe we'd have to talk about other things as well. Like about what was going on in the Admin Core.

Sometimes, after we finished, I'd lie there and think I heard things. Laughing, sometimes. Shouts, now and then.

And other things. Moans, maybe. Crying.

I'd tell myself that wasn't what I was hearing. I was hearing the wind. I was hearing stray cats.

I think now that I didn't really hear that stuff. Not any of it. No moans, no stray cats. My mind was just filling in the blanks, of what I knew and didn't want to see.

CHAPTER FOURTEEN

Harrison Wang's dinner is at a space in 798, the old East German factory complex at Dashanzi. Artists colonized it in the late '90s, carving out studios in the middle of machine tool factories and industrial laundry facilities. Now it's mostly galleries and bars and restaurants. That's what always happens. Artists come and make something cool, and then everybody wants it, and the people who made it cool can't afford it any more.

I wander among red-brick buildings, cement-block dorms, tangles of pipes and water tanks, and weird industrial detritus that the artists left here, even after the factories departed. I'm looking for a space called 'Door.' I've never been there, but I'm pretty sure it actually exists – it was listed on one of the signboards by the gate.

But I can't find the damn place. It's dark, they don't light things well, and the signs aren't clear. I hear snatches of music, a party going on somewhere; people gather outside an Italian restaurant, waiting for their table. Here's a photo gallery having an opening, BMWs and Mercedes parked in front. I turn a corner. Find myself walking down a narrow path between two long red-brick buildings. Darkness. Galleries, boutiques, a few studios. All closed for the night. Nobody here but me. And a surveillance camera, the black dome in the plastic frame an oily bubble emerging from white.

Keep walking, I tell myself.

I come to the end of the row. Facing me is what looks like the back wall of a factory building. Two stories high, gymnasium-wide. It's blank brick.

Except for a big brass handle in the middle of the wall with the single character for 'door' stenciled above it in white paint.

Cute.

It's a door, camouflaged in the brick.

I pull it open. And immediately feel underdressed.

'Good evening, Miss. May I have your name, please?'

The door opens into a foyer. A hostess in black silk smiles at me. Behind her, water runs down slate onto perfectly round gray stones, interspersed with stalks of bamboo.

'Ellie Cooper.'

She runs a manicured finger down a smoked Plexiglas clipboard.

Watch me not be on the list, I think. God, I hate this kind of shit.

'Thank you, Miss! Enjoy your evening!'

Inside, huge paintings hang on white walls above a black granite floor, interspersed with giant red doors studded with brass knobs and lion's-head knockers, like something out of the Forbidden City. Ambient techno fills the room, playing at just the right volume. People sit at tables or drift amongst them, socializing. Waitresses in beautiful embroidered *qipaos* glide between the tables, keeping everyone supplied with drinks and hors d'oeuvres.

A waitress approaches me with a tray full of wine.

'Would you like wine? Red or white?'

'Uh, red.'

I'm not a big wine drinker. But a drink sounds like a good idea.

I wander around, snagging a couple of snacks off passing trays, and wonder how this works. There are a hundred people here, at least, not exactly what came to my mind when I got the invitation to dinner. Do I grab an empty seat at any old table? Does that mean I have to talk to people I don't know? I hate that.

'Ah, Ms Yili. So glad you could come.'

This, as I recall, is Harrison Wang.

He's handsome, elegant, in a snowy white shirt that seems to glow, it's so clean. Mid to late thirties, though he could be older – he's one of those guys who's very well kept, probably works out every day and does yoga or Pilates or whatever. He's perfectly groomed. If I stroked his cheek, I know it would be smooth, with just a hint of beard beneath the skin.

I bet he exfoliates.

'Thanks for having me,' I say.

'My pleasure.' He takes my hand, clasps it gently.

I'd assumed he was Chinese, but there's a sort of European cast to his features, which makes me wonder where he's from, and his English is perfect. Unaccented. He smells nice. I'm a sucker for that.

153

'I've been anxious to talk with you since I heard about your association with Zhang Jianli.'

'Oh. Well, it's not like I'm . . . I mean . . .'

I don't know what to say.

'I don't represent him, or anything like that,' I manage.

He gives my hand a gentle squeeze and lets go. 'Of course. I know the two of you are good friends. That's all.'

He checks his watch – a real Rolex, I'd bet. 'We'll be serving dinner in about a half hour.'

His eyes meet mine, and he smiles. 'You're seated at my table. We'll have a chance to talk then.' And with that, he excuses himself to go play host.

Maybe Harrison is interested in Lao Zhang's art.

He's definitely interested in something, and I doubt it's my good looks and charm.

Halfway through my glass of wine, someone taps me on the shoulder. 'Oh, Yili. How nice to see you again.'

Lucy Wu.

'Likewise.'

Tonight Lucy's wearing a scarlet silk shirt with a neckline that plunges practically to her crotch, Capri pants, and espadrilles with embroidered Eiffel Towers on them.

'So, I didn't realize you were acquainted with Harrison,' she says.

'I'm not. I mean . . .' I drink some more wine. It's not bad, I've decided. 'He just invited me to dinner.'

'Because of your connection with Jianli?' She doesn't wait for an answer. 'I see.'

'Hey, maybe you know,' it occurs to me to ask. 'What's Harrison do, exactly? Is he an artist?'

She giggles politely. 'Oh, no. He's a collector.'

Then she leans forward, puts her hand on my shoulder, and practically whispers in my ear, 'You should be careful with him.'

'Careful? Why?'

'He sometimes takes advantage, that's all.' Lucy Wu ducks her head, seemingly embarrassed. 'I shouldn't have said anything. It's only that I know when you're a foreigner, it can be difficult, knowing who to trust.'

Like I trust *you*, honey, I want to say, but I don't. 'Thanks for the warning.'

She giggles again. 'Don't take me too seriously. I'm told I tend to be dramatic.'

She gives my shoulder a little squeeze. 'We should have lunch. Can I call you?'

'E-mail me. My phone's not working too well.'

'Good. We'll be in touch.'

With that, Lucy Wu gives me a good-bye hug and pitter-patters off.

But it won't be a *real* party until Creepy John shows up.

'Glass of wine?' a waitress asks.

'Sure.'

I'll drink this one slowly, I tell myself. Because it's just about time for dinner to be served, and I'm sitting at Harrison Wang's table, which means that I shouldn't get too drunk, in case he tries to take advantage of me.

A hostess guides me to Harrison Wang's table. Sloppy is there, deep in conversation with a familiar-looking European woman wearing an embroidered jacket from Yunnan, reddish hair forming a frizzy halo around her long, pale face.

'Oh, Yili,' Sloppy says. 'This is Francesca Barrows. You remember. From Simatai Great Wall.'

'Sure,' I say, trying to find my place. There are two empty seats, next to each other, at the six-person table. I sit down next to Sloppy.

About a minute later, Harrison Wang slides into the last remaining chair, next to me.

'Miss Yili. I hope you're enjoying yourself.'

'I am. Thanks.'

I'm enjoying the wine, anyway.

'A French Meritage,' Harrison explains, gesturing toward my glass, 'though they've adopted a more New World style, I'd say. But try the white with the first few dishes.'

Okay.

Dinner arrives, and I enjoy that too. The food, at least. Lots of small plates. It's not exactly Chinese, but still sort of Asian.

'This is delicious,' I comment over an appetizer, which tastes like custard flavored by the ocean.

'The uni?' Harrison asks. He notes my look of non-comprehension. 'Sea urchin.'

'Oh.'

The conversation is similarly rarefied. There's an American professor who's writing a book on the Star Star Exhibit and Democracy Wall; he keeps talking about 'misty poetry.' All I know about Democracy Wall is that it happened before I was born, back in 1979. The other guy at the table, a Chinese artist, leans back, chuckles, and makes sweeping statements about Star Star artists' 'derivative naiveté.' Sloppy practically leaps across the table at this.

'You say that, but they took real chances. They moved people. Art was important then.'

'It could get you arrested, anyway,' Harrison says dryly. 'But I think political art is rarely good art, detached from its politics.'

'What about *Guernica*?' asks Francesca, equally dry.

'I would argue that *Guernica* was a personal expression before it was a political expression. And ahead of either of these is Picasso's artistry. The work has form, organization. Picasso views the event with a sense of aesthetics. He makes art out of it.' Harrison sips his wine. 'Genius is rare. Polemics, unfortunately, are not.'

The Chinese artist, Zhou somebody, nods vigorously. 'Yes. This is the problem with modern art in China. Still too much of this nonsense performance art. Just because it shocks people –'

'Threatens authority, you mean,' Francesca interrupts.

'Art is powerful when the state is afraid of ideas,' Harrison interjects smoothly. 'The simplest way to defuse art's power is to ignore it, or co-opt it.' He smiles. 'Make it into an advertisement, if possible. Or a tourist attraction. Like *this* place.'

Everyone laughs.

I've sat here the whole time, taking in this conversation – trying to, anyway, as most of it is way over my head, and I've also had a lot of wine.

Maybe it's the wine that prompts me to ask: 'So, Lao Zhang . . . Zhang Jianli. His work. I mean, it's really cool. I think. But I don't know that much about art. So I'm wondering . . . what's it about, for him? Art or politics?'

157

'I've always considered Jianli fundamentally a political artist,' Francesca Barrows says. 'The majority of his pieces have a political theme or context. Which would explain why he hasn't joined the ranks of China's artist millionaires,' she adds, with a pointed look at Zhou.

'Yue Minjun –' Zhou begins.

'Can't show his Tiananmen painting inside China,' Francesca interrupts. 'Then there are the artists here at 798 who've had their leases cancelled because of their political content.'

'Zhang Jianli doesn't make very much money because he doesn't care to try,' Zhou says, exasperated. 'I hear he has rooms full of paintings he won't show anybody. But maybe they aren't very good.'

'They *are* good,' I protest.

Zhou focuses his attention on me, his face lit by sudden interest. 'You have seen them?'

'Uh, yeah. I've seen them.' My face flames red. 'I mean, I think they're good. But I don't know that much about art.'

Sloppy tugs on her braid and seems to focus on her food. 'Jianli once say he paints for himself, just what he sees in his head,' she says quietly.

Harrison smiles at me. 'To answer your question, Yili, I believe Zhang Jianli's art is difficult to categorize in so Manichean a fashion. If I were to look for a common theme, I would say his work deals with the meaning of community in a post-Mao, post-democracy era, in the greater context of globalization.'

Francesca Barrows arches an eyebrow. 'That's an interesting analysis.'

'I'm speaking primarily of his performance pieces and

installations, since I haven't seen much of his painting.'
He turns to me again. 'What do you think?'

I catch a whiff of his aftershave.

I think of all the times Lao Zhang talked about living a creative life, about what that means, how hard it is to do in a world of mega-malls and labor camps.

'Yeah,' I say slowly. 'Yeah, that sounds about right. I mean, look at Mati Village. He pretty much started that place, didn't he?'

Harrison nods. 'In a way, you could consider Mati Village his most elaborate piece. Of course, it's nothing if not a collaborative project,' he adds, with a smile in Sloppy's direction.

I think of the Great Community. Of the Game.

Harrison rests his hand on my arm, just for a moment. 'Perhaps Jianli has things to teach us,' he says. 'More wine?'

'Sure. Thanks.'

Harrison Wang lifts his hand to signal a waitress, then orders more wine for the table. 'Something special, this time,' he says, with a mischievous smile.

Harrison Wang's special bottle of wine tastes pretty good, so far as I can tell. We drink that, then he orders another, and I'm a little fuzzy on exactly what happens after that. It's not like I intend to get hammered, but this stuff is easy to drink, and it feels so good to finally relax, to let go.

At one point, I remember Sloppy looking concerned and tugging on my sleeve.

'Yili,' she says, 'why don't you come with Francesca and me? Maybe get some sleep?'

'Nah, that's okay. I'm not tired.'

'So, where you going to stay?'

I shrug. I'll figure that out later.

The music gets louder. I laugh a lot, even dance a little, with the Chinese artist and the American professor, and I must be pretty drunk because that's what it takes to get me to dance these days with my leg like it is. But I'm having fun for a change, so why not?

After a while, it's like somebody flips a switch, and all of a sudden I just want to get out of here. Go home. Wherever that is.

I stumble toward the exit. I'll catch a cab at the gate, I figure. There's gotta be a cab, right? And I'll go . . . someplace. Maybe Chuckie's place at Wudaokou. They're not going to think to look for me there. They think I moved out. It's probably safe for one night. Maybe.

Or I could get a hotel. I know a couple cheap dives not too far from here. Maybe that's a better idea.

'Ms Yili? Are you leaving?'

Harrison Wang has appeared at my elbow.

'Yeah. Yes. Thanks. I had a really great time. But it's getting late, and . . .'

'I hope you're not planning on going to Mati tonight. That's a long way.'

'No. I'm staying in town.'

Harrison Wang hesitates. Cups my elbow in his hand, just for a moment. 'I'm leaving too. Can I give you a ride?'

I shiver a little, and I'm not cold. He's attractive and polished and rich. Everything I'm not. He's way out of my league. And he takes advantage – that is, if I can believe Lucy Wu. Which is a big 'if.'

I shouldn't, I think. I'm drunk, and I know it.

'Sure. I'd appreciate that.'

Harrison Wang not only has a car, a Lexus SUV hybrid; he has a driver.

'Would you like a drink?'

The two of us sit in the back seat. I make a noncommittal noise. I know I shouldn't, but I wouldn't mind having another drink.

Harrison Wang reaches into a storage compartment behind the driver's seat and pulls out two tumblers and a bottle of something – Johnny Walker Blue – and pours.

'Cheers,' he says, lifting his tumbler.

'Likewise.' Which is a stupid thing to say. Harrison pretends not to notice.

We drink. Dang. I could start drinking whiskey if more of it tasted like this.

'Where can I drop you?' he asks after we've both had a few sips.

'Oh. There's a hotel not too far from here. It's, uh, it's called . . .'

I can't remember the name. It's close to here, though. Greenish.

'Do you have a room there already?'

'No, I mean, I . . .'

'There's no need for you to find a hotel, Yili,' Harrison Wang says gently. 'I have an apartment in Chaoyang I use when I'm in town. Please, be my guest for the evening. There's plenty of room.'

I know I can't trust him. I'm just not sure that I care any more. Whatever happens, happens, right?

What difference does it make?

'Thanks,' I say. 'That's really nice of you.'

We drive south, deeper into Chaoyang District. I drink my whiskey and do my limited best to make conversation.

'So, Harrison . . . you're an art collector?'

Harrison shrugs. 'I enjoy art. I try to support what I like.' He freshens our glasses. 'What about you? I know about your association with Zhang Jianli, of course. But what do you do here, in China?'

I snort. 'That's a good question.'

But it's not one I can answer, really.

Harrison stares at me for a minute. Then he rests his hand on mine. 'Sorry. I don't mean to pry.'

'Hey, it's not prying till you ask me how old I am and how many kids I have.'

He chuckles. 'I see you've spent a fair amount of time in China.'

I lean back in the padded leather seat and watch the lights on the sagging skyscrapers go by, the ones built twenty years ago that already look like they're about to fall down. Billboards for expensive watches, medicinal herbs, fancy shoes, cars, new housing developments with names like 'Good Fortune Silver City' and 'Laguna Beach Resort Lifestyle Homes' flash by like we're in some howling, neon-encrusted canyon.

Harrison lives off Jianguomennan Dajie, not too far from the Ancient Observatory, in one of those luxury complexes perched on top of a Hong Kong-funded shopping mall. It's so easy when you have money. The driver pulls up to the private apartment entrance and drops us off. We go up in a brass-lined elevator to the penthouse.

'Here we are,' Harrison says.

The elevator opens onto a foyer, for proper *feng shui*

purposes. He leads me past the sculpture there, a parody of revolutionary imagery, which, instead of featuring your typical stalwart peasants and soldiers, has a guy carrying a briefcase and a woman talking on her cell phone, both casting beatific gazes towards the left of heaven.

He wasn't kidding about having plenty of room.

We step into a living room where the entirety of one wall is given over to a huge picture window. Below us are the lights of Beijing, glittering in their Christmas-tree colors. I see a sign for China Rail, the encircled hammer. Next to that, the golden arches of McDonald's. And, of course, a Starbucks.

'Nice,' I say stupidly.

Harrison shrugs. 'It's all rather crass. On the other hand, there's no escaping reality.'

The floors are polished granite. A fountain runs down the middle of the space, channeled over an arrangement of boulders tumbled near the window wall. On the other walls, paintings are hung, lit by discreet spotlights.

'I just keep a few pieces here,' Harrison is saying. 'The rest are at my other houses and in storage.'

I don't know what to say to this. I wander through the living room – gallery space is more accurate – sipping the remains of my whiskey.

Huge canvases, bleeding landscapes, gaping mouths and eyes and grasping hands. Toy tanks marching across cartoon geography.

I try to keep it all straight. In focus. My eyes burn. Just close them for a minute, I think. Rest.

'Can I show you your room?'

Harrison has appeared at my side.

163

'Thanks,' I say.

We go down a hall hung with smaller works, a few statues tucked into alcoves.

Here is my room, a large bedroom with a picture window shuttered by automatic blinds, a bathroom off to one side.

A maid lays out a pair of silk pajamas on the turned-down bed and smiles at me nervously as she ducks her head and backs out of the room.

'You should have everything you need,' Harrison says, 'but if not, just call for the maid.' He points to a button on a small console sitting on the nightstand.

I stand there awkwardly for a moment. 'Thanks, Harrison,' I say. 'I really appreciate this.'

'Don't mention it.'

With that, he leaves.

I somehow manage to undress and change, even fold up my clothes and place them on a chair, because it seems wrong to leave any kind of a mess in this pristine space. I brush my teeth (there's a fresh toothbrush waiting for me in the bathroom) and swallow a couple of aspirin and vitamins from bottles conveniently left out for me on the counter. Then I crawl into the king-sized bed.

For a couple of minutes, I play with the console, which not only calls the maid but also controls all the lights, the blinds, and the electronics.

No disturbing images hang on these walls. A wash of color here, a traditional nature scene there, some delicate purple flowers, a few stalks of bamboo.

I switch off the lights and open the blinds. Here is Beijing, around and below me, the harsh neon diffused by the treated glass and by distance. Across the way is another penthouse, muted lights softly glowing. It's quiet, so quiet. No noise but the breeze-like whisper of the penthouse's conditioned air.

I close the blinds, and then I close my eyes.

CHAPTER FIFTEEN

I just wanted to sleep.

Trey and me were lying on the cot in the Admin Core. I didn't want to be there. It's not him, I told myself. This isn't some random hookup. I love him. It's this rusty cot, the scratchy blanket, this stupid little room.

I didn't like doing it there. Didn't like walking into the Admin Core, past the guard, with a wink and a nod.

I almost said something then. I should have. I didn't.

'What did this used to be?' I asked instead.

'This building?' Trey shrugged. 'A government complex.'

'But it's not, like, the mayor's office or something. It's not even in town.'

'Yeah.' Trey tapped out a cigarette and offered it to me. I took it. Between the cigarettes and the dust, my throat was raw all the time, and my chest nearly always ached. 'Well, it was a Baathist complex. You know? They had a company of Republican Guards garrisoned here, to keep the LNs in line.'

LNs = local nationals. Trey was hitting the acronyms pretty hard at the time.

'Oh.'

I remember staring up at the ceiling, at the yellow waterspots and peeling paint.

'You know, sometimes I think this place is haunted,' I said.

Trey frowned and lit a cigarette. 'You're kidding, right?'

I forced a smile. 'Yeah, I guess.'

I was so tired all the time that it was like a weight in my bones: from the weird work schedule, from the mortars and RPGs going off every night – which hadn't stopped, even if we *had* caught the muj in charge.

Sleep felt better than anything. Better than being awake ever felt.

Better than being with Trey.

I was sleeping in my bunk one late afternoon when Trey's OGA buddy Kyle came around.

'Hey. McEnroe. Ellie. You in here?'

'Yeah. What?'

I'm thinking: fucking Kyle. Because I was actually alone, for once. I didn't know where Greif and Pulagang were, and I only cared inasmuch as I was hoping they wouldn't come back for a few hours so I could sleep uninterrupted by Pulagang slamming shit around or Greif's constant tapping on her keyboard and muttering Arabic phrases to herself.

'Hey, Kyle,' I said, sitting up slowly. I was wearing a T-shirt and panties and nothing else, so I pulled the sheet around myself. 'What's up?'

Kyle was doing this thing with his hands, slapping his

open palm over his fist. 'So . . . you've been helping Trey out with the PUCs, right?'

I had to think about this for a minute.

'Oh. Yeah.'

'Great. 'Cause usually we use Hilliard, but he's still OC.'

'OC?' I asked, as it was an acronym I'd never heard before.

'Off campus. You know, he was evac-ed out.'

'Oh, right.'

Hilliard was the guy with dysentery, only whatever was causing it we couldn't knock out, and he kept getting sicker until all of a sudden he was exhibiting signs of toxic shock: so good-bye, Hilliard.

'So now we have this situation with one of the PUCs,' Kyle was saying.

'Oh. Okay. Give me a minute.'

I kicked Kyle out and got dressed, threw on my field jacket because it was close to dusk and the weather had finally started to cool. We'd even had rain once, turning the dust briefly to mud.

I started heading toward the aid station to pick up a medical bag, but Kyle stopped me. 'We've got a kit on site,' he said. 'It has everything you'll need.'

Kyle and I entered the Admin Core the same way Trey and I did, passing a soldier standing guard who'd seen me there before. I could tell what he was thinking, me going in with Kyle, and I wanted to say: that's not it, it's nothing like that; but it's not like I could really say anything.

We walked down the familiar hall, past the rooms with the file cabinets, until we came to the wider corridor that

I'd always passed by before. This time, we turned down it.

I'd always seen a few soldiers down at the end of this corridor, and they were there tonight too, three of them, hanging out around a card table they'd set up, drinking water and shooting the shit. They were guys I'd seen around the base, in the DFAC for chow, playing pool in the MWR. I'd treated one of them for a sinus infection two weeks ago.

Just ordinary guys.

'Hey, McEnroe,' one of them said, 'what are you doing down here?'

'She's helping me out with Sneezy,' Kyle told him.

'Oh, man. Did you tell her to bring a facemask? 'Cause he's just reeking.'

'Yeah, yeah.' Kyle patted me on the shoulder. 'McEnroe here's a pro. Nothing she can't handle.'

I didn't ask questions. I didn't say anything. I tried to smile, to show I was one of the guys.

We turned the corner, and I couldn't pretend I didn't know any more.

'So this was, like, the jail?' I asked. 'I mean, before.'

My voice sounded small. Weak.

'Yeah. Not for car thieves or burglars or that kind of thing. More for regime opponents. Draft-dodgers. Or folks who pissed off the local sheik.' Kyle grinned. 'Pretty convenient, huh?'

I nodded.

One of the soldiers – one of the guys – unlocked the door to a cell. Because that's what this was, down this hall: it was a row of cells; and this one, I could smell the stink before he even opened the door. We went inside, into this tiny room, lit from above by a stark, bare bulb, and I swear to God, to my buddy Jesus, there was this naked guy lying on the floor, his wrists and ankles cuffed in front of him, chained to this big bolt drilled into the cement floor.

'What the fuck is this?'

'He's non-compliant,' Kyle explained.

This guy was filthy and moaning, and he smelled like shit and he was lying in a puddle of piss.

I just stood there, my mouth hanging open, because even though none of this should have been a surprise to me, I still didn't know how to make it make sense.

'What do you want me to do?' I asked.

'Well, you know, check him out.' Kyle shifted back and forth, shuffling his feet like he'd been caught cheating on a spelling test or something. ''Cause he's just lying there, he won't talk to us, so we were thinking maybe he's sick.'

It was one of those times when I didn't know what to say. When the obvious words out of my mouth should have been something like 'Well, what the fuck do you expect, dickwad? He's naked, and he's chained to a bolt on a cement floor, and he's lying in his own – I hope – piss!'

But I was a good girl, and I didn't say stuff like that back then.

What I said was: 'Okay. Get me your med bag. I'll check him out.'

Sneezy was young, in his twenties, maybe even his teens, kind of skinny, with tangled hair and a beard even scruffier than most of the local terrorists. I checked him over, and I didn't think he was that sick, but he was pretty out of it, banged up some, a little hypothermic and dehydrated.

'When did he eat last?' I asked Kyle.

'I dunno, a couple of days. He won't eat.'

'He drinking anything?'

'Not much. Doesn't wanna drink either.'

'Nice,' I muttered.

'I think he's mental,' Kyle explained. 'We brought him in; after a day he started acting crazy, throwing shit and spitting at everybody. His own shit, I mean. So we restrained him.'

It was weird; the whole little drill from EMT class was going through my head: 'Is the patient oriented times three? Does he know who he is? Does he know what day it is? Does he know who the president is?' And I almost laughed, thinking: yeah, who's the president, you poor pathetic motherfucker?

'Okay.' I stood up. 'We should get some fluids in him. And you need to get him warmed up. Get him off the floor and in some blankets.'

Kyle got this irritated look on his face and checked his watch. 'He good for another couple of hours like this?'

I stared down at the PUC, who lay there, shivering and making little nonsense sounds, somewhere between moans and a kid's nursery rhyme. 'Lah, lah, lah . . .'

'Like this?'

'Yeah.' Kyle nodded vigorously. ''Cause obviously we don't want to restrain him like this if he's in serious distress. But the protocols are, we can do him another couple of hours if it's not really gonna hurt him.'

The light in there was so bright, it hurt my eyes.

'I don't understand,' I finally said. 'I mean, if he's got psychiatric problems, what's the point?'

Kyle leaned toward me, rested his hand on my shoulder

like he was about to share a big secret. 'He could be faking it. He had explosives residue on his hands. So we're pretty sure he's a bad guy.'

'I don't think this is a good idea,' I said, stammering. 'I mean, I don't think he'll die or anything, but . . . but I don't think this is a good idea.'

'Okay, Doc,' Kyle said, patting my shoulder again. 'I appreciate your feedback. So, can you give him fluids like this? Or would it be easier if we put him in a different position?'

I thought about it.

A woman's voice drifted down the hall. Speaking Arabic. Sounding pissed.

Kyle rolled his eyes. 'Oh, man. Sounds like the show's starting. Listen, I gotta go ride herd. Andretti's just outside the door if you need anything.'

I nodded. And he left.

I walked around the PUC a couple of times, assessing the situation and mapping out where I might want to stick him. I was thinking cephalic vein or maybe accessory cephalic vein, if the cuffs made the cephalic too problematic.

I knelt down by the guy, checked out the veins, and scrubbed both sites with Betadine while he lay there, babbling and trying to spit, except his mouth was too dry to work up a good loogie.

Then I learned why they called him 'Sneezy': his face wrinkled up and he practically convulsed, making this 'chuh, chuh, chuh' noise and bobbing his head like some long-necked choking bird. I'm thinking, should I use a saline lock? Is there any point? Or should I just hang fluids and leave it at that? And where am I going to hang the bag, anyway, in this barren little cell? On the window bars, maybe?

Then I noticed, above my head, screwed into a ceiling beam, what looked like a rusting meat hook made of thick, pitted iron.

That could work.

Whatever was going on down the hall kept getting louder, the woman's voice punctuated now and again by male laughter.

'Lah, lah, lah,' said Sneezy.

I stared at the meat hook, thinking I'd need a chair to climb up there.

And that was when it occurred to me that this was completely, irredeemably fucked up. I mean, what was I thinking? Here was this stinking, crazy naked guy caked with shit and lying in piss, chained to the fucking floor, and I was just going to give him IV fluids and leave? What the fuck was wrong with me?

'Okay, Sneezy,' I said. 'Okay. You need some fluids, but you really need to be in a bed. This is bullshit. I'm gonna take care of this, okay?' I searched through the med bag and found an emergency thermal blanket, one of those things that looks like folded tinfoil and fits inside a baggie. Better than nothing.

I covered him with it. 'I'm sorry, Sneezy, I'm really sorry,' I said. Tears were running down my face, and I didn't know why, considering that this guy was some hajji who wanted to kill me and I really didn't care what happened to him. 'Just hang in there, okay? I'm gonna figure this out.'

Sneezy chuffed a couple of times and stared at the floor. Then his head rolled up, and he stared at me.

'Cunt,' he said. 'Cunt whore.'

I had to laugh.

'Wow. You *do* know English.' I patted him on the shoulder. 'Be right back.'

Outside the cell, Andretti leaned against the wall, playing on his Game Boy.

'Problem?' he asked.

'I need to talk to Kyle.'

He jerked a thumb down the hall. 'That way.'

I could have just followed the sounds, the woman's angry Arabic, the occasional barked laughter, coming from the cell at the end of the hall. Nobody really stood guard; there were a couple of guys clustered by the door, but why would they be worried about somebody like me?

'Hey,' I said to the soldiers by way of greeting. And I stepped inside.

First thing I noticed was Kyle, sitting on a folding chair near the door, tilted back against the wall like he was watching a movie and working on a giant tub of popcorn. A couple other guys stood next to him, guys I didn't recognize, other OGAs maybe, no names on their fatigues.

Second thing I noticed was two more naked PUCs. One of them had his hands cuffed behind him, the cuffs threaded through one of the window bars so that he was half-kneeling. I learned later that this position is called a 'Palestinian hanging' and that it can put enough pressure on the lungs and diaphragm to cause respiratory compromise. An Iraqi general died at Abu Ghraib after being put into this position with broken ribs.

But I didn't know that then.

The second naked hajji was kneeling in front of the first. His hands were cuffed behind his back.

174

There was this woman, a small woman with brown hair and delicate features, stalking around them like some kind of predatory cat.

My roomie, Greif.

She yelled something, and one of the OGAs grabbed the second naked guy by his hair and jerked his head back.

Greif got in his face. Screamed at him.

Second naked guy turned toward first naked guy. His mouth and tongue sought out first naked guy's dick.

Kyle tilted back his chair, snorting with laughter.

It wasn't enough for Greif. She lifted up her T-shirt, grabbed her left tit, freed it from her bra, and thrust it in the second hajji's face, pointed with her free hand at the other guy and screamed at them both.

I just stood there with my mouth open like the fucking clueless idiot I'd been all along.

'Hey,' Kyle said. 'Hey, McEnroe. What's up?'

'I, uh.' My mouth was dry. I swallowed hard. 'I, uh.'

Kyle giggled. 'Yeah, ain't this the shit?' He rocked forward and stood up, propelled out of his chair like he'd been sitting on a cartoon spring.

'Hey, McEnroe,' Kyle said, standing close enough to me that I could feel his warm breath, 'why don't you show them your tits? You got a way better rack than Greif. C'mon, they'll be begging for it. Show them your tits.'

Greif whipped her head around. She saw me, and there was this moment – I'm not sure what it was. Like there was this emptiness in her face, a sort of blankness.

And then fury.

'What's *she* doing here?' she snapped.

Kyle threw up his hands with exaggerated flair. 'Hey, she's just helping me with a PUC, that's all.'

'She shouldn't be here,' Greif said, biting off each word. 'She's not authorized.'

'Sorry,' I said. 'Sorry. I – the PUC – he's . . .'

'Shit, don't tell me he's dying on us,' Kyle muttered.

'No. No . . . I just . . .'

Then I heard footsteps echoing down the hall, coming at a fast clip. I knew who it was even before I saw him, and the relief that flooded through me at that moment was as palpable as water. He'll fix this, I thought.

Trey pulled up in the doorway and took in the scene. He crossed to Kyle, and for a moment I thought he was going to grab him by the collar. 'What the *fuck*, Kyle? What the fuck is this?'

'Jesus, Cooper. You said she's been helping you with the PUCs. I needed some help. What's the big fucking deal?'

Trey turned to me. I couldn't figure out his expression. Somewhere between stunned and ashamed.

'Ellie, you shouldn't be here,' he said. 'Go wait outside. I'll be there in a minute.'

'There's a PUC,' I began, 'and he's –'

'I'll take care of it.'

I did what he said. I went down the corridor, turned right, turned right again. Passed by Andretti playing his Game Boy, by the other soldiers hanging out around the card table, by Morris standing sentry at the entrance. I went outside, into the cool night air, shivering a little in my field jacket, stopped for a moment to light a cigarette in the shelter of the entrance. Then I just walked until I came to the berm. I gathered up some rocks, and I sat down.

It didn't take Trey long to find me. It's funny how we used to be so in sync. I heard him coming up behind me, but I didn't turn around. I picked up a rock, sized it up in the palm of my hand, took my time. Then I hurled it at the shed.

I missed.

'Ellie,' Trey said. He sat down next to me.

I picked up another rock.

'You shouldn't have seen that.'

My hand tightened on the rock. I felt the edges cutting into my hand.

'Then why'd you take me there?'

'I didn't think . . .'

He sighed. A real sigh, like he was expelling any hope that he might have once had. 'Things get out of hand sometimes.'

I looked up at him. Took in the stubble on his cheeks. Marked his hopeless eyes.

'I don't understand,' I finally said.

He lit a cigarette. 'These people respect power and fear. You come across weak, they'll rip your throat out the minute your back's turned.'

'But . . .' I struggled to find the words. 'Some of that . . . I mean . . .'

'This is a shame-based culture,' Trey mumbled. 'Stuff like that, it makes them feel vulnerable.'

'Well, no shit.'

Trey stared at me, the glint in his eyes hard, and my hand closed around the rock again.

'You think I'm freelancing?' he said. 'You think this is my idea?'

'No, I just –'

'I'm doing what I was told to do. CO told us the gloves have come off. That we needed to step it up, get more intel.'

His hands clenched, and then he drove his fist into his thigh. 'The whole thing's fubar,' he muttered.

Right then, I just wanted to take him in my arms, tell him it wasn't his fault. That it was all going to be okay.

'There must be somebody up the chain. Somebody we could tell.'

'Are you fucking kidding me?'

It was like how he spoke Arabic. Angry. Hard.

'Don't you get it, Ellie? Don't you get whose operation this is? It's not mine, it's not the Army's. It's the OGAs'. They do what they want. And you do not fuck with them.'

I weighed the rock in my hand. I threw it at the shed. It hit the door with a clang that echoed like a cowbell.

'The PUC,' I said. 'The guy they call Sneezy. He needs fluids. But not like that. Not on the floor.'

Trey nodded. 'We'll bring him to you.'

I treated him. Got him warm and hydrated, and then they took him away.

I treated PUCs. That's what I was supposed to do. I did my job.

CHAPTER SIXTEEN

I wake up around nine A.M. It's the best I've slept in a while, which is strange, because usually, when I've had that much to drink, I don't sleep well at all.

It's just so comfortable here.

Then I think about last night, about how drunk I got, what an ass I probably made of myself.

If I'm lucky, maybe I can sneak out without having to talk to anyone.

I look over at the chair where I left my clothes, and they're gone. In their place is a new fleece robe and a pair of slippers.

This is what happens sometimes when you think you don't care: you wake up the next morning and realize that you *do* care, but you can't find your clothes.

What if I can't leave?

Okay, I tell myself. Okay. Maybe there's some other explanation, one from the planet of the normal people, like, the maid hung up my clothes while I was passed out.

I check the closet. No clothes. My stinky Pumas are

there, though, which makes me feel a little better. Because if Harrison was planning on imprisoning me here in his luxury penthouse, he wouldn't have left me my shoes, right? And my leather jacket's hanging on a padded hanger, and my little backpack's next to it as well.

I put on the robe and the slippers and cautiously pad down the hall.

I wander into the gallery. The trickle of the fountain echoes in the conditioned air.

'Ellie. Good morning.'

Off to the right is a breakfast nook, a small dining table and a bar with tall stools that borders on a kitchen. Harrison Wang sits at the table, sipping a cup of coffee, typing a last word on his laptop. He's dressed, of course, in a suit jacket and another one of his collarless shirts.

'Hello,' I say. I find myself clutching the collar of my robe together.

He indicates the chair across from him. 'Would you like some coffee? Breakfast?'

'Thanks.'

I sit. Out of nowhere, a woman appears with a cup of coffee. 'Cream? Sugar?'

'Black is fine.'

'For breakfast? You would like eggs? Croissant? Congee?'

'I, uh . . . whatever.'

'Did you sleep well?' Harrison asks.

'Very.'

'The housekeeper sent your clothes out to be cleaned. It's her habit when she sees any clothes left out. They should be back soon. I hope this doesn't inconvenience you.'

180

'No, it's . . . nice of her.'

The coffee's excellent, which doesn't surprise me.

Harrison closes the lid of his laptop. 'So, Ellie. What are your plans?'

'In what sense?'

Harrison chuckles. 'I was only thinking as far as today.'

I drink some coffee and try to think of how to answer. I shrug. 'Nothing much. You know, check some e-mail. Stuff like that. How about you?'

'Meetings,' Harrison says with a sigh. 'Nothing very interesting.'

'So, do you have some kind of business, or . . . ?'

'Investments, mostly. Venture capital. Real estate.' He smiles. 'You can see why I collect art. It's really much more satisfying.'

'I'm starting to get that,' I say.

The maid returns from the kitchen carrying a tray holding a bowl of congee, little dishes of condiments, and a croissant.

I flavor my congee with pickles and dried fish and screw up my courage. 'You know a lot about Lao – Zhang Jianli.'

'I know a little about his art,' he says, watching me.

'It seems like you know a lot,' I say, and I try to smile. Like it's a compliment. 'I was interested in what you said last night. About community.'

Harrison nods. Waits for me to continue.

'That doesn't have to mean a real place like Mati. Does it?'

'I'm not sure I understand what you mean.'

Oh, you know, like a secret society inside an online game.

'Well, what you were saying last night. About . . .' I try to remember through the haze of wine. 'Post-democratic communities.'

'Ah.' Harrison waits for the maid to refill our coffees. 'Forces of globalization tend to have an atomizing effect on traditional communities. The resulting clash and mix can be both exhilarating – and disorienting. One response is the rise of fundamentalism and nationalism. In Zhang's work, I see an ideal of transcending nationalism and creating new forms of community that oppose globalization's homogenizing tendencies.'

I had to ask . . .

'When you say new forms of community . . . what does that mean?'

Harrison shrugs. 'It can mean a number of things. But basically, I refer to people coming together for a common purpose. Lovers of opera, perhaps. Or for saving the pandas.'

'Huh,' I say. 'So, communities like that . . . people wouldn't have to be in the same place, would they? I mean, you could have your panda lovers in Beijing and your panda lovers in San Diego. You know? And they still come together somehow. Like on the Internet. On Facebook. Or something.'

'Certainly,' Harrison says. 'That is, if we are talking about pandas.'

There's this energy between us, like a static charge.

'I've never heard Lao Zhang talk about pandas,' I say.

Harrison stares at me. 'Pandas are something of a cliché in contemporary Chinese art.'

'Oh, yeah?'

I stir a little cream into my coffee. 'So . . . do you believe in all that? I mean . . .'

I meet his eyes. They're hazel, verging on green.

I continue: 'What Lao Zhang believes in?'

He blinks. It's almost a flinch. Then he smiles.

'I'm not an idealist by nature. But I appreciate the artistic results.'

Now the housekeeper has returned with a perfect cheese-and-chives omelet.

Harrison takes a sip of coffee and puts down his cup with an air of finality. 'I'm afraid I have to go. Please don't rush your breakfast. Stay here as long as you'd like.'

Seeing as how I don't have my clothes, I'm not in a position to rush.

'I'm sorry we didn't have more of a chance to talk,' he continues, 'but maybe we can meet again later in the week, if you're available.'

'Sure,' I say. 'Let's keep in touch.'

He nods and rises. 'Here's my card.' I take it. 'Do you have one, or –?'

'No, not right now. I'll write down my information for you.'

'Thank you.' He extends his hand, clasps mine for a moment. 'It's been a pleasure.'

I can feel myself blush. 'Thanks again,' I manage.

He turns to go. Then, almost as an afterthought, he says: 'If you find yourself in town, and you don't have anywhere to stay, feel free to use this place. I'm not here that much, and, as you can see, I have plenty of room. Just ring the bell. The housekeeper is always here.'

After Harrison leaves, I pick at my breakfast. Mostly I drink coffee and surf on Harrison's laptop. I think about checking my e-mail, but I'm too paranoid. As soon as my clothes get here, I'll find a random *wangba* and do that.

I don't know what to think about Harrison.

A half hour later, the housekeeper comes in, bearing my clothes in a shopping bag, every piece folded and wrapped in paper, tied up with string.

'Here you are, Miss,' she says with a smile. 'Sorry so slow.'

'No problem.'

She hands me the bag and goes back out into the kitchen. A few minutes later, she comes back, bearing a small lacquer tray. 'So sorry!' she says. 'These are yours also.'

On the tray are a few coins, a folded wad of bills, a couple crumpled receipts, and several business cards. The stuff that was in my pockets.

Here are the two cards from the Suits, William Carter and George Macias. Here's one from Lucy Wu. And here is the card from creepy John – Zhou Zheng'an, representing a company by the name of Bright Spring Enterprises.

I tap the edges of the cards to line them up straight. I think about Harrison maybe having seen these cards.

I have a last sip of coffee, get dressed, and get out of there.

I walk until I see a China Construction Bank. I can use their ATM to pull some cash from the stateside account where my disability pension is deposited. I hardly ever touch it. I try to forget it even exists. It's not enough to live on or anything. But I figure if I ever want to go home, at least I'll have a little something socked away. Something I can use to start over.

That's where I hit the wall every time. Start over, doing what?

The one job I was good at, being a medic, I don't think I can face.

Standing there, waiting for my money, I feel a little nervous. I always do. Like they're not going to give it to me. Like it's not really mine, or I did something wrong. But the money slides out, just like it always does.

I stand there for a moment, shivering in the massive shadow of concrete and marble and glass.

I head in the direction of the Beijing Railway Station, which is a good place to pick up the local train to Mati and where there's bound to be a few Internet bars. Sure enough, I find one within sight of the station's entrance, between a McDonald's and a Starbucks. It's full of smoke, young guys wearing headsets and shouting curses when they get blown up, upholstered metal chairs with gaping holes in the cushions, and posters for the latest games: warriors and fast cars and half-naked women.

I sign in, buy a bottled Wahaha, and settle in at a terminal.

I check my e-mail. A bunch of spam for Viagra and stock tips. From my mom comes the latest in Jesus e-mail, one where you drag your cursor across snow to show God's invisible footprints, because He always walks with you, and another that says '8 angels R sent 2 U, U must send them to 8 people including me. In 8 minutes U will! receive something U have long awaited. Have faith!' This is apparently something I was supposed to have acted on a couple days ago for the angels to bring me my long-awaited whatever, so I guess I'm shit outta luck as usual.

My eyes are so glazed over from reading another one of these Jesus missives that I'm hovering over the 'delete' button before I notice the 'P.S.' at the end of the e-mail.

'Some changes at the office,' my mom writes. 'Probably best if you don't call me there or use my work e-mail. Love you, honey. Write soon!'

Fuck. What's that mean?

I can't worry about it, I think. My mom can take care of herself. It's not like I can take care of her. Given that I'm not doing such a bang-up job of taking care of me.

Here's an e-mail from Lucy Wu, complete with cool flash animation of . . . art, I guess.

'Ellie, hello. Hope this e-mail finds you well. Are you able to have lunch later this week? I'm anxious to move forward on an exhibition of Jianli's work. Of course, I understand the difficulties, given the current situation, but I have a few ideas how we might proceed.

'If nothing else, we can at least have lunch! I know a fun place by the Drum Tower.'

And here's an e-mail from Trey.

I stare at my inbox. Do I really want to open this?

Finally, I click on the e-mail.

'Ellie, you can't keep doing this. You can't keep ignoring me. Okay I know some bad shit happened and that some of it was my fault, but that was a long time ago. Are we just supposed to keep going on like this? With nothing changing and nothing getting decided? You know I tried to help you but nothing I did was good enough so it's clear I'm not the man for you anyway. So okay it's time we both move on and try to have better lives for ourselves.

'You don't want help from anyone Ellie but you can find help if you want to because Jesus is always here for you. If you let Him back into your life He will heal you and take away your pain. I know He can because He did that for me and I'm a worse sinner than you could ever be.

'Please call me Ellie. It's better if you do. Things are kind of heavy and I don't know if you understand that yet. You don't want to get in the middle.

'Call me when you get this. Trey.'

I sit back in my chair. I chug my water like it's wine. I wish it was.

There are so many things I want to say. So many that I can't think of anything at all.

I start to type.

'So you get to do whatever you want and Jesus makes it okay? Well, it's not okay, you don't get to just make it okay like that. You act like you did everything you could, and that's bullshit, because you could have just loved me and that would have been enough. And you said you did and that was just another lie. You don't even know the meaning of the word, you selfish piece of shit.'

My mouse hovers over the send button.

Instead, I press down on the backspace key, watching it swallow every one of my angry words, the cursor gobbling up my bile and rage, and I think, this is what the Chinese mean when they talk about 'eating bitterness,' about how life is a struggle and you just have to accept your fate because you don't have a choice about it.

'Trey,' I type. 'I know we need to talk. I'm busy right now. I'll write you later. Ellie.'

Busy. That's a laugh.

I have to figure this out, I think, have to figure out what I'm doing. At least what I'm doing next.

I log on to the stupid game.

It's not like I've learned anything by playing so far, but, still, it's the closest thing I've got to a clue.

I figure I'll give it one more shot, and that's it. And this time I'm going to be direct about it.

After logging on, I go to the Yellow Mountain Monastery, make myself anonymous, and type 'Hail, the Great Community!'

Mist drifts down from the mountain, swirling around my legs. I walk up the path. Water drips from condensation on the pine needles.

Nobody's responding. No Cinderfox, no Monk of the Jade Forest. No Water Horse or Golden Snake.

And no Upright Boar, that's for sure.

Goddamn it, Lao Zhang. Do you even have a clue what kind of mess I'm in?

'Okay guys,' I type. 'It's me, Little Mountain Tiger. Anybody out there?'

Just an animated owl, flapping its speckled wings and landing on a pine branch above my head.

'I did everything you asked me to. Can you just give me a hint? Who I should talk to? What I should do? What do you WANT, anyway?'

The owl sitting on the branch above me hoots: once, twice. Then the bird swells to about twice its original size, and some kind of energy beams shoot out of its eyes.

'Hey,' I mutter. Fucking NPC. I raise the shield above my head, which protects me from the beams, and the owl dives at me.

I wind up my staff like I'm swinging at a baseball and nail the thing. The owl flutters to the ground, losing a few speckled feathers in the process.

I have to give them credit for some killer animation.

The owl lies on the stone path, yellow feet sticking up in the air. I guess it's dead. What was *that* about, I wonder? I'm anonymous. Why am I getting attacked by homicidal birds?

I use my wisdom to verify that it's dead and that it's no longer dangerous. Then I pick it up, on the off chance that it contains some hidden power or message for me.

Nothing.

I start walking up the path again, thinking maybe I'll try to find the Yellow Mountain Monastery, which I haven't actually seen yet.

I'm trying to remember the significance of owls in this game. It isn't wisdom, I don't think. I have the vague memory that it's something bad, bad luck, a bad omen, something like that.

This notion is confirmed for me when a pack of Hopping Corpses comes at me from out of the woods.

'Shit.'

I remember the Hopping Corpses. They're these zombies that have long tongues and will try to suck the life force out of you. They're dressed up in fancy, if rotting, robes, like Qing Dynasty officials, and they get around by, well, hopping. They're pretty easy to kill, though. I reach into my knapsack and get out my sheaf of yellow spell paper and type the 'attack' command. The yellow sheets peel off and fly toward the Hopping Corpses, clinging to their faces like Saran Wrap. One by one, the Hopping Corpses collapse. I don't know if you can say that they die, because technically they were already dead.

I take a couple hits from their tongues, which weakens me slightly, but I more than make up for it with the points I get for – I guess – re-killing them.

189

By now I'm just a bit pissed off.

'What's up?' I type. 'Did I do something wrong? Give me a hint, okay? Did I talk to somebody I shouldn't have? Not do something I was supposed to? Come on, this sucks!'

No response. I start walking up the path again, looking for the Yellow Mountain Monastery.

Then, at the edge of the screen, I see a figure – a man – with reddish hair. Cinderfox?

'Hail, Little Mountain Tiger.'

'Hail, whoever you are.'

'Cinderfox,' he confirms. 'Something wrong. Log out and try again later.'

'OK.' I type in the command.

But nothing happens. I'm still there, still standing on the mountain path, looking at Cinderfox in the distance.

Right about then, something really nasty swoops down from the sky.

This thing, it's sort of a bird, but it's huge, and it has a bunch of heads – I can't even count how many – and it's spitting fire from each of them, and even though I raise my tortoiseshell shield, I can't protect myself from all of them.

'Log off!' Cinderfox types. 'LOG OFF!'

I try to log off again, but I'm still stuck here. And I'm remembering something, something about the game, about one of the strongest demons in it, something called a 'Nine-Headed Bird.'

I run down the mountain, holding my shield over my head, throwing every spell I have at the demon, but it's too fast and too strong, and I make a stupid turn and practically run into a granite cliff face. I think: cave.

190

Maybe there's a cave I can hide in while I try to log out again. But there's no cave, and finally what happens is the Nine-Headed Bird catches me in one of its beaks, and though I manage to slice off two of its heads, the one that has me in its mouth tosses me against the granite rock face again and again, and the hit points keep climbing, and, all of a sudden, Little Mountain Tiger goes limp in the Nine-Headed demon's beak. It drops me to the ground, and I'm dead.

Little Mountain Tiger is dead.

I mean, what the fuck?

CHAPTER SEVENTEEN

The way the military determines if you have post-traumatic stress disorder is, they look at how many traumatic and stressful things you personally experienced. Things like being in combat, seeing your buddies get blown up, things like that. So, I wasn't in combat, and even though I was a convoy medic for a while and that was pretty fucking stressful, I never saw my buddies get blown up, only some already blown-up hajjis and the soldier nobody knew who blew his brains out. As for the gunfire and mortars and RPGs going off all the time, almost everybody in the sandbox had to deal with that, so that wasn't enough. You try to make a claim based on that, they say either you're faking it, or you had some pre-existing mental health problem, which, if true, might lead you to ask, then why the fuck did you send me off to war in the first place?

Trust me, they don't have a good answer to that.

Of course, I did get blown up myself. Here's why that didn't count:

I was on my way to the DFAC for chow. Middle of the day. And what happened was, some hajjis decided to launch a couple mortar rounds, just to show they could, I guess, because they almost always did that at night. And one of them landed close by me, and I got hit pretty good by shrapnel and the concussion from the explosion. But I don't actually remember that part.

What I remember is leaving my hooch and being kind of hungry and hoping there were still some tacos left, because Pulagang had already eaten, and she'd told me the tacos were pretty good. And then I remember lying on my back, staring up at the yellow sky. Everything was really quiet, I guess because I was deaf from the shock or the explosion for a little while. It was actually kind of peaceful. I just lay there, blinking at the sun, watching clods of dirt rush toward me and land in little puffs of dust.

Next thing I remember, I was lying in the aid station. Blanchard was working on me, and in spite of his being a dickhead, he was actually a pretty good medic, and he got me packaged up and ready to go in record time, all wrapped up in tubes and gauze and air-filled plastic like I was some kind of extra-fragile FedEx. I was so fucked up, I can't even describe what I was feeling as pain; but I got some morphine, and I could nod and respond and grab his hand, and holding somebody's hand never felt so good or important, like it was going to save my life.

After I was more or less stabilized but before the copter got there, Blanchard let Trey come in to see me.

'Oh, Ellie. Oh, Jesus.'

He was crying. Tears streaming down his face. He

covered my hand with his, gently, like he was afraid he might break it. 'Don't worry,' he said. 'It's gonna be okay. You're gonna be okay. I'll be there as soon as I can. I promise. I swear.'

I didn't see Trey at the hospital at Camp Screaming Eagle Whatever, and he didn't come to Landstuhl, which is where I went next. He couldn't request emergency leave under the circumstances – technically, we weren't supposed to be fucking.

But not too long after I got to Walter Reed, when it still wasn't clear whether I'd keep my leg or lose it, I was lying in bed in a haze of morphine, watching some dumbass reality show about celebrities eating bugs, and I looked up, and there was a man standing in the doorway. He was tall, broad through the shoulders, wearing an Army dress uniform, and juggling this oversized bouquet of yellow roses, a teddy bear, and something else, I couldn't see what.

'Trey?'

'Hey, Ellie.'

He stood there awkwardly. I couldn't do anything much, as I still pretty much felt like I'd been hit by a truck. I think I smiled a little.

Trey put the roses on the nightstand by my bed, where I could smell the sap from their fresh-cut stems. He held on to the teddy bear for a moment, chewed on his lip, and finally placed it on the pillow next to my head. Then I could see the other thing. He'd somehow gotten my red Beanie squid, the one I'd taken over there with me. I almost cried when I saw it. Maybe I did cry. He put it in the teddy bear's lap.

'Thanks,' I said.

'How're you doing?'

'Okay.'

'I miss you,' he said.

'Me too. I mean, I miss you too.'

Trey bowed his head. Like he was ashamed about something.

'Ellie,' he said abruptly, 'I want to take care of you. Let's –'

On the TV, some supermodel shrieked about having snakes crawling on her.

Trey found the remote and turned it off. Then he knelt down at the side of the bed.

'Do you want to get married?' he asked. It was weird the way he asked it, like it was something that had just occurred to him.

He stared at his hands. They were clasped together, resting on the edge of the bed.

'I know I'm a sinner. And I don't think I deserve you. But . . . I want to get better. I want to be a better man.'

I can't really say that I thought about it. I was on so much morphine that thinking about much of anything was beyond me.

But what I felt, for just that moment, was that I was finally safe.

'Sure, Trey,' I whispered. 'I'd like that.'

Anyway, back to my PTSD claim. Like I said, they base it on the fucked-up shit you personally experience. And I wasn't in combat, I didn't see my buddies get blown up, and I couldn't even remember much about my own injury.

195

What about what happened in the Admin Core, you might ask?

Well, here's the thing. In order for it to count, you have to tell them about it.

CHAPTER EIGHTEEN

I walk out of the *wangba*, and I'm pretty shook up about being dead.

Of course, being dead isn't permanent in the Game. I can resurrect Little Mountain Tiger if I'm willing to put in the playing time. But the whole other aspect of it, the idea that Cinderfox claimed to be Lao Zhang's friend, that I joined their Guild, and then out of nowhere just about every bad demon in the game arrived to take me out . . .

Well, that's disturbing.

I can't even begin to sort out what it all means.

I see the green-and-white Starbucks sign, and all I want to do is sink into that familiar environment, with the wood-grain tables and the cool jazz music and the nice coffee smell and the hiss of steaming milk.

I go in, order a Grande Mochachino from the cheerful barista, and sit by the window that faces the train station.

The Beijing train station is big and brown and flanked at intervals by towers topped with pagoda roofs – another attempt to put Chinese lipstick on an architectural pig. It's still better than the Beijing West train station, which is like the same thing but on steroids and gray, with a massive upside-down U at its center that squats there like some kind of Stalinist wet dream, as British John would put it. But hey, who died and made me Beijing's architecture critic? Especially considering that right now I'm dead myself.

Sometimes I lose track of where I am. I'll end up someplace and wonder how I got there. Or I'll be somewhere and completely space out. Disassociate. Part of the fun of PTSD. It's what happens when I'm exhausted from being hyper-vigilant.

Which is why I don't notice the two guys coming up from behind until they sit down on either side of me.

'Mrs Cooper,' one of them says briskly.

It's the Suits – the GSC guys.

The thinner, younger one – Carter or Macias? I try to remember – does his best impersonation of a concerned expression. 'Sorry to intrude, Mrs Cooper. Or do you prefer McEnroe?'

'What do you want?' I say, as soon as my heart stops hammering enough for me to speak.

'You've been spending some time out in Mati. And with some interesting people. We were hoping you might have news for us.'

'I already told you –' I begin.

'And we don't believe you,' says Suit #2, the bulky, meaner one.

'Why not?' I don't have to fake sounding angry. 'It's

198

just a coincidence that I even met the guy. You think I'm some kind of terrorist?'

'We think you have information that you're not sharing due to some misguided loyalty to your boyfriend,' Suit #1 says. 'And while we understand that, we just don't have time for it right now.'

'What, the Uighur's gonna set off a nuke in Manhattan?' I snark.

Suit #2 clamps his beefy hand on my forearm.

'I'll scream,' I say.

Suit #2 shrugs. 'Go ahead. You think anyone will care? Let the foreigners deal with their own problems. That's what they think around here.'

'We really need your help, Mrs Cooper,' Suit #1 says. 'We thought, with all the time you've been spending in Mati, that you might be trying to help us. It's disappointing that you're not.'

I'm still more pissed off than afraid. 'So what are you gonna do? Dress me in an orange jumpsuit? Fly me in a Gulfstream to Bumfuckistan?'

'You think we can't take you out of here if we want to?' Suit #2 says in a low voice, fingers tightening on my arm. 'You think we can't make you disappear? Who'd blink twice if we did? You're *nothing*, you get that? We can find you any time we want, and we can take you any time we want.'

'People'd notice,' I say in a small voice.

Suit #1 nods in agreement. 'You're pretty close to your mother, aren't you? The two of you seem to communicate pretty regularly. I gather she's been having a rough time lately, with her employment situation. And her relationship isn't going so well either. But that's a pattern with her, right? Bad choices with men.'

I stare at the hand on my forearm. It's rough and reddish and has the kind of spots you get from sun and age. The weird thing is, the nails are neatly trimmed. Polished, even.

'First thing,' I say, 'take your hand off me, or I really will scream. You want a scene in Starbucks? Go ahead. I'll make one.'

Suit #1 nods slightly. Suit #2's hand withdraws.

'I don't know if I can help you,' I finally say. 'I really don't. Maybe I can try. But first you gotta tell me some things.'

'If we can.'

'Why do you want Hashim? The Uighur guy. What did he do?'

'It's what we told you before,' Suit #1 says. 'He's connected to Islamic extremist organizations that are working against U.S. interests.'

'What's that mean, exactly? He wants to blow up the Mall of America or something?'

Suit #1 hesitates, but only for a moment. 'I'm afraid I can't discuss specifics.'

Well, no surprise there.

'What about Lao Zhang?' I ask.

'What about him?'

'I mean, what do you want with him?' I feel like my gut's stuck in my throat. 'You want to take him to some recycled gulag, or what?'

Suit #2 barks out a laugh. 'I wish. We lost the EU facilities thanks to that bitch from the *Washington Post*. Now, *there's* somebody I'd like to render unto Caesar.'

'Ha-ha,' I say uncertainly.

'Mrs Cooper,' Suit #1 says, 'we all know there were

some abuses in the past. But that's not how we do things now. We're very careful about how we proceed.' He smiles at me. 'We're just after the bad guys.'

'Lao Zhang's not a bad guy.'

'I don't get why you're protecting him,' Suit #2 says suddenly. 'You're just a piece of ass to him, don't you get that? His token white girl. He dumps you in a pile of shit and leaves. When are you gonna wise up?'

My hand makes a fist, like I'm not controlling it. 'What do you know? What the fuck do you know about it?'

The businessman at the next table stares at us.

'Everybody calm down,' Suit # 1 says. 'We're not after Lao Zhang. We want to find the Uighur. That's all.'

Funny, but I don't exactly believe him.

'Okay,' I finally say. 'Maybe I can help you find the Uighur. But that's it. I'm not helping you find Lao Zhang. And you'd better not fuck with my family.'

Suit #1 gives me this wide-eyed look. 'Who said anything about that?'

You did, asshole, I think; but I don't say anything.

'All right, Mrs Cooper. When can we expect to hear from you?'

'If you can find me any time, why are you even asking?'

He lifts his hands. 'We don't want to crowd you. We'll give you some time to do what you need to do. Within reason.'

'A couple of days,' I say, my thoughts scrambling around in my head like panicked mice. 'Till the weekend.'

'Agreed.'

The two of them rise. 'We'll be in touch,' says Suit #1.

201

After they leave, I sit at my table for a while, sipping my Grande Mochachino and staring out the window at the train station across the way, thinking: I just gave myself four days to do something, and what the fuck am I going to do now? Because Little Mountain Tiger is dead, which means I can't go to the Yellow Mountain Monastery. I log on to the game, and I'll be in Hell, and I'll have to face Ox-Head and Horse-Face, the guardians of the Underworld, and it will take hours of playing time just to resurrect myself to a basic level, which I don't think will get me into the Yellow Mountain Monastery, and who's to say every monster in the game won't show up to kill me again?

I could try resurrecting myself and going to the Teahouse where I met Cinderfox, but I don't know if he hangs out there at all or whether it was just a convenient place to meet a low-level player like I was before.

Maybe he'll send me an e-mail, I think. He's got my address. I don't have his. The invitation came from the Game, not a private e-mail address.

And if he did write me, then what?

He's my only connection to Lao Zhang right now, and I don't even know what that connection means.

Even if I could contact Lao Zhang, there's no way I want to put the Suits onto him. Even if he did leave me in a whole heap of shit.

He didn't mean to. I don't think.

That's the thing, the real pisser of it all. A part of me thinks Suit #2 is right.

Not that Lao Zhang meant to get me in trouble, but that it doesn't really matter to him that I am.

202

How can I know? What are we to each other? Right now, I don't have a clue.

Then I remember the painting, the portrait he did of me. I don't get what it means, with the three-legged dog and the scared cat and all, but I remember how he made me look: strong. Calm.

That's how he sees me. Even if I'm not.

How do I see him?

I picture him painting. I think about sitting on his couch, watching him, and how that made me feel.

Like I was welcome someplace. Like I was home.

So, okay. That leaves the Uighur. Maybe he really *is* some kind of major terrorist. Which would mean my helping the Suits find him is the right, moral, *patriotic* thing to do.

Ha-ha.

Or I could just tell the Suits about the Game. Hey, look, guys! Terrorist sympathizers hatching their plots through PlayStations! That would be enough, wouldn't it? Enough to take care of me and my family, and fuck everyone else.

After I finish my latte, I walk over to the train station. I can't help it. The thought that there's this place with trains getting the fuck out of town every few minutes attracts me like some kind of drug. I walk into the main lobby, into the hordes of people going here and there, riding the escalators up and down, the migrants from the countryside clutching their cardboard suitcases and faded striped shopping bags, the giggling students sharing iPod earbuds and ringtones, the middle-class Beijingers in their Polo shirts and fake Prada, the PA announcing arrivals and departures, all punctuated by the red diode signboards blinking destinations, and I think: how far away could I get? Is there someplace I could go where they can't find me?

How *did* they find me? Can they find me when my phone is off? Can they track my e-mail to whatever Internet bar I happen to log in at? Or was it from using the ATM, from getting money out of my U.S. account?

Or maybe it's something more low-tech. Like Harrison Wang works for them, and he told them I was at his place, and they followed me from there.

I stare at the red diode signboards above the escalators to the second floor. I just missed a train to Harbin. Too bad. Harbin is pretty far away. In three hours, I could catch a train to Xiamen. People tell me Xiamen is nice. Warm. It has a beach. That's tempting. Here's another going to Inner Mongolia. Could I get to Outer Mongolia from there? That might be far enough.

Here's a train to Taiyuan, in Shanxi, leaving in thirty-eight minutes.

Taiyuan, I think. Chuckie's family lives around there.

Chuckie, with his seventh-level Qi sword. His hacking skills. Chuckie, who's played *The Sword of Ill Repute* way longer than I have.

Maybe he's not part of the Great Community, but who better than Chuckie to help me get Little Mountain Tiger back in the Game?

I watch the red letters on the signboard shuffle and reassemble. Train to Nanjing in an hour. One to Lanzhou in two.

I think: maybe Chuckie won't help me. I think: even if he does, maybe I won't get anything more from the Game than I already have, which adds up to pretty much nothing.

But what else am I going to do? Stumble around Beijing for a couple days? Wait for the Suits to pick me up in some random Starbucks?

Right now, the Game is all I've got.

And leaving town in thirty-eight minutes sounds good.

CHAPTER NINETEEN

I was lucky. My leg was totally busted up, multiple frac-
tures, shredded muscles, lacerated blood vessels, but I
didn't lose it, even after the post-op infection and compli-
cations from blood loss; they did skin grafts put in an
intramedullary rod and five titanium screws to hold it all
together. I had broken some ribs and fractured two verte-
brae too. I had a major concussion but no long-term brain
injury, at least that's what they said. At first they weren't
sure, because for a while I had a hard time putting
sentences together, and I'd get these headaches that were
so bad I'd want to die. That made them wonder if some
of the psych symptoms I exhibited were organic, as
opposed to just me being crazy. But they cleared me of
any permanent brain injury.

I know I was lucky. I told myself that every time I saw
some of the guys in the hospital. The guys with
'polytrauma.' That's what they call it when you have more
than one serious injury at once, usually an amputation
combined with head trauma. The guys who had to learn

to both talk and walk all over again. The guys who couldn't get that far. Who would never be able to hold a real job, because their brains just wouldn't work right any more. Smart guys, funny guys, with chunks out of their skulls, indentations like somebody'd taken an ice-cream scoop to their heads, who'd smile sometimes when they couldn't keep up, like they knew they were missing something, but didn't know what. The guys who were worse than that. The ones who weren't really there at all any more, who needed tubes to breathe and tubes to suction out their mucus and tubes to pump liquefied pudding into their guts and take away their piss and what passed for their shit. I'd go by those rooms on my crutches, the pain in my leg so bad that even through the haze of narcotics I'd have tears streaming down my face and not even realize I was crying, and I'd see families in there sometimes, sitting around the bed, holding the guy's hand, telling him how he was going to get better soon, and they were going to take him home. He'd be home, and it would all be better.

People kept telling me how brave I was. I didn't get that. I mean, how brave do you have to be to get blown up? But I'd smile and nod anyway. I just did what I was told. Walk to the end of the rail; lift your leg; tighten your belly; four more times; come on, you can do it; pump, pump, pump! I worked my ass off, like a good little soldier.

But the first time I really saw myself in the mirror, when I was finally able to go into the bathroom with the help of an attendant, no more bedpans and catheters, I could hardly believe the face that stared back at me. I'd lost something like twenty-five pounds, and I hadn't been heavy to begin with. I looked like a little old man. Some shriveled-up circus monkey. My eyes were sunk into their sockets, surrounded by bruised, black lids, black holes that were going to swallow me up inside them.

'Hey,' I said to the attendant, this Haitian guy who was built like a statue. 'Hey, I look like shit, don't I?'

'You don't look so bad,' he said, resting his heavy hand on my shoulder. 'You'll get better. Don't you worry.'

I was in the hospital for over a month. After the first two weeks, my mom had to go back to work. She said she could come and see me on the weekends, but I told her she should save her money. As much as a part of me wanted her there, wanted my mommy to stay and take care of me, another part of me wished that she hadn't come. Because I could see how much it hurt her to see me like this, her little girl, how painful it was for her. I could see her eyes fill with tears as she looked at me, when she didn't turn away in time. I didn't want to be responsible for that.

Trey couldn't stay long either. He had to get back.

I'd wanted to wait and have a real wedding, that whole princess fantasy, me all in white; but Trey had more sense about this than I did.

'No,' he said. 'We should do it now. Just in case.'

'Don't think that way,' I said.

'Ellie, we *have* to think that way. If something happens to me, you'll have my benefits. That's not much, but it's something.'

I finally decided that he was right. That it was practical. Or maybe I just wanted to please him. It was what he wanted, after all. And I wanted to make him happy.

A chaplain came and married us, me lying in my hospital

bed, Trey in his dress uniform, my mom and his parents standing by. This was the first time I'd met his parents, naturally, and in my morphine-addled state it was hard for me to form much of an impression of them, except that I could see Trey in them both, distorted, fun-house mirror versions of Trey anyway. They smiled a lot. They seemed tense.

'You just let us know if you need anything,' Trey's dad told me. He was an executive in an insurance company.

'We just want to welcome you to our family,' Trey's mom told me. She sold real estate at the time.

'Thanks,' I said. 'Thanks very much.'

Trey's mom clasped my hand. 'Such a brave girl,' she said.

The night before Trey had to report, he brought dinner for me. Mexican food. I'd been saying how much I wanted some decent Mexican food, because nothing at the hospital tasted good, and I never felt like eating. I needed to eat. I'd lost too much weight, and I needed to eat, everyone kept telling me, to get my strength back.

If I could only have some Mexican food, I was sure I'd feel like eating.

So Trey went out and got all these dishes from a local restaurant – enchiladas and burritos and chile rellenos – and served them to me on the plastic tray that swung over my bed.

I pretended it was great, but it wasn't. Soupy red sauce, too much sour cream, and guacamole that only vaguely tasted like avocado.

'If you need anything, just call my folks,' Trey was

saying. 'They really want to help, so don't feel shy about it.'

'I won't,' I said.

I was having a hard time swallowing. The enchilada seemed to stick in my throat. I had the idea, suddenly, that the food was getting stuck on all the words down there, the words I wouldn't say, and that was why I couldn't eat.

I was pretty high from the morphine at the time.

'That stuff,' I said. 'The stuff we did. Are we going to get in trouble?'

Trey's fork froze halfway to his mouth.

He took the bite. Chewed. Swallowed. 'We didn't do anything wrong,' he said quietly.

'We didn't?'

'Things look different from here,' he finally said.

He put his hand on mine. 'Look, most people aren't going to understand. They weren't there.'

'I don't know, Trey.'

My eyes teared up. That happened a lot. I couldn't control it. Sometimes I didn't even think I felt sad.

'Ellie. You can't talk about it. This is about OpSec. You violate that, you're putting the mission at risk. You don't want to do that. Right?'

He spoke so soothingly. Like I was a child. And I was. Helpless. Needing to be fed. Tuck me in, Daddy.

'No.'

'Good.' He leaned over and gently kissed me. 'Just get better, Ellie. That's all you need to think about right now.'

I saw a shrink a couple of times. That was standard operating procedure. They had this rhetoric about how the sooner you start treatment, the less likely you are to develop major psychological problems. But this was more of an evaluation. A cover-your-ass move. I got the usual questions: 'How are you feeling?' 'Are you experiencing any intrusive thoughts?' 'Any nightmares?' 'Anything you'd like to talk about?'

'Fine,' I'd say, which of course was a big fucking lie, considering how much pain I was in. But the pain drove out most intrusive thoughts (as did the narcotics), and I wasn't having nightmares. Not then. Those started later.

The only question I'd get stuck on was that last one: Anything you'd like to talk about? 'No,' I'd say. 'I'm okay.' But I knew what was hovering at the edge of my thoughts, wanting to push its way in, and every once in a while I'd get this flash, this vision, like a snapshot, of Sneezy chained to the floor of the Admin Core, of Greif flashing her tit. Of me and Trey fucking in that horrible little room.

I guess those were intrusive thoughts.

I'd push them all away. I could do that then. Sometimes I could hardly remember anything about those times. I'd had this strange interlude on the other side of the planet, but it was over, I was home now, and I could forget about it.

I just had to get better, that's all.

The shrink, this middle-aged major – looking back, he wasn't a bad guy. Maybe I should have talked to him. I wonder, would I have gotten better if I had?

But I couldn't talk about it, could I? Not about what happened in the Admin Core. I'd get in trouble. I'd get Trey in trouble. They wouldn't understand.

The third and last time Major Shrink saw me, after I

told him I wasn't having any intrusive thoughts, no nightmares, I was okay, he leaned back in his chair and pushed his glasses onto his forehead.

'I'm glad to hear that you're feeling good, Ellie,' he said. 'You've been through a really rough time. Just because you weren't in combat doesn't mean you didn't experience a significant amount of stress. Now, you're a medic, so I think you'll understand what I'm going to say. These kinds of symptoms can take a while to develop. Three, four months; it's not unusual.' He closed his eyes for a moment and tapped his pen on the edge of the desk a few times. 'I'm glad to hear you're feeling good,' he repeated. 'Just keep in mind, if you have any problems, there are resources available that can help you.'

'Thanks,' I said. 'Appreciate it.'

I wonder now, how did he know? Could he see it in my face? In my eyes? Was it something he understood because he'd been there? Or was this just his standard-operating-procedure CYA line of bullshit? 'Patient was informed of treatment availability. Patient reported no significant symptoms and declined further treatment.'

CHAPTER TWENTY

I'm sitting on a hard seat, drifting in and out of sleep.

It's a ten-hour train ride to Taiyuan, arriving at 11:00 P.M. Hard sleepers are sold out, and I don't want to pay for a soft sleeper when I'm not traveling overnight.

The open compartment is packed, as is usual for hard seats, with everybody and their *xiao didi* along with this crazy assortment of bags and boxes and suitcases crowding the aisles. People stand, squat, perch on the little tables, sit on their luggage. I'm lucky to score a seat by the window. Before long the compartment smells like cigarettes and stale sweat and shit from the squat toilet two rows away.

A middle-aged woman who's traveling with a little kid sits across from me. Auntie obviously thinks this kid is the most adorable, talented ankle-biter ever, and okay, she's pretty cute: red-cheeked, hair as black and shiny as obsidian, dressed in a pink jumper with little cartoon mice appliquéd on it.

It's my fault for playing peek-a-boo with the kid. After

213

that, Auntie offers me some of her sweet and spicy peanuts, and little Meihua climbs up on my lap, unafraid of close contact with the foreign devil.

'Meihua, don't bother the foreign miss,' scolds Auntie.

'It's not a problem,' I say, though to be honest, having her there is making my fucking leg hurt and I end up taking one of my last Percocets with a swallow of Auntie's lukewarm tea. After that I hardly notice Meihua. I just doze, drifting in a warm, waveless sea.

We roll into Taiyuan as scheduled – one thing about China, the trains are nearly always on time. My leg buckles when I try to stand up; the muscles wake up like they've been lit on fire.

'You're not well? Let me help.'

Auntie takes me by the arm and guides me down the train compartment's steps, even though I'm only carrying my little backpack and she's got a rolling suitcase, a giant shopping bag, and a shoulder duffel.

Since Auntie has her hands full, I take Meihua's hand, and the three of us exit the train station.

Taiyuan smells like coal dust and is bathed in yellow light from the low-sodium street lamps. Taxis wait in line by the curb, the drivers mostly napping in their seats, a few smoking cigarettes and drinking tea in glass jars where it's probably been steeping since this morning.

It's not too late for the touts, though, and a bunch of them swarm me, not quite touching me but coming close, saying things like 'Miss! Miss! Need good hotel? Nice price!'

'Stop bothering her!' Auntie snaps. She turns to me. 'Where are you staying tonight?'

I make a noncommittal response. I'll figure out something.

Auntie whips out her phone and starts rattling away in the local dialect.

'Okay,' she says when she gets off. 'I have a nice room for you. Very good price. My friend is the driver. He comes in a minute.'

'You are very kind,' I say, 'but –'

She pats my hand. 'Don't worry.'

This guy in a black VW Santana shows up, Auntie's friend: middle-aged, skinny, face seamed by lines blackened by the coal dust, like he's some kind of comic-book drawing.

'Please, get in,' Auntie says, gesturing toward the back seat, with its white seat covers. 'We'll take you to the hotel.'

I've had things like this happen to me before in China, but I only used to worry about stuff like, am I supposed to pay the driver? Am I going to end up in a hotel I can't afford?

Now I'm thinking, what if they're working for someone? The PSB or Creepy John?

She's an auntie traveling with a little girl, I tell myself. They were already in the train compartment when I got there. Weren't they?

Auntie gestures again toward the back seat.

I climb in. Auntie gets in front, riding shotgun.

Sitting in the back seat of the Santana, Meihua snoozing on my thigh, I stare out the window at the broad, anonymous streets of a city I've never seen. Auntie and the driver chat in the local dialect, and I can't quite figure out what they're talking about. 'Foreigner,' I hear, and 'money.'

Auntie turns toward me. She smiles, revealing a gold

215

front tooth. Her eyes look like black stones behind her glasses.

Mouth dry, I keep my hand on the door handle.

After maybe a fifteen-minute drive, we turn down a narrow lane and stop in front of an entrance wedged between an office building and a clothing store.

A signboard in gold letters says 'The Good Fortune Guest House.'

Inside, there's a modest front desk that looks like it doubles as a bar, with stand-up ads for beer and Nescafé. Auntie negotiates with the clerk behind the counter, in spite of my protests that I can take care of it myself. 'You know, some Chinese people try to cheat foreigners,' she whispers darkly. 'They think all foreigners have money.'

A couple of minutes later, negotiations concluded, I show my passport to the clerk and am given a keycard to a room on the second floor. 'Nice room, quiet,' Auntie says. 'You won't have any troubles here.' Then she reaches into her purse and extracts a card case. 'You have any problem, you call me,' she says, pulling out a business card.

I take it from her in the polite manner, with both hands. I'm so embarrassed, I don't know what to say.

'Thank you,' I manage.

Auntie smiles. 'Welcome you to Taiyuan,' she says, beaming.

I make my way upstairs to my little room. Brown and tan walls, a hard, single bed, a window draped with blackout curtains, no fridge, just an electric kettle and a teacup.

But it's mine, my own small, private space. At least for the night.

I brush my teeth with the hotel toothbrush and overly sweetened toothpaste from the miniature tube, spit out a few shed bristles. Then I take off my shoes, jeans, and bra and crawl into bed.

I probably shouldn't feel so comfortable here, I think. After all, I gave the clerk my passport number. Assuming China's got some central foreigner-tracking system, who's to say that Creepy John won't be knocking on my door tomorrow?

I have this sudden vision of him sitting on the edge of my bed in his faded Beijing Olympics T-shirt and cheap leather jacket, smiling at me.

It takes me a while to fall asleep after that.

In the morning, I limp downstairs and order up a double Nescafé, which should tide me over till I find some real coffee. Chuckie was always bitching about what a backwater Taiyuan is, but three million people live here – there's got to be a Starbucks somewhere, or some Chinese rip-off version, Star Cup or Moonbucks or something.

Fueled by Nescafé, I smile at the desk clerk and go outside.

Pollution in Beijing is pretty bad, but Taiyuan puts it to shame. Everything is covered with a layer of sticky black dust; the sun struggles to shine through a greenish sky, and the air smells like chemical soup. A few years ago, Taiyuan was the world's most polluted city. Now they don't even have that distinction going for them; it's maybe the fourth worst. What's the point of that? No one cares about Number Four. You're out of medal contention.

I find a coffeehouse, have a decent cup of coffee and a limp bagel, and then sit there for a while in a little booth by the window, watching people pass by on the grimy sidewalk, nurse a second cup of coffee, and try to figure out what I'm going to do.

I decide to call Chuckie. I step outside and find a public phone, duck into the egg-shaped booth, and punch in Chuckie's number.

'*Wei?*'

'Chuckie? *Shi nide lao tongwu.*'

Your old roommate.

There's a long pause. 'Hey,' he says.

'Look, I need a favor.'

'Ahhh . . .' A longer pause. 'Maybe not convenient now.'

'You owe me,' I snap. Truthfully, he doesn't owe me shit, but it sounds good. 'It's nothing that's gonna cause you any problems.'

Of course, I have no way of knowing if that's true.

'Okay,' he finally says.

Chuckie and I arrange to meet at a karaoke bar on the fringes of Taiyuan. Karaoke bars usually have a lot more than just karaoke going on. Prostitution, drugs, bribery – they're the Amazon.com of vice. A lot of the time karaoke places are hole-in-the-wall joints, attached to hotels, next to restaurants and discos, set apart by the letters KTV outlined in neon.

This one is more ambitious. It's called 'The Parthenon,' and it looks like a Greek temple – that is, if the temple's architects had dropped a lot of acid before they built it. Marble columns with flashing strings of green and red diodes snaking around them, naked statuary lit by colored spotlights, and a fountain that dances around vaguely in

218

time to the latest Taiwanese pop blaring from the outdoor speakers.

I pay the taxi driver, thinking this might be an appropriate occasion for a Percocet.

Inside is a large main room, a dance floor encircled by booths, with a long bar cutting the space practically in half. Illuminated plastic signs at the back of the room, where the private rooms are, read KTV. It's still early, and the place is pretty empty. The DJ plays Mandarin rap in a mash-up with the Carpenters. I decide it's definitely time for that Percocet.

I'm supposed to meet Chuckie at the bar. I try the local draft, called 'Yingze Cleaning Flavour Beer.' I'm a little disappointed that it tastes like any other bland Chinese lager.

I'm about halfway through my pint when Chuckie shows up.

'Hey, Chuckie. *Hao jiu bujian.*' Long time no see.

'Yili, *ni hao*. How's it hanging?' he adds in English.

'Dude, you don't say 'how's it hanging' to a girl,' I say, exasperated. 'Because you're asking about, you know, which side of the pants your *jiba* and *dan* are hanging on.'

Chuckie's face flames red. 'Oh. I thought this was same as hanging out.'

'Well, maybe, sometimes,' I relent, because this really isn't the time for me to try and upgrade his English slang. 'You want something to drink?'

'Beer is good.'

I order two more.

'So, how's Taiyuan?'

'Okay,' he says nervously. 'Kind of boring.'

The beers come. I lift my mug. Chuckie lifts his in

219

return, leaning back on his barstool and eyeing me over the mug's rim.

'So, Yili,' he says. 'You say you need some help from me. Right now, maybe it's bad time for me. But tell me anyway.'

Good, he's not in the mood for *keqi hua* either.

'Okay, here's the deal. You know my character in *Sword of Ill Repute*? Little Mountain Tiger?'

Chuckie nods.

'Well, she got killed. I need you to help me bring her back.'

Chuckie takes a swallow of his beer, frowning. 'So, that's easy. You just have to play some rounds in Hell. Meet Horse-face and Ox-head. You know how to do that.'

'I don't have time.'

People are starting to arrive, groups of students and middle-aged men accompanied by much younger women wearing stilettos and short skirts. I figure they'll be ordering up the Courvoisier or Dom Pérignon or whatever overpriced bullshit middle-aged Chinese yuppie guys buy to impress their hooker girlfriends.

The music's changed too: it's harder-edged, faster, and the volume's cranked up to the point where I start to get nervous. I chug the rest of my first beer and start on the second. I can do this. I just need to have the rest of this conversation, and then I can get out of here.

'See, Chuckie, the thing is, my character was a lot higher ranked than before. And . . . I kind of need her to be that high-ranked again, and right away.'

I can tell that Chuckie's having a hard time absorbing this, considering that I'd never shown much interest in the game before. 'What level?'

'Ummm . . . eight . . . I think.'

'Eight? But you only . . . you are just level one or two before.'

'Yeah. But, you know, I, um, played a lot after you left Beijing, and –'

'You can't just become level eight after so little playing time,' Chuckie protests. 'Takes maybe a few months of playing, and playing many hours.'

'Yeah . . . well . . . it just kind of happened.'

Chuckie stares at me, aghast. 'You cheated?'

'No, I didn't cheat. Somebody helped me out. That's not cheating.'

'This is what ruins games!' Chuckie says furiously. 'You can just buy what you want, not earn it.'

'Hey, you lent Ming Lu your whatever-the-fuck-level Qi sword! How's that different?'

Chuckie slams his beer mug on the bar. 'It was for specific quest! That is part of this game!'

'Okay, so this was part of a specific quest too,' I retort. 'And things got fucked up, and they need me for this quest, and you gotta help resurrect me!'

'So, what kind of quest?' Chuckie asks.

Oh, shit.

Chuckie ran all the way to Taiyuan to get away from whoever was threatening him in Beijing. To get away from me. He's not exactly thrilled to see me as it is. If I tell him any portion of the truth, he'll probably bolt to Tibet.

But lying to him? I can't do it. For one thing, I suck at lying.

'It's important,' I say. 'And it's really better if I don't tell you what it's about.'

'I don't understand,' Chuckie says with a frown. 'If this

221

is for the Game, you can tell me. Maybe I can help you on the quest.'

Is Chuckie a part of the Great Community? It would make sense. It's his Game too.

But what if he's not?

I take a deep breath. 'I can pay you.'

Chuckie bows his head, practically resting his chin on his beer mug. I'm pretty sure he's deeply offended.

''Cause I got these cool weapons,' I continue. 'This really tall staff that shoots Qi energy. And, um, this tortoiseshell shield. And I get those back once I'm resurrected, right?'

Chuckie's head pops up. 'Turtle shield? You got a turtle shield?'

'Yeah.'

'That protects against almost anything,' he breathes in wonder. 'So, how did you die?'

'Nine-Headed Bird.'

'Ah.' Chuckie nods in sympathy. 'Almost impossible to kill Nine-Headed Bird. You must use turtle shield and Mutual Rings, if you have them. And call for phoenix intervention.'

'Oh. Phoenix intervention. Forgot about that.'

I'm feeling a little calmer. Probably because the Percocet's kicking in. 'Look, Chuckie. You can have my turtle shield just as soon as I'm through with this quest. I promise.'

Chuckie sighs heavily. He doesn't like it. But you know what they say: every man has his price.

CHAPTER TWENTY-ONE

Trey came home five months after I got blown up. He was still a soldier, so he found an apartment for us near his base, in one of those sixties or seventies tilt-up complexes with parking underneath, held up by skinny metal poles. Before that, I'd been living with my mom, which hadn't worked out too well. It was a long way to the VA Hospital from where she lived, and every time I rode in a car I worried about getting blown up again.

Trey's and my apartment was pretty basic, a cheap, two-bedroom place with shiny beige walls and pressboard wood paneling. Minimally furnished, half from Wal-Mart, half from thrift stores. It was clean, at least, thanks to Trey, who, whatever other shitty things I could say about him aside, was always neat and tidy and made the bed every day – well, he made it on the days I'd get out of it, at least.

The one thing I insisted on was a high-speed Internet connection. I'd gotten kind of hooked on Web surfing during my recovery. It was an activity that pretty much fit my level of concentration, which is to say transitory and fragmented. Plus there was always the possibility of some kind of connection. That one of my buddies would write me. That dog Turner, or Kim, or Mayer. Pulagang or Torres, Palaver or Madrid. And then I could write back. And we could maybe talk about how we were feeling and what we were going through, but we could still hide, from each other and the world.

We had about six months together before Trey was redeployed. That time was okay. We were both trying. I went to the base for physical therapy, three, four times a week. I wasn't ever going to be a hundred percent, but the PT helped, and it gave me something to do. Trey kept the house clean, brought me little presents now and again.

But it seemed to me that we had a lot of silence between us. Because what we had in common was the war. Was Camp Fucking Falafel. And neither one of us wanted to talk about that.

It was like before, where we'd fuck and not talk about it. Except that the fucking part, which was one thing we really had going for us before, wasn't the same. I was still pretty messed up, and Trey would treat me like a piece of spun glass, because he never knew what was going to hurt me.

I didn't like leaving the apartment. Hated having to do pretty much anything. Shopping, forget it. I'd get too nervous. Paying bills, hated that. Taking out the trash, could barely manage it. Doing dishes, making the bed, no way. Too much effort.

Though I liked going to the base, actually. I liked

entering through a guarded gate, liked being protected by razor wire and guns. Seeing guys in their battle dress, seeing Humvees, going to the PX; all that stuff felt familiar. Safe.

Just throw in some mortars and IEDs, and I would've felt right at home.

Turns out I'm going to have to pay Chuckie some real money in addition to a virtual turtle shield. 'Not for me,' he insists. 'For some other guys.'

I'm not thrilled about somebody else being involved with this. 'What other guys?'

'Some other guys. Don't worry. They do this all the time.'

'I'd have to give them my password?'

'Soon as they finish, you can change it.'

'I don't know.'

At that, Chuckie takes a big swallow of his Cleaning Flavor beer and shrugs. 'Maybe, if this is too much trouble, we should not do it.'

I'm tempted to agree with him. Give some stranger my password? Maybe I should forget the whole thing and run like hell to Outer Mongolia. I could live in a yurt. Ride camels.

Chuckie must see the doubt on my face, because something shifts in his. Maybe he's thinking about that turtle shield slipping from his grasp.

'Look,' he says, 'these are okay guys. Friends of mine. You can come meet them. Bring them some Jack Daniels or something. You'll see.'

'Okay,' I finally say. 'Okay.'

I ride with Chuckie on the back of his moped, which can't

go very fast with the two of us on it, so at least it's not too scary. We stop at a little 24-hour market run by Koreans, and I buy a bottle of whiskey. Then I hang on to Chuckie's waist, and we ride down Taiyuan's wide coal-choked streets.

Eventually, we come to what looks like an older area of town: random twisted pipes, rusting oil cans, and busted chairs piled in front of cement and white-tiled-front buildings, cracks and holes in the Day-Glo-colored plastic signs, everything greasy with black grime. There's a night market here, tumbling out of an alley, a burst of music and noise, sizzling meat and garlic.

We drive around the back of the market. Chuckie parks the bike and locks it to a rack. Trash spills out of bins. There's one pathetic sodium light over a doorway, bathing the entrance in a sickly yellow glow.

'This way,' Chuckie says, and he leads me through the door and down a flight of stairs.

In China they don't believe in lighting hallways unless they have to. Apparently we're supposed to make our way here by the light that seeps out from under the doors of the occupied offices. Or, given the hour, we aren't supposed to be here at all.

But here we are.

At the end of the hall is a double door. Chuckie raps his knuckles on it a couple times. After a minute, the door opens. A skinny guy wearing a stretched-out V-necked undershirt, cigarette dangling from the corner of his mouth, claps Chuckie on the shoulder. 'Hey,' he says. 'What's up?'

'Not much.' Chuckie gives a nod in my direction. 'Li Ke, this is a friend of mine, Yili. She has a little problem. Maybe you can help her.'

Li Ke nods noncommittally, and we follow him inside.

It's a big room, divided into cubicles, maybe a hundred or so, and at first I'm thinking particularly sleazy Internet bar, because every cubicle has a computer with a guy sitting in front of it, and there's a lot of noise from various games: music and combat sounds and animated screams and laughter. Cigarette smoke hangs in the air; there are junk-food wrappers and soft-drink bottles lying on the ground, and the place has this funky smell of smoke, sour sweat, stale grease, and mildew.

The weird thing is – and it takes me a few minutes to figure this out – nobody looks like they're having any fun. They're just sitting there in front of the terminals, hollow-eyed and bored, punching keys and toggling joysticks like they're transcribing medical records or something.

Meanwhile, Chuckie leans in close to Li Ke's ear and explains my problem.

Li Ke shrugs. 'Sure,' he says. 'We can do that.'

He pivots and heads down an aisle, taps a guy on his back, mutters some explanation, and points in my direction. The guy stands, sees me, smiles in an embarrassed way, and nods at me like a bobble-head doll.

'What is this, Chuckie?' I ask in a whisper.

'Gold farm,' Chuckie says tersely. 'They play for you. Kill monsters. Get you gold and spells and treasure. Then you can move up levels.'

Okay. I try to wrap my mind around this. 'So, they play as me? As Little Mountain Tiger?'

Chuckie nods. 'Right.'

'And they do this for a living?'

'Sure. Lots of rich players want to move up fast, go on better quests, without taking the time.' Chuckie snorts. 'It's cheating, I think. People with more money, they don't have to work. Have these guys farming for them. Get high-level spells and weapons, and they don't earn them at all.'

'So, how do you know these guys?' I have to ask.

'I do some server work for them,' Chuckie mumbles. 'But I play my own game,' he adds defiantly.

Li Ke slouches toward us. 'How soon you need this?' he asks.

'Soon,' I reply.

'So, we can put both shifts on it,' Li Ke says with a shrug. 'Maybe take three days.'

Shit, I think. Shit, shit, shit. I told the Suits I'd have something for them in four days. This isn't going to work.

I stare at the young guy Li Ke tapped to work on my job, pounding down a Stalking Tiger Energy Formula, the Chinese equivalent of a Red Bull. In the cubicle next to him, a man sleeps with his head resting on his keyboard, mouth open, snoring as easily as if he were in a luxury suite at a Hilton.

What choice do I have? I'll just have to stall the Suits, somehow.

'Okay,' I say. 'How much?'

I hang out a little while longer with Chuckie and Li Ke and one of the game farmers who's going to kill monsters for me, a guy named 'Leopard,' drinking shots of the whiskey I bought, in an unoccupied cubicle by the back door. All around us, bored, pasty guys kill low-ranking monsters, farming for virtual gold.

'Hey, Chuckie,' I say, after I get a little drunk. 'You're a good friend for hooking me up with this.'

Chuckie shakes his head. 'Not so good. I run away and hide.' He takes a swig of whiskey, then shrugs. 'I'm just . . . a dickhead.'

'No, you're not.'

'I am.'

'You're not. Look. You don't know me that well. I could be a spy, or a foreign splittist, or something.'

He looks at me. 'Are you?'

'No,' I say with a sigh. 'I'm . . . another dickhead. I mean, a female one. Whatever that is.'

'What can you do?' He sounds agitated now. 'They have all the power. All the money.'

'Yeah.' I think about the Suits. I think about Harrison Wang, that huge penthouse suite, the statues and paintings. Must be nice, having that kind of money. Enough to insulate you from some of the bullshit.

Chuckie pours more whiskey into my teacup and then his own. We sit in silence while Leopard and Li Ke play some kind of drinking game with a pair of dice.

'Hey, Chuckie,' I say. 'If I wanna e-mail somebody, and I don't want them to know where I am, what's the best way to do that?' I'm thinking: proxy servers. I've used them before when I wanted to surf someplace the Net Nanny doesn't like, but the ones I know don't work any more. The Great Firewall finds them, blocks them, then new ones pop up. Like the Chinese government is the little Dutch Kid, and the Firewall's a leaking dike.

Chuckie thinks for a minute. Then he reaches into his shoulder bag, into one of the compartments, grabs some-

229

thing small, and puts it in my open hand, gently closing my fingers around it.

'Fuck the authority,' he whispers gleefully.

After that, Chuckie offers to drive me back to my hotel. I hesitate, because by now I feel like I owe Chuckie big-time, and I don't want to put him out. Plus, the moped is pretty uncomfortable. But there aren't any cabs around, and besides, this is the first time since all this shit started happening that I haven't felt alone, and all of a sudden I realize that I don't want that to end.

Fuck the authority!

Chuckie seems to be in a similar mood, because he's singing this cheesy Communist Youth anthem I recognize at the top of his lungs as we swing too wide around a corner; the back tire skids a little, but we don't fall, and we are both laughing our asses off, and for whatever reason I start singing 'The Star-Spangled Banner,' and we both laugh at that too.

'No, no, wait, I got a better one!' I manage between giggles. 'Welcome to the Hotel California!'

'Such a nice surprise —' Chuckie sings.

'For your alibis!'

Finally we pull up in front of the Good Fortune Guest House.

I swing my bad leg over the rear tire, clutching Chuckie's shoulders for support.

As my foot touches the ground, the air around us turns blue-white.

Headlights.

I blink. Make out a car parked just up the block, nearly hidden behind its high-beam curtain.

'Ellie, get back on!' Chuckie whispers. 'Let's go!'

'No,' I say before I can stop myself. Because it's not fair for Chuckie to get dragged into my shit. Because the two of us on a moped can't outrun a car.

Because the only chance I have right now is to get back in the Game, and I can't do that without Chuckie.

The car doesn't move.

'Take care of Little Mountain Tiger for me,' I say. 'It's really important.'

Chuckie hesitates. 'This isn't right,' he whispers.

'It's okay. Come on, I'm a foreigner. Worst thing that could happen is they kick me out of the country.'

Or it's the Suits, and then I don't know what the worst thing that could happen is.

I steady myself. Chuckie's still sitting there on his moped, the engine firing like a badly tuned lawn mower.

'Just don't go home tonight, okay?' I say, my voice cracking. 'Go someplace else for a couple days.'

I think, that's what Lao Zhang said to me, and it didn't do me much good.

Walk away. Walk away now.

That's what I do.

Behind me, I hear the moped stutter, rumble, and recede.

I am bathed in light as I walk into the Good Fortune Guest House.

Inside, sitting on the gray upholstered couch, are two Chinese men in suits. One short, one tall. Neither of them wears a tie.

The shorter one rises.

'Ellie Cooper?'

I nod.

'If you could come with us.' He smiles. 'Just to have some tea.'

CHAPTER TWENTY-TWO

Trey's contract was up a couple of months after he got home from his second deployment. I thought he'd re-up. If anyone was a lifer, I figured it was Trey. Because he believed in it all.

But then one night I came out from our spare bedroom, where I'd been hanging out online, like I did all day, every day. Trey was sitting on the couch watching TV, a cable news report about this mosque in Samarra, the golden one that got blown up. It was a Shiite mosque, a particularly sacred one that held the bones of these prophets or something. After this mosque got blown up, that was when things really went to shit, as if they hadn't gone to shit enough already.

And Trey – I guess Trey knew what the consequences of this were likely to be. Because he just sat there, glassy-eyed, clutching a beer in one hand, staring at the footage of the mosque, of what it had looked like before, golden domes against a bluebird sky, of what it looked like now, collapsed piles of gray cement, the gold vanished like it was some kind of illusion, one of those fairy tales where the treasure is nothing but straw.

'I'm not going to re-up.'

When he told me, we were in bed. It was one of the few times since I'd gotten blown up that we'd had a good time in the sack. I was feeling okay, and Trey, he was so pissed off that he wasn't obsessing about how I was poor damaged little me; we were just going at it like we used to, all desperate and energetic, and for once I could forget about how fucked up things were; it was just me and him and his smell and the hairs circling his nipples that I gathered up with my tongue and the beard that burned my cheek like some kind of sandstorm.

'Oh,' I said. 'So, what do you want to do?'

Trey flopped onto his back. Clasped his hands behind his head.

'I've gotten offers from some private contractors. The pay's three times as much as what I'm making in the Army.'

I don't know why it bothered me. What difference did it make, really? But I couldn't help it: I thought of Kyle. Thought of him snickering while Greif flashed her tit at the PUCs. Remembered how he stood so close to me, his breath in my ear.

'You sure you want to do that?' I asked.

He shrugged. 'Work's not that different. Money's a lot better. It'd be good for us.'

What he didn't say was that since the Army'd settled my disability claim and I no longer got active duty pay, I wasn't bringing in much money. Kind of hard to work when you can barely bring yourself to leave the apartment.

'I could do more,' I said, though I wasn't sure if I

actually could. 'I mean, if you want to stay in. I was thinking, I could go to school, do that physician's assistant program. P.A.'s make pretty good money. It's just a few years. We could manage till then. So you wouldn't have to, if you don't want to.'

'That's not it.'

Trey stared up at the ceiling. 'There's just no point, you know? The whole thing's fubar.'

'But . . . wouldn't you still have to go back?'

'Yeah. But at least I'll be making bank.'

I think there was another reason too. Contractors got away with shit you could never pull in the Army. Maybe Trey thought, if he had to do stuff like he did in the Admin Core, why not have some protection?

Why not get paid?

Trey took the gig with GSC. I'd never heard of them before they hired Trey. They keep a low profile, not like Halliburton or Blackwater. But GSC's connected. I'm pretty sure, though of course no one will come right out and say it, that the CIA uses GSC as a cover. Or that at least GSC is a CIA asset. Nothing official. But still. Look at Trey. Trey worked in Military Intelligence as an interrogator, 'liaising' with the locals. Isn't that why GSC hired him?

After Iraq, Trey went to Kabul. After Kabul, Baku; after Baku, Bishkek. I stayed home. Too rough for fragile li'l me, according to Trey. I don't really know what he did during those times. He could have been fucking around all along, and I wouldn't have known. He came back for two weeks three times a year, and every fifth quarter he was rotated to headquarters in Houston, our new home. Where I knew nobody.

What did I do? I stayed in our nice new condominium, bought with GSC's money and what was left of my settlement, with our plasma TV and our high-speed Internet. I drank beer, I watched TV and DVDs from Netflix, and I surfed the Net. Checked my e-mail over and over, hoping for a message from one of my buddies.

It's not like I was housebound. I did go out sometimes. One of the times Trey was home, I even went to a party. Early one evening, as I sat in front of the computer, I saw Trey walk by carrying a dress shirt in a dry-cleaning bag.

I followed him into the bedroom. 'Where are you going?'

'PSOI reception tonight. At the Hilton. I told you about it.'

'You did?' He might have.

'Yeah. Drinks and rubber chicken. The usual.'

I watched him undress, step into the shower. He still looked good.

'You want me to come along?' I asked.

'Sure.' He sounded surprised, standing behind the dimpled, steamed-up glass. 'A lot of the other wives'll be there. Some nice girls.'

Right, I thought, picturing a lot of big hair, gold jewelry, and gleaming teeth. I knew I wouldn't fit in.

But Trey was my husband, and as much as I felt like I was a kid playing house, dressing up in somebody else's castoff grownup clothes, I thought maybe if I acted the part a little better, I'd learn how to do it for real.

The party was at a banquet room – white tablecloths, gold-flocked wallpaper, champagne fountains, banners welcoming the Peace and Stability Operations Industry Association to Houston.

For the first part of the evening, we were supposed to mingle. Mingling was not one of my strong points. I hung back on Trey's arm while he introduced me to a bunch of guys with buzz cuts and women with names like Tiffany and Madison.

After a while, Trey ran into a buddy of his —'Hey, Ellie, you remember Franklin, from the base?' – and ten minutes into their rehash of old missions, I slipped away to find another margarita.

I liked it better in the back, by the bar. I could look out over the gold-flocked room crowded with couples beneath brass chandeliers, let the music and conversation recede to a dull buzz, and drink.

I drank my margarita, and then I ordered another one. I leaned against the wall. I couldn't see Trey from where I was. Just a blur of sports coats and polo shirts and big hair.

Then, someone in focus. Sharp. Tight. A small, taut woman with short brown hair and a tailored black suit approached the bar. I caught a glimpse of her face before she turned to the bartender: pale, almost luminous in the yellow light of the chandeliers.

That's different, I thought, before I figured out why I'd even thought it.

She'd always been so tan before.

My heart started pounding. A wash of cold sweat covered me like a shroud.

Okay, I told myself. Okay. Turn and walk away. She hasn't seen you. You can still get away.

But I didn't. I froze, like I was paralyzed.

Like I wanted her to see me.

She got her drink and turned. Stopped.

'Hey, Greif,' I said.

She blinked.

She still wore glasses, a fancy, rimless pair, but she had on makeup now, which was also different for her. Subdued shades. Classy.

'Ellie McEnroe?' she asked slowly.

'Yeah.' I straightened up. 'How've you been?'

'Good,' she said, with a slight stammer. 'I've been well.'

'I can tell.'

That suit she wore, so perfectly tailored, good fabric, and those buttery leather boots, an elegant gold necklace and sleek watch – yeah, I could tell.

'What are you doing here?' she blurted out. Like I was the last person she expected to see.

Like I didn't belong.

'My husband, Trey. He works for GSC. You remember Trey, right? Trey Cooper.'

If anything, she got a little paler. 'Of course. I remember hearing the two of you got married. That's . . . great.'

I couldn't tell you how I felt, seeing her then. Mostly what I felt was the tequila. The feelings underneath that churned around in water so murky, I couldn't quite make them out.

'So,' I said, 'I guess you're not in the Army any more.'

'No. No, I got out a couple years ago.'

'You with GCS? Strategic Solutions? One of these guys?'

'I'm a liaison.'

'Oh, yeah? A liaison for what?'

'Congress,' she mumbled.

She's scared of me, I realized.

I liked that.

Greif checked her watch. 'I'm afraid I've got to run. But it's great seeing you again. Maybe we can get together while I'm in town –'

'Hey, Greif,' I said. 'You know, after I got hurt, all the girls wrote me. Pulagang, Palaver, Torres, Madrid. Everyone but you.'

She flushed, a red that crept up her neck and spread across her pale cheeks. 'I'm sorry about that,' she said quietly. 'I really am. I didn't know how to get ahold of you, and . . . well, I should have made more of an effort.'

I shrugged. 'No hard feelings.' I smiled at her. 'You know, the rest of us, we're still in touch. We e-mail. Talk on the phone sometimes. It's nice, having those guys to talk to. You know? People who understand what it was like.'

She nodded, her eyes fixed on mine.

'I really have to go,' she said. 'I've got a panel in a few minutes, and they're expecting me.'

'A panel? Where's it at? I'd be real interested to hear what you have to say.'

'It's a closed session,' she said, with a trace of her old condescension. 'I'm afraid you'd have to have an invitation.'

'Oh. Too bad.'

'But let's keep in touch. I know you've had a rough time. Maybe I can help.'

Maybe she was sincere, in her way. Maybe she felt sorry for me, the drunk, crippled loser, the weakling who couldn't handle what needed to be done in a war – not like her; oh no, she'd handled her shit, and look at her now.

The corners of her mouth turned up, an attempt at a friendly goodbye.

'Hey,' I said. 'Are you gonna show them your tits? 'Cause that used to work pretty well for you.'

She flinched. Then I saw it: the empty look, followed by rage, quickly masked and swallowed.

She took a step toward me. Then another, so the tips of her buttery boots nearly touched my shoes.

'I hope you understand that that is still a classified operation.'

'Seriously? I thought they would've given you a medal on the White House lawn by now.'

Her glasses magnified her eyes, but there was nothing there. I heard her take a breath. Exhale.

'I'd advise you to think very carefully about what you say. There might be consequences you won't like. Do you understand me?'

'Sure.' I smiled at her. 'It's been great catching up.'

She nodded fractionally and turned to go.

'Knock 'em dead at the panel!' I called after her.

That was fun, I thought. Fuck being quiet, being good.

I'm gonna start having fun again, I told myself. Start telling the truth.

I was well into another margarita before Trey came and got me.

'Let's go, Ellie.'

'Why? I'm having a good time.'

'Let's just go.'

Trey didn't talk much on the ride home. Neither did I.

Finally, as we pulled into the garage, he said: 'You shouldn't have done that.'

'I didn't do anything,' I mumbled.

I pushed past Trey into the kitchen and got a beer out of the fridge. Opened it. Trey's hand closed around the bottle and yanked it away.

'Fuck! Give that back!'

'No.'

He grabbed my wrist, pulled me into the living room, and practically pushed me onto the couch.

It was the closest he'd ever come in our time together to hurting me.

'You listen to me, Ellie.'

Drunk as I was, something in his voice told me I'd better.

'You should not have done that.'

'What, give Greif some shit? Like she doesn't deserve it.'

'Greif is not somebody you want to mess with.'

I snorted. 'You're afraid of Greif? What, she's your boss now?'

Trey paced a couple of steps, like he couldn't contain himself. 'You can't maintain security, the people I'm working for, how do you think they're gonna react to that?'

'So, this is about your job?'

He stopped, the muscles bunching in his shoulders. 'She's connected, Ellie. Can't you fucking get that?'

I googled Greif. Just to see who was paying for those nice outfits. There wasn't much on her, but it was enough. A transfer to the Department of Defense. A fellowship at a think tank. Most recently, an adviser to a senator on the Intelligence Committee. There was a press photo

241

of her standing behind the senator, dressed in her neat, tailored suit, her eyes watching him, her lips slightly parted.

I stared at the screen. Thinking about how much I wanted to bring her down.

Maybe I would have tried. Gone to the press. Done something.

Instead, when Trey got transferred to Beijing, I went with him.

Trey's idea.

What happened was, about a week after the party, Trey came home from work and said 'Hey, why don't we go to Casa Lupe's?'

Even though I didn't much feel like going out, I did like Casa Lupe's, especially their chile rellenos.

I liked their margaritas too, but I figured I'd better stick to beer.

We sat in the back, underneath the cheesy mural of Aztec warriors and corn maidens with humongous tits, and shortly after our beers arrived, Trey told me his news.

'They're transferring me to Beijing this time. A promotion.'

'Wow. That's great.'

In fact, I didn't really give a shit. What difference did it make where he went, what they paid him? It wasn't like anything changed for me.

'The thing is, this assignment's a little different. It's long-term. And Beijing's not like the other places I've been, Ellie. It's pretty chaotic, but it's a real city. There's all kinds of shopping malls and nice restaurants, stuff like that.'

Trey shifted around in his chair, one of those barrel-shaped ones with rawhide straps. 'I thought maybe you might want to come along.'

I didn't get it right away. 'Go to China?'

'Yeah.' He looked away, like he needed some extra time to choose his words. 'I know it's been tough, being here on your own all the time. I just thought . . .'

He looked at me, almost pleading. 'We could try.'

Something inside of me softened, like the lump of calcified rage sitting in my chest had slowly started to dissolve.

We could try.

'That sounds good,' I said.

It really did.

I wonder now why he wanted me to come with him. Did he worry about what I'd do if he left me behind? Did he just feel sorry for me? Or had he really meant what he said, that he wanted us to work on our marriage? To build a life together.

Okay. I decided I wouldn't mess with Greif. I'd leave all that in the past, where it belonged. I'd go to Beijing with my husband.

What's that line about the past not really being past?

It's got to be Greif, I think now. She's got the pull, the connections. If she wanted to keep an eye on me, how hard would that be? To have them monitor my e-mail. Tap my phone. See where I went. To make sure I wouldn't cause any problems.

Why not? It's easy to do that stuff. What's stopping them?

If I saw her again, I'd tell her, look, I don't really know anything. The interrogations I saw, I didn't understand what they were about. What was asked or what was said.

I don't know who the detainees were, whether any of them were important.

I know what went on was wrong, that she – that all of us – could still get in trouble over it.

I'd tell her I'll stay quiet. I'll keep my mouth shut. I promise.

CHAPTER TWENTY-THREE

They're from the PSB. They say they are, anyway, and one of them shows me a badge in a leather case. I go with them. What else can I do? I cringe as we pass the desk clerk, because even though I'm in all kinds of shit, I keep thinking how embarrassing this is, how Auntie is going to lose face for bringing a troublemaking foreigner to her favored hotel.

The three of us get into the car parked in front of the hotel. I can see it, now that I'm not looking into the headlights: some plain-wrap black car that smells like stale cigarettes. A driver waits.

One of the Chinese Suits sits in the back with me. He's slight and moon-faced and wears a perpetual smile.

'How do you like Taiyuan?' he asks me as the car pulls away from the curb.

'I, uh . . . it's . . . interesting,' I manage.

He nods. 'We have some very interesting scenic places. The Jinci Temple. It is special architecture, unique to Taiyuan. Have you visited?'

'Not yet.'

'In general, foreign visitors don't spend much time here. With emphasis on heavy industry, perhaps cultural development has suffered neglect,' he admits. 'But our vinegar and noodles are the best in China.'

That's when I remember: Chuckie's device.

My heart beats like I'm running a race now; I can see the pulse in my chest, and I think: this guy can probably see it too.

Where did I put the jump drive? In my backpack?

No. In my jeans pocket. I can feel it there, against my thigh.

'Are you nervous?'

'Shouldn't I be?'

His smile broadens. 'If you haven't done anything wrong, then there is nothing to worry about.'

We drive a while, maybe a half hour, finally pulling up to a metal gate flanked by cement walls, stained by rust where the bars pierce the concrete. There are no government seals on the pillars here, no guards in uniform, just some guys wearing white polo shirts and black jackets.

We pull into the courtyard and get out of the car. A few bare floodlights throw crazy shadows on the stained concrete. It's a U-shaped complex, maybe three stories high. The white tile walls are streaked with black grime.

There are other people here too, a couple dozen of them huddled by one of the L-shaped wings of the complex. Old people. Middle-aged. Women, one with a kid hugging her thigh. A young guy missing a leg, leaning on a crutch.

They see me and start calling out, and I don't understand what they're saying, except, 'Miss! Miss! Please, can you help?' Some of them clutch papers that they thrust in my direction.

'They think you are reporter,' Smiley says.

One of the guys in black jackets goes over, shouts something; a middle-aged man goes toe to toe with him and shouts back, something about his daughter and justice. Black Jacket slaps his face, shoves him, once, twice, till he stumbles and falls.

They take me to a little beige room with a couple of chairs and a small table.

We sit.

'Do you know why you are here?' Smiley asks me.

His companion doesn't smile. He sits, slightly behind Smiley, arms folded across his chest, eyes dull, face lifeless.

'No,' I say.

'You don't have an idea?'

Tell them, a voice in my head says. Go ahead. Just say something. About Lao Zhang. About the Uighur. The Game.

'I really don't,' I say.

Smiley leans back in his chair. Exhales heavily.

'Why do you come to Taiyuan?' the other guy asks abruptly.

Like Smiley said, foreigners don't generally spend a lot of time in Taiyuan. They mostly come here because it's a major rail hub, the best place to make connections to a number of more scenic locales.

'I'm going to Pingyao,' I blurt. 'I've – I've never been there before. I've heard it's really interesting.'

'Pingyao is very interesting,' Smiley agrees. 'The entire city is a World Cultural Heritage site.'

'Why did you come to China?' Scary asks.

'Because my husband did.'

'You're traveling without him,' Smiley points out.

'He left me. For a Chinese woman.'

The two exchange a look.

You see a lot of Western men with Chinese women. Sometimes Chinese men get pretty pissed off about that.

'So you are only taking a vacation?' Smiley asks.

'Yes. I was upset. About my husband. I just wanted to get away for a while.'

'So you visit to Pingyao.'

I nod.

Scary, meanwhile, puts on a pair of latex gloves and starts going through my backpack.

'And will you see anyone there?' Smiley continues.

'No. I don't know anyone in Pingyao.'

'And here. Do you know anyone here?'

A wave of nausea hits me so hard I think I'm going to puke right in front of them. I don't. I swallow.

'No . . . not really – I partied with some guys I met last night. But it's not like I know them.'

'How did you meet them?'

'I was at a karaoke bar. I met one of them there.'

'What was his name?'

'Chao . . . something.'

'And the others? Where did you meet?'

'We went someplace. Some office. I don't know where it was.'

'What were their names?'

'I don't know. This guy Chao. Leopard somebody. A guy named Li.'

Smiley shakes his head. 'You spend the evening with these men, but you don't know very much about them.'

'It wasn't anything. We just hung out. Talked. Had a few drinks.'

Scary pulls my Beanie squid out of the backpack. Looks at it. Looks at me.

'It's my good-luck squid,' I explain.

'Ah.'

Scary puts the squid back in my bag. He turns to me. 'In China, leniency for those who confess. Severity for those who refuse.'

He says this like he's talking about, I don't know, vinegar and noodles. Best in China.

'You know, it is good to confess,' Smiley says in soothing tones. 'Bad things can disturb the mind. Don't you think so?'

I can feel the tears gathering behind my eyes. Don't, I tell myself.

'When you tell the truth, you take the power away from the bad things,' he continues. 'So really, if there is something you should confess, it will be better for you.'

All of it, all of it rushes up, and I can't hold it in any more. I sob, once, twice, and the tears pour out like water.

'It's just . . . It's just . . . '

'What? What, Mrs Cooper?'

'Trey,' I sob. 'And that . . . that *Lily*!'

I don't know how I latched onto it. Like I'm King Kong, with all those airplanes buzzing me, and this is the one I pulled out of the sky.

Use it, I tell myself.

Smiley looks confused. 'Tray?'

'My husband. Trey. And the Chinese girl he's gone off with.' I wipe the tears from my eyes with the back of my hand. 'How come so many American guys want Chinese women? And the Chinese women, they just go for it, you know? I mean, why? They've got their own men. Why'd she have to take mine?'

I snuffle loudly. 'It's just not right.'

I steal a glance at Scary. He's looking down at my backpack, his jaw tight. Smiley's smile looks a little frozen.

For a long moment, no one says anything. I sit there with my head bowed, looking, I hope, suitably anguished.

Finally, Smiley heaves a great sigh. 'Is there something else you wish to tell us?'

I half-shrug and shake my head.

'Are you certain?'

'Be careful how you answer,' Scary says. 'If you lie, we will know it.'

'No,' I say, and my voice cracks a little. 'There's nothing.'

Scary zips up my backpack. Smiley rises, walks to the door, then pauses, hand hovering over the doorknob.

He suddenly turns and approaches my chair. Stands in front of me, hands clasped behind his back.

'So, how will you go to Pingyao? By train or bus?'

'Uh . . . train?'

He checks his watch. 'The bus is more convenient this time of day.'

'Oh.'

Scary tosses me my backpack.

Back in the courtyard, the petitioners surround me again, waving their letters, their evidence, shouting their recitations of wrongs. My house. My husband. My son. The guys in black jackets herd them back. We get into the black car.

The sun struggles to rise, melting the chemical soup in the air to a dull orange.

On the way to the bus station, Smiley details Taiyuan's local delicacies, which include 'the steamed dumpling and the Sausages and Mutton Soup.'

As they let me off in front of the station, Smiley has one more thing to recommend.

'I hope you will remember to always cooperate with the authorities, Ms Cooper, and avoid unpleasant characters and rascals. You will have a much better stay in China if you do.'

Even on the local bus, it takes less than two hours to get to Pingyao from Taiyuan, which is still way too much time for me. It's already dawn, but sleep feels like something I've forgotten how to do. My mouth's dry, and a headache pounds behind my eyes; I taste bile in my throat, and there's not enough water in the bottle I bought at the station to wash it down.

So they let me go. For now. I'm not kidding myself that I've gotten away. They were playing with me, playing their own Game, and I'm a newbie. I don't have a clue how to get to the next level.

That place they took me to – it didn't look exactly official. I've read about places like that before, 'black jails.' That's where they take you when somebody in power wants to do something that isn't legal by China's own laws.

Off the books.

Like with the OGAs, now that I think about it.

When I get to the Pingyao bus station – which is basically the parking lot of the Pingyao train station – the place looks like any other Chinese town to me. White-tile disease, taxis, construction cranes, noise, and dust.

I don't have to go far before I see the difference: a looming wall, complete with towers and battlements, that surrounds an antique city.

I think about getting a room in the new part of town because it would be cheaper, in the Oil & Gas Industry Guest House maybe, but I'm supposed to be a heartbroken tourist, so I figure I'd better play the part and go for quaint and scenic.

I find a room in a traditional hotel in the old city. The Yi De Inn is a remodeled Qing Dynasty courtyard house; the rooms have round, Shanxi-style doors, and the bed in my room is on top of a kang.

The only clothing I've got with me aside from what I'm wearing is a change of underwear, and my T-shirt's greasy with sweat, soaked through in places, from an excess of whiskey and fear.

Now that the adrenaline's gone, everything aches. I feel like I'm a hundred years old. Like someone's been twisting my muscles like they were wringing out a wet rag.

I've got three Percocets left. I take one, stretch out on the hard mattress, and sleep for a while.

By the time I wake up, it's around noon. I have a pot of tea in the Qing Dynasty dining room and score a few snacks for the road at the sundries counter.

Armed with a foil pouch of Pingyao's special 'Five Aroma Beef,' I set off.

I wander around Pingyao's narrow streets and alleys, past temples and courtyard mansions and crenellated towers, all hung with red lanterns. Bicycles pull carts laden with water bottles and scrap and the last honeycombs of coal needed before the summer heat. It looks like the China I pictured in my head before I came here but which hardly exists in real China. Like a giant outdoor movie set, or a theme park.

I buy a couple of souvenir T-shirts and a pair of fake Nike sweat pants. Visit a temple and the Risheng Exchange House. Play tourist for Smiley and Scary's benefit, in case they're watching. I assume they are.

I'm as ready as I'm ever going to be to call the Suits.

I know I need to call them. There's no way I'll know anything by the old deadline, which is less than three days from now. I'll barely have Little Mountain Tiger resurrected by then, and I don't know what I'll be able to find out when I do.

I find a phone booth on a corner across from the north gate of the city wall. I try Macias first – I think he's the younger, thinner one – and get his voicemail. I'm about to leave a message, but then I change my mind and hang up. What am I going to say?

So I try Carter. On about the fifth ring, someone picks up.

'Hello?'

Definitely the older, meaner one.

'This is Ellie Cooper.'

'Yes?'

'I, uh . . . I'm working on that thing you asked me to. But it's going to take a little longer than I thought.'

There's a brief pause. 'Look,' he says. 'Don't think you can stall us. Because that's not going to work.'

'I'm not,' I say, and I know I sound desperate. 'I'm really not. It's just – it's just a little complicated.'

'Complicated is one thing. But if you're trying to bullshit me, you're not going to like the way it plays out.'

In spite of how scared I am, this really pisses me off.

'I'm not bullshitting you. PSB picked me up. They *said* they were PSB, anyway.'

'Oh, yeah?' Now he sounds interested. 'So? What did they want?'

'I don't know. They asked me a bunch of questions, and then they let me go.'

'What did you tell them?'

'Nothing. I mean, they didn't ask me anything about . . .' I trail off. 'You know. My friend.'

'I get it,' he says.

'I don't.' And I really don't. Why did they pick me up? Why did they let me go?

'Could be they just wanna rattle your cage. See what you'll admit to right off the bat. Maybe they don't know anything and they're working for someone who does. Could be State Security.' I hear a long, slightly phlegmy exhalation on the other end of the line. 'Where are you?'

I can't help it. 'You don't know?'

He chuckles. 'Look, whoever's on your ass, you better decide what you wanna do. They want something bad enough, they don't care if you're a foreigner. The gloves come off.'

The gloves come off. Step it up. Get more intel.

'I told you, I'm trying. It's complicated. I need more time.'

'How much longer?'

'I, uh . . .' I squeeze my eyes shut. You can't fucking panic, I tell myself. Figure it out. 'A week,' I say. 'If things go well. It might take a little longer, if things don't.'

'You're stalling.'

'I swear. If I can't do it by then, then I'm not going to be able to do it at all.'

'You'd better hope that's not how it goes,' he says flatly.

'What the fuck do you think?' I snap, before I can stop myself. 'I just want this done. I just want you out of my life.'

He chuckles again. 'Call me on Friday. Give me your report, and we'll take it from there.'

I start to object, but he cuts me off.

'That's three more days than you asked for originally. We'll look at extending the deadline after that. But if I think you're shitting me? We're pulling the plug.'

After that, I decide to take a walk around the city wall. I turn down the pedicab driver, which I might regret, because it apparently takes at least an hour and a half to make it all the way around. But I need some time. Time to calm myself down. Time to think.

So I take my time. Stop and stare out over the medieval roofs, into crumbling courtyards. Here are workers, repairing the intricate tilework atop the wall of what was a Qing Dynasty banker's home. Here are wooden and wire cages, filled with minks. There's an old woman, practicing tai chi.

Those PSB guys, or whoever they are, they could be working for anybody. The central government, some local authorities, a PLA general, a random billionaire. You don't know in China. The central government isn't a monolith; what goes on in the provinces isn't necessarily under Beijing's control, and the different factions in Beijing have their own agendas as well.

Okay, I think. I don't know how they found me in Taiyuan – maybe through my passport when I checked in at the Good Fortune Guesthouse. Well, there's nothing I can do about that. I have to show my passport when I check into a hotel.

No matter how they found me in Taiyuan, they know I'm in Pingyao now. Smiley practically carried me onto the Pingyao bus.

As for the Suits, who knows how they keep finding me? I called Carter on a public phone, but I'm wondering: do they have some way to track that? Something as simple as caller ID, maybe?

If it's electronic, like if I use a credit card or an ATM, I can avoid all that stuff the next place I go.

Except for e-mail. But I have Chuckie's device for that.

I get more cash out of my disability account from an ATM next to the Oil and Gas Industry Guesthouse, as much as the machine will let me withdraw. Then I buy an overnight ticket to Xi'an for tomorrow.

I'm supposed to be a tourist, and Xi'an is a big tourist destination. Everybody goes there to see the *Bingmayuan*, the tomb of the First Emperor Qin with his terra-cotta army. I've seen it – ranks of soldiers, thousands of them, each one unique, some with chariots and horses. It made me think of that poem we had to learn in high school, the one about a toppled statue in the desert, covered by drifting sand, of some king named Ozymandias, and on the statue it says 'Look on my works, ye Mighty, and despair!'

The point being, I guess, some kind of cheap irony about how you're still going to die and all your works crumble to dust, no matter how big your clay army is.

CHAPTER TWENTY-FOUR

I was doing better in Beijing. That was the funny thing. You'd think with all the noise, the confusion, the overwhelming masses of people and lights and cars and chaos, that I would've stayed in our apartment above the mall, maybe made it downstairs to the Starbucks now and again at best. But China was so different that sometimes I forgot who I was, what I'd done, what had happened. Like the noise of Beijing crowded out the noise in my head, at least for a while.

'I was thinking maybe I should learn some Chinese.'

I mentioned this to Trey one night after he got home from work. We were at the Cantonese restaurant down in the mall, a Hong Kong chain, a little less greasy than Northern-style food, popular with the Taiwanese crowd of students and businessmen.

'That's a great idea,' Trey said. He smiled at me and stretched his hand across the glowing Lucite table and rested it on my forearm. 'I'm glad you like it here.'

'I guess I do,' I said. I was surprised to hear myself say it. But it was true.

I took the subway and then the train to the Haidian District four times a week for Chinese classes at Beijing Language and Culture University. I wasn't the most brilliant student, but I did okay. And I met people. Chuckie, for example, who was hanging out in the Sauce, looking for students to tutor him in English.

I had my backpack with my textbooks; I was making friends; I was doing a pretty good impression of a normal person. I still worried about getting blown up, but I started turning it into sort of a game. Like, oh, there's a truck hauling giant cement cylinders and PVC conduit. You could pack enough explosives in there to blow up the Great Hall of the People. And how about that guy with the bicycle cart full of winter cabbage? Perfect cover for IEDs.

Then I'd laugh at myself and stop to buy a steamed bun from a street vendor.

I'd see Trey at night, after he'd get off work. We didn't talk that much, but then we never had. Maybe the sex part wasn't all that great or all that frequent, but he was busy. So was I, finally, for once.

I thought things were going okay.

Then came the day I left school early because I wasn't feeling good. One of those gastrointestinal bugs I'd catch every couple of weeks when I first moved to China. Bad cooking oil, bacterial contamination, or god knows what else that had gotten into the food chain.

I felt so nauseous that I decided to take a cab home; I figured the traffic at that time of day shouldn't be too bad, and maybe a cab would be faster than the train and the subway.

The traffic still sucked. Every time we'd get stuck behind

some old beater, I'd get a whiff of raw exhaust that would send my stomach heaving.

I must have looked pretty green when the cab dropped me off in front of our building, because the cabbie patted my hand, told me to drink some warm water and go take a rest.

I thanked him and tottered inside.

Using this entrance, I could bypass the mall and go directly to the elevators that serviced the apartments upstairs. I pulled out my keycard, thinking: Pepto-Bismol, do we have any? Maybe I should go to the drugstore in the mall first and pick some up. But I didn't, because by then I was really feeling like I was going to throw up.

I went into our apartment, tossed my keys and my keycard in the brass bowl on the table in the entry, and tried to decide if I wanted to drink some Coke or just head straight to the bathroom.

That's when I heard something.

It was the middle of the day, right after lunch. It's not the house cleaner, I thought. It was something moving around, coming from the master bedroom.

I approached, slowly.

I heard moans. A squeaking mattress.

The bedroom door was open. I stood in the doorway.

I don't know why I even looked. I already knew what I was going to see: my husband's naked ass pumping on top of some strange woman.

I stumbled backward, rushed blindly into the bathroom, and threw up all over the toilet seat.

'Ellie? *Ellie?*'

I glimpsed Trey over my shoulder, now wearing a pair of boxers, and I was aware that there was this chaos going on – a woman gasping and making little sobbing sounds, Trey retreating from the bathroom and saying something to her in a low voice – but I was really too busy throwing up to process it all. Doors opened and closed softly; at some point she left, and meanwhile Trey held my hair out of my face so I could throw up some more.

After I threw up everything humanly possible, Trey made me take a Dramamine and some Pepto-Bismol and guided me toward the bedroom. Our bedroom.

I finally found my voice.

'I am not getting in that fucking bed,' I managed. 'I'd rather lie on the fucking floor than in that fucking bed.'

'I'm sorry,' Trey muttered.

'Sorry? You're *sorry*? You fucking asshole.'

I wanted nothing more than to walk out the door right then. Be some place, any place, other than there.

But, ha-ha, I was too sick to move. I parked myself on the futon in our guest bedroom, with Trey's help. I threw up a couple more times. And then I slept the sleep of the utterly depleted.

Maybe I could have let it go. We were supposed to be building a life together. I know I would have tried.

Joke's on me, as usual. Because when Trey and I did sit down to talk, for once, right before I packed up my duffel bag and split for Chuckie's place, here's what he said:

'I'm in love with Lily.'

And that wasn't all.

He sat there on our couch, staring at his hands. He wouldn't look at me when he talked about Lily. At first I couldn't say anything. Then I yelled. A lot. Called him every name I could think of.

After I'd screamed myself quiet, he did meet my eyes. 'You don't need me any more, Ellie,' he said.

We arrive in Xi'an around six thirty A.M. I've had another shitty night's sleep on a hard sleeper, kept up by a group of guys drinking *baijiu* and the thoughts in my head that won't stop, like the little hamster on a wheel going nowhere.

I find a reasonably priced hotel down by the Big Wild Goose Temple. Have my second-to-last Percocet and a beer in my room and collapse on the bed, covering myself with stiff, clean sheets that still smell faintly of detergent.

I wake up around noon again. Take a shower. Put on one of my new Pingyao T-shirts.

This hotel is a cut above the other places I've stayed on this trip. My room has a fully stocked mini-bar and a fridge and a window that actually looks out onto the street as opposed to an airshaft or brick wall. Downstairs is a fancy lobby with marble floors and a coffee shop with decent coffee. There's a gift shop selling reproductions of terra-cotta warriors, embroidered padded silk jackets, T-shirts, and jade bracelets. Tour groups gather by the front desk – Western retirees, most of them.

I sit by the rail that separates the coffee shop from the lobby and watch the tourists check their camera bags and purses under the soft spotlights, making sure they have sufficient batteries, money, and anti-bacterial wipes for the day's expedition.

I finish my coffee. Time to go.

Outside, the air is dry, the sun diffused by dust.

I find an Internet bar close to the Big Wild Goose Pagoda, bordering a plaza/park with big water fountains and green lawns and statues where the locals like to hang out amidst signs that say things like 'Enjoy the city sculptures with your intelligent eyes, but do not damage them with your hands' and 'The grass longs to grow up strong and healthy.'

The device Chuckie gave me looks like a flash drive. It masks the IP address I'm coming from and automatically finds proxy servers to operate through. So if the Suits or the PSB have some kind of tap on my e-mail account – and I assume they do – at least they won't be able to figure out where I'm logging on from.

I have way too many e-mails. A lot of them are junk: spam that makes it past the filter, horoscopes, petitions, shopping deals, cool downloads. Messages from various mailing lists: my high school, some veteran's groups.

Here's an e-mail from Lucy Wu, an invitation to her latest opening, with a note saying she hopes we can have that lunch soon.

And here's my e-mail from Trey.

'Ellie, hope you're doing okay. Heard you got in touch with our friends from the office. That was the right thing to do. You help them out and they'll help you out for sure. Anyway hope you're doing okay and that you're watching out for yourself. Let those guys do the heavy lifting, okay?

'Love you, Ellie. I know you don't believe that and I guess I haven't shown it very well, but I do. Take care.'

He's right. I don't believe him.

Then there is the latest in Jesus e-mails from Mom:

The Concert

The concert was about to begin when the mother returned to her seat and discovered that her child was missing. Suddenly, the curtains parted and spotlights focused on the beautiful Steinway on stage. In horror, the mother saw her little boy sitting at the keyboard, innocently picking out 'Twinkle, Twinkle, Little Star.'

At that moment, the great piano master made his entrance, quickly moved to the piano, and whispered in the boy's ear, 'Don't quit. Keep playing.'

Then, leaning over, the famous pianist reached down with his left hand and began filling in a bass part. Soon his right arm reached around to the other side of the child and he added a running obbligato.

Together, the old master and the young novice transformed what could have been a frightening situation into a wonderfully creative experience.

The audience was so mesmerized that afterwards they couldn't recall what else the great pianist played. Only the classic, 'Twinkle, Twinkle, Little Star.'

Perhaps that's the way it is with God. What we can accomplish on our own is hardly noteworthy. We try our best, but the results aren't always graceful flowing music. However, with the hand of the Master, our life's work can truly be beautiful.

The next time you set out to accomplish great feats, listen carefully. You may hear the voice of the Master, whispering in your ear, 'Don't quit.' 'Keep playing.'

May you feel His arms around you and know that His hands are there, helping you turn your feeble attempts into true masterpieces.

And remember,

'Don't quit.'

'Keep playing.'

It goes on to say how, since the lives of the people we touch are more important than the things we acquire, I should reach out and touch a few people by passing this message along.

But above all this is an actual message from my mom.

'Hi Honey,' it begins. 'Hope things are going okay with you. It's been really hot here this week, and the air conditioner isn't working that great. So I've been spending a lot of time at Sunrise. Actually, there's an opening in the bookstore for an assistant manager, and I'm thinking about applying. You know things at the office aren't that great lately. They say there's going to be another round of lay-offs, and I wouldn't be surprised if I'm on that list to go. So even though the Sunrise job won't pay as well, I am thinking that it might be a good move for me. At least I would be in a Christian atmosphere 24/7!'

As I read this, there's that pull on my gut, like I'm feeling the black waters below. No job's stable any more; you're lucky to have a fucking job; I get that. I grew up with that. But my mom, my mom's fifty; she's worked like a dog for more than twenty-five years, busting her ass for shit money, for lousy vacations, for health benefits that don't cover anything; she's got a crappy townhouse that's falling apart in a complex with an underfunded condo association that doesn't fix stuff and a used car she can't afford to drive.

'I sure do miss you, Honey. I take comfort in knowing that you're living with a Godly man. Even if we're half a world away, I know that Jesus holds you in his arms, and I hold you in my heart.

'Love, Mom.'

Okay, I never exactly told my mom about the problems Trey and me were having – I would have ended up with twice as many Jesus e-mails and even more pleas to get my sorry butt home.

And I don't want to go home. Go home to what?

For a moment I sit there, shaking. Then I go back to my inbox.

Finally, here's the e-mail I've been waiting for:

'Best stock options! High growth, hot stock! Sinogram Medical Devices. Shanghai Exchange Best Pick!'

It's from Chuckie, the signal we agreed upon. And it means that Little Mountain Tiger is back in the Game.

CHAPTER TWENTY-FIVE

Armed with my turtle shield, a Korean version of Red Bull, and a bottle of Wahaha, sitting in an Internet bar by the Big Wild Goose Pagoda, I'm ready to kick some ass.

I log on.

I'm not dead, and I'm not in Hell, and I don't have to deal with Horse-face and Ox-head.

Instead, I'm back on the path leading to the Yellow Mountain Monastery, right where I was before I got killed.

I back out, go to my profile and change my password, then head to the Midnight Bazaar for some Mutual Rings, in case I need to kill another Nine-Headed Bird.

The Midnight Bazaar is really jumping, in spite of the fact that it's just after two in the afternoon here in Xi'an. All kinds of avatars cluster around the various booths, shopping for weapons and spells, checking out the fare at the Food Court. I buy some Mutual Rings, and then I think I should get Little Mountain Tiger some *jiaozi*. She's got to be hungry after being killed and getting resurrected.

So I find a *jiaozi* stand, and as I'm coming out of the Food Court, an avatar approaches me. Female, copper armor that hugs her body like scales. Gold letters sparkle above her head.

Golden Snake.

'Hail, Little Mountain Tiger.'

'Hail.'

'You're not anonymous,' she points out.

'Had to buy some stuff.'

'Can we talk?'

'Okay.' I guess.

I start to type the anon/group command.

'No need,' Golden Snake says quickly. 'Let's talk like this.'

The anon/group command means only members of my Guild, the Great Society, can see me.

So, does Golden Snake want someone else to see me?

'How come I got killed?' I type.

'Ask the Monk.'

'You don't know?'

'I wasn't involved.'

Which doesn't mean she doesn't know.

'What about . . .'

I stop there. I'm afraid to type his name. Even his avatar's name. Because I don't know who's watching.

'What about our friend?' I type. I don't know if she'll get that or not.

'Ask the Monk,' she repeats.

I have a hard time reading what she's saying, because all around us, more and more avatars crowd into the Bazaar: warriors, gods, wizards, and half-beasts. Text balloons pop up, overlap, disappear, filling the upper half of my screen like some kind of sudden storm. 'Protest!' I read. 'To the Governor's mansion!' 'Support Glorious Rooster!' 'Storm the gates!'

'What's this?' I ask.

'Demonstration. Protesting detention of high-ranking player.'

Real or virtual, I wonder, but there are too many avatars, and I can't think straight.

'What did he do?'

'Called the Governor a tyrant and demanded his overthrow. So much going on, easy for us to talk.'

I don't know what to say about that. 'What do you want?' I ask instead.

'Just to see what you think of the Game.'

'Free Glorious Rooster!'

'Demand new Constitution!'

I don't know what I think.

'I want to help my friend,' I type.

Golden Snake's scales glisten. A forked tongue flicks out between her lips.

'There are other Guilds.'

'Can they help?'

'Perhaps.'

Is this a real offer? Some kind of test?

'Hang the Governor!'

'Burn the Capitol!'

'I'll think about it,' I write. 'I'm going to do what you said first. Go ask the Monk.'

Golden Snake doesn't move. I watch her scales shimmer.

'Very well. I will be in touch,' she finally says.

And Golden Snake is gone. Logged out.

I can barely move, there are so many avatars gathered

269

in the market, on their way to the Governor's mansion. I don't know if I just did the right thing or if I totally fucked up.

Now, suddenly, there are soldiers swarming the Bazaar, and a large text box pops up with red letters saying: *'This is an illegal activity. You are in violation of the Terms of Service.'*

I figure that's my cue to leave.

I make myself anonymous and go back to the Yellow Mountain Monastery.

Like the last time, fog swirls around my ankles. Somewhere an owl hoots.

'Hail, the Great Community,' I type.

Nothing. I continue up the path.

'It's Little Mountain Tiger,' I type. 'I need to talk to Upright Boar. I'm in big trouble, okay?'

I continue on, alone in an empty landscape, talking to myself.

'Come on,' I type. 'This is bullshit. You guys invited me, okay? Are you really there?'

There's a bridge up ahead, a rope bridge that sways in the virtual wind. I approach it. The bridge spans an abyss. Boulders tumble down its sides, disappearing into inky black.

I wonder what happens if I commit virtual suicide. Just leap off the bridge, into nothing.

'Where's the Great Community?' I type. 'Is there one? Are we really in this together, or was that a bunch of shit too?'

No one answers. I cross the bridge, and it creaks with my every step.

Don't quit. Keep playing. Ha-ha.

Now I can see it, perched on the side of the mountain, carved into the cliffs – the Yellow Mountain Monastery.

'Because right now, I just want to go home,' I type. 'I've had it. I'm done. I just don't know where home is any more.'

And I can see, standing on a terrace of the Yellow Mountain Monastery's far pavilion that juts out over the gorge, a tiny avatar.

I keep walking, listening to the slithering of pebbles beneath my feet, the rasp of crows, the *erhu* and *pipa* music, which has taken on a decidedly mournful tone as I climb the winding path to the Yellow Mountain Monastery. No Nine-Headed Birds, anyway. A few NPCs that ignore me. My anonymous command seems to be working okay this time around.

Finally I reach the monastery gates. The doors are massive, red studded in brass. And they are locked firmly shut.

Fuck. Are they enchanted? Is there some spell I'm supposed to use to get in? Am I supposed to batter them down with my magic staff and my Mutual Rings? Or what?

I just don't give a shit.

I command my avatar to sit by the gate. I eat some virtual dumplings and drink some tea that I picked up at the market, because Little Mountain Tiger's energy is running a little low. Then I type 'Okay. I'm here. You want to talk to me, come and talk to me. Give me a reason not to bust you guys. Because I am in some big trouble and you aren't helping.'

After a minute, the monastery gate slowly swings open. A figure steps out. The Monk of the Jade Forest.

'You would not want to do that,' he says.

'Why not?'

'Because you would hurt your friends.'

I think about this. 'My friends?' I type. 'You mean Upright Boar?'

'Upright Boar and people who think like him. Who don't care about governments and their rules. Who want to help each other.'

Nice-sounding rhetoric. But what does it really mean?

'Why was I attacked?' I type. 'Why the Nine-Headed Bird?'

The Monk of the Jade Forest sits down next to me. 'A test.'

'A test? Of what?'

'To see if you are willing to struggle. To fight and not give up.'

I have to sit there for a moment.

'Okay,' I type. 'You put me through this bullshit test to see how I play some stupid fucking game when in real life I have real-life people who are threatening me and my family so you know what, fuck you. I need to know what to tell these guys so they'll leave me alone. I don't want to get anyone in trouble especially not Upright Boar so you have to give me a hint here what I'm supposed to do.'

I stare at Monk of the Jade Forest, but of course he's an avatar, an animated character, and he just sits there, blinking according to the dictates of his program.

Finally the words appear, floating above his head like a comic-book thought balloon.

'Wait one day. Log on then. We will instruct you.'

I really want to object. To tell him that I'm pretty sure

272

this whole thing is full of shit, that I'm going to tell *someone* – the Suits, Creepy John, the PSB – about this stupid game. That I'm going to, I don't know, go home, enroll in a community college, and study dermatology or something, hope I get a job, pretend that I don't know anything about how the world works, about the thin ice and the cold, dark waters beneath when you find yourself, by mistake, someplace you never wanted to be.

But I don't do any of that. 'Okay,' I type.

After that, I go outside. I start walking, no destination in mind. Eventually I make my way up to the old city, which is marked off by medieval walls and gates. I visit the 'ancient culture street,' where you can buy calligraphy brushes and knockoffs of classical Chinese paintings. I sit and have a local brew at a beer garden in the shadow of the Drum Tower.

I end up in the Muslim quarter.

It doesn't look that different from the other old parts of town: low, gray buildings made of medieval bricks. Stalls crowd the narrow streets, selling leather shadow puppets and Mao memorabilia, sesame oil and spices, flatbread stuffed with meat and pickled vegetables. Mopeds and bicycles weave in and out of the crowds. Now and again I see Hui Muslim women wearing headscarves. But this is still China. It's nothing like where I was before.

It's mid-afternoon, just after three o'clock. The streets are too narrow for cars; maybe that's why it seems so quiet. There's a covered market here, selling mostly souvenirs. More leather shadow puppets. They seem to be a local specialty. Hui ladies call out to me, wanting me to come in and see their goods.

One of them comes out from her stall. 'Miss,' she says,

'Miss. Come look.' She's a middle-aged woman, the plains of her face broad, her cheeks slightly reddened, as though she's wearing rouge. To my eyes, Hui people don't look any different than a lot of northern Chinese. It's only the headscarf that lets me know.

She smiles at me. There's something kind about her smile.

'Sure. Okay.'

I go inside. She pats the seat of a metal folding chair, gesturing for me to sit. She brings me tea in a glass. At the back of the stall, a young boy is curled up by a stack of paper kites and folk paintings, doing his homework. Her grandson, she tells me. 'Very smart. Good in school.'

She asks me the usual questions; I answer the usual answers; and finally, because she gave me tea, because she's kind, I buy some paper cuttings, tranquil countryside scenes, which I tell her I'm sending to my mom. Who knows if I really will? I say I'm going to do a lot of things that I never do.

I exit the stall. As I do, I notice a man looking at the leather shadow puppets at the stall next door. Pretending to, anyway. He barely moves his head, and I can't see his eyes through his fake Ray-Bans, but I think he's looking at me.

I turn away. So what? People look all the time. He probably wants to sell me something.

Fake Ray-Bans, white polo shirt, black jacket.

I keep walking, down a cramped lane that runs along a low whitewashed wall. I hear footsteps behind me. Measured, calm. I slow down, pretend to examine a tray of Little Red Books and calligraphy sets. The footsteps slow.

I start walking again. The footsteps follow. This is crazy. I'm in the middle of a market that sells tourist souvenirs. What's he going to do?

I think about running. I think about screaming. I feel like there's a target on my back, between my shoulders, and all the muscles there clench and spasm, waiting for the bullet.

I whirl around. There he is, maybe two yards away.

'What the fuck do you want?' I shout. 'Who the fuck are you?'

The man lifts his hands in mock surrender and grins.

'What do you want?' I ask again. A sob catches in my throat.

He laughs. Takes a couple steps toward me, with an exaggerated limp. Imitating my walk.

I stand there. My hands ball into fists. I want to kill him. I think, if I had a gun, I'd shoot this motherfucker.

He smiles at me.

Don't be such a bitch.

I turn around. I walk away.

I make my steps as steady as I can. I hear him follow. Not closing the distance. Just following me along the narrow lane by the whitewashed wall.

Up ahead is a ticket kiosk. Above it, a wooden sign: 'The Grand Mosque.'

I hesitate, and then I buy a ticket.

'The Mosque closes soon,' the ticket-taker says.

'*Meiguanxi*,' I mutter. Doesn't matter. I head toward the turnstiles.

Right before I enter, I turn around, and he's standing there. Not smiling now. Just watching me.

But he doesn't follow.

I've never been inside a mosque before.

This one looks like a Chinese Buddhist temple, overall. There are dim galleries and overgrown gardens, carved gates and wooden pavilions, but there are no statues, no gods and goddesses. I see maybe one or two other tourists who stop now and again to take photos. It's very quiet here. Peaceful.

I stop at a marble bench and sit for a while, gazing at the pavilion in front of me. Above the archway is a wooden signboard with carved Arabic calligraphy. I stare at that a while. I have no idea what it means.

Finally, I head for the exit. I don't see my stalker. Whoever he is. He could be anybody, or no one.

As I leave, I notice that there's another entrance to the complex, farther down the wall. There are no ticket-takers, no turnstiles. Hui men wearing white skullcaps and robes enter there. Muslims going to what remains of the real mosque, the place where they worship, a place where I'm not allowed.

I go back to my hotel with a couple bottles of beer and some snacks. Kick off my shoes, climb into bed, and turn on the TV.

Do I stay in Xi'an and play the Game, or do I run somewhere else?

Run where? From whom?

I decide, why not stay here? When I take a minute to be honest with myself, I figure I'm pretty much screwed no matter what I do.

Maybe I should buy another ticket to the Great Mosque and go sit on the bench in that courtyard and stare at the calligraphy I can't read until they come and pick me up. Whichever 'they' happens to find me first.

What difference does it make?

Don't quit. Keep playing. Ha-ha.

I'm not really thinking any more, if I ever was: I'm just reacting. But that was always what I did. What I was good at. When I was a medic, I had to deal with what was on my plate. I didn't go seek stuff out; it came to me. Then I handled it.

But this? How do I handle this?

Another day. How many days has it been? How many days do I have left?

What's going to happen to me?

I hole up in my room, watch TV, have instant coffee and crackers for breakfast, shrimp chips and beer for lunch.

Around two P.M., I go out. Gray dust washes out the sky, fades it like an old photograph. I walk down the cracked rubber sidewalk, turning down offers of phone cards and lottery tickets and fake Rolexes. Buy myself some flatbread stuffed with pickled vegetables and spiced meat.

Next to the stall where I get my snack is a street market – booths selling cheap clothes and shoes and luggage, toys and appliances.

'iPod!' a hawker cries out. 'You need iPod? I have real thing!'

On the second floor, next to a teahouse, is an Internet bar plastered with LED ads for the latest movies, Chinese, Korean, and American. Swords flash, lips kiss, things blow up.

Up I go.

The Internet bar is dark, smoky, and probably unlicensed. Well, good. I like that. Plus they sell beer. I like that too.

I sit down with my big bottle of Xian Beer, and I log

on. I pick up where I left off, with Little Mountain Tiger sitting in front of the Yellow Mountain Monastery's massive brass-studded gate.

'Hail, the Great Community,' I type.

I get about halfway through my bottle of Xian Beer before the gate slowly swings open and an avatar strides out, sword in hand – Water Horse.

'Hail, Little Mountain Tiger.'

'Long time no see,' I type. I get my turtle shield ready, just in case.

'Sorry for your trouble,' Water Horse says.

'That's the rules of the game, right?'

Water Horse sheaths her sword and approaches me. 'Maybe not everyone agrees how to play.'

'Right,' I type. 'So you guys have me running around wasting my time because you can't agree on the rules. Thanks.'

'It's not just the four of us you meet in our Guild. We have to be careful. We have to make sure we can trust you.'

'Fine.' I fall back in my chair, take a couple slugs of my beer. I'm so pissed off, and I'm so tired.

'Just tell me what to do,' I finally say.

'Can you go to Chengdu?' Water Horse asks.

Chengdu is the capital of Sichuan, practically in the furthest southwest corner of China.

'Why?'

Water Horse just stands there.

'Why Chengdu?'

'To help Upright Boar.'

'How does me going to Chengdu help him?' I type furiously. 'What do you want me to do?'

A pause.

'Maybe Chengdu too far for you.'

I think about this. I drink some more beer. 'Maybe you'd like it if I give up.'

'No,' Water Horse protests. 'I think you are Upright Boar friend and you want to help him.'

'Okay,' I type. But how do I know what's true? Water Horse, Golden Snake, Cinderfox, the Monk – they could all be the same person, or they could be lying about what they want and whether they're on my side or not.

Maybe Water Horse is some fat dude sitting in a comic-book store in Cleveland.

'I'll go to Chengdu,' I finally say.

I've already gone this far, haven't I?

CHAPTER TWENTY-SIX

It's a fifteen-hour train ride overnight from Xi'an to Chengdu. I end up on a hard sleeper, in the middle, which is the best berth, because if you're on the bottom everybody sits on your bunk, and if you're on the top your nose is practically touching the ceiling and it's usually stuffy and also a long way down if you miss a step trying to get to the toilet in the dark.

I don't make conversation. I climb up on my bunk with a big bottle of Xian's finest lager and my last Percocet, and between those and the fact that I'm so exhausted that I can barely haul my gimpy leg and tired ass up there, I fall asleep about five minutes after I finish the bottle, pulling the quilt over my head like a shield.

When I wake up, I'm in a different country.

Everything's green here, unlike the dry, yellow north. There's soft mist poured over the fields and hills and stands of trees and bamboo.

It's raining when the train pulls into Chengdu.

The Sichuan earthquake in 2008 killed tens of thousands

280

of people; no one knows how many. They don't want anyone to know how many children died up in the mountains in collapsing schoolhouses that weren't built right, constructed out of tofu, people say. But I can't see any signs of quake damage here. Maybe it's been covered up, plastered over, like so many inconvenient wounds.

There's a hotel I've heard of in Chengdu, a cheap backpackers' hangout, and I figure I pretty much look like a cheap backpacker, considering that all I'm carrying is an overstuffed day pack and a plastic shopping bag from the Number 2 Pingyao Department Store. I catch a cab outside the train station, take note of the giant statue of Mao with his arm outstretched like he's directing traffic – or maybe he's just trying to greet the patrons of the shopping mall and the Starbucks down the street.

I get to the backpackers' joint, wedged between a hotpot restaurant and a camping-supply store on a narrow lane.

'No baggage?' asks the . . . clerk? Manager? You can't call somebody a 'concierge' when he's sitting behind a scarred desk in a beige room containing a bulletin board leprous with notices about treks to Tibet and Jiuzhaigou and dubious job offers to teach English, a pressboard bookcase overflowing with paperbacks, and a pile of backpacks heaped in one corner.

'My bag got stolen,' I explain. 'In Xi'an.'

The hotel guy, a compact man of indeterminate age wearing a Madras shirt and khaki shorts, makes a sympathetic noise. 'Lots of thieves in Xi'an,' he says. 'I show you your room.'

Another cheap hotel room, beds with pressboard mattresses, pebbled brown vinyl on the walls. Backpackers wander the halls. My age, most of them. All of them fit, tanned, and relaxed. Laughing. 'Yangshuo was awesome!' 'Have you checked out Hei He?' Couples holding hands.

Shiny, happy people. Isn't that the name of some old song?

But where there are backpackers, there must be Internet connections.

Sure enough, out in the courtyard, beneath a gray-tiled roof that I'm told dates from the Ming Dynasty, is a teahouse. In the back of the teahouse, a row of computers.

I order a pot of Dragon Well and retreat to the darkest corner. Plug in Chuckie's little anonymizer and log on to the Game.

And here's Little Mountain Tiger, sitting on a rock in front of the big red doors of the Yellow Mountain Monastery. Sulking, if I can attribute a mood to an avatar.

'Hail the Great Community,' I type. 'Yo, Little Mountain Tiger here. I'm in Chengdu.'

After a minute, a text box pops up, framed in gold, containing the Chinese characters for 'Da Tong' and, in English, 'Message From the Great Community.'

The characters are a live link. I click on it.

'Changqing Shan. The Taoist Scholar Cave. Tomorrow. 3 P.M.'

CHAPTER TWENTY-SEVEN

Changqing Shan, 'Evergreen Mountain,' is a Taoist sacred site, a mountain honeycombed with temples, sixty or seventy of them, connected by steep stone paths that wind over and around the peaks. The entrance to the mountain is the front gate and galleries of a temple – carved peaked roofs rising to points, painted dragons perching on the roof tiles, surrounded by a riot of ginkgos and palms and plum trees. Behind it, the low mountain rises, swaddled in green and mist.

I get there early, catching a ride from the hostel's minibus.

I pay my entrance fee and go inside.

Walking through the first temple, I think: that Chinese guy kneeling in front of the Guanyin altar with his incense sticks – he could be part of the Game. Or that European woman in cargo shorts and a camera vest taking photos of an ornate bronze caldron. The worker sweeping the temple courtyard.

Any of them. None of them.

I walk up a slate path that is slick from the drizzle, my sneakers squeaking as I step. Changqing Shan isn't as crowded as a lot of Chinese tourist traps. I don't know if it's because of the weather, or if the complex is so big, with so many temples and galleries, that it somehow absorbs the visitors, renders them nearly invisible, like they're a part of the landscape.

Maybe it's the mist. I feel like I'm walking through a cloud. I turn my head and see a little shrine tucked into the rocks. In another direction, a pavilion, with two women and two men dressed in traditional costumes – musicians with stringed instruments and hand drums. Poised as if they're about to start singing, but they don't: they just stand there like a freeze-frame in some movie.

Above them, nestled in the rafters of the pavilion, is a surveillance camera.

I keep walking. Behind me, I hear the echo of strings and the quaver of a woman's voice.

I have over two hours before I'm supposed to go to the Taoist Scholar's Cave. I have to do something, so I keep moving. I take the chairlift, just a raw wood-and-iron bench painted a thick, peeling green, to the top of the mountain. My feet seem to skim the tops of the trees. This little chant goes through my head, something I learned in a Chinese class: '*Ren fa di, di fa tian, tian fa dao, dao fa ziran.*'

Man follows Earth, Earth follows Heaven, Heaven follows the Way, the Way follows Nature.

I'm not really clear on what that means, because, as it was explained to me, all things arise from the Tao, from the Way, the union of opposites, and that would have to include nature, wouldn't it? So maybe it's all one big circle. Big wheel keeps on turning, right? The Tao keeps rolling along.

Yeah, I think. Yeah. Who cares about all the rest of it, all the details? I listen to the silence, the occasional creak of the iron cable that hauls me up the mountain, the crows that ruffle the treetops.

At the summit is a teahouse. I sit by the window, near a family playing cards and a young couple holding hands across the table, and have a pot of tea and a bowl of spiced melon seeds. I look out the window, staring down at the clouds.

Finally, I go looking for the Cave of the Taoist Scholar.

I pick my way down the slippery path, following the carved wooden signboards. There's a Temple of Utmost Purity, a Palace of the Creation of Good Fortune.

And here's the Cave of the Taoist Scholar.

I walk inside. It's simple, with unfinished earthen walls that recede into darkness. A young woman and her five-year-old daughter hang out behind a low wooden counter at the entrance. A snack bar in the sacred site. There's a little TV at the end of the bar, playing cartoons at low volume, and they're half-watching it as mom braids her daughter's hair.

I go further into the cave. The walls narrow, then widen into a small chamber. I see what looks like an altar, with this twisted brass candle-holder with many branches, like a bare tree, surrounded by red strips of paper with black writing on them fluttering in the dim candlelight.

There's a plain wood table in front of it. On that is a carved wooden cylinder, with the patina of age. It's filled with flat bamboo sticks, tipped in red.

I've seen this before. It's for fortune-telling, I think. They have it in front of temples sometimes.

'Do you want to try?'

Standing there is a monk. He's wearing plain blue robes and a round hat that has a red knob on top, like some kind of spiritual bellhop. He's middle-aged, the lines of his face softened by the candlelight.

I shrug. 'Sure.'

He picks up the canister and hands it to me. 'You just shake,' he says in English. 'Like playing dice.'

I've never played dice. 'Right.'

I shake the canister, thinking things like: this sounds like bones rattling around, but that's stupid, because I don't know what rattling bones would actually sound like; it's just the kind of thing that you're supposed to think of when you're doing some creepy Chinese fortune ritual.

A bunch of the sticks starts to slide out. Slowly. I keep shaking. A couple teeter on the brink. Then, finally, one falls.

The monk picks up the stick. 'Number forty-eight.' He smiles a little.

'So, what does that mean?'

'Every number has fortune to go with it.' He lightly touches my forearm. 'Come, and I get you Taoist fortune.'

I hesitate. The monk smiles at me.

'Come, Little Tiger. I get you your fortune.'

I follow him.

He leads me through a wooden doorway, into a little room off to one side. One wall is the side of the cave. The others are wooden screens, heavy, blackened cabinets, and bookcases filled with scrolls, books, and stacks of paper. There's a small traditional scholar's desk, with ink-stone and calligraphy brushes.

And a computer.

'Are you Monk of the Jade Forest?' I ask.

'No. Just a monk.'

'Where's Upright Boar?'

'Upright Boar could not come. He would like to. But is not safe for him.'

'What about Cinderfox? Or Water Horse?'

The monk shakes his head. 'I'm sorry. I do not know them.'

'Golden Snake?'

'Sorry,' he says again. 'I don't know.'

So much for my Tao mellow. 'What *do* you know, then?'

The monk nods and reaches into the drawer of his scholar's desk.

'For you.'

He extracts a rice-paper envelope, so thin that I can see the folded sheet inside.

'This is from Upright Boar. Instruction to manage his art. He names you to be manager. It says you get money for doing this.' The monk grins, showing crooked, tea-stained teeth. 'A percentage.'

I just stand there. 'I don't understand,' I finally say.

I guess I was hoping for something bigger. Like, if the Game is this great conspiracy, shouldn't we be over-throwing a government or something?

'He request someone to help him in this way. You take care of his art. You put money aside for him. He put his chop on this paper. So it is legal document.'

'Why me?'

287

'He trusts you. And you are foreigner. So you are protected, a little, from Chinese government.'

The monk lays the envelope on the desk. 'But still, this can be a little dangerous for you, I think. People maybe can ask you, where is Upright Boar? Of course, you don't know. But you are still in charge of his art and his money. So maybe they will bother you about this.'

'Can't they just freeze the funds?' I ask. 'If Upright Boar is some kind of criminal?'

'Not a criminal. No one says that he is charged with anything. But, maybe. We don't know.' The monk shrugs. 'Maybe it is not safe for you.'

A chuckle escapes my throat. I haven't been safe for so long that I've forgotten what it feels like.

'I don't know anything about managing art,' I say. 'What am I supposed to do?'

'I am just a monk. This is nothing I can tell you. I think, just take care of the art and make money.'

I try to take this in, what it means. Do I say 'yes' and get even more tangled up in the Game, or turn around and leave? Just walk out of here and go . . . somewhere.

Maybe my being a foreigner protects me a little from the Chinese government, but it's not going to protect me from the Suits.

And then I could hit myself, because I'd almost forgotten about the most important thing.

'The Uighur. The one who stayed the night at Lao Zhang's place.'

The monk shakes his head with a placid smile. 'I don't know who you mean.'

'Are you sure?' I insist. 'Because I'm in some serious shit

288

because of this guy. He's supposed to be a terrorist or something. That's why they're after us. And, I mean . . .'

Now the thoughts are scrabbling around inside my head again, trying to get out. 'It's not like I wish this guy any harm,' I say. 'But if you want me to help . . . I gotta get these spooks off my back.'

'Spooks?' the monk asks, with a puzzled frown. 'Those are . . . ghosts?'

'Shit,' I mutter under my breath. 'Secret officials,' I say in Chinese, because I don't know the word for spies. 'They want the Uighur. And . . . if he's really a terrorist, maybe it's not worth my life or Upright Boar's to protect him.'

The monk's expression is sympathetic. Maybe even sad. 'I am sorry, Little Tiger,' he says. 'But this is nothing I know about.'

'You don't know?'

I cannot fucking believe this.

'I come all the way to Sichuan to get some answers, and I almost forgot to ask the fucking question. And you're telling me you don't know? Why should I believe you?'

'Each one of us only knows what we must,' the monk says gently.

'Oh, great. That's just great.'

Like I need this Zen crap right now.

What I need is something – *anything* – that's going to get the Suits off my ass. I don't care what it is any more. Just give me a reason not to give up.

To keep playing.

'Look. I have to talk to Lao – to Upright Boar.'

The monk shakes his head. 'He is not online.'

'But I need – I need some help.'

I try to keep the edge of desperation from my voice, and fail.

'I can't help you,' the monk says.

He sounds so kind, and the wrinkles on his face look like a map of compassion. For all the good that does me.

'I am so fucked,' I mumble.

He gestures at the envelope. 'Maybe, then, this is something you don't want.'

I stand there, staring at the envelope. The monk picks it up, holds it out to me with both hands.

'Do you want it?' he asks.

I don't have a clue what I want. Instead of too many thoughts racing around my head, my mind suddenly feels empty.

Ren fa di, di fa tian, tian fa dao, dao fa ziran.

I shrug. 'Okay.' I take the envelope.

It's probably a bad idea. But, you know, whatever.

The monk walks me toward the door, then clasps his hands together. 'Ah. I forget your fortune.'

'Don't bother,' I say, because some corny Chinese fortune is the last thing I care about right now, but the monk has already turned away. He goes to a bookcase that is divided into little cubbyholes filled with scrolls the size of fat cigarettes. He retrieves a scroll tied, like all the others, with a long length of red silk string.

'Number forty-eight,' he says, handing it to me. 'The, the *zhegu* changes into a *luan*.'

'The what?'

'*Zhegu* . . . this is . . . a small bird. A plain bird. Brown,' he adds helpfully. 'The *luan*, this is . . . very big.' He stretches his arms wide above his head. 'Not real . . . it is a bird like . . . like a *fenghuang*, but even bigger.'

290

Like a phoenix. 'Okay, so the *zhegu* turns into a *luan*,' I say. 'Then what?'

'The *luan* flies higher and higher, above the clouds,' the monk explains. 'More free than any other bird can be.'

I think about this. 'So, that's a good thing, right?'

The monk gives me his I'm-so-spiritual smile again. 'The meaning is, big changes. Sometimes good, sometimes bad. Depends on your actions.'

Given my track record, this isn't very comforting.

Sitting on my bed at the backpacker's hotel, I study Lao Zhang's letter.

The paper is very thin, like the envelope. Just one page. I can understand a few words here and there – Lao Zhang's name, my name, 'American,' 'art.' With enough time and a decent dictionary, I could probably work out what it says. For now, I figure it means trouble. Proof that I've been in contact with Lao Zhang.

Now that I've got it, all I want to do is hide it. Bury it, like a cat covering up a turd in the litter-box.

I'm coming up on Carter's deadline, and I've got nothing. Nothing but a piece of paper that's going to get me in worse shit than I already am.

Here I go again, I think. Some guy I'm sleeping with asks me to do something, and I'm so pathetic, I just go along with it, no questions asked. Help Upright Boar! He *needs* you!

When's Upright Boar going to help *me*?

Fuck you, Lao Zhang, I think. It's all a game, and I'm just a piece in it. More important than a pawn, I guess, but still one that gets sacrificed along the way. A knight, maybe, or what's the one that looks like a tower?

291

But he trusts you, another part of me insists. He trusts you with something important. His art. His work. He chose you out of everyone he knows to take care of it.

Big deal, I snap back. It's still all about him. What *he* needs. Not about me.

Maybe he doesn't know, the *nice* girl pleads. He's been on the run, in hiding. He could be in Bumfuck Guizhou or Gansu or out of China altogether; he might not know anything about what's going on, with the Suits, with the Game. He could be on fucking *dial-up* for all you know.

And he did help you. All those times you went over to his place. The times he came over to yours. He didn't judge. Didn't demand. Didn't treat you like a victim. Like a loser.

I sit cross-legged on the pressboard mattress, staring at the letter, and my butt's falling asleep because it's like sitting on Monk of the Jade Forest's meditation stone.

I think, if I fold the letter in half lengthwise and then in half again, it's about the same width as my Taoist fortune scroll.

So I fold it. Make a sharp crease with my thumbnail. I unroll the Taoist fortune scroll and I line up Lao Zhang's letter against that. Then I roll up the whole thing, with Lao Zhang's letter inside, and tie it up with the scroll's red silk thread.

After that, I think about where to put it. I take everything out of my little daypack in search of a good hiding place.

Here's my faithful Beanie Squid.

I stare at the silly thing, at its floppy Day-Glo orange legs, its shiny black eyes.

I take the red silk thread and tie the scroll around my Beanie Squid's neck.

That's when I realize I've made a decision.

It comes down to this: I like Lao Zhang. And I'm not sure what we are to each other, except that he thinks I'm better than I am, and I'd rather be his version of me than the one living in my own head.

I don't know exactly what he's up to, but I know he's created things. Helped people. Maybe what he's doing, what he's done, is more important than what I'm doing. Than what I've done.

What have I ever done that meant anything?

Then I think, what I did at Camp Falafel, *that* meant something all right.

Okay. I'll be a part of something good this time. I'll help Lao Zhang. Help him build his post-modern communities, or whatever they are – places where people can live decent lives. Even people like me.

Hey, maybe I'll even make some money. Didn't Lucy Wu say we could all profit?

That is, if I don't get arrested. Or thrown out of the country. Or . . .

My mind stops there. I don't know what they'll do, and I can't think about it now.

What I do know is that I have to go back to Beijing.

Sure, I could try to run. Chengdu has an international airport. I could go to Singapore or Amsterdam or Bangkok. But what would be the point? They'd find me eventually, and I'd look even guiltier than I already do.

And where would I end up? How would I live? What kind of life would that be, always running from place to place? Until I get caught.

It doesn't matter where I go. There's nothing I'm going to learn that will rescue me. No one who can help. I'm not going to find the Uighur, which is just as well, because do I want that guy's life on my conscience?

No. I've had enough of that. I'm not playing that game any more. I'll tell the Suits I'm done, and what happens happens.

Lao Zhang's art is in Beijing. If I'm going to take care of it, that's where I have to go.

CHAPTER TWENTY-EIGHT

I don't have enough cash for a plane ticket, and I don't want to risk using an ATM or a credit card. There's an express train leaving tomorrow morning, but I don't want to wait that long. Now that I've decided, I want to get back. To go home.

So that's how I end up on a slow train from Chengdu to Beijing. A thirty-two-hour ride, leaving Chengdu tonight.

This way, I'll arrive in Beijing early Wednesday evening, ahead of Suit #2's Friday deadline.

I'll call him and tell him I'm back. I don't have a clue what I'm going to tell him after that. A piece of the truth, I guess. That I tried. That I couldn't find out what they wanted to know. That I'm not going to cause anybody any trouble. What else can I say? I'll just have to bluff it out.

Maybe it will help that I'm willing to face him. Maybe it won't.

I have a soft sleeper, at least, which will make the next thirty-two hours or so a little more comfortable.

Even better, as the train pulls out of Chengdu, I have the compartment to myself.

Okay, I think. Okay. I'm going to my doom; I might as well enjoy the ride.

After the conductor comes and checks my ticket, I go down to the dining car and buy myself two large bottles of Blue Sword Premium Beer. Then I retreat to my quiet compartment, sit on the slightly dingy white seat covers on the bottom bunk, sip my beer, and stare out the window into the dark. There's something comforting about the noise and the rhythm of the train, the wheels on the tracks, the occasional deep hoot of the horn. When I get bored with that, I climb up to the upper bunk. I finish my beer, feeling the exhaustion seeping into me like rainwater staining discarded paper.

I pull the quilt over myself and fall asleep, rocked by the rhythm of the rails.

I'm dreaming about something; I'm not sure what, but there's clouds everywhere, and I'm still on the train, like it's open to the sky, when I feel a gentle hand on my shoulder, hear a soft voice in my ear:

'Ellie. Ellie. You should wake up now.'

So I do.

A hand covers my mouth. Gently. And when I open my eyes, I see John's face, John's eyes, staring at me.

'Please don't be upset,' John says quietly. 'I hope you can not make a fuss. I'll take my hand away if you promise to be calm.'

I nod in agreement.

John takes his hand away.

And I open up my mouth and scream 'Help!'

John slaps his hand over my mouth again. He's straddling me, so I can't kick him; I try clawing at his face, but he does something, presses his fingers into a spot at the base of my neck, and it's so painful that I'm practically paralyzed, and all the while, John is saying 'Ellie, Ellie, stop. I don't want to hurt you. Stop. Be calm. Just listen.'

I stop. I stare at his face. His lip is bleeding, and there are red marks raked across his cheek.

John slowly lifts his hand.

'Okay,' I say. 'I'm listening.'

'You need to get off the train,' he says. 'People are coming for you.'

I almost laugh. 'And you're, like, what? Here on a friendly visit?'

'I am your friend,' he insists. 'We will stop in a few minutes at this town. We can get off there.'

'Who's after me?' I demand. 'I mean, how do you know –?'

'I hear a guy ask about who is in this compartment. This guy, he is a bad-looking guy,' John says, sounding very sincere. 'He and some other guys, they are in the soft sleeper car next to this one. Maybe they are State Security, but undercover. Maybe somebody has paid them.'

I shake my head, like that's somehow going to clear it. But I'm pretty sure that this is one significant ration of bullshit.

'Okay, John,' I say. 'You've been, like, stalking me. You drugged me. You show up in my train compartment in the middle of the night. Why am I gonna believe anything you say?'

'Because I'm Cinderfox.'

CHAPTER TWENTY-NINE

Well, okay. It's not like I suddenly trust Creepy John, who did, after all, drug me and stalk me and wash Chuckie's and my dishes, which is just perverse. But I've already let Cinderfox and his buddies lead me from one side of China to the other. Am I really going to stop now?

Besides, I'm tired. It's the middle of the night, and I don't have time to think about what to do.

'Okay,' I say, shouldering my backpack. 'Let's go.'

John puts a finger to his lips and helps me down from the top bunk, slides the compartment door open quietly as he can. We step into the narrow corridor that runs along the sleeper compartments. One guy sits on the jump seat at the end of the car, toward the train engine, reading a magazine in the passage's dim light. He looks up as we head the other way, toward the rear of the train.

The train slows. Sways like a snake. We reach the end of the corridor, and John opens the doors that lead to the vestibule between the cars.

Behind us, a compartment door opens and slams shut.

I look over my shoulder. Two men. Jogging toward us.

The steel plates where the cars are hitched together move in opposite directions, and I step wrong and stumble, see the diamond patterns in the metal outlined in grime as I start to fall. John hauls me up and drags me into the next car. Another soft sleeper. We push past a conductor as the train continues to slow, make it to the car after that. A hard sleeper. Passengers stir, grab their bags, their jars of tea, ready for a quick exit. We keep going.

'Do you have your ticket?' John hisses.

'I, uh –'

'Just follow me.'

Cheery arrival music plays. The ubiquitous woman's voice comes on, announcing the stop. John pushes past a couple of peasants clutching faded striped totes and ripped canvas duffels, dragging me with him into the next vestibule and down the three iron steps onto the station's platform.

Knots of people push past us, getting on the train. I glimpse dreary cement, peeling white pillars, a vendor with a cart piled high with packaged noodles and sugared nuts and bottled water. John keeps his hand clamped around my wrist, and I follow him down the platform, toward the back of the train and the hard-seat cars.

'Ticket,' he whispers, steering me back toward the train. I try to remember where I put the fucking thing. In my wallet? My backpack? John already has his out to show the railway worker standing at the compartment's entrance, the usual neatly made up young woman in a peaked blue cap. He starts up the three stairs, pulling me with him.

'Your car is up front,' I hear the ticket-taker say.

'*Meiguanxi,*' John mutters.

'*Xiaojie, nide piao,*' she demands crisply, pointing at me.

Your ticket.

'*Ta you, ta xianzai bushufu le!*' John snaps. She has it; she's not feeling well. Which is not too far from the truth.

Pants pocket, I think, and there it is, my little pink ticket, stuck between a couple of ten-yuan notes.

'*Duibuqi,*' I say automatically. Sorry. We board the train.

The compartment to our right is a hard sleeper. Inside, only a few passengers stir: a couple of new arrivals settling in, a group of guys playing cards in two of the lower bunks, a girl texting on her cellphone.

We make our way through the car, go on to the next and the one after that. As we pass the toilet compartments, John jiggles the handles – locked, as they generally are for arrival at a station.

In the third car, the door opens.

John silently gestures for me to go inside. I do. He follows me, closes the door, and locks it.

The two of us stand in the tiny cubicle, me with one foot on the step of the squat toilet, which by this time in the trip is spattered with piss and shit and hunks of sodden toilet paper.

Did we lose those guys? Did they follow us back on the train? I don't have a fucking clue.

The train slowly starts to move.

'We stay here,' John whispers. 'Another stop in a quarter hour.'

I clutch the iron bar by the toilet as the train lurches forward and picks up speed.

We're standing inches apart from each other but barely say a word. I listen to the rhythm of the wheels on the tracks and think of how seductive the sound is, how much I'd like to find a bunk and crawl into it and sleep. Just sleep.

Somebody comes and rattles the door handle once, but they leave.

Fifteen minutes go by. It feels like hours. The train slows.

'Okay,' John says, unlatching the door. We step out into the passageway.

The omnipresent woman's voice announces the stop. Some town that, if I heard correctly, is called 'Treasure Chicken Village.' I think: that can't be right.

We exit the train. No one follows us. No one I see, at least.

A little station, not much more than a platform and tracks, dark except for flickering halogen lights. Steam rises from the train, smelling of diesel and rain. The station is pushed up against the base of a hill or maybe a mountain, a dark mass that rises to some indeterminable height.

A few people climb onto the train. A couple of ticket-takers stand around in their blue uniforms and peaked hats, looking bored.

'This way,' John says.

I follow him past the red-brick station building, glimpse a couple of people inside, sleeping amongst their bags, stretched out across the orange plastic seats beneath the dim fluorescents.

We follow the tracks a ways at a half-jog.

'Where are we going?' I ask in a whisper.

'Don't know.'

Up ahead, there's a break in the hills, and a road, a darker black against the gray.

We pick our way along the side of the road in the dark, heading downhill. I'm glad that I don't have any real luggage. Only my little daypack and my shopping bag. 'I can carry that,' John offers. He too has a small backpack. He's wearing that cheap leather jacket. I keep glancing over at him in the dark, trying to get a glimpse of his T-shirt to see if it's that same Beijing Olympics one. I don't know why I care, and, anyway, I can't tell. Everything's faded to grays and blacks, the color leached out by night. It's quiet except for an occasional car or truck rattling up the hill to the train station.

'Okay, Cinderfox,' I say. 'That night. The night of the party. What the fuck was that about?'

John gives me his best wide-eyed, innocent look. 'That night? You were sick.'

'Would you stop bullshitting me?'

I'm surprised at myself, at how loud my voice is. How strong. It's like somebody took the gag out of my mouth, like I'm waking up after a long sleep.

'You put something in my beer. You drugged me and you asked me a lot questions. How come?'

John hunches in his leather jacket. I think maybe he's blushing. 'We just need to know, can we trust you?' he mumbles. 'Some people think maybe you are not reliable. Maybe you would betray us. Maybe you don't really care so much for Upright Boar.'

I feel a surge of bile in my throat. 'Did *he* think that?'

'Upright Boar?' John shakes his head. 'No. I don't think so. He worry about you. He does not want to ask you

302

to do something that is too hard for you. He only says we should ask you if you can do this favor for him.'

I stop. Just stop. Stand there in the middle of the road in the dark, somewhere out in the Chinese countryside.

'And that was your way of asking?'

John hangs his head. 'Not everyone agrees with Upright Boar.'

I want to sit down, find some patch of grass or boulder at the side of the road and sit there like Little Mountain Tiger in front of the red gates of the Yellow Mountain Monastery. Wait there until I get some real answers.

But apparently this is as good an answer as I'm going to get.

'What's wrong with you people?' I mutter. I straighten my pack and start walking.

John grabs my arm.

I whirl around, my hand closed in a fist, and I start to swing, but he pulls me down with a little move that knocks me off-balance, and I land on top of him by the side of the road. We're face to face, and he says, 'Car!' and points uphill, toward the train station. I roll off him, and we scuttle into the brush, bellies down on the dirt.

I hear a car engine, and headlights sweep past us, slowly, silhouetting the bushes in front of us so they look like black paper-cuttings.

Finally, the engine noise recedes and the road is silent again.

'Sorry,' John says, his face inches from mine.

'What the fuck was that?'

'I thought it could be those guys,' he mutters.

'It was a car. We're on a *road*. Where cars drive!'

I stand up. My leg wobbles and I stumble a little. John

scrambles to his feet, steadies me. I shake him off. Dust off dirt and grass and head down the road.

We walk a while in silence. I don't want to look at John, but I'm aware of him next to me, carrying my shopping bag. He doesn't want to look at me either.

'How do you know Upright Boar?' I ask.

'The Game.'

'You met online?'

He nods. 'I get an invitation,' he says. 'From the Great Community. I play for a while. For a long time.' He shrugs. 'Finally they accept me.'

'Who are they?'

'I don't know. I mean, I know some. But not many. Just the screen names.'

'Why?' I ask. 'Why did you join them?'

For a few minutes, all I hear are our footsteps, and then a distant train whistle.

'I have a sister,' he finally says. 'She is, you know, a blogger. Just writes about her thoughts and her feelings. And then about some historical incidents. Just things she has learned. She lived in London for a while. And when she came home to China, she still is thinking like that overseas person. Like she can say what she wants.'

'She got in trouble,' I conclude.

'Yes,' he says very quietly, like he's still afraid of being over-heard. 'This is . . . maybe six years ago. One day, the PSB comes and takes her away. I am her brother. I think it is my duty to look after her. I think, there must be a mistake. She is not challenging the government. She is just talking. I talk like this with my friends, all the time. We don't know why her. No one will tell us. She isn't charged with anything. We cannot see her. We cannot talk

304

to her. I go to the PSB. I go to the Ministry. To the Municipal Government. I fill out forms. I am only following the Chinese Constitution. I do all these things.'

He laughs. 'I am young. I am graduated from college. I have a good job. I am making money. I have a fiancée. A nice apartment. A car. I believe in a prosperous future. I believe in China. I think: this is a mistake, and I can correct it.'

I want to laugh myself.

'So what happened to your sister?' I ask.

'She is in our home town now. She was gone for two years. Two years!' He stops in his tracks and swings my shopping bag in the air, in utter frustration. 'For the first two months, we can't find out anything. Then they charge that she is disturbing the social order. I got a lawyer. They followed him. Called his office and made threats. He still tried to present her case, but it doesn't matter. The court says she is guilty. They send her to labor camp. Then one day they just let her go. They don't say why. They just let her go. No apology. Nothing. And I think, where is the justice? Where is the right? Not with my government. But some of her friends here in China and some of her foreign friends, other bloggers, they are writing letters, they are writing every day, and I think, who are my friends?'

He stares at me. I can only imagine his face, his expression, because it's too dark to see it. 'Do you understand, Ellie?'

I shrug. 'I guess.'

We start walking again.

'I am Chinese,' he says, almost to himself. 'I am a patriot. I love China.'

At the bottom of the hill is a cluster of lights – a gas station, some square darkened buildings. I guess this is Treasure Chicken Village.

'What happened to your fiancée?' I ask.

I can see John's face now, and he looks embarrassed, almost hurt, like a kid who's been slapped and told he's a fuckup.

'She does not like that I am angry. Spending so much time on my sister's case. I explain, this is my family. Don't Chinese people care about family any more? But my fiancée says, your sister is a bad social influence. Maybe she needs this lesson. And anyway, if you complain too much, you won't have success.'

Then it's his turn to shrug. 'Actually, she is a bitch.'

I laugh. I think this is maybe the funniest thing I've heard in years. I just keep laughing until I'm out of breath and my stomach hurts and I have to stop and rest my hands on my thighs for a minute.

John gets that scrunched-up, confused look on his face. 'Is that word . . . does that offend you?'

'Fuck, no,' I say, catching my breath.

'Because she really is a bitch,' he explains earnestly.

'I believe you.'

And I do. Finally.

Up ahead, the road widens into a square. A collection of anonymous buildings are strung out around us along a few anonymous streets: Treasure Chicken Village.

There's not a lot to see in Treasure Chicken Village – and, since it's after midnight, what there is to see is mostly closed: a market, a restaurant, a car-repair place. The main street has a fresh asphalt glaze; my sneakers stick on the blacktop, and the air smells like oil. There's what looks to be a karaoke bar that's open; a neon sign glows outside of it, at least.

'I think maybe I can go there,' John says. 'Find someone with a car. Those guys, maybe they can figure out we got off the train here. We should not stay.'

'Yeah,' I say. 'But, I mean, if some guys are chasing us, if they're State Security . . .'

I look around at the little town, at the dark hills rising up around it. I don't know where we are, other than someplace between Chengdu and Beijing, but it's cold in these hills.

' . . . where are we going to go? Where's safe?'

John hesitates. 'Maybe, since you're an American, we can go to your embassy.'

I think about the Suits and shiver in my light jacket. 'I dunno, John. That might not be the best place.'

Which reminds me of something.

'What do you know about the Uighur? Hashim . . . somebody.'

'The Uighur?' John gets that confused look again. 'What Uighur?'

'Never mind.'

I gesture in the general direction of the karaoke place. 'So, let's go check out Treasure Chicken's nightlife.'

'Maybe this is not a good idea, Ellie. That kind of place . . . maybe it's not a nice place for you to go.'

Coming from a guy who drugged me and who's seen my tits, I find this concern for my delicate sensibilities a tad annoying.

'What am I supposed to do, just hang around outside? What if those guys show up? Wouldn't I be safer inside with you?'

John frowns, thinking it over, and then he nods. 'Okay. I think so.'

I'll admit, when we walk into the karaoke bar, I do have a few second thoughts.

This place is about as low-rent as they come – cheap plastic tables, Christmas lights for decoration, some tattered posters of Korean pop singers and, of course, the Beijing Olympics. A drunk guy yells into the microphone over a cheesy synthesized karaoke track, following the words on a video shown on a flat-screen TV sitting crookedly on top of a table. Most of the couple dozen people in the bar are men, and if the few women who *are* here aren't hookers, they must play them on television.

We go up to the bar, which is really just a counter with some bottles displayed on a couple of wall shelves behind it.

Everyone in the bar stares at us.

It's way more common to see Western men with Chinese women than the other way around. When it's a Chinese guy with a white girl, a lot of times you get the feeling the guys are going to high-five behind your back. Everyone knows about those insatiable white chicks. Way to go, dude!

People don't seem hostile. It's more like we're Martians, because how many times has a mixed-race couple walked through the door of this dive in Treasure Chicken Village in the middle of the night?

Great, I think. Like we're not going to stand out here. Like we wouldn't have been better off staying on the train till we got to someplace larger, more anonymous.

I'm feeling like this whole thing might be some weird number of John's and I fell for it.

I look at the people staring at us: the young drunk guys

gathered around the karaoke mike, the railway workers, faces seamed and tanned from endless days working outside, the chicken girls in their sequined baby T's, and I think any one of them could be working for somebody. For the PSB or State Security. For whoever John is really working for.

'Two beers,' John tells the woman working behind the counter, which on the one hand is annoying, because he didn't ask me what I wanted, but on the other hand, he does know I like beer, and I could sure use one right about now.

Undrugged, preferably.

He gets the beers and pays, and we find an empty table behind the karaoke speaker where it's not quite so loud.

'Okay, Ellie,' John says, after a few sips of beer. 'I try to find us a car now.'

He goes back to the counter and starts talking to the barwoman.

Meanwhile, one of the chicken girls sidles up to my table.

'Hello,' she says brightly.

'Hello.'

'Is that your husband?' she asks.

I shudder. 'No, he's not.' Then I think, that sounded a little harsh. 'Good friend.'

'Not too many foreigners come to Treasure Chicken Village.'

'Right,' I reply. 'We're . . . sightseeing. And we heard . . . the temple near here is really beautiful.'

There's always a temple around someplace.

A puzzled frown creases the girl's powdered forehead. 'Temple . . . Oh! You mean Moon Hill Monastery!'

309

I nod vigorously. 'Yes. That's what I mean.'

'But you should stay in Yilin Village, not here. Much closer.'

'Oh, is that right? I guess we didn't read the guidebook carefully enough.'

The girl pulls out one of the plastic chairs and sits.

'There's really nothing interesting around here,' she confides.

'So, if we wanted to get a ride to Yilin Village, is that possible?'

'Bus goes three times a day.'

'What about now?'

'Oh, it's too late for the bus now.'

'Do you know anyone who has a car, or . . .'

'Long drive. Maybe two hours. Maybe no one wants to go there so late at night.'

'We can pay,' I said. 'It's just that . . . we don't have a place to stay tonight. And Treasure Chicken Village looks . . . very small.'

She giggles. 'Oh, *Upper* Treasure Chicken Village isn't very interesting, but *Lower* Treasure Chicken Village is more fun. More things to do. Bus runs from here to there all night, and I think you can find a place to stay.'

Right about then, John returns to our table.

'John,' I say brightly. 'We should have gone to Yilin Village. It's much closer to Moon Hill Monastery.'

I give John some credit. He closes his eyes for a couple of seconds, but it's more like he's suffering from allergies than, say, he doesn't have a clue what the fuck I'm talking about.

'Oh, really?' John says.

'Yes. And it's too late to get there tonight, but we can

go to Lower Treasure Chicken Village and find a place to stay.'

'Ah.' John sits down in the vacant plastic chair. 'Yes. That's what the bartender told me as well.'

This is what we learned: that Upper Treasure Chicken Village is essentially a railroad stop, that there's nothing much up here that isn't connected with the train, that the patrons at this karaoke bar are mostly railway workers, and as for the girls, they commute from Lower Treasure Chicken Village, which apparently is where the action is.

So, we drink a couple of beers to be polite, and after that, we catch the 2:15 A.M. bus to Lower Treasure Chicken Village with our new friend Madonna.

I can't really say what sort of expectations I have about Lower Treasure Chicken Village, because honestly, I'm not thinking much. I'm stressed out, I'm sleep-deprived, and luckily I'm a little drunk, which makes the being-in-fear-for-my-life thing seem kind of laughable. But what I'm not expecting – and I should know better, given how long I've been in China – is that as our bus trundles down the mountain road, me feeling every bounce and pothole thanks to the non-existent suspension, I look out the window, and spread out below us in the valley is Lower Treasure Chicken Village, and it's not some little Podunk town. It's this fucking *city* in the middle of Bumfuck China. A million people, maybe? Who knows? Who's ever heard of Lower Treasure Chicken Village? Is it in my *Lonely Planet Guidebook*? Hah! Why would it be? What's here? Why would anybody in his right mind come and visit this place? It's just another anonymous white-tile-infested Chinese city in denial, pretending it's a village. There's nothing charming about

311

it. No sights to see. Why would anyone ever go to this pimple on China's backside of beyond?

And yet here we are.

The lights twinkle and wink and seem to ripple as swaths of the city suddenly go dark.

'Oh,' says Madonna, 'another blackout.'

I stare out the mottled Plexiglas bus window, etched with graffiti that I can't read. Outside, the lights stutter, like an engine misfiring and then suddenly catching hold.

'Okay,' Madonna says, resting her manicured nails on my unkempt hand, 'I have a recommendation where you can stay.'

I turn to John. He's hunched over, hugging himself, looking almost sullen.

'What do you think?' I ask him in English.

He shrugs silently.

We get off the bus three stops into Lower Treasure Chicken Village. I have no idea where we are, what part of town this is, what any of it means.

'This is a friend of mine's place,' Madonna babbles. 'You can stay here. Very private.'

We enter through a storefront that I think is a beauty salon or something like that – there are mirrors and chairs and plastic tubs that look like foot-baths, anyway.

We walk up a staircase to the faint sound of Taiwanese pop.

Here's a narrow dark hall with doors on either side. I'm not sure what I'm hearing – a TV, maybe. Somebody laughs.

'No one's using this room,' Madonna says, jiggling a doorknob. 'You can stay here.'

A dark little room with a window overlooking the

street. A hard mattress on the floor. It's stuffy. I go to the window, which is covered by a dust-coated shade, brittle and yellowed from sun and age.

'How much do we owe your friend?' I hear John ask.

Madonna murmurs a figure. 'Ah,' John exclaims, 'are you trying to cut me? Come on. Be reasonable.'

I open the window. The streetlights are out, but there's a big neon sign for a karaoke place across the way that casts a dim green light. I hear it buzz and crackle.

After Madonna leaves, I kick off my shoes and sit down on the narrow mattress. John does the same. 'I think her friend will demand more money from us tomorrow,' he mutters, disgusted.

'I've got some money.'

'People have no morals. They just care about making money.'

I shrug. 'Yeah.'

'There is no trust. That is the biggest problem in China today.'

'Right.'

We sit there in the dark, side by side, for a long, silent moment. 'We should get some sleep,' I finally say. 'And get out of here as soon as we can in the morning.'

'Yes.'

'Okay.'

I lie down and roll over to face the wall. John lies down too. I think he's facing away from me, but I don't look. I'm going to sleep in a bed with Creepy John, and I'm thinking some weird things. Like, if John is just some young businessman with a tragic dissident sister, where did he pick up this weird skill set he has, knowing how to drug people and interrogate them and press his fingers

313

into your neck so it hurts so bad that you can't move?

I stare at the wall, which is tinged green from the neon across the street. I hear John breathing behind me.

He's Cinderfox, I tell myself. And even if I don't really know what that means, he's a friend of Lao Zhang's.

I think.

I reach into my daypack and feel around for my Beanie squid. Here it is. I feel its familiar weight in my hand, the little pellets it's stuffed with beneath the neon orange-and-red plush. Here, around its neck, is the Taoist scroll. And Lao Zhang's letter, naming me manager of his art.

Okay, I think. Okay.

I press Beanie to my chest. I curl in on myself. I will make myself small. I will hide. And I will be safe.

CHAPTER THIRTY

I do sleep – for a while, anyway. Not well. I'm having these dreams about things blowing up. *I'm* not getting blown up; I'm standing back a ways, watching the explosions on the horizon, thinking: I wonder how close this is going to get to me? And there's this plane, like a passenger jet, that's all lit up and on fire, plummeting toward the earth, and I think: should I run? When it hits, is the wreckage going to take me out too? Then there's all this shouting, and I think: I'd better run, right now.

I wake up.

It's still dark, but rectangles of dim light tilt through the window, into the room. The shouting is real. I bolt out of bed and hobble to the window, where John already stands.

'What's going on?' I ask.

'Something. Some protest.'

I look out the window. People pour down the street, carrying signs and flashlights. Some have pots and pans that they're banging together. Others have clubs.

'Shit.'

John checks his watch. 'Not even six A.M. This must be big.'

There are lots of protests in China. Eighty, ninety thousand of them last year at least, over things like illegal land seizures, pollution, unemployment. Farmers get thrown off their land and don't get shit for compensation; a factory complex pollutes so badly that crops die and people get sick and babies are born with deformities – these things happen all the time, even though the central government makes laws that are supposed to prevent it. There are just too many people, too many places like this too far from Beijing where the local authorities do whatever the fuck they want, like a bunch of modern-day warlords.

The Emperor is far away.

People keep coming, banging on their pots in rhythm now.

'Well, hey, at least it's not about us,' I say.

'No,' John says, staring down at the street. 'But I think we should leave. If this gets too bad, maybe riot police come, seal off the town. Then we can't go.'

We gather up our stuff while the crowd passes by, walk as quietly as we can down the stairs, through the storefront, whatever it is – a pedicure place? – where a tiny woman wearing an *Ice Age 2* sweatshirt who looks like she's about a hundred years old shuffles around, spraying the plastic tubs with some mutant offspring of ammonia and jasmine.

'Hey,' she says, her voice a rusty quaver, 'you don't leave without paying.'

'We already paid,' John snaps, steering me toward the door.

'I call the police!' she screeches.

'Shit, John, let's just give her some money.' I pull out a wadded hundred-*kuai* note from my pants pocket, straighten it out, and fold it in half. 'Thanks, Madame, this is a very nice place you have here, and we really like it. Very comfortable.'

She takes the note and gives me the evil eye like I'm some cheap foreign slut.

'That is plenty,' John says, grabbing my wrist. 'Come on. We are going.'

I don't like the way John grabs me, and I pull away. But I follow him out the door.

A few stragglers make their way down the street. There's a vague glow in the sky, not bright enough to cast shadows, but it must be nearly dawn, muted by a thick layer of clouds.

We go down the street in the general direction of the protesters. At the end of the block, John stops and swivels his head, scanning up and down the intersection.

'Where are we going?' I ask.

'Bus station,' he says shortly. 'Or just find a car to hire.'

John pulls out a smartphone from the inside pocket of his jacket. A nice, sleek one that looks brand-new. I peer over his shoulder. He's pulling up maps of China.

'Hey, that's pretty cool,' I say, because it's hard to get good maps in China with stuff labeled. It's like the government's afraid you might find out a state secret if you know how to get around Lower Treasure Chicken Village. 'Where'd you get it?'

He shrugs. 'Online.'

And I'm thinking weird things again, because I've never seen a database of Chinese maps on a smartphone before.

317

Google Earth's mapped Treasure Chicken Village?
Seriously?

Maybe it's some kind of, I don't know, GPS service.
They have GPS mapping for cities like Beijing.

But for Treasure Chicken Village?

Right.

'Okay,' he says. He checks the street sign, checks his
phone, and tilts his head to the right. 'This way.'

We head down the street, turn onto a broader avenue.
The gray sky whitens, seeming to suck the light from the
streetlamps until they hiss and fade. People filter onto the
street, emptying trashcans, sweeping sidewalks, riding
scooters with stacks of plastic cartons strapped flimsily to
the luggage racks. Street vendors set up bowls of congee
and fry *you tiao*, twisted strips of dough, to dip in it. The
normal stuff of daily life.

But now and again I hear something else. Shouts.
Breaking bottles. Wooden spoons banging on pots.

Here's the bus station.

It's basically a big parking lot packed with buses and
a small, low terminal with a shiny plastic façade and
white-tile-clad walls. A couple of taxis wait by the curb.

John approaches one of them.

'Hey,' I say, tugging on his sleeve, 'where are we going?'

'Maybe just to that place you mentioned. Yilin Village,
with the monastery. Do tourist things.'

'Okay. I guess.'

I stand back. Let John handle it. It makes sense for us
to act like tourists. What are our options, really?

If he's some undercover State Security guy, I'm pretty
much fucked anyway.

The taxi John hires is a piece of shit. The seats are

sprung, the seat covers are stained; it smells like gas and sweat and burning wire.

Oh, well.

'What's this protest about?' John asks the driver, as we pull away from the bus station.

'Turtle egg officials and rich men ripping off the common people, like they always do,' the driver says. 'But this time it's too much. The people can't stand for it. Half the town marched yesterday.'

I close my eyes as the driver launches into the saga of the Treasure Chicken Village Rebellion. It has something to do with land seizures and factory layoffs and I don't know what else; I can't understand it all. The dialect here is pretty thick, even though he's trying to speak Mandarin. But I've heard it all before. Like the driver says, it's the same fucking story as always.

'Yesterday we blockade the factory,' the driver says. 'Keep the trucks from leaving. That really pissed them off.'

'And today?' John asks.

'Surround the county government office. Demand justice. People have rights. The laws say so.' He waves his cell phone. 'I get a message, I text everyone I know. Today's demonstration even bigger than yesterday's.'

John settles back in his seat, mouth tight, eyes grim.

We drive a while. I'm not paying too much attention. We're on this road with two lanes, one in either direction. We pass an intersection, a crossroads, where a smaller road climbs up a mountain on one side and winds down a hill on the other.

Up ahead, there's a mob of men blocking the road.

'*Ta ma de!*' the taxi driver yells. He hits the brakes.

The men, six of them, carry clubs. They wear dark clothes. No pots. No protest signs.

'The Party Secretary's dogs,' the driver spits. 'Making sure the protest leaders don't leave town.'

'Turn around,' John says urgently, grabbing his arm. 'Just turn around.' I see him pull out his phone, hit a couple buttons.

The driver shoves the gear into reverse; it grinds, catches, and we jerk backward. He twists the wheel; the tires spin and rubber burns; the car lurches forward, back the way we came.

A car pulls up in front of us, blocking our way back.

'What's going on?' the driver yells, sweat and panic on his face. 'Who are these motherfuckers?'

John ignores him. He puts his hand on mine. 'Ellie, I am going to open the car door and get out. When I do, you should run. Just run.'

That's stupid, I want to say. There's one of you and at least six of them. And I can't run. Not very well. I'll never outrun them.

But I don't have time to say that. John opens the car door.

He gets out, raises his hand, and walks toward the men behind us.

'Hey!' he calls out. 'What's this about?'

I guess this is my cue to run.

A couple of the men take a few steps toward John.

I'm thinking: run where? The road is blocked in both directions. The only way to go is up the mountain road. But it's stupid. I'm never going to get away.

I get out of the car. I run.

I see, out of the corner of my eye, the men swarming

John. I see him kick, hit, see one of the men clutch his knee and fall. Clubs lift and descend.

I run up the road. Stumble a little. I look back over my shoulder.

John's on the ground now; they're kicking him, hitting him with clubs, kicking him in the ribs, the head. He's got his arms raised, trying to ward off the blows, but his arms are sinking, slowly, like they're in water.

I can't say that I like Creepy John, but I'm not going to get away, am I?

So I turn around. And I run toward these guys, screaming, 'Hey! HEY! Leave him alone, you cocksuckers! Leave him alone!'

I'm screaming in English, but I get their attention.

They stop. It's almost funny. They all kind of freeze in various positions, some crouching, some standing, some in mid-kick, and stare at me. Like, who's this crazy bitch?

I don't hear them come up behind me. Arms circle around my waist; fists push up between my ribs, knocking the breath out of me. I gasp as someone kicks my legs out from under me, and before I catch my breath, someone puts a black hood over my head and wrenches my hands behind my back and clamps the flex-cuffs on my wrists, and there are no thoughts in my head, just fear so intense that my mouth tastes like metal.

A shot. I hear gunshots. Two. Three. I can't see; I can't see anything. A hand pushes in the center of my back; another grabs the flex-cuffs and yanks them up. Pain shoots through my shoulders, and I stagger forward. The car, I think we're at the car; my shoulder hits the door-frame; then the hand lets go of the flex-cuffs, pushes my head down, and shoves me forward. I fall inside. The door slams shut.

I just lie there for a minute.

I think: this bag on my head, it smells like one of those woven plastic shopping bags the peasants carry, like a plastic tarp.

I struggle to sit up.

The car door on the other side opens. I hear a cry of pain, sounds of struggle; then the seat bounces, and some-thing – someone – falls against my side with a moan.

'John?' I whisper.

The car door slams. Someone gets in the front seat; I can feel his presence; I know he's there, this solid object that displaces air. Someone else gets in the passenger side, doors slam, then the engine starts, and suddenly we're moving, fast.

'John,' I say. 'John, can you hear me? Are you there?'

'*Bi zui*,' one of them says.

Shut up.

Someone turns on the radio. Chinese hip-hop. '*Daibiao wo hutong*,' the rapper chants. Represent my home.

We hit a pothole. John's head slides down onto my lap. I try to reach him, stretch my hands from behind my back. I strain, and my fingertips graze the back of his neck. I try to reach his carotid to check for a pulse, but I can't.

My fingers come away slick and greasy, and I know it's blood.

I think I can hear him breathing through the plastic hood, over the radio and the engine. I think I hear a rattled breath, filtered through snot and blood. He's not dead, I'm pretty sure. I feel the weight of his head on my thigh, and it's warm, so he can't be dead.

As we drive, I feel the warmth spread, and I realize his blood is soaking me.

I don't know how long we drive. At some point, they switch the radio to a talk show. I can't hear it all that well, but I think it's a call-in show about people's sex problems. Every once in a while the driver and the passenger chuckle in response.

I'm going to die, I think. They're going to kill me. I'm going to die. I'm breathing too fast, I can't breathe in this fucking hood, I'm going to suffocate, I'm going to die.

Shut up, I tell the voice in my head. Just shut the fuck up. I can breathe. And they don't want to kill me: they think I know something.

Okay, I think. Okay. So . . . so what? So they're going to try and get me to tell them things. Things I probably don't even know. Well, okay, I know how that goes. I know the kinds of things they'll do.

Lah lah lah. Stupid cunt.

Oh, Jesus, I think. Can't you help me out here? Can't you give me some strength? So I can suffer, like you did, and still be strong?

But I'm just praying into my hood. No one answers. A part of me thinks that means my faith was never strong enough. That I'm not good enough. Then I think: that's bullshit. You accept Christ as your personal Savior, and it doesn't matter what kind of miserable piece-of-shit sinner you are, what horrible wretched things you've done. You get forgiven anyway. Free pass!

I'm thinking about all this, and there's just silence. No words of comfort from my former best buddy Jesus. There's only me, cut off from the world by the hood. There's John's head in my lap, his ragged breathing and blood. On the radio talk show, the hostess berates a caller, and the driver laughs.

I stretch out my arms so I can touch the back of John's neck again. 'Hang in there, John,' I whisper. 'Keep playing. Okay?'

'Shut up,' the driver says.

Then I know that I'm not forgiven. It matters what I do.

Okay, I think. I've got to do this right.

Shit, I really have to pee.

The car pulls over. Stops, though the engine keeps running. The passenger door opens with a metallic creak. Someone gets out. Opens the back door.

A hand grabs the collar of my jacket and pulls it off my shoulder.

'What are you doing?'

The passenger ignores me. Lifts up the sleeve of my T-shirt.

I don't think. I just react. I jerk back, then slam my head and shoulder as hard as I can at the hand, and I think I hit his head.

'Fuck!' he says. In English.

He slams me back against the car seat. His forearm pushes against my throat, like a metal bar. I can't breathe.

I feel a sharp prick on my shoulder, a burning in the muscle. The arm comes off my throat. I suck in air, gasping.

Oh shit. Oh god. I don't . . .

My breathing slows. I feel the air move through me, like warm water.

I can't lift my head. It's all water.

'Hey,' I manage. 'Hey . . . why'd you do that?' My voice slurs.

'Because you're taking a little trip,' he says.

CHAPTER THIRTY-ONE

Cold. I'm cold.

I open my eyes, and it's all white.

White walls. Cold white light.

I'm lying on my back on a cement floor, one arm flung out, the other shading my eyes from the fluorescent glare.

My leg hurts; my hips and shoulders ache. I remember . . . what?

My mouth tastes like copper.

I try to sit up. Oh, shit, I think I'm going to throw up. My head pounds like it's about to burst.

I lie back down and close my eyes.

When I open them again, I pull my legs up, knees bent, feet on the ground. My legs are bare. I'm wearing a T-shirt. That's it.

Then I remember. My jeans. Blood. And I think maybe I pissed in them. I kind of remember doing that.

I remember a little more. The car. John's head in my lap.

They drugged me.

Where am I?

Small room. White walls. Cement floor. One door. Two metal chairs, one with short legs, like it's built for kids.

I try to sit up again. Slowly. I lean against the wall. Wrap my arms around myself. It's like a meat locker in here.

The door opens. A guy comes in, wearing a tracksuit and a mask – a ski mask – and rubber gloves. The tracksuit is red with yellow trim. Adidas. I can still see his eyes. He's Asian, thick, squat, built like a wrestler.

'Sit in the chair,' he says. He sounds American.

I try to stand up, but I just can't. I'm too dizzy and my head hurts.

He grabs my wrists and pulls me to my feet. I feel the rubber on my skin. He pushes me into the low chair.

'You do what you're told. Understand?'

I think he might be the guy who came to the Liangs' place, to Tongren Village. I nod.

'Stay there.' And he leaves.

So I sit. I sit for what feels like hours, shivering. I stare at the white walls. I think I hear something, the call to prayer from a mosque, so faint I'm not sure, and it reminds me of those times. I think: I can't be there, but maybe I am. How long was I out? I don't have a clue. I could be anywhere. I strain to listen. The chair is hard and too small, the seat at a funny angle, and after a while it hurts for me to sit in it. I'm cold, and I'm so thirsty. My tongue sticks to the roof of my mouth. I think: I can't stand this; I really can't.

Finally, I think: fuck these people. I stand up. My legs and back are so cramped that I almost fall over, but I stay on my feet.

327

Immediately, the door opens. The Chinese (American?) guy strides across the room. Puts his thick hands on my shoulders and shoves me into the chair. 'What did I tell you? What did I tell you?' he yells.

'Fuck you,' I say, voice cracking.

He slaps me across the face. I smell rubber and talcum powder.

'You're going to do exactly what we tell you. Sit in the fucking chair. Don't fucking move.'

He leaves me there.

After a while, I start crying. I don't want to. I know they're watching me. I don't want them to see me cry, but I can't help it.

Then I stop. Wipe the snot off my face with the back of my hand. I stand up.

And in pops the same guy. In my head, I name him Charlie. 'Sit in the fucking chair!' he screams.

I laugh.

He doesn't hesitate. He grabs my wrist and forces it behind my back, pushes down, and the pain nearly drops me to my knees, and I'm in the chair. With his free hand, he pulls a pair of handcuffs out of his pocket. Metal this time. He fastens one ring around my wrist, threads the cuffs around one of the chair's back struts, then secures my other wrist.

'You're going to sit,' he says. 'You wanna play it this way, then that's how we'll play it.'

And he leaves me there.

Hours go by. Maybe days. I notice the subtle gradations of white on the walls. My teeth chatter. My hands feel numb. My shoulders burn. I've got to pee again.

I think: if I don't drink something, I'll pass out.

Then I have a new idea. I'm cuffed to this chair, but that doesn't mean I can't stand up.

I stand. I can't stand up all the way. The cuffs slide along the strut to the backrest, and the fucking chair is heavy. I take a few steps, hunched over, dragging it behind me.

The door flies open, and here's my new best friend.

He hits me. I sit. He yells: 'You think this is some kind of game?'

I look up at him. 'Yeah,' I manage. My lip is bleeding. 'It's called, I stand up and you come running.'

I wait for him to hit me again, but he doesn't. So I keep going: 'It's like, it's like . . .' I laugh; I can't help it, but I can't catch my breath, and it's more like a wheeze. ' . . . musical chairs. You know? Musical chairs. But there's no music. You should work on that.'

Even with the mask on, I can still see his eyes. He looks confused.

'Hey, I need some water,' I say.

'You need to sit down and shut the fuck up,' he says, trying to recover his inner bad-ass.

'I'm dehydrated, you stupid fuck,' I say. 'You wanna keep playing here, you'd better get me some water.'

His fists clench and unclench, like he really wants to do something, but he doesn't know what.

'Come on,' I say. 'What's your problem? You don't wanna get me some water, you can just hit me again. I'm sitting right here. Not going anywhere. Come on, you fucking pussy. Don't you wanna hit me?' I stand up again, lift the chair legs off the ground, take a couple steps balancing the chair on my back like I'm some Chinese peasant with a bushel basket of rice. 'Look, I'm not sitting! Come on! Do your job, asshole!'

He puts me down, of course. It takes a couple of seconds, and I couldn't even tell you how he did it, except suddenly the chair's on the ground, my butt's in the chair, and I feel like I'm going to puke.

He has a roll of duct tape. He doesn't say anything, just pulls off lengths of it, looking pissed off, and he wraps it around my ankles, securing them to the chair legs.

But he doesn't hit me again. He doesn't meet my eyes.

'Heckuva job, man,' I say. 'You should be real proud of yourself.'

He tears off another piece of tape and stretches it across my mouth.

'Shut up,' he says.

Fuck, I am so thirsty.

I guess I do pass out, finally. I can't breathe that well through my nose, and then I can't hold my head up. But when my head falls forward, that wakes me up, and I jerk my head upright, and think, okay, I'm still here.

I can't really stand up with my ankles taped to the chair legs. I can scoot the chair across the cement a little, which makes a really irritating scraping noise. I do that for a while. No one comes in.

Come on, I think. Come on. You can't just leave me here. You can't.

Days go by. Years.

I can't hold it any longer, and I piss myself. The puddle spreads out on the metal chair, drips down my thighs. I stink. I'm wet. I'm cold.

The pain between my shoulders feels like a hand reaching beneath my skin and twisting the muscles.

330

Spasms travel down my back, down my legs, the nerves on fire.

I can't stand it.

I just want to lie down.

I push myself hard, and I fall to one side. I crack my head against the concrete, and the last clear thought I have is: maybe that wasn't so smart.

The door opens; everything seems to be dissolving around the edges, and it's hard for me to hold the picture together. Somebody, Charlie, I think, squats next to me, frees my hands, then my ankles. He half-carries, half-drags me over to the wall and leans me up against it, which is what you're supposed to do with a head injury, keep the head elevated, and I feel like congratulating him for doing the right thing, but then he rips the duct tape off my mouth, and that really fucking hurts, and the pain is like plunging my head in ice water, and all of a sudden I can almost think again.

He checks my pupils with a little flashlight, probes the area around my temple with his fingertips, then says over his shoulder, 'Yeah, she's okay.'

The person he says it to crouches down into my field of vision. He's holding an open bottle of water. I take it, suck it down.

'Told you I needed water,' I say.

It's Suit #1 – the younger, thinner one. Macias.

'You're in a serious situation,' he says.

I want to laugh. 'Really? No shit.' I look around the cold, white room. 'Where's your buddy? Beating on women seems like something he'd like.'

Suit #1 blinks and furrows his brow. 'Why are you escalating this?' he asks.

331

The weird thing is, he sounds genuinely puzzled.

'You threaten me, you kidnap me, and *I'm* the one who's escalating? That is just fucking hilarious.'

Suddenly I realize something. This isn't the scenario they gamed for.

'Oh, I get it,' I say. 'You think I'm this loser headcase, and the minute you started playing Gitmo with me, you figured I'd cave.'

Now I do laugh. 'I mean, you let me keep my T-shirt. That's pretty fucking lame. Don't you get how it's done?'

'You want to us to take it?' Macias asks. 'Because we can make this a lot worse. Is that what you want?'

He stares at me, unblinking.

He'll do it, I know. He'll do whatever needs to be done.

'No,' I say.

He stares at me a moment longer. Then he takes the water bottle out of my hand. Puts it down beside him.

'I want to be very clear with you,' he says. 'We have everything we need to lock you away someplace where you'll never see the sun. You'll live in a cell. You'll never see a lawyer. You won't get visits from the Red Cross, or from your friends and family either. We can do that. Do you understand?'

I don't say anything. I don't nod. I stare back at him. My heart's pounding in my chest, the sweat's pouring off me like water, and I know I'm not fooling him. But I'm not saying anything. I'm not.

He reaches into his suit pocket. 'We have this paper,' he says, 'assigning you authority to manage Zhang's artwork and finances. Where did you get it?'

I shrug. 'He left it for me.'

'Who gave it to you?'

'I found it.'

'Bullshit.'

'At his place,' I improvise. 'In the frame of one of his paintings.'

Okay, it sounds like a bad spy movie. But I see the doubt in Suit #1's eyes.

'I don't know where he is,' I state, and this should sound plausible, because I really don't know. 'I don't know where the Uighur is either.'

'Then what was it you were doing? You said you could get us the information we needed. We gave you time to cooperate. You went to Taiyuan, Pingyao, Xi'an, and Chengdu. You had us chasing you all through China. You wasted our time. Why?'

I stare down at the bare concrete floor. Is this it? Is this what I'm going to see, from now on? White walls and gray cement?

'I got scared.' I make my voice small. It's not hard. 'I didn't know what to do, and I got scared. I got on the first train I could catch. Then, I just, I just kept going.'

I look up at him. I figure I must look pretty pathetic. His expression is a blank. I can't tell if he's buying this or not.

'The man you were with,' Suit #1 says flatly. 'Zhou Zheng'an. Who is he? How do you know him?'

'Oh, John?' It suddenly comes back to me, John's bloody head on my lap. 'He's just, he's just a guy. A guy I met in Beijing. He, he kind of has a thing for me. He was going to Chengdu, for business. He said maybe I should go there. We could . . .' I look away. 'You know. Get together.'

'Why did you get off the train?'

'Because of the temple. The, the Moon temple. John said it was nice. And a good place for us to, just, hang out.'

Suit #1 stares at me. He knows I'm lying, I'm pretty sure.

'Look, I was lonely. I needed . . . I needed someone . . . to just . . .' My voice trails off, caught in my throat.

'Is John okay?' I ask then. And I really want to know. 'Where is he?'

'He's being taken care of,' Suit #1 says.

For a moment, I'm so scared that I almost tell him everything.

No, not scared. Hopeless. Like, what's the point? Just tell him. We're all fucked anyway. What difference does it make?

You said you wouldn't tell, I tell myself. So, don't.

He stares at me. I look into his eyes, and I see it all. What he's done. What he's willing to do.

I know I can't win.

But I don't look away.

Then, a funny thing happens: Suit #1's phone rings. His ring tone is a song by Tupac.

'Yeah?'

He listens. Something in his expression shifts. He stands up and paces toward the door.

I just sit there.

Suit #1 signals to my buddy Charlie, who's been standing beside me like a block of wood. The two of them leave.

And here I am, by myself again. But nobody's ordering me to sit in a chair.

I lean against the wall, shivering. Tilt my head back, close my eyes, and think about things. I think about sitting on the couch at Lao Zhang's place, watching him paint. I think about these goofy Chinese girls who got up that last karaoke night at Says Hu and tried to do some ghetto hip-hop number.

I think about Trey, and the things we did together.

Finally, Charlie comes back in, a pair of sweats draped over one arm. He's holding something else too, a tall plastic tumbler.

He tosses the sweats at me. 'Put these on.'

I do, teeth chattering.

'Here.'

He holds the tumbler out to me. It's pink, with cartoon characters on it. I can smell the alcohol.

'Wow, Hello Kitty,' I say.

'Drink this.'

I think about objecting. I think about spitting it in his face.

What's the point?

I take it. I drink. Vodka.

I get about halfway down and stop. 'I can't drink any more.'

'Finish it.'

I can feel the tears, and I tell myself, don't. Don't give in.

Keep playing.

'Why? What are you gonna do?'

'Drink it.'

I think: he'll pour it down my throat if I don't.

I take a few more swallows. I have these weird thoughts, like this is a movie, right? Where they get somebody drunk, and then, I don't remember what happens after that. A car crash or something.

My stomach twists. Bile rises up in my throat.

'That's it,' I manage. 'I can't drink any more.'

He takes the cup. Looks to see how much vodka is left. Looks at me.

I'm feeling kind of loaded.

'Okay,' he says. He reaches into his pocket. 'Put these on.'

He hands me these, these sunglasses. Like ones you'd wear for skiing, almost like goggles. Dark.

I try to put them on, but I miss my head and stab myself in the eye with an earpiece.

Shit. I am so wasted.

'Oh, man, this is ridiculous,' I say.

'Here,' Charlie says, exasperated. He puts the glasses on me. I see them coming, like they're this special effect in a movie. The bad spaceship. Big black glasses, blotting out everything.

Then I can't see.

'Don't take them off,' he says. 'Don't even try. Or I'll cuff you. Understand?'

'Yeah,' I say. Then I laugh. Sure, I understand. Right.

'Shit,' he mutters. 'Okay, we're standing up now.'

He helps me up. Guides me to the door. I can't see a fucking thing.

I don't know where I'm going. I have no idea. I'm stumbling around in the dark with this guy holding me up. I think we turn and turn again, but that might just be me. There's an elevator, I'm pretty sure. Going down. At one point, I collapse. The glasses come loose. I see, glimpse, concrete stained with oil. A car tire. An open car door.

A hand pushes the glasses back on.

336

'In you go,' says Charlie. He guides me into the car. The door slams. The car lurches back, then forward.

We drive and drive. Everything's spinning.

Somebody sits in the back seat with me, making sure I don't peek.

I think it's Suit #1. It must be. Because after we've driven for hours, forever, he puts his hand on my shoulder and says to me: 'This is what I want you to understand. We will be watching you. We'll be listening to you. Always, from here on out. There's no place you can go where we can't find you. So don't try to run. There's no such thing as running. Are we both clear on that?'

I'm staring into the inky black. I can see patterns in it if I really try.

'Uh-huh,' I say.

The car slows. Stops. 'Here's where you get off.'

The door opens. Somebody helps me out. My butt hits cold concrete. I hear a muffled thud as something lands next to me.

'Don't turn around,' Suit #1 says.

Hands take off the glasses.

I blink in the night.

Behind me, with a soft squeal of tires and a low hum of its engine, the car pulls away.

My head falls back. A streetlight, glowing around the edges. A tall building. Lift up your head, I tell myself. Hard to do when your head feels like a big lead balloon.

In front of me, gates. Cheerful signs. Little cartoon kids. Trees. Grass. A park. It's dark. Night. A lone worker sweeps the gutter with a straw broom. I see big characters on the sign: 'North . . . something . . . park.'

337

I'm still in China.

I pat around on the sidewalk next to me.

Here's my day pack. My jacket. My shoes.

My mouth feels like about a hundred miles of bad road. My stomach – I think I'm going to be sick.

I throw up in the gutter.

A couple of guys walk past, stare for a moment, and continue on.

'Okay,' I mutter. 'Okay.' I fumble with my shoes. Get them on my feet. Try to tie them.

I stand up, and I can tell I'm really loaded.

For a minute, I think about approaching the street sweeper over by the park entrance. Asking 'Hey, did you see who brought me here? How they dumped me out on the sidewalk?'

But what's the point? Chinese people mostly mind their own business. There's an expression for it – *ma mu* – meaning 'wooden-headed.'

Numb.

Nobody's going to have noticed anything, and so what if they did? What would it prove?

'Ha, I'm gonna go to *The New York Times*,' I mumble, stumbling down the street. 'Gonna go to CNN. To Huffington Post! Tell 'em all about this shit. Ha-ha.'

Where the fuck am I?

I walk and walk and walk.

I get so tired. My leg hurts. My head hurts too.

Finally, I stop and hold on to a skinny tree trunk. Close my eyes. Still not as dark as the glasses, I think.

'Miss? Miss?'

I open my eyes. A taxi. A Beijing taxi.

'You want taxi?' A cab driver, brown wrinkled face,

338

tea-stained teeth. Straining to get the English words out through a thick Beijing accent.

I burst into tears.

'Yeah,' I say, snuffling into my sweatshirt. 'Yeah.'

CHAPTER THIRTY-TWO

The cab driver, my new best friend, gives me a lecture as we drive down the 4th Ring Road.

'You see, this is a problem with modern society. You meet strangers. You don't know what kind of people they are. You shouldn't be so trusting.'

'True,' I agree.

It would have been simpler if I'd kept my mouth shut, but I'm drunk. And maybe high on something else – who knows what else was in that vodka, and the Suits sure like their drugs. So I told the cab driver a story about how I was out at this club and I met these two guys and they put something in my drink. I didn't say what happened after that, but the driver wants to take me to a hospital or, alternately, Public Security.

'That's okay.'

'Maybe you're right, Public Security is worthless. But I know some other people . . .'

He starts hinting about some cousins of his with Triad connections; at least, I think that's what he's getting at.

'I just want to go home,' I blurt out.

'Okay, okay. *Nide jia zai nar?*'

Where is your home?

I laugh to myself.

We're at the northern end of Chaoyang District. 798 Factory is near here. So is the Capital Airport. I get that urge again, the one that says: go to the airport. Catch the next plane out. Just like when I went to the train station and took the train to Taiyuan.

Maybe that's not the best way for me to think any more.

Mati Village, I think. That's where my stuff is. I could go there, even though it's kind of far.

Then I realize, I don't even know if I have any money.

I check inside my backpack. Flick on the little flashlight I keep attached to the ring inside. Well, that's still there.

So is everything else. Here's my iPhone. My wallet, with 2,000-plus yuan still inside. My passport, in the hidden pocket.

Here's Beanie squid. With the Taoist fortune and Lao Zhang's letter tied around its neck.

That's just weird.

For a moment, I think: Treasure Chicken Village, John getting beat up, the little cement room – maybe none of that really happened. But I know it did. I guess I just somehow hope that really wishing it hadn't might make it so.

My head pounds, and I think I might throw up again.

All I want to do is lie down.

If you find yourself in town, and you need somewhere to stay, feel free to use this place. Just ring the bell.

Harrison told me that.

341

'Miss? Where do you want to go?'

I give him the address.

It's just like Harrison said so long ago. It feels like years. How long ago was that? Two weeks?

It's the middle of the night, and I don't even know what day it is.

But I ring the bell, and the housekeeper answers.

Of course, Miss, Mr Harrison is happy to have you as his guest. You should treat this like your home.

Harrison isn't there. Didn't he tell me that he hardly ever was?

'Please,' I ask, 'can you tell me when Mr Harrison is returning?'

'Mmm, not sure. But maybe on Tuesday.'

I'm too embarrassed to ask how far that is from now.

So here I am, in Harrison's empty luxury penthouse. His gallery. The air conditioning whispers; the air is vaguely scented with cedar.

I wander around in my bare feet. Dangle my toes in the channeled fountain. Stare at the art.

Looking at the work here, I think Lao Zhang's paintings really are good. They're about something. I'm not sure what, but I can tell, they're real. Substantial. No wonder Harrison wants some for his collection.

I'm going to do the right thing, I vow. I'm going to make sure they're protected. Appreciated.

Lao Zhang trusts me. I'm not going to fuck up.

I stagger into the bedroom I stayed in last time. No pajamas on the bed. I search the dresser drawers and find a stack of silk pajamas, still in their wrappers.

Funny, I think. I wonder who else stays here. How

many women? Or how many men? I'm really not sure, in Harrison's case.

I pick a pair I think will fit and change in the bathroom. Brush my teeth. Stare at my face in the mirror. Yeah, I look like shit. There's a bruise spread across my cheek. How did that happen?

Oh, yeah. When I landed on the concrete floor.

The swollen lip . . . Right. I remember that too. When he hit me.

I fall into the large soft bed. Eventually the room stops spinning. And finally I sleep. Or pass out. Sometimes it's hard to tell.

The next morning, the coffee is already brewing when I wander into the kitchen. 'For breakfast, what would you like?' the housekeeper asks.

'Anything is fine.'

I sit at the dining table. Here's a laptop, with an open browser.

I click on to Yahoo. It's Friday, April 23. 10:12 A.M.

I try to think. I lost . . . I lost . . . two days? Three? I can't remember.

The housekeeper brings me coffee, a bowl of tofu with pickled vegetables, a croissant, and a bowl of fruit.

'Thanks,' I say vaguely. I surf the Net a while.

I think about checking my e-mail.

Why not? If the Suits can find me no matter where I go and no matter what I do, what difference does it make?

Something stops me. Something about not wanting to involve Harrison, even if I already have, just by being here.

Or something about how he might be one of them.

I really should leave.

But I don't. Instead, I sit around in silk pajamas and watch TV. Nap. Eat the great meals and drink the tea and fine wine brought to me by the housekeeper, a woman from Fujian nicknamed Annie who treats me like I'm a convalescent. Which in a way I guess I am.

I don't check my e-mail. I don't try to log on to the Game.

Nobody bothers me. No one at all. If the Suits know where I am, they choose to leave me alone.

After three days of this, when the bruise on my face has faded to a light green, I figure it's time to go.

I thank Annie for her kindness and tell her to give Harrison my thanks for his hospitality.

Then I go out into the world.

It's blistering hot. First thing, I go to the nearest mall and buy myself a couple of T-shirts and some shorts. I used to hate wearing shorts because of the scars on my leg; but now I think: fuck it. It's hot.

I ride the escalators up and down. Have a bite to eat at the food court in the basement. Stop in at Starbucks and order a latte. Listen to the Afro-pop they're playing today.

Then I find a Net bar.

The clerk here asks for my passport. I hand it over. I don't much care any more. She enters it into a computer. Damn, I think, that's actually efficient. But then this is a classy-looking Net bar. No gaming posters on the wall. An espresso-and-tea station along with the usual cold drinks. Comfortable chairs.

I log in to my e-mail.

My inbox is loaded.

I answer Lucy Wu first: 'Hi, Lucy, I'm back in town

now. Let me know when you'd like to have lunch. I might have some ideas on that exhibit you're interested in.'

Read an e-mail from one of my buddies, that dog Turner: 'Hey, Baby Doc, hope this finds you doing okay. Guess where I am? Ha ha, that's right, redeployed to the sandbox. Ain't life a bitch? But I'm in KBR-land, near the Pizza Hut, so I guess I won't complain too bad. Attached is a recent pic of me and the family. The new addition is baby Nicole, she's seven months.

'Take care of yourself, Doc.'

KBR-land is a section of Joint Base Balad. It's like Little America, they tell me. Most of the guys never leave the base. Same thing with the other three bases they built, bases with air-conditioned Conexes wired with the Internet, football fields, Pizza Huts, and, yeah, Grande Mochachinos.

But still.

Another buddy in the kill zone, in the war without end.

I write him back. Give him some shit and tell him I'm fine and say what a good-looking family he has.

There are a bunch of e-mails from my mom.

'Well, it looks like I'm taking the Sunrise job,' she says in one of them. 'Things will be a little tight but I feel that this is what God wants for me and with His help, everything will work out fine. Hope you're okay sweetie. Write me, would you? It makes me nervous when I don't hear from you for a while.'

I blink a few times and stare at the screen.

'Hi Mom,' I finally type. 'Sorry I haven't written sooner. I got kind of sick while I was traveling. Nothing serious but I slept a lot and couldn't get to an Internet bar for a few days. I'm back in Beijing now. Everything's fine.'

345

I hesitate. I just can't decide what needs to be said right now.

Then I think of something.

'Remember that e-mail you sent me? The one about the kid playing piano, with the famous musician telling him to keep playing? That was good advice. Thanks for that.'

I hit send.

There's nothing from Trey.

What did they tell him, I wonder? The Suits. What did they say? 'Hey, no need to worry about your wife any more, 'cause we're taking care of that problem for you. Enjoy life with your girlfriend, buddy!'

Why did they let me go?

I find Harrison's card with his e-mail address and write a note thanking him for letting me stay in his apartment. I want to say something, to explain how fucked up I was, how much I needed some sort of refuge, some quiet place. But what can I say? How can I explain?

'Hope I didn't take too much advantage of your offer,' I write. 'But I really appreciate it. I wasn't feeling too well and having somewhere to stay in town for a couple days really helped me out. Thanks again.'

I should send some flowers, I think. Something for Annie. I'll do that, I decide. I have to learn how to do that kind of stuff. How to do it right.

Hey, if this thing with Lao Zhang's art works out, I'll cut Harrison a good deal.

I go through every e-mail. Even the stuff that looks like spam. Just to make sure that there isn't some hidden message, some communication from the Great Community.

Nothing.

I log on to the Game, using a proxy. I figure I'd better not try using Chuckie's anonymizer, not since the Suits got their hands on it.

Little Mountain Tiger is where I left her, sitting in front of the Yellow Mountain Monastery gate.

'Hail, the Great Community.'

No one answers. I sit for a while. Listen to the wind howl through the peaks of the Yellow Mountains.

By the time I log out, it's about five o'clock.

Out on the street, it's as hot as it was before, and the wind has kicked up, carrying with it a haze of yellow dust. I walk a ways. I don't know where I'm going. Mati Village, I guess. Eventually.

Where I am now, it's all apartment blocks, office buildings, broad streets, and traffic.

I'm tired. My chest aches from breathing dust. I see a Mexican restaurant, the Sombrero Café, on the first floor of a new tower, a squat space with a thick, tinted Plexiglas window. It looks like it's being crushed by all that weight above it.

In spite of that, I go inside. I'm thinking maybe I'll try their fajitas.

But I'm not really hungry. I sit at the bar and order a beer.

It's dark and cool in here, at least. Embroidered sombreros and piñatas dangle from the ceiling. The chips are passable, the salsa oddly spiced, and the bar is fake walnut.

I drink the beer down and order a second. I'm thinking about, I don't know, cement rooms and lying on that hard mattress next to Creepy John.

I'm pretty spaced out. Disassociating again.

Which is why I sit there like an idiot when Suit #2 – the older, meaner one – slides onto the stool next to me.

'Calm down, Doc,' he says immediately. 'I'm just here for a drink.'

He lifts his hand. 'Tequila. Reserva de la Familia. Two.'

I unfreeze. 'What the fuck do you want?'

'Like I said.'

The bartender, a guy who actually looks Mexican, comes over with two shots of tequila.

Suit #2 – Carter – pounds his down. 'Keep it coming,' he says. He turns to me. 'Come on, aren't you gonna join me? All that time you spent in Arizona, I figure you must like tequila. And this is the good stuff.'

'I don't want it.'

'Shit. Considering I liberated your ass, the least you could do is have a drink with me.'

I should leave. I know I should. 'What do you mean?' I ask.

'Listen, if it were up to Macias, you'd still be a PUC.'

Person under control.

I sip the tequila. It really is good.

'Fucking cowboy,' Suit #2 says, tossing back his second shot. 'Guys like that, they just make everything harder.'

'I don't get it,' I say. 'Why did you help me?'

'We don't do that kind of shit to our fellow Americans.' Then he snorts with laughter. 'Much.'

The bartender comes over and refills our glasses.

'You threatened me,' I say. 'You told me there'd be consequences.'

'Yeah, well, I was trying to *scare* you, sweetie. See, that's the thing. Most of the time, you let people know what they're up against, they fold.'

'And if they don't?'

'Well . . .' Suit #2 contemplates his shot glass. 'Well, that all depends on what's at stake.' He turns to me and smiles. 'Hey, we're the good guys, remember? Macias was just fucking with you. He probably would've let you go eventually.'

I drink more tequila. I'm feeling this energy. It might be rage.

'I don't get it,' I say.

'We can't have people fucking with us,' Suit #2 explains patiently. 'We're operating in a tough neighborhood. That means you gotta show you're strong. Someone like you, maybe you think you can yank my chain and get away with it. But those aren't the rules any more, okay? You fuck with us, we fuck you back, and it's asymmetrical warfare, honey. The guns are on our side.'

It's not like I don't know this. It's not like I didn't see it, before. Except I was on the other side back then.

A gun doesn't care what it shoots.

'So why'd you help me?' I ask again. 'If you really did.'

'Fucking Macias, he never knows where the line is,' Suit #2 says, disgusted. 'You fuck with an American citizen, that's a whole clusterfuck, right? But Macias, he's impatient. He's gotta get what he wants right away.'

Suit #2 stares off at some point in the middle distance. There's no way I want to know what he's seeing.

'If you hadn't called, I would've brought you in,' he finally says. 'But not like that. That was over the top.'

I almost laugh. 'So . . . what? You felt sorry for me?'

He shrugs. 'Big fucking drama for no reason. I got us what we needed my way.'

I don't want to ask. But I have to. 'Lao Zhang?'

'Nah. He's the Chinese government's problem. Too bad. He'd be better off with us.' He signals the bartender. 'Just bring us the bottle, okay?'

There were two things they wanted. Lao Zhang was one.

'The Uighur?'

'Mmm-hmmm.' Suit #2 tops off our shot glasses. 'Thanks to you.'

'Me? But . . . I didn't know anything.'

''Course you didn't. But I got a tip. From somebody who did know something. You know, it's horse-trading.'

'I don't understand,' I say. But I already do, at least part of it. Before he even says it.

'I want something; my new buddy wants something. So, Macias grabbing you, that wasn't totally wasted. He gave me something to trade. Something that was worth more to my new buddy than that poor pathetic son-of-a-bitch Uighur.' He lifts up his glass in a mock toast. 'Here's to you, sweetie. The superior horse.'

The tequila I've had burns in my empty gut like acid.

'Is this someone I know?' I ask shakily.

'You think I'm gonna tell you that?'

'What about the Uighur?'

'What about him?'

'What happened to him?'

'You really wanna know?'

I think about this. I stare at the shot glass. Fuck him, I think, and his stupid macho drinking contest. I take a sip. 'Yeah. I do.'

'Traded him to Uzbekistan,' Suit #2 replies, almost merrily. 'Poor ol' Hashim's an Uzbek national. Regime wanted him for subversion. Of course, it doesn't take much to be a subversive in Uzbekistan. Nasty mother-fuckers. You know they like to boil dissidents alive?'

'I didn't know they had Uighurs in Uzbekistan,' I say stupidly.

'Yeah. Lots of them.'

I just sit there. What am I supposed to say to this? Finally, I come up with: 'Why?'

'Natural gas. Oil. Bases. You heard of the Shanghai Cooperative Organization?'

I shake my head.

'Joint security and development group. China, Russia, and a bunch of the 'Stans: Uzbekistan, Kyrgyzstan, Kazakhstan, couple others I can't remember. Lovely bunch of dictators and assholes, doing their best to cut us off from Central Asian energy markets. So, we run a counteroffensive, okay? Do these guys some favors. Cut them some deals. You want a quesadilla?'

I don't get to answer this question, because Suit #2 has already signaled the bartender and ordered two quesadillas, along with a side of guacamole, before I can even open my mouth.

'Couple of years ago, some of the liberals at State got their panties in a wad about Uzbekistan's human rights violations,' he continues. 'Made a big public boo-hoo about it. We lost our military base there. We want it back. Thus, the Uighur. See, he's their superior horse. We give them the Uighur as a gesture of good faith. They see we can deliver. They give us something back. Simple, right?'

'You're fucking sick.'

He laughs. 'Like your hands are clean. C'mon, honey. You think I don't know what you and your hubby did in the war?'

If you're going to get gut-punched, it might as well be while holding a shot of tequila. I drink.

'I didn't do anything,' I say. I sound like a sullen kid.

'Oh, that's right. You just helped.'

'I treated detainees. That's it.'

'A regular Suzy Nightingale.'

I let that go. 'I was a medic. What was I supposed to do?'

'You could've blown the whistle. You could've told someone.'

'I got blown up, remember?'

Suit #2 shrugs. 'You wanna tell yourself that, go right ahead.'

I think about what he's said. But it's not like I haven't thought about it before.

'I had a few weeks,' I finally say. 'Maybe a month between when I figured out what was going on and when I got hurt. I was confused. But I didn't hurt anyone. I treated a few detainees. I did my job.'

Suit #2 laughs and pours us both more tequila. 'You signed off on it, sweetie. You signed their reports. You gave them cover. "Injured during extraction." Or maybe you didn't do paper on a few of them at all. Right?'

I don't say anything. I can't.

'All you had to do was tell the truth,' he says, like it was no big deal, like we're talking about copping to a traffic ticket, 'if you really gave a shit. Maybe you could have stopped it. Ever think about that?'

Like it was the easiest thing in the world.

'Fuck you,' I whisper. 'I was nineteen years old.'

'Sorry,' he says, without an ounce of sympathy. 'You don't get a pass for that.'

I feel like I'm shrinking into myself again. Like I want to hide forever. Like I've felt for almost seven years.

I can't feel this way any more.

'Yeah, okay,' I say. 'I was young and stupid. But I've learned. So what's your excuse?'

He grins. 'If I told you, I'd have to kill you.'

Our food arrives. Believe it or not, I eat some. I figure I'd better.

'What happened to John?' I think to ask.

'John?' he says, between bites of guacamole-covered quesadilla.

'Zhou Zheng'an. The guy I was with when your pals grabbed me. He got beat up really bad.'

'Oh, that guy?' He takes the salsa bowl and dumps a puddle on his quesadilla. 'Shipped him off to Kabul.'

Then Suit #2 gives me that shit-eating grin and tops off my tequila. 'Just kidding. They dropped him at some rathole hospital out in the boonies. He was alive when we left him there. Hopefully they didn't kill him.'

After that, I don't have much appetite. Suit #2 does, though. He finishes off his quesadilla, using the last wedge to wipe up the remains of the guacamole.

Then he slaps a stack of hundred-yuan notes on the bar. 'Well, I'm outta here. I'll try to keep Macias off your back. But you better be smart. You start acting stupid, there's not much I can do.'

I nod. What can I say?

Then I think of something. 'How'd you guys keep finding me?'

'Trade secret,' he says with a snort.

'Give me a hint.'

He considers. 'Well, we don't depend on any one thing.

Redundancy, right? So, we have our HUMINT, and we have our SIGINT – the high-tech stuff.' He leans toward me, like he's about to share a particularly juicy piece of gossip. 'Take your passport. It's got an RFID chip embedded in it. That chip's got all kinds of personal information.'

I've actually heard of this. RFID chips are in a lot of stuff these days – passports, ID badges, keycards, cars, consumer goods. They track goods and people from one point to another.

'But that only works at short range,' I say. 'The chip has to be within a couple of feet of a scanner.'

'Unless it's active, with its own power source. We can pick those up from satellites. How's about *that* for Big Brother?'

He grins again and pats me on the shoulder. 'Hey, I'm just giving you shit. Your passport doesn't have one of those.' He tops off my shot glass one last time. 'Tequila's on me. Enjoy.'

CHAPTER THIRTY-THREE

I take the tequila with me – he's right, it's good stuff – and even after I pay the tab, I've got about nine thousand yuan left over. That's pretty funny, I think. Like, a thousand bucks or whatever it is these days is some kind of bribe? What's to stop me from going to some journalist and telling them everything that's happened to me?

Aside from the fact that I have no proof of anything and it all sounds pretty crazy, that is.

The Suits know it. They've got nothing to worry about.

I use some of the money Suit #2 left on the bar and hire a cab to take me to Mati Village.

Lao Zhang's place looks the same as I left it, like no one else has been here in the meantime. Who knows if that's true?

I don't do much my first night here – drink some beer, watch movies, surrounded by stacked canvases and the smell of paint thinner.

The next day, I wake up pretty early, fix myself a double espresso, find a notepad and a pen, and do some work.

I have no clear idea what I should do, but I figure I should start with an inventory, get an idea of what's here. There's a lot, I don't know how many canvases stacked up against the walls of the main room and bedroom and kitchen, and then I remember that there's a storeroom on the side of the house as well.

What I do is, I assign a number to each piece, starting with the ones in the bedroom, and I describe the subject and the size next to it. Lao Zhang made things a little easier for me by writing the date of each work under his signature. I have a vague memory of him doing this each time he finished a piece.

I work all morning, and I realize that it's going to take me a while to go through everything. Besides paintings, there are photographs, DVDs of performance pieces, and video art. Jesus. This is the work of someone's life, and Lao Zhang's no slacker. As I recall, he has a storage space at the Warehouse as well.

Around two in the afternoon, it occurs to me that I haven't eaten anything other than a small bag of snack crackers I found in the kitchen, and I'm getting pretty hungry.

I decide to go to the *jiaozi* place.

It's after the lunch rush, and the restaurant is pretty quiet, just a few young guys leaning back against the wall in one corner, drinking beer and smoking cigarettes. I order some dumplings and green vegetables and a Yanjing beer. I have the strangest feeling, like if I sit here long enough Lao Zhang will walk in, dressed in some raggedy old T-shirt and skullcap, sit down and order up another round of *jiaozi*. He won't talk much – he hardly ever does – but he'll smile in that crooked way of his and every now and then look up, thick shoulders hunched over his

356

plate, and try to explain to me what some painting or performance piece is really about. It used to be when he'd talk about stuff like that, I'd lean back in my chair and nod and drink my beer, and most of what he said would go right by me.

I'm thinking now, I'm ready to listen, and I could really use a few explanations.

I could use his company even more. Just having him sitting here, eating *jiaozi* with me.

I'm almost done eating when Sloppy Song and that Western woman, Francesca Barrows, walk in. The two of them scan the room, stopping when they see me. They seem surprised. Concerned, even.

'*Yili, hao jiu bu jian*,' Sloppy says.

Long time no see.

'*Ni hao*. I've been a little busy.' I gesture at the table. 'Please join me.'

They sit. Sloppy tugs on her braid in a way that looks more pissed-off than distracted.

'You're at Lao Zhang's place?' Sloppy asks.

'Yeah. Trying to do an inventory of his art.' I watch her closely, thinking that she could easily be one of the players in the Game, and it's not so much what she asks me as what she doesn't.

'Good. You going to the Warehouse?'

'The Warehouse? I was going to do that last.'

'Don't wait,' Francesca says. 'Haven't you heard?'

'I've been out of town. Heard what?'

And at that, Sloppy bursts into a torrent of heavily accented Chinese, most of which I can't understand, but I catch 'government,' 'demolish,' 'vacation homes,' and, I think, 'auto dealership.'

357

'Auto?' I repeat.

'Volkswagens,' Francesca spits out. 'Fucking bastards.'

'Wait. What?' I ask.

Sloppy tugs on my sleeve. 'Better you see.'

We walk a block on Heping Street and turn the corner onto the street leading to the Warehouse.

For a moment, I don't know where I am.

There used to be a bunch of outbuildings ringing the Warehouse: residences, little shops, a couple of restaurants, all decrepit and seeming on the verge of collapse. Now one side of this is gone, smashed into rubble. Migrants in tattered trousers and T-shirts pick through the piles, separating bricks from trash. Bulldozers are parked to the side, their toothed jaws slack and empty. Waiting for their next meal.

'What happened?' I ask.

'The government's seized the land around the Warehouse,' Francesca says in clipped, bitter tones. 'They've ordered it demolished to make way for vacation condominiums and a car dealership. They're planning additional land seizures in Mati Village as well. The area where Lao Zhang lives, for one.'

Vacation homes I can kind of get. It's pretty scenic around here, actually. But a car dealership? Do people buy cars when they're on vacation?

'What's this really about?' I ask.

Sloppy shakes her head.

It could be what Lao Zhang and I had talked about before. The government doesn't like it when too many people get together with a common purpose. Even if that purpose is just making art.

Then there's Lao Zhang. If the Suits were flipping out

about him, god knows what the Chinese government's doing.

Maybe this is their response. They can tear down what he helped to build.

'Is there anything . . . ? I mean . . .'

Sloppy shakes her head again.

'I've contacted a number of Western media outlets,' Francesca says. '*The Guardian* and the *LA Times* are interested in doing stories. But that won't stop this.'

'What would?' I ask.

'Short of massive bribes . . . I can't think of anything.'

I think about this. 'What about Harrison?'

'Harrison Wang?' Francesca lifts an eyebrow. 'I can't say I'm on those sorts of terms with him.'

Can I say that I am?

'I could let him know what's going on,' I offer. 'Maybe he might have some ideas.'

'I suppose it couldn't hurt,' Francesca says, but it's clear from the way she says it that she doesn't think there's a chance in hell it'll do any good.

Inside the Warehouse, people are packing up exhibits, gathered in small knots engaged in tense conversations.

I approach a group where I know a couple of people – Xiao Zhang and this photographer, Fuzhen. They're sitting with a couple of guys I don't recognize on a sprung couch next to a video installation, drinking tea and eating sunflower seeds.

'*Ni hao,*' I say uncertainly, because even though I hang out here, I'm not really a part of it, and what I'll lose is only a small piece of their loss.

'*Yili, ni zenme yang?*' Xiao Zhang asks. He gestures at the couch.

'Okay. Busy.' I sit.

Fuzhen pours me some tea in a plastic cup. 'Heard from Lao Zhang?' she asks.

'Not for a while. But he asked me to look after his art.' We all sit in silence for a minute.

'How long before they knock this down?' I finally ask.

'Not sure,' Fuzhen says. 'One official says he can delay it a few days. But we can't be sure he's in charge.'

That's typical. You got one guy who tells you one thing and another who says the opposite, and it's not necessarily that either one of them is lying; it's just that it's not clear who has the authority to decide.

'What are you going to do?' I ask.

'Looking at a space in the Wine Factory,' one of the men I don't know replies.

'Maybe Tongzhou. Maybe Caochangdi,' Fuzhen says.

'I don't know,' says Xiao Zhang.

At the back of the Warehouse are a bunch of storerooms. Inside the storage space belonging to Lao Zhang are more canvases, a couple of stacks of dusty boxes of CDs, DVDs, and VHS tapes, binders of photos and negatives, some odds and ends that might be sculpture or might be junk. There's a lot of stuff here. I'll need a truck to get it all out.

I spend a while trying to figure out what's there, take some notes, try to determine how big a truck I'll need and where I'm actually going to put all of this once I move it.

I debate about whether I should call Harrison or e-mail him, and settle on the electronic. Not because I'm paranoid that my phone is a global tracking device – who knows? Maybe it is. Maybe I've got a microchip in my butt, for all I know.

I decide on e-mail so I can think about what I want to say, so I can say it right.

I go to Comrade Lei Feng's (how long will this place last if they tear down the Warehouse and start evicting artists?) and log in to my e-mail account.

'Dear Harrison,' I type. 'I'm back in Mati Village. I found out that Lao Zhang wants me to handle his art while he's away. It's a lot of work, and I hope I can do a good job with it. Things are a little complicated here, though.'

I go on from there, explaining what the government is planning. And I finish with: 'I'm wondering if you might have any ideas of any options we could pursue. This is a great place, and it would be really sad to see it destroyed. Best, Ellie.'

Then I go home. I mean, I go to Lao Zhang's. It's not really home. I don't know how much longer it will even be here.

The next morning, I get up and make myself a double espresso and try to figure out what I should do first. Hire a truck, I guess, and move the stuff out of the Warehouse and bring it over here. Even if the plan is to tear down this block of studios, no one's come and painted '*chai*' on the wall yet. I probably have a little time.

But then what?

I'm thinking: Lucy Wu. She's been all hot to arrange for an exhibit – unless, of course, that was all bullshit and she's just another operative – but if she really does have some fancy art gallery, maybe I can work a deal with her for storage.

I'm thinking about all this when someone knocks on the door.

I almost drop my coffee cup. Okay, I think. Okay. Deep breaths. Public Security, the Suits, some random Beijing officials – I'm just hanging out. I don't know anything, and I'm not doing anything wrong.

Not that it matters.

I open the door, and Harrison Wang stands there, dressed in a black silk shirt that seems to soak up the surrounding light and shimmer with it.

'Harrison,' I say stupidly. 'Hi.'

'I hope this isn't a bad time.'

'No, it's – it's fine . . .' I smooth my hair with one hand and gesture awkwardly with the other. 'Come in.'

I steer him toward the couch in the main room, grabbing a couple of empty beer bottles that have congregated on the coffee table. 'Espresso?'

'I'm fine, thanks.'

I go make him one anyway. Because that's what you do, to be polite, and I'm trying to figure out how to act like a grown-up.

When I come back in with the espresso, Harrison sits on the couch, staring at the canvases stacked against the wall beneath the skylights.

'This is impressive work,' he says.

'Yeah.' I put the espresso cup on the coffee table in front of him, snatching up a couple of snack-food wrappers and a plate of sesame-seed shells. 'I mean, I don't know anything about art. But Lao Zhang's stuff. I see it, and it . . . it makes me feel something.'

Right now, I feel myself blushing, because I sound like such an idiot.

'Yes,' Harrison agrees. 'In an art form like painting, where seemingly everything has been done before, for the artist to move the viewer really means something.' He squints, as though he's trying to make out fine detail in one of the paintings. 'Plus the theme and the execution are both very sophisticated. And powerful.' He turns back toward me. 'I can understand why you want to protect all of this.'

'Yeah,' I say, since I can't come up with anything else. I sit down in the chair across from the couch.

Harrison sips his espresso. 'I'd already heard about the situation here in Mati Village. Unfortunately, it's complicated.'

'Complicated?'

I hate that word.

'The development project has the support of some powerful people in the government. There's a lot of money involved.'

Not like that's a huge shock. 'But what about that Vice Mayor?' I ask.

I can't remember his name, but he's always talking about how art is this engine for cultural and economic development. Look at 798 – it's a tourist attraction.

'Mati Village has its supporters, it's true. I considered proposing an alternate development plan myself, with a consortium of investors.'

'So maybe there's a chance we could stop it?' I ask.

'It's not clear to me that we should try.'

Now Harrison puts down his espresso and stares at me. 'Which is more important, do you think? The community itself, or its members?'

Another thing I hate. Brain teasers. 'Well, the community is made up of its members,' I say. 'So I don't see how you can separate one from the other.'

'True. But some members are more vital than others. Wouldn't you agree?'

'I guess.'

All of a sudden, I get it.

'That was the trade-off,' I say. 'Lao Zhang for Mati Village.'

'I don't have that kind of power,' Harrison says, with a sad shake of his head.

'But you do have influence.' Even though I don't understand exactly what it is that Harrison does, one thing I know is that he's got a lot of money. And influence is one thing that money can definitely buy.

'So, how'd it go?' I ask. 'You come up with this competing plan, and then you offer to drop it if they leave Lao Zhang alone?'

Harrison says nothing. He stirs his espresso with the little spoon I gave him.

'Where is he?' I ask.

'I have no idea.'

Something else occurs to me. 'But the Uighur. You knew where the Uighur was.'

'The Uighur? What are you talking about?'

Oh, he's a good liar, I have to give it to him. But a little too smooth. No ragged edges around his denials.

'Yeah,' I say. 'The Uighur. Why was I worth more than the Uighur, Harrison?'

'You don't have a very high opinion of yourself, do you?' Harrison says after a moment. He finishes his espresso. 'I came to see if you needed some help moving Lao Zhang's art. I have a truck I can send over and plenty of room in my storage units.'

A lot of stuff goes through my head all at once. Stuff

like: who gets to decide what's more important? what's more valuable? who gets saved, and who doesn't?

Who gets to decide? The person who has the power, that's who.

Beyond that, it's all chance. Or fate. Or God and karma. Who the fuck knows?

'Thanks, Harrison,' I say. 'I could use your help.'

The next day, I'm running around Mati Village, trying to co-ordinate with the truck driver Harrison's hired to move Lao Zhang's stuff, when my phone rings. I'm yelling at the driver, who's overshot the loading dock at the Warehouse, so I kind of juggle the phone and answer it without seeing who's calling me.

'*Wei?*'

'Ellie. It's Trey.'

I stare at the phone, heart pounding.

'Hi, Trey. Can you hang on a second?' Then I yell at the truck driver, 'Pull up here! Just back in! Wait a minute, I'll be right over.'

'Okay, okay!' the driver shouts back.

'Ellie?' I hear Trey's voice come over the cell.

'Sorry. You got me in the middle of something.'

Naturally, he doesn't ask what.

'So . . .' he says, and then there's this silence. 'So I heard you're back in town.'

I'm thinking all kinds of things, but what comes out of my mouth is: 'Yeah. Yeah, I'm back.'

'So . . . so everything's okay?'

I hear this. I open my mouth to say something, but I can't. I'm struck dumb.

Then all at once the words rise up and tumble out.

'Oh, yeah. I'm okay. I'm just fine. Everything's great. What the fuck is wrong with you?'

'Ellie, I just –'

'What did your friends tell you, Trey? What did they tell you about what they did? Did they tell you how they picked me up? What they did to me? Did they talk about that?'

'No!' he says. 'No. They just said . . .' Something stops him. Like the words get tangled up in his throat.

'I told you to not to mess with those guys,' he finally says.

'Right. You did. Because you knew what they'd do. And you just let them, right? You didn't even *try* to help me.'

'Ellie . . .'

He's crying now. I can hear it. Deep, choking sobs. 'I'm sorry,' he manages. 'I didn't . . . I told them . . .'

He can't finish.

'Whatever, Trey,' I say. 'Look, I've got things to do. Why don't you go fuck yourself?'

I hang up on him. It feels good.

That was my revenge, I guess. But I wake up the next morning, and I think, how stupid is this – this mean, trivial payback?

Why not let him go?

So I do. We meet for drinks at a fancy bar in a five-star hotel, just me and him, and I sign the papers. We sit there across from each other at a little round table in a red-lit room while a jazz trio plays standards, the singer going on in her husky alto about love gone wrong, or whatever – isn't that what all of those songs are about? Trey's wearing a sports coat and an open-necked shirt, and he

366

looks so handsome, and I feel it in my gut, everything all at once, how I thought I loved him, how – in spite of everything that had happened, in spite of everything that had gone wrong – I thought we could still have a life together, and then how he betrayed me, how he stabbed me through my soul, and I'm not even sure when that betrayal happened. Maybe the whole thing was spoiled from the beginning.

I'm staring at him, sipping my wine, and it's like something shifts. Like something's pulled away, some lens I'd been seeing him through, and all of a sudden, I see him clearly. He's just this guy. He's not going to save me. He's not going to ruin my life either. That part's pretty much up to me. Or maybe the Suits. But not Trey. He doesn't have that kind of power any more.

'I'm sorry, Ellie,' he keeps saying. 'I'm so sorry.'

I almost ask him, sorry about what? About what you did in the Admin Core? About how you treated me?

That's when it hits me. We did those things together. What he did on his own, to the PUCs, what he let happen there, okay, that's his burden. But the two of us? Our marriage, the life we had? The secrets we kept?

We were in it together all the way.

We have one last blowout at the Warehouse before they knock it down. The musician who lives on Lao Zhang's courtyard spins his new tunes; we have food brought in from the *jiaozi* place, buckets of beer, all kinds of liquor, and hashish from the local Kazak dealer. Various people make attempts at live music, most of which suck, and I find out that Francesca Barrows plays the drums pretty well, and Fuzhen likes to sing pop songs. People get up in front of the mike and drunkenly recite poetry. Overseeing the whole thing, like some mute MC, is a cardboard cutout of Lao Zhang that somebody made and put up on the stage; and when one of the artists asks 'Lao Zhang' to say a few words and sticks the microphone up to the cutout's face, waits a long minute, and then says, 'These are our guiding principles!,' I laugh so hard that I spit out my Yanjing.

Mostly, I stand toward the back and watch. But that's okay. Because standing here, I feel surrounded by something, something good. I feel like I'm part of this. Not that I'm an artist, or anything like that. And I know Mati Village isn't some utopia either. The people here gossip and screw each other and have their little dramas, just like everywhere else I've ever been.

But still, this place, these people, it means something. Even if I'm too plastered to figure out exactly what.

Later, I sit on the sprung couch, nursing a beer, wishing I hadn't joined in the maotai toasts, because that stuff's pretty foul, as befitting something that comes in what looks like a Drano bottle. Eventually I'm joined by Sloppy and Francesca.

'Did you ever talk to Harrison Wang?' Francesca asks.

'Yeah.'

'Did he have any ideas?'

I'm not sure what to say. I settle on: 'Yeah. But it's complicated.'

Francesca snorts. 'Why am I not surprised?'

'It's not like that,' I protest. 'I mean . . . some stuff's more important than buildings.' I'm having trouble remembering exactly what.

Sloppy sits there, tears running down her face. 'I'll miss all of you,' she says.

Oh, yeah. People. That's it.

'We can stay in touch,' I say. 'Hey, we could start a blog. You know? The Mati Village refugee blog.'

I don't think Sloppy understands the word 'refugee,' but she still nods thoughtfully. 'I think blog is a nice idea,' she says.

CHAPTER THIRTY-FOUR

So, I'm pretty sure Harrison's the Monk of the Jade Forest. The Monk fits him. The way the Monk talks – well, types – he sounds like Harrison. Like Cinderfox sounded like Creepy John, when I stop and think about it.

And I think Harrison is Suit #2's asset. Who else could it be? Harrison had access to the Suits' business cards, the ones in my pocket, when I stayed at his place. I guess I should be grateful that he talked to Suit #2 – to Carter – and not Macias. Otherwise . . . otherwise, who knows what might have happened?

Harrison has connections. Has juice: the money and the power. He could horse-trade if anyone could.

But Harrison won't come out and cop to it. Oh, he drops hints now and then, stuff about the nature of power, the tyranny of the State, of corporations when they're essentially arms of the State – or is it the other way around? Fuck me if I can keep that straight.

Mostly he talks about the need for artists, the necessity

for them to create freely, and I think that's what really motivates him.

Or maybe it's just a game. Something to play when he's bored.

There's a lot of stuff I don't know and probably never will.

Here's what I did figure out: it's all insider trading. The powerful making deals with the strong. A bunch of us scrambling for our places, working to get our little piece. A whole lot of folks sliding off the end of the greased ladder.

I keep thinking that someday, something will rise up from that pit at the bottom. Something deep, strong, and full of rage, a tsunami sweeping everything away into a jumble of broken trees and twisted metal and trash and bloated bodies. Then the tide goes out, depositing the rubble where it doesn't belong: boats on top of buildings. Fish in the forest. Up is down, and the underdogs stake their claims. Like what happened in China some sixty years ago.

The problem with revolutions is that eventually the whole fucking thing repeats itself. You know?

I'm having one of those nights. One where I don't go to sleep like I should. I try, but I can't stop thinking about things.

I think about the Uighur a lot. Hashim. I should call him by his name. That's the least I can do, right? It's not like I knew him, but he seemed like a nice guy. And nobody deserves what he probably got.

I don't pray. I don't believe in that any more. But I think about him.

Overall, I'm doing better. I've got this decent apartment

in an older, five-story building in Tuanjiehu – a cute neighborhood close to Sanlitun and the Embassy district in Chaoyang. My apartment's pretty cheap, owned by a pair of retired college teachers who moved to their condo in Miyun Resort Village, and though the building itself isn't anything fancy, they did a nice job remodeling the place inside. I can't complain. I like it, actually. I can go outside, watch the little kids playing at the elementary school down the block, stop in at my local market in the narrow tree-lined lane and buy Yanjing Beer for four yuan. There's a great Xinjiang lamb place close by and one of the best Peking Duck restaurants in all of China just a ten-minute walk away. It's nice here.

But I still have these nights, sometimes, when I think about things. When I try to figure out what happened and why.

The Great Community's no help. Every once in a while, I log on. Type 'Hail, the Great Community!' No one answers. Maybe it's not safe there any more.

I wonder about other people, who else might have been in the Game. Sloppy Song? Her friend Francesca Barrows?

Lucy Wu, I don't think so. My best guess is, she really *is* just a Shanghai art dealer. At least she has this cool gallery near the French Concession, in a rebuilt *shikumen* – the traditional Shanghai apartment building. I've seen the gallery, and it looks pretty cool to me anyway.

I'm guessing that when Lucy found me in Lao Zhang's place that morning, she figured I was the channel to get to his art. She'd met me at the *jiaozi* place, seen Lao Zhang and me together at the Warehouse – with him gone, I was the girlfriend, someone she could either work around or work with.

372

When I ask her about the keys she had to his place, she just giggles.

Oh well. I'm the one with the piece of paper from Lao Zhang, right?

The funny thing is, after all that, and in spite of the fact that she's tiny and gorgeous, I've decided that Lucy Wu is pretty much okay.

We're working together on Lao Zhang's art, Lucy and me. There's a lot of buzz, and the fact that he's disappeared makes it even more intense. Lao Zhang's like this underground figure who everyone's heard of but hardly anyone's seen, and people want to know: is this guy some kind of undiscovered genius? Do I need to get a piece?

We haven't shown his work yet – as Lucy put it, 'Maybe it's too complicated right now.' But we've sold a few paintings, to foreign and local collectors, and so far that's been okay. Lucy takes a percentage. So do I. I'm not getting rich, but I'm making enough to live on. The rest of the profit goes into a trust, a foundation 'to support the arts.' We do charitable work to make it legitimate, art programs for poor migrants' kids, stuff like that.

Harrison helped with that part, with drawing up the papers. 'We'll put in a back door for Jianli,' he explained, 'so that he can claim the majority of the profits, should he want to.'

And I've got my work visa, finally. Harrison set me up with that. I'm the director of the foundation, which is licensed through one of his businesses somehow. I'm not sure how I feel about that either, being in Harrison's pocket, but here I am.

The Chinese government could still decide to boot me

out, to not renew my visa, but they haven't yet, and you know, there's no guarantee of anything.

I study. Read articles. Go to galleries. Ask questions. A lot of the time I just shut the fuck up and listen. I'm in way over my head, but what else is new?

I do my best. Shit comes at you, you handle it. That's what they taught me when I was a medic, and I was pretty good at that job.

A couple days ago, I went out for a walk around the neighborhood. It's fall, the best time of year in Beijing. As ugly as they've made the city in general, there's still something about the air in autumn, how crisp and clean it feels, about the light, the gray-and-red-washed walls against the blue sky, the lengthening shadows in the golden hour.

I was thinking: I wouldn't mind a latte.

So I wandered over to the neighborhood Starbucks. I'd downloaded a new book onto my iPhone; I figured maybe I'd hang out, drink coffee, and read for a while.

I got my latte, sat by the window, and read my book, now and again glancing out at the cyclists passing by beneath the falling leaves.

The book was pretty stupid, so I switched over to a TV show I'd downloaded but hadn't seen yet. It was okay, I guess. I watched for a while, until I finished my latte.

Then I powered down my phone, put it away in my little pack, and stretched out in the chair for a moment.

When I looked up, I saw John standing near the entrance.

This weird combination of feelings rushed over me. My

gut hollowed out. My heart started pounding. I was scared all over again.

But I was glad too.

John approached my table, tentatively, with a hitch in his step, not a limp, more like a hesitation.

'Can I join you?' he asked.

'Yeah. Sure.'

He sat.

I wouldn't call him baby-faced any more. Now I could see what his bones looked like, how big his eyes were in their hollow sockets. There was a scar across his forehead, cutting into one brow.

But he was still wearing that same cheap leather jacket. Either that, or he has a closet full of them.

The T-shirt was different, though. Just a plain black crew-neck.

'I'm glad you're okay,' I said awkwardly.

He nodded. 'Yes. I was in the hospital for a while. But I feel better now.'

We sat there in silence.

'I'm sorry,' I finally said.

I'm not sure why I said it. I was sorry he got hurt, I guess. I was sorry I hadn't tried to do anything. To find out where he was, or what had happened to him. I could have at least tried.

Except, of course, he still kind of scares me.

John managed that squinty-eyed look.

'Ellie,' he said, 'I don't remember what happened. I remember, we get off the train. I remember, we stayed in that place, and there were . . .'

He wrinkled his forehead, seeming to struggle for the word. 'There were those people. Who were on the street.

The, the protesters. And I remember, you and I, we find a car to drive us away.'

He smiled. 'I don't know what happens after that.'

'Some men stopped us on the road. You don't remember that?'

He shook his head.

Lucky John, I thought.

I wondered what I should tell him.

'They beat you up,' I said. 'Some other guys chased them off. Those guys, they –'

'What guys?' he asked urgently. 'Who were they?'

I remembered the white room. I saw it like the wall was right in front of me, the slightly uneven paint, the different subtle shades of white.

It wasn't that bad, I told myself. I'm okay now.

'American guys. They'd been after me. I guess they took you to the hospital.'

He nodded slowly. 'And they let you go,' he said, almost like it was an afterthought.

'Yeah. They let me go.'

He stared at me with those eyes of his, so dark it's hard to see the pupils. 'What did you tell them, Yili?'

I stared back. 'Nothing. I didn't tell them anything.'

'Then why did they let you go?' he asked, sounding genuinely puzzled.

'They got what they needed from somebody else.'

There was a long silence between us.

'They were looking for the Uighur, that's all,' I finally said. 'When they found out where he was, they let me go.'

He frowned. Like he didn't really believe me.

Well, fuck him if he doesn't, I thought.

376

'That story about your sister . . . that was bullshit, right?'

Because if he wanted to play Who's the Big Liar, I was all in.

He drew back: surprised, I guess, that I'd call him on it. 'No. It was the truth.'

'And you don't really work for a joint venture company, do you?'

He looked a little startled. 'I do. Just like I tell you.'

'Bullshit,' I repeated. 'For one thing, you don't dress the part. Where's your designer golf shirt? Where's your man-purse?'

He looked truly confused at that. 'My . . . man . . . ?'

'Never mind.'

I let out a big sigh. I was so tired of this. People lying. Covering up. Not saying who they really are.

'You're some kind of cop. I know you are. What I don't get is how come you haven't started busting people yet. Or maybe you have, and I just don't know about it.'

'No.'

The way he said this, simple and strong, almost made me believe him.

'These people, the Great Community, I believe what they believe. They are my friends,' he said.

'But you still don't know who most of them are in real life, right? Is that why you kept playing?'

I remembered when John carried me into my apartment, when he told Mrs Hua to mind her own business, the cold quality of his anger. I caught a glimpse of that now, and then a flash of hurt, before his self-control returned.

'Yili,' he said, 'things are not always so . . . so straight-forward.'

377

'Oh, yeah? Tell me about it.'

He ducked his head in that awkward, embarrassed way of his.

'There was a guy, this big official, back before Jiang Zemin was Chairman,' he finally said. 'This official, he was called Qiao Shi. He had a lot of jobs, but he was head of Internal Security for a while, so he sees all kind of things. After that, he is in charge of National Peoples' Congress. NPC at this time doesn't really have very much power, it only approves what the central government tells it to. Qiao Shi wants to change this. He talks a lot about reform, about the rule of law. Because he saw before what happens when there is just the Party and no laws can control it.'

Then John shrugged. 'This guy, this official, he lost, I guess you can say. Jiang Zemin doesn't like him. When Jiang Zemin becomes Chairman, Qiao Shi must retire.'

I sat there for a minute. 'So, what's your point?' I asked, though I had a pretty good idea what he was getting at.

'Just that it is hard to change things. And most of us, we can only do some small thing.'

He looked up at me. There was something pleading in his look.

'But maybe if enough of us try. If we can connect, all our small things together.'

He reached out his hand, like he was going to take mine, but he didn't. He put his hand on the table. I could see the tendons and muscles tense, then relax.

'This is what matters,' he said. 'That we can connect.'

He looked away. That was as much as he was going to give me.

Then it hit me, something that was beyond a thought; it was something I felt, like a blow.

Maybe I was wrong about Harrison. Maybe John was the guy who had something to trade. He could have seen the Suits' business cards that night in my apartment. The Chinese government's not crazy about Uighur activists, after all, and neither are a lot of Chinese people. Why not give Hashim to the Americans? Sure, China and America fight over all kinds of things in public, but who knows what kind of cooperation goes on behind closed doors? Who knows what they might be trading?

And John – wouldn't he have picked me over Hashim? I have a feeling he would have.

We sat there for a few more minutes, until it started to feel way too uncomfortable.

'I should go,' John said. 'I have a meeting. For my company.'

He rose slowly. 'Maybe I see you again, Ellie.'

I stood up too. 'Maybe.'

I wouldn't be surprised.

'Hey,' I said, as he started to turn away. 'I'll tell you what I do believe.'

He stopped.

'The part about your fiancée. She really is a bitch. Right?'

He smiled. 'Yes. She really is.'

I haven't seen John since then, but it won't exactly be a shock if he turns up again. Maybe it's true what he said, about the *hong xian*, the red thread of fate that connects certain people together, that tangles but doesn't break.

Or maybe he's this creepy stalker guy, and you know how hard it is to get rid of people like that.

It's a cold, rainy night, and I'm hanging out in my apartment, checking my e-mail and surfing the Web.

These days I use a VPN, a virtual private network, that lets me bypass the Great Firewall and surf anonymously. When I'm at a Net bar, I use a little flash drive with a similar program, like what Chuckie gave me before. I've learned a little since then. I don't take any chances.

Nothing's perfect, of course. The government comes up with new ways to spy and to censor, choke points along the Cisco routers; the privacy folks circumvent them.

I'm not sure who's winning.

I read an e-mail from my mom, skimming the part comparing cell phones to Bibles –'We wouldn't have to worry about being disconnected, because Jesus already paid the bill!'

'Thank you for my new water heater!' she writes. I sent her some money this month, for her birthday. I had a little extra, thanks to a painting we sold for a particularly good price. 'Do you think you'll be making a trip home soon? I miss you. Love, Mom.'

'I'll try,' I write back. 'I'll let you know.'

It all depends. Assuming we can get some of Lao Zhang's paintings out of China, Lucy knows a gallery in Los Angeles that wants to exhibit them. That could be good for Lao Zhang. Good for us.

I'm not sure how I feel about going home, on my own, without Trey. But if I do, at least I can tell myself I'm not a total fuckup. I'm doing something now. At least I'm trying to.

I'm not hurting anybody; I'm not helping anyone hurt anybody. I'm not participating in anything that does.

First, do no harm. I'll start from there.

I visit the 'Leaving Mati' blog. Francesca and Sloppy set it up, after Sloppy's studio got destroyed and she moved to a little town near Mutianyu Great Wall. The blog's in English, because the government doesn't watch English-language blogs as closely as Chinese ones, and, even if they did, there's nothing subversive or political about it. It's just a place where Mati Village artists can post about what they're doing now, their art, their upcoming shows, their new lives.

This big company bought six of my paintings. I've gone back to Hubei. I have a new daughter. We're having a party, please come!

It's just people talking to each other, right? What could be subversive about that?

I start to read the latest posts, but I get distracted by a new batch of e-mail. One from Palaver and Madrid, who have a new baby, thanks to the help of a gay male friend. Another from my mom, about how chocolate is better than men (though she's pretty happy with her new boyfriend).

One e-mail in particular catches my eye. From 'Monastery Pig.'

I don't know that handle, but my heart starts beating a little faster when I see it. In Chinese tradition, monks who live in monasteries are vegetarians, so a 'monastery pig' is a happy pig, a pig who's found himself a safe haven.

And 'pig' is another way of saying 'boar.'

The subject is: 'Invitation to An Opening.'

Inside, it looks like spam for a stock offering. Typical stuff: 'This is our Pick of the Year! We don't see this slowing down! We know many of you like momentum! This is a must-watch! Buy aggressively!'

Right in the middle, there's a hot link.

Maybe it's spam. Maybe it's just a weird coincidence about the handle.

I click on the link.

It takes a while to load. Maybe I'm being shuffled from proxy to proxy to get to it.

When it does load, it's like I'm inside a painting. A seaside landscape, with rolling waves and sand blowing across the dunes that drift down to the water's edge. I say it's like a painting because, though I've seen a lot of fancy computer graphics and game environments, I've never seen one quite like this: soft around the edges, with brushstrokes here and there, but somehow more vivid than most. More real.

It's peaceful. No stupid soundtrack. No shrieking demons or aggressive swordsmen.

No other players, not that I can see. Just a generic female avatar dressed in casual clothes.

That must be me.

I walk along the beach. Seagulls wheel above me. A dog dashes along the shore, splashing water from an incoming wave.

Here's something funny: a giant Mao statue, bleached by the sun, half-buried in the sand.

A little further along, a faded pink Cadillac, planted fins-up.

I see a path that leads up a hill, toward the interior. I turn up it. There's a little building up ahead of me. Plain. White tile. With red Chinese characters that say 'Fanguan.'

'Restaurant.'

I go inside.

It looks familiar. White plastic tables. Fading posters

on the wall for the Beijing Great Olympics. A little shrine to Buddha. But it's empty. No customers. No waitresses. Only me.

I sit. I wait a while.

A man walks in. Stocky. With a goatee and a beanie.

A text box appears.

'Glad you made it.'

He sits down across from me.

'Glad to be here,' I type. I'm not sure what else to say. I'm not sure what's safe. I'm not even sure if it's him. How can I be? He's an avatar on a computer. He could be anyone.

Except . . . this place . . . this landscape . . . it doesn't just look like a painting. It looks like one of his.

'What do you like to eat?' he asks. 'Not much on the menu yet. Still building this place. But I have two things you like.'

I think for a moment.

'Jiaozi,' I type. 'And Yanjing Beer.'

A smile icon appears in the text box above the avatar.

'That's what's on the menu.'

Dumplings and beer appear on the table. We sit.

'So,' I type, and then I don't know what to say.

'The Game,' I finally ask. 'What was it for?'

'To go on quests. Kill dragons.' I imagine him chuckling in the pause that follows.

'To help friends,' he eventually continues.

'Your friend.' I won't type his name, not now, not even here. 'Your friend of a friend. He's not okay.'

A longer pause. 'I know.'

'I'm sorry.'

'Not your fault.'

I'm not so sure about that. It seems like my fault, somehow.

'Where are you?' I ask. 'Are you okay?'

'I'm in a good place. Safe. But you?'

'I'm good.'

'I hear you had problems.'

I hesitate. 'A few. But I'm okay now.'

Our avatars stare at each other across a white table heaped with virtual dumplings and beer.

'I thought I was helping you,' he says. 'I thought you need something to do. I did not think you would have trouble with your own people. I hope you can forgive me.'

'They're not my people,' I type, before I can really think about it.

But that's not really true. I brought them to Mati Village, didn't I? Like I was carrying some disease.

That's what it feels like, anyway.

'There's things I never told you,' I say. 'Things I did before.'

The words appear over his head: 'Not important. I know what you do now.'

I think about it. Had I balanced things, somehow? Was it enough?

Maybe it never is. What's done is done, and I can't take it back.

But maybe that's not the point.

'You're right,' I type. 'I needed something to do.'

'Are you sure?'

'I'm sure.'

'I think it's time to end the Game,' Lao Zhang says. 'To start something new.'

384

He stands up. 'Do you want to see?'

'Yes,' I say.

I follow him outside. 'I want to build a lot more,' he explains. 'Now I work on this house.'

We walk up a winding path that roughly follows the edge of a cliff, overlooking the ocean.

A sleeping Chairman Mao with the proportions of a baby drifts by on a pillow of clouds.

Here's the house, against a backdrop of twisted pines.

It looks more Japanese than Chinese, with a wood deck that wraps all the way around, huge open windows, rounded gray stones.

Here's the dog from the beach, a big dog with three legs. It barks, then halts, wagging its tail, pink tongue hanging out of its mouth.

A small orange cat sleeps curled up on the stoop. As we approach, it stands, stretches, and sits on its haunches. I hear faint purring as we cross the threshold.

I still have the portrait Lao Zhang did of me. Harrison wants to buy it, but I'm not sure I want to sell. It's not mine, of course, but it's *me*. The painting sits, safely wrapped, in the small bedroom closet of my apartment. I haven't figured out where to hang it. My apartment is small, and I don't have a lot of wall space.

Here, in Lao Zhang's world, the living room is big and empty, filled with light. The beams are polished, dark wood, so finely rendered that you can see the knots and whorls of grain.

'I need to make some furniture still,' he says. 'And make more rooms.'

'It's beautiful,' I type.

But it isn't real.

'I guess you can't come back to Beijing,' I say.

'Not right now. But the situation will change. It always does.'

I can't nod, seeing as how I'm just an avatar. 'I understand,' I type.

'I invite more people here in the future,' Lao Zhang says. 'Build more houses. Create a place for all of us. But this one house is for you. Come back any time. I will be here.'

It's not what I want. Not what I'd choose. But if we can talk, if we can connect, that means something, right?

Maybe it's real enough, for now.

I sit in my cozy Beijing apartment, listening to the rain pounding on the balcony, the fresh ozone scent drifting in through the window I have cracked open, staring at a computer screen, at the view of a virtual house overlooking a virtual sea, my good friend standing next to me.

'Thank you,' I say. 'I'd like that.'

ACKNOWLEDGEMENTS

To everyone at Soho Press, with particular thanks to Laura Hruska and to Katie Herman, whose attention to both the big picture and the tiniest details blows me away.

To my parents, Carol, Bill, Ray, and Gayle, and my family, with a special shout-out to my mom, Carol, whose research assistance was invaluable.

To my friends for putting up with my craziness, especially beta readers Billy Brackenridge, Nikki Corda, Christy Gerhart, and Jenny Brown; Pilar Perez, Anna Chi, Kathleen Cairns, and Ebbins Harris for their all-around support, Jim Bickhart for the margaritas, and Mimi Freedman and Jon Hofferman for Buffy nights.

My China buddies, in particular Richard Burger, Fuzhen Si, and Shanghai Slim.

The Writing Wombats, whose camaraderie and humor have brightened my days for over two years now. I must mention Ken Coffman, Sherrie Super, Judi Fennell, Pat Shaw, Beth Hill, Jamie Chapman, and Dale Cozort in particular, for their very concrete help and encouragement.

T. Jefferson Parker, who taught me something about the first fifty pages.

Kerrin Hands, for making the book look great, Anne Fishbein, for making me look good, and Ryan McLaughlin for the awesome website.

The Lurking Novelists, who have been with me every step of the way – Dana Fredsti, Bryn Greenwood, Elizabeth Loupas, Maire Donivan, Maureen Zogg, and our newbie, Heather. You guys are beyond awesome. I can't wait to see every one of you in print.

And finally, Nathan Bransford, whose hard work, editorial eye, patience and constant good cheer made this debut possible. It would not have happened without you.

Read on for an exclusive preview of
Lisa Brackman's next thriller

Day of the Dead

CHAPTER ONE

Michelle dropped the sarong she'd started to tie around her waist onto her lounge chair. Nobody cared what her thighs looked like.

Sand burned the soles of her feet as she walked down to the water. Look at these people, she thought. Foreigners, mostly. Like her. Older, a lot of them. Sagging, leathered skin, the ones who'd been here awhile. Pale tourists, big-bellied, pink-faced, glowing with sunburn. A family of locals – Mexicans anyway, who knew if they were really from here? Dark, short, and blocky, eating shrimp on a stick from the grill down the beach, giant bottles of Coke tucked in a Styrofoam cooler.

Out of shape. Lumpy. Flabby. Aging.

Nobody cares.

And her thighs weren't bad, anyway.

She stood at the water's edge, watching the rainbow parasail from the real-estate company lift a middle-aged woman into the soft blue sky, the motorboat gunning its engine and heading out into the bay, avoiding the banana boat undulating up and down as it hauled a load of college kids south toward Los Arcos. She watched them gripping the yellow tube with their knees, shrieking with laughter, several clutching beers, tanned and young and healthy.

They'd drink until they puked, screw each other till they passed out, go home and post about their awesome vacation on their Facebook pages.

She waded into the water until it was up to her hips. Warm as a bath, but the surf was pounding. She stood there trying to resist the pull as the receding waves sucked the sand out from under her feet.

After a while she'd had enough and went back to her lounger beneath the *palapa*.

She tried to read her book. It was about a woman whose marriage had broken up, and she'd learned to bake bread. Bread and muffins. After about thirty pages, Michelle was willing to bet that the heroine would end up with the overly educated woodworker and not the stressed-out options trader.

'Ma'am? Can I get you something? Something to drink?'

The hotel waiter, dressed in a white guayabera and smudged white pants, stood above her, round, sweating, tray in hand. Nutbrown, gray-haired, creases marking his face like wrinkles in a crumpled shirt.

She thought about it. 'A margarita, please.'

Why not? She didn't need to be sober to follow this plot.

They'd already paid for the vacation. It still seemed like an extravagance. She and Tom were going to go together. A getaway. A celebration, he'd said.

She wondered what it was that he'd wanted to celebrate.

She must have fallen asleep for a while. That was sort of the point with these vacations. You partied at night. Got up earlier than you'd like. Grabbed your *palapa* while the sun was still low behind the eastern mountains, spread out your towel on your blue canvas chair, put on your sunblock, found your place in your novel. First cocktail at lunch, to wash down the greasy quesadillas brought out to you on a paper plate. Try to ignore the vendors selling jewelry, blankets, offering to braid your hair, massage your feet. At some point you'd close your eyes, tired as they were from reading in the shaded sunlight, irritated from the sunscreen sweated into them.

When she opened her eyes, it was late afternoon. She'd been dreaming, about something. About being too hot. About . . . what was it about? About somebody breathing in her ear. Leaning over, touching her shoulder. A man, but not Tom. *Didn't you forget?* he'd asked. *Didn't you forget?*

A few clouds had come in, but it was still hot, and the sun glared in her eyes. She blinked a few times. Then something blotted out the light.

A parasail, between the beach and the sun.

It took a moment for her eyes to adjust. The parasail was its own small eclipse, dark against the sun. Now she could see it – the blood-red parachute, white letters glowing.

TOURISM KILLS! they spelled. In English.

Michelle blinked again and stood.

An atypical crowd had gathered on the beach. Elegantly dressed men and women—a wedding party, she thought at first. Waiters rushed to fill shot glasses with tequila. Photographers ringed the group, pointing their cameras at the parasail, which was heading back from the bay.

Now she could see the person in the harness. Even at this distance, he appeared huge, roughly as spherical as a balloon. As he descended, she saw that he wore a three-piece brown tweed suit and a red plaid tie.

She wished she had her camera. But it was locked up in the hotel's safe – too valuable to risk leaving on the beach while she napped or waded.

The parasail crew – tattooed, in surfwear T-shirts and baggy trunks – kicked up sand as they staggered under the parasail rider's weight, trying to guide him to his landing, and for a moment Michelle thought they would all collapse in a heap. But at the last second a third man dressed in a crisp linen suit stepped forward, bracing his hands against the fat man's chest, pedaling backward until at last the body in motion came to rest.

The people in the crowd cheered and raised their glasses in a toast.

'That was different.'

Michelle turned.

The man next to her smiled.

'Yes,' she said. 'What was it, exactly?'

'Arts festival. It's running all this week.'

He was an American, or sounded like one. About her age. Tanned so dark that the creases around his eyes fanned out like tiger stripes.

'Should be interesting,' he said, 'if you like that kind of stuff.'

He wore a pair of baggy swim trunks and a faded batik shirt. Gray flecked his hair and the stubble of his beard, but he was rangy trim. A fit fortyish.

'Do you?' she asked.

'It's kind of fun,' he said with a shrug. 'I mean, art, you hang it on a wall or put it on a pedestal. I'm not sure what this is.'

'Performance,' Michelle murmured.

By now a procession had formed around the fat man: the well-dressed crowd, the photographers, and a group of young musicians wearing matching T-shirts, singing 'Paperback Writer' in perfect harmony. Together they set off down the beach, north toward the pier, laughing, drinking tequila. A brown dog followed in their wake.

'I was going to get a drink,' the man said. 'Would you like to join me?'

His name was Daniel. 'I live here part-time,' he explained. 'Got a condo on Amapas.'

'Are you retired?' she asked.

He drew back, mock offended. 'Wow. I hope I don't look old enough to be retired.'

'Not at all,' she said. 'But you never know what people's situations are.'

'Well, I'm not loaded either,' he said with a grin. 'I'm a pilot. The work is sort of freelance. So I have some flexibility about where I spend my time.'

They sat at a table under a *palapa,* on the sand. The sun wouldn't set for another few hours; the restaurant staff had just begun to bring tables out to the beach for dinner. Michelle expected that the restaurant would not be full, even with the arts festival. Memorial Day weekend was the last gasp of tourist season in Puerto Vallarta, and it was still pretty quiet. Too hot this time of year. The crowds came earlier, for Easter and spring break, and later in the fall, after the rains.

'A pilot. For an airline?'

'No. Private company. We fly Gulfstreams and Citations mostly. Rentals.'

He scooped up guacamole with a chip, spooned salsa on top of that. 'You know, businessmen who can't afford their own but want to impress a client. Rich guys who want to get to a golf course or a football game in a hurry. That kind of thing.'

She nodded and sipped her margarita. They made good ones here. Not too sweet. You could taste the lime. 'Sounds fun,' she said.

He smiled. 'Works for me.'

The sun had moved behind a bank of clouds, illuminating them like a bright bulb in a shaded lamp.

'Check it out,' Daniel said.

She looked where he pointed. A pair of dolphins surfed at the crest of a wave. They leaped above its crest, plunged back into the water, caught the next swell, then shot up again, twisting in mid-air like a pair of dancers.

'Better than SeaWorld.'

She nodded. 'It's beautiful here.'

Daniel leaned back in his chair, took a final sip of his drink. 'How long are you staying?'

'I'm not sure. My flight's on Sunday. I might change it.'

She wasn't sure why she said it. She had no real intention of changing her flight. It was just that when she thought about what was waiting for her in Los Angeles, it was easy to indulge in the fantasy of staying a little longer. Of never going back.

'Nothing pressing back home?'

He was looking at her in that way, sizing her up, what her intentions were, what she might be willing to do.

She shook her head.

'Are *you* retired?'

She laughed briefly. 'I'm between things.'

He didn't ask questions. Michelle wasn't sure how she felt about that. She wasn't ready to talk about any of it, certainly not to a stranger, but on the other hand one does like to be asked.

'This is a good place to be,' he said. 'When you just want to relax and figure things out.'

Maybe that wasn't such a bad answer.

He was a good-looking man, she thought, with sharp cheekbones and a firm jaw, sky-blue eyes that stood out against his black hair and dark tan. The gray in his hair, the crow's-feet around his eyes, made him more attractive. To her anyway.

Otherwise he would have been too perfect.

Men like that could have anyone.

'Another margarita, ma'am? Sir?'

Daniel grinned. 'I'm up for it if you are.'

She hesitated. This was her second of the day, and she hadn't eaten much.

Losing control would be a bad idea.

'How would you feel about dinner?' she asked.

They had another drink so they could watch the sunset, ate some more guacamole to absorb the tequila. 'There's a restaurant not too far from here I like,' Daniel said.

397

'I'm not really dressed.' She'd only put on a gauzy white blouse over her bathing-suit top, wrapped the sarong around her hips.

'What you're wearing is fine,' he said, giving her a quick, appreciative look. 'It's a casual place. Lots of people go there after the beach.'

The restaurant was a few blocks away, on a street that ran up from the beach and bordered a small plaza, where there were a number of restaurants that catered to tourists. Further up the street were shops, mostly clothing stores and handicrafts: Huichol beadwork, hand-tooled leather, embroidered blouses. Michelle had walked up there the day before.

'There's always lines out the door,' Daniel said. 'It's one of the only decent places to get Mexican food around here.'

They waited outside, by the open-air grill, where a woman made tortillas and a man tended meats.

'Really?'

He shrugged. 'Well, I'm sure there are some places the locals go to that I don't know about. Here in Zona Romántica – you can get better Mexican food in Los Angeles.'

Michelle nodded. 'I'm from Los Angeles,' she mentioned.

'Oh, yeah? I love L.A. Where do you live?'

'Brentwood.'

Of course, that wasn't exactly true. The storage space with her things in it was in Torrance.

But she'd lived in Brentwood, before.

'Nice,' Daniel said. 'Good weather, right, that close to the ocean?'

It was hot inside the restaurant, even with the fans, even though the front was open to let in whatever breezes there

398

were. There weren't any. The air was weighted down by heat and humidity, immobile.

Daniel recommended the tortilla soup. They both ordered a bowl. Had another round of margaritas. Mariachis played, whether anyone wanted them to or not.

'Hey, Danny!'

The man who approached their table was soft-featured, in his thirties, wearing Dockers and a polo shirt.

Daniel shifted in his chair. 'Ned, hey.' Something close to a frown creased his forehead.

'Man, I can't believe I ran into you here. I was just, you know, on my way to the restaurant, and I saw you.'

'Yeah, well, we're having dinner,' Daniel said.

Ned shuffled from one foot to the other, rubbed his hands together. 'I don't want to interrupt. But, look, I really need to talk to you. When you have a chance. Are you around, or . . . ?'

'Can you make it to the board meeting? We can talk then.'

'I guess . . . I'll try . . . It's just . . . kind of time-sensitive.' Ned looked around, eyes darting, still rubbing his hands. He reminded Michelle of the tweakers she used to know in high school. 'Hey, you could come by the restaurant tomorrow night. I'll hook you up. We're running some great specials. Surf and turf. Got some good wines in, too.' He finally focused on Michelle. 'You could bring your friend.'

'This is Michelle,' Daniel said. 'From Los Angeles.'

'Oh, cool.' He extended his hand to her. She took it. Sweaty, not surprisingly. 'My place is just down the street. The Lonely Bull.' He smiled at her for a moment and seemed to lose focus. 'Hope you can make it.'

'I don't know, man,' Daniel said. 'I've got some stuff going on. Look, just give me a call tomorrow, okay?'

Ned nodded like a bobblehead doll. 'Okay. Great. I'll call you.'

'The board meeting?' Michelle asked after he'd left. 'Are you in business together?'

Daniel snorted. 'With Ned? No.'

By now their carnitas had arrived, along with another round of margaritas.

I'm getting pretty buzzed, she thought. She no longer cared.

'The board meeting, it's just a bunch of us expats who get together on Fridays, at El Tiburón. We hang out, watch the sunset.' He stared at her. 'Think you'll be around?'

'Maybe,' she murmured. 'Tiburón. Like the town in California?'

'Maybe.' He grinned. 'It's Spanish for "shark".'

By the time they finished eating, it was almost eleven. Not that late, but after all the drinks and a day in the sun Michelle had to step carefully off the high curbs onto the cobblestones. That was the thing here – the curbs were not a uniform height, you couldn't just assume you knew how to judge the distances.

'Whoa!' Daniel said, catching her elbow, steadying her.

Michelle giggled. 'Glad I'm not wearing heels.'

Now they had reached her hotel, bypassing the open-air lobby and entering through the arches that bordered on the wide, cobblestone drive.

'Which way is your room?'

'Through the courtyard, to the right, in the tower overlooking the beach. Watch for the slick terra-cotta tiles, the sand gritting underfoot. Wait for the elevator, and when it doesn't come, climb the stairs to the fourth floor.'

Michelle felt around in her sisal tote bag for her key, found the hard plastic wedge stamped with the room number, the key attached. Her hand closed around it.

She turned, her back to the door.

'Well,' she said.

'Well.'

He leaned down and kissed her. She tasted salt – from the drinks? From the ocean? She leaned into him, let her hand rest above the small of his back. He pressed against her, hard. She wrapped her leg around his, felt his hands on her ass, lifting her up.

'Wait,' she said. She showed him the key.

He grinned. 'I was hoping you'd ask me in.'

The room was stifling. She'd turned the air conditioner off, out of habit. She switched it on, and the unit rattled to life. It smelled musty, like the spoiled damp of an old refrigerator. Still, with the sliding glass doors that led to the balcony left open, you could hear the ocean, catch a whiff of its brine.

Daniel stood and watched her, a dark silhouette.

'Come here,' he said.

By the time they'd made it to the bed, the air conditioner had chilled the room enough that Michelle was grateful for the warm breeze that blew in from the balcony.

'You have a beautiful body,' Daniel said, running a hand lightly over her belly.

'So do you.'

The words sounded stupid as soon as she said them. You don't tell men they're beautiful.

401

Daniel didn't seem to mind. He looked pleased. 'Gotta keep in shape for the things I enjoy.'

He had a nice body, he really did. Lean but not stringy. Energetic. She hadn't been with anybody like him in a long time. Certainly not Tom, and she'd stayed faithful to Tom.

Tom with his big belly, his barrel chest. Twelve years older than her and not exactly a stud.

'Hey,' Daniel said. 'Hey, what is it?'

She was crying, goddamn it. She rarely cried. She hated it.

'Hey.' He smoothed the hair around her face.

He was looking at her now, and she could tell what he was thinking: Great, I'm in bed with a crazy woman.

'Sorry,' she said. 'I'm sorry. Don't . . . It's stupid.'

'Listen, I mean, if you're not into this . . .'

He tried but could not quite keep the irritation from his voice.

'I am. I'm sorry. It's just . . .' She tried to smile. 'I haven't dated in a while. My husband . . .'

'So . . . you're married?' Now the irritation seemed mixed with curiosity.

No disapproval at least. Perhaps a calculation about whether this was worth it.

'No. Not anymore.'

'Oh.' Daniel rolled over onto his side, propped himself up on his elbow. 'Yeah. It's tough getting back into things after you split from somebody you've been with for a long time.'

'My husband died, actually.'

She enjoyed it in a way, getting the reaction, seeing the look on his face, the shock, the embarrassment.

402

'I'm really sorry,' he said.

The way he said it, so simply, made her flush with guilt.

'No, don't be, I really . . .' She wanted to reach out, wanting to touch him, to encourage him, but it felt so awkward, so phony.

'I want to,' she finally said. 'It's just a little hard.'

Daniel extended his hand, rested his palm on her cheek for a moment. 'Look. We both had a lot to drink. This is all kind of intense. Maybe I should just go.'

This time she did reach out. 'No. Stay. If you want.'

They tried again. But the energy that had gotten them into bed was gone now, dissipated, and after a few perfunctory thrusts Daniel stopped and mumbled, 'I'm sorry. I'm really tired.'

'Don't apologize.' She tried to smile. 'You've been great. I haven't.'

'Don't worry about it.'

His face was dark above hers, but she thought his expression was kind.

She kissed him, slowly.

'Mmmm. That was nice,' he said.

After that they both fell asleep, not spooning but close together, Daniel's hand resting on the hollow above her hip.

So many noises here. The familiar: unmuffled motorcycle, snatches of music, pounding surf. The unfamiliar: songbirds singing foreign tunes, parrots squawking, the *toc-toc* cry of geckos.

What woke her?

A muffled thud. A clatter. She blinked her eyes open. Two men, one entering from the balcony, the other crouched over the chair, Daniel's shorts in his hand, her tote bag on the floor by his feet.

'Hey!' Daniel flung the sheet off, bolted out of bed.

Now Michelle saw they wore kerchiefs over the lower halves of their faces. The second pulled something from his pocket, something dark that he gripped in his fist. For a moment Daniel froze as the man took two quick strides to him, raised the hand that clutched the black pistol, and smashed it against his temple.

Daniel crumpled, as surely as if he'd been shot.

It happened so quickly that Michelle didn't scream; instead she gasped and clutched the sheet.

The man with the gun turned to her.

He was close to the bed. She could see that he wore dark clothes, a black T-shirt, jeans, and he took another step toward her. He had on a belt, woven brown and white leather; she could see it clearly in the light that leaked in from the balcony.

The buckle was a gun, and there were letters in the weave. She saw those as he tugged at the tongue of the belt to unbuckle it.

'*¡Pendejo!*' the other man spit, gesturing toward the balcony.

The man with the gun stared at her a moment longer before he turned and followed his companion out the sliding glass door, into the night.

CHAPTER TWO

There was a lot of blood.

Headwounds bleed a lot, Michelle thought vaguely. She'd read that somewhere. Or seen it on television.

It didn't mean that Daniel was dying.

But by this time the blood had covered one side of his face, was dripping onto the tiled floor, and he was unconscious, moaning now and again. Michelle couldn't decide what to do next.

Clothes, she thought, I have to put on some clothes. And I have to call someone. And get a towel, for the blood. Which first?

Phone.

She wasn't sure who to call or how it worked, so she punched 'zero' on the room phone, and finally a woman's voice answered, asking a question. '*A sus órdenes,*' Michelle made out.

'Help . . . I need help . . . in Room 452. I need a doctor.'

'You are having an emergency?'

'Yes. Someone's hurt. They came in, and . . . Please, just send help.'

She grabbed a T-shirt and a pair of shorts, thinking, I'm putting on clothes, and this naked man is bleeding on my floor. I should be doing something for him, but I need to get dressed, don't I? And it took only a minute or two, and by the time someone pounded on the door, she'd crouched down by Daniel, had covered him with a sheet, was pressing a towel to the bleeding gash on his scalp. No one needed to know she'd gotten dressed first.

Two hotel workers had come, men who handled luggage, patrolled the grounds. Seeing Michelle at the door holding a bloody towel, Daniel lying on the floor behind her, one immediately reached for his walkie-talkie.

The first set of police arrived just before the ambulance did.

'He's not my husband,' Michelle tried to explain. 'He's a friend. *Un amigo*.' The blood had soaked the towel, had gotten all over her hand, and she wiped her hand on her shorts.

One of the policemen handed her a fresh towel. White, like the uniform he wore, white polo shirt and cargo shorts, black baseball cap.

The other policeman knelt down next to her. 'Let me help you, señorita,' he said, taking the towel. 'You can rest if you like.'

Suddenly she felt dizzy. 'Thank you,' she said. Somehow she made it to the bed, her hand reaching blindly for the solidity of the mattress. She sat on the edge of the bed, watched the ambulance attendants arrive and tend to Daniel with a minimum of fuss, bandage his head and lift him onto a gurney.

By now he was conscious, somewhat. 'Hey,' he said. 'What . . .?'

'Where are they taking him?' Michelle asked the policeman.

'CMQ Hospital. Don't worry. It's a good place. He'll be fine.'

Two more men arrived. 'Judicial police,' the patrolman explained. 'They can take the statement from you.'

The new policemen wore plainclothes. Polo shirt again and khakis on one, a madras plaid and Dockers on the other, ID and badges hung on lanyards.

One of the ambulance attendants asked her a question. It took a couple of times for her to understand.

'*Su nombre,*' she heard. He pointed at Daniel. *His name.*

'Daniel.'

'The family name?'

Of course she didn't know.

The faces of the ambulance attendant and the policemen stayed studiously blank.

'So he is not your husband,' one of the new policemen stated, the one in khakis. 'Or a boyfriend.'

'No.' Her face flamed red. 'Just a friend.'

His partner lifted Daniel's shorts off the floor, patted the pockets, and retrieved his wallet. The policeman in the khakis gave a little wave to the ambulance attendants, who bundled Daniel out the door.

He was younger than she was, the policeman, in his early thirties, she thought: tall and well-built, with a relaxed, loose way of carrying himself. Something about his accent, the cadence of his speech, was familiar, but she couldn't quite place what it was.

'Can you tell me what happened?' he asked.

There wasn't much to tell, really. She skipped how she and Daniel had met. They'd had dinner. Come back to the hotel. Were sleeping.

'So these men,' he said when she'd finished. 'Anything you can tell me, about how they looked? Were they tall? Short? If we showed you photos, could you identify them?'

She shook her head, 'No. They wore scarves across their faces. They were . . . I don't know.' She tried to picture them, that moment when she saw them entering from the balcony. 'One was skinny. Not very big at all. Short. The other, he wasn't tall either, but he was stocky. Like a wrestler.'

The one who'd approached her bed.

'He had on a belt,' she said suddenly. 'With a buckle shaped like a gun. And there were letters woven in it. ERO.'

'Guerrero?' the policeman asked.

'Maybe. Yes. I think so.'

He nodded. 'Okay,' he said, standing up. 'Sorry this has happened to you and your friend. It's not so common in Vallarta, but it happens. If you give me contact information, I'll let you know if anything comes up.'

'What's Guerrero?' she asked.

'State next door. Lots of thieves come from there.'

The other plainclothes policeman nodded. 'And *narcos*,' he said. 'Always causing problems. Even now in Vallarta.'

After the policemen left, Michelle stayed where she was, sitting on the edge of the bed. Little piles of clothes lay scattered about, like the aftermath of a freeway car wreck. She could see the blood as well, the blood on the tiled floor. She'd gotten blood on her T-shirt and shorts, too.

What was she supposed to do now?

There was a knock on the door.

'Señorita?'

And naturally there was blood on her hands. She almost laughed at that. She hadn't done anything wrong, and she still felt guilty.

'Señorita Mason?' It was a woman's voice. 'Can we come in?'

'Who is it?'

'Claudia, from the front desk.'

She thought she remembered a Claudia, but she couldn't be sure. She got up, went to the door, put on the chain, and cracked it open.

A woman stood there, middle-aged and stout, wearing a blue shift that looked like a nurse's uniform. Michelle recognized her. Behind her was a man she'd seen sitting at a stand resembling a portable bar up at the entrance to the hotel driveway, where taxis dropped off guests.

'We are here to help you,' the woman said.

Michelle nodded. 'Okay.' She undid the chain. 'Thank you.' It made sense, she thought, that they'd send someone. To clean up.

They came in. The man spotted the bloody towel on the floor. He picked it up and put it in a trashbag. He wore latex gloves, like you'd use to do dishes.

Michelle sat back down on the bed. She didn't know what else to do.

The woman immediately squatted by Michelle and covered her hand with her own, which was dry and a little rough.

'This is terrible,' she said, 'and we are so very sorry. These things should not happen in Vallarta.'

'Things like this happen everywhere,' Michelle murmured.

'I think we can move you to another room, right? A better room.'

Michelle thought about it. She stared at the heaps of clothing, the puddle of blood now drying in the refrigerated air.

'Yes,' she said. 'Yes. I don't want to stay in this room anymore.'

They moved her to a suite in a newer wing, one with a separate bedroom and a bar, a wide balcony with wrought-iron furniture. She checked the balcony first thing. It could not be reached through another suite; there was no way to climb up to it that she could see.

After the woman from the front desk and the man from reception moved all her things, hung the clothes that had been in the closet, arranged her toothbrush, cosmetics, and moisturizers on the bathroom counter—after all that had been done, the offer of tea by the hotel staff turned down, Michelle stepped into the shower and stood under the spray for a very long time.

When she got out, she slipped into the silk pajamas she'd packed, the sleeveless top and shorts. She considered having a whiskey from the minibar, thinking it might relax her, might help her sleep, but she already had the beginnings of a headache, so instead she took an Ambien. Tom's prescription. Why let them go to waste?

She climbed into bed, closed her eyes. What replayed in her head was not the robbery, the assault, but Daniel's face, over hers.

Maybe I should have gone to the hospital, Michelle thought as the drug began to take hold. Would that have been the right thing to do? But she barely knew Daniel, after all. Couldn't even ask for him by name.

The breeze from the ocean billowed the gauzy curtains on the balcony. I should get up, she thought. I should close the door. But she was safe here, wasn't she? And she was so tired, and the air smelled good.

She watched the curtains expand and contract, as though they were breathing.

Eventually her breaths slowed down to match, and then she slept.

'We hope you can stay a little longer, Ms. Mason.'

The woman behind the front desk, a different woman from the one last night, briefly rubbed her hands before composing herself. She was trim, perhaps Michelle's age, carefully made-up, with a gold necklace and gold earrings that looked to be a set. Even in the heat of the patio that served as the hotel lobby, only the faintest dewy perspiration dampened her forehead. Michelle was already dripping sweat.

'We are so sorry about what happened. We'd like for you to stay as our guest and enjoy yourself.'

Everyone was being very kind, Michelle thought. Probably they were worried about lawsuits.

The robbers had somehow gained access to a vacant room next to her old room, and climbed from that balcony onto hers. Obviously the security was not what it should have been. If she were in America, she could probably sue.

But in Mexico? How did things work here? Would it be worth it to try?

'Right now I'm scheduled to leave on Sunday,' she said.

'Of course, of course. We could make an arrangement for you to stay here in the future, if you'd like to return. Or if you decide you'd like to stay a little longer, we can do that as well.'

'Thank you,' Michelle said. 'I'll think about it.'

Even with what had happened, it was tempting. Spending time on the beach, drinking margaritas on the hotel's dime, sounded better than her current life in Los Angeles. Living in her sister's spare room. Listening to Maggie's fights with her boyfriend, to her son Ben's tantrums. It was why she'd come on this vacation in the first place, to get away from all that for a few days.

A giggle rose in her throat as she walked up the stairs from the reception area to her tower. Maybe she just wouldn't leave. See how long the hotel's free room was good for. They hadn't really said.

I'll live off room service and peanuts from the minibar, she thought. Let my hair go gray, my thighs get fat, get a couple of cats and a chihuahua. Fill the room with purchases from the beach vendors: loud serapes, wooden dolphin statuettes, flying Batman parachute toys, piled in stacks, all smelling vaguely of cat piss. Take her chihuahua on walks down the Malecón. Maybe one of the cats, too.

She felt, for the first time in months, light. Unencumbered. Free.

The feeling wouldn't last long, probably, but why not enjoy it?

Maybe I'll take some pictures, she thought.

Get out the good camera. Wander around. See what caught her eye. She hadn't done that in ages, hadn't done it here at all, not even a few snapshots with her point-

and-shoot, and she was a pretty decent photographer – or had been, once.

She decided to change out of the sundress and into some shorts and a tanktop. Better for taking photos, in case she needed to climb or crouch.

The hotel people hadn't arranged things the way she would, naturally, and she had to hunt inside the wardrobe to figure out where they'd put her clothes.

Underwear on one shelf. Blouses and skirts neatly hung. Sandals lined in a row.

Including one pair that didn't belong. A pair of Tevas, too big to fit her feet.

Hanging on the closet pole, a faded batik shirt.

Daniel's clothes.

She found the swimming trunks on the shelf with her bathing suit and sarong.

Holding up the trunks, she felt a surge of irritation. How could they have forgotten his clothes? What was she supposed to do with them?

Maybe she'd give them to the beach vendors, to one of the Indian kids peddling garish magnets made in China.

It's not right for me to feel this way, she thought. She should care – shouldn't she? – about what had happened to him. Maybe he'd just needed stitches, maybe he was resting at home right now, or even back on the beach looking for some other tourist to fuck, but what if he'd been badly hurt? A skull fracture, bleeding in the brain, something like that.

But ever since Tom had died, she didn't seem to feel the things she was supposed to feel.

And maybe it wasn't so strange, not wanting to see Daniel, after what had happened. What did she know about him, really? Just that he was attractive, and after she'd taken him to her room, they'd been attacked.

It could have been a lot worse.

She shuddered thinking about it.

Just some clothes that he wasn't going to miss. Not her problem.

There was a sudden burst of music. She flinched, almost flinging Daniel's trunks in the air. What *was* that? Not the stereo from the beach bar, it was definitely inside the room. A rock song, something familiar. She finally recognized it as Offspring's 'Pretty Fly.' Coming from inside her tote bag. It was her iPhone. I've never used that ringtone, she thought. She grabbed it from her bag, hit ANSWER.

'Hey, Danny?' A male voice.

'No,' she said. 'Who's this?'

'Oh. Sorry. Wrong number.' The call ended.

She stared at the phone. The wallpaper on the screen was wrong—an ocean wave rather than the rows of mountains she used. A moment later it rang again. NED G came up as the caller. Same ringtone.

'Hey,' the same male voice said. 'This is Danny's phone, right?'

CHAPTER THREE

She hadn't thought it was Daniel's phone. It looked exactly like her phone. It was a black iPhone, for chrissakes; they all looked pretty much alike.

'Who's this?' she asked again.

'It's Ned. So is Danny around?'

'No. He isn't.'

'Oh.' A nervous chuckle. 'Well, sorry to bug you. But, um . . . is this Danny's number? Maybe my phone's screwed up somehow.'

She stared at the iPhone. 'I don't know,' she said. She didn't know what else to say.

'Okay,' the voice said. 'But you know him, right?'

She hit DISCONNECT before she could even think it through.

When she slid the bar to unlock the phone, ENTER PASSCODE appeared on the screen. She didn't use a passcode.

She had Daniel's phone. So where was hers?

She tossed his phone on the bed. Used the hotel phone to make an international call and dialed her own number, waited for the ringtone she used for unidentified callers, the default marimba.

Nothing.

The call went directly to voice mail, and then she remembered that she'd turned it off to avoid roaming charges. To avoid calls from her attorney. From the creditor who'd somehow found the number.

'Oh, fuck,' she said.

'Leave a message,' her own voice said.

Beep. She hung up.

She tried to remember where she'd put the phone last night. It had been in her tote at the beach, she remembered that.

Where she'd found Daniel's phone.

She checked the tote. Her phone wasn't there.

Then she remembered: the tote, knocked over, its contents spilling out onto the floor. The man, going through Daniel's shorts.

If she had Daniel's phone, maybe Daniel had hers.

The phone rang again, and she lunged for it. 'Hello?'

'Look, I'm really sorry to keep bugging you.' It was the man who'd called before – Ned. 'But if Danny doesn't want to talk to me, could I, like, leave a message or something? It's kind of important.'

Ned. That was the man who'd come up to Daniel in the restaurant the previous night. Tweaker Ned. Daniel didn't seem particularly happy to see him, but that didn't mean they weren't close, close enough at least for Ned to maybe know where Daniel lived.

'Is this Ned?'

'Yeah, it is.' He sounded relieved, like he was happy to have been recognized. 'Who's this?'

'Michelle. We met last night at the restaurant. I'm Daniel's . . . Danny's friend.'

'Great. So can you give Danny a message for me?'

'No, he . . .' How to put it? 'He had a little accident last night. They took him to the hospital . . . He . . .'

'Fuck. Shit. Really? What kind of accident?' It was more than concern in his voice, she thought. There was a distinct note of panic.

'A robbery. I mean, he's okay,' she said, even though she didn't know that for sure, 'but he probably needed some stitches. And I ended up with his phone, and I think he has mine.'

'Oh, man,' Ned said. 'Oh, man.'

'So I was wondering . . . Do you know where he lives? Because I'd like to get this back to him.'

'No. No, I don't know. I always just . . . you know, call him.'

'Great,' Michelle muttered. 'Okay, thanks.'

Well, that was useless, she thought, hitting the red 'disconnect' bar.

She couldn't call Daniel's contacts. Couldn't access any information he might have on the phone.

Maybe she'd try the hospital.

'Discharged,' the woman at the hotel front desk said.

Michelle had asked her if she would make the call, in case the hospital receptionist didn't speak good English.

'So it must not have been serious?'

The woman gave the suggestion of a shrug. 'I think probably not.'

'Did they tell you . . . is there any way I can get a hold of him?'

As soon as she'd said it, she knew it was a waste of time. Hospitals weren't going to give out that kind of information.

'They say if you want, you can leave a note with them. That he must come back in a week or so for removal of the stitches.'

A week. She couldn't wait that long, could she? That would mean staying here till next weekend, at least.

Today was Friday.

Friday was when Daniel's friends met. At El Tiburón. The Shark.

El Tiburón was one of a string of bars just north of the small cement pier at Los Muertos Beach, where people caught fishing charters and the water taxi south to villages like Yelapa. Like most of the beach bars, it had a palm-thatched roof, wood floors, and a wooden rail running along the front, where a few vendors quickly draped their serapes and blouses and sarongs to display to customers before a waiter shooed them away.

We hang out, watch the sunset, Daniel had told her.

One of his friends would know how to find him.

She'd brought his things, on the off-chance that he'd be there. Stopped at one of the little stores by the pier to buy a tote bag to put them in. Her choices were Frida Kahlo and Che Guevara, their faces outlined in black against fluorescent shades of green, red, and yellow, stamped on woven plastic. She chose Che.

Now Michelle stood on the beach boardwalk a few yards from the rail, squinting into the darker bar. That group at the long table, was that the board meeting?

She climbed the three steps that led into the bar, stood

there a moment. It must be that table, she thought. There were about a dozen people there, and she thought they mostly looked like Americans, or maybe Canadians. White people, mainly. One black woman, an Asian man, and a guy who might have been Mexican.

Mostly middle-aged or older. Ordinary.

Certainly not dangerous.

Stupid, she told herself, it was stupid to even think that way. What had happened in the hotel room, that was just a robbery. Not Daniel's fault. Nothing involving any of these people.

'Miss? Would you like a table?'

'I . . . I'm looking for . . . There's a group that meets here?'

The waiter, a young man tanned as dark as strong coffee, gestured at the long table she'd already noted.

She took a tentative step forward, toward the table. Stopped.

This is silly, she thought. Just get it over with.

'Here for the board meeting?'

The man who spoke was hollow-cheeked thin, with a white-stubbled beard. He wore a Clash T-shirt, collarbones protruding above where the neck had been cut out. A blurred tattoo ran down his shoulder, below the ripped-off sleeves.

'I'm . . . a friend of Daniel's. Michelle.'

He might have been in his sixties, but he looked like he'd lived hard. 'I'm Charlie.' He smiled, revealing yellow, channeled teeth, an obvious hole where a tooth should have been and a bridge wasn't. 'Danny's coming tonight?'

'I'm not sure I . . .' She felt herself flush. 'He got hurt last night, and I was wondering if . . .'

'Danny got hurt?' He sounded concerned.

'Is he okay?' a blond woman sitting across from him asked.

'I think so,' Michelle said, and then Charlie patted the empty chair next to him.

'Sorry, my dear, I didn't mean to make you just stand there. You want something to drink?'

She sat. He seemed nice. Harmless at least. And he knew Daniel.

'Thanks. Yes, I would.'

'I wouldn't have the margies here,' he confided. 'They use Sprite.'

'Have the piña colada,' the blond woman said. 'Two for one during happy hour.' She was large, on the far side of middle age, the blond an obvious dye job, wearing a Hawaiian shirt patterned with orange and white hibiscuses.

'Piña colada, I guess.'

'I'm Vicky.'

Her smile, unlike Charlie's, showed gleaming white teeth.

'Smoke?' Charlie asked.

'No thank you.' Not surprising that he smoked. She could smell the cigarettes on him, layer upon layer of smoke on his T-shirt and shorts that no amount of washing would vanquish, on his index finger and thumb as well, browned and baked by burning tobacco.

Their drinks arrived, Michelle's piña coladas coming in two large plastic cups. She sipped one. The rum cut through the sugar with a tang of kerosene.

'What happened to Danny?' Charlie asked.

'It was a robbery.'

'Oh, my God,' Vicky said with a gasp. 'That's terrible!'

420

'He's okay,' Michelle said quickly. The more Vicky reacted, the less she wanted to talk about it. 'But I have some of his things.'

Both Charlie and Vicky had Daniel's cell number, but no landline. No address.

'You know who I bet does?' Vicky said suddenly. 'Gary. He told me he was stopping by tonight, and if he doesn't, I can call him.'

'Great,' Michelle said. Maybe she'd get her phone back. That would make the evening worth it.

'Oh, Gary. He's delightful,' Charlie muttered.

Vicky grabbed her wadded-up napkin and tossed it at him. 'Now, come on,' she said. 'Gary's . . . a good person. He really likes to help people.'

'He's not my sort,' Charlie said in an exaggerated whisper. 'He *golfs*.'

Michelle smiled, for a moment forgetting that she didn't want to be here.

She'd waited for almost an hour, listening to the blur of smalltalk around her and sipping her piña colada, when Vicky said, 'Oh, here's Gary.' She waved in the direction of a man who'd just come in. He wore a neat, expensive Lacoste shirt and khaki shorts, Ray-Bans pushed up onto his forehead.

'Well, hey there, Vicky,' Gary said. He made his way up to the table, next to Michelle, and gave her a long, thorough look. 'I don't believe we've met.'

Michelle wasn't sure how old he was. He had a face that seemed out of balance, his cheeks and lips plump like a baby's, the knowing eyes above peering out from wrinkled, puffy lids, all framed by blond curls.

'Michelle.'

He took her hand, gave it a little squeeze. 'Can I get you a drink, Michelle? You look practically empty.'

He signaled to the waiter before she could say yes or no.

'Michelle's a friend of Danny's,' Vicky said. 'Did you hear . . . ?'

Gary found a chair and pulled it next to Michelle. 'Oh, man, I sure did. So that was you in the hotel with him?'

She'd thought she was beyond embarrassment by now, but she wasn't. She kept her voice level. 'It was.'

'I'll tell you, this town . . .' He shook his head, his bow lips curved in a little smile. 'It's getting kind of crazy here.'

'What happened to Danny?' an older woman a few seats away asked. Karen, or was it Kathy? Michelle had been introduced to too many people to keep track. She was thin, tanned almost as dark as the waiter, her hair in a long gray braid.

'Oh, well, the way I heard it, some *narcos* tried to rob him, cracked him on the head.' Gary spoke loudly, so that others sitting at the table could hear him, even over the blare of Steely Dan playing on the bar's speakers.

'How do you know they were *narcos*?' the older woman asked, but no one paid attention.

'The *narcos* are out of control,' said a middle-aged man sitting two seats over. 'Did you hear about what happened by Bucerías yesterday?'

Everyone started talking at once. A battle with machine guns and grenades, between drug gangs and police. *Narcos* incinerated in cars. Police ambushed at a crossroads in retaliation.

Michelle felt dizzy. She closed her eyes. Clutched her

422

drink. Took another long sip through the plastic straw. Like a pineapple milkshake.

'Fucking Sinaloa cowboys,' someone said. 'They ought to put an electric fence around that whole shithole state. Save us all a lot of trouble.'

'Guerrero,' Michelle said. 'They were from Guerrero.'

'It's just really sad.' Vicky's eyes glistened. 'I hate seeing this kind of thing happen in Vallarta.'

'If this were St. Louis, or New Orleans, no one would even blink,' the older woman said. 'But here in paradise we expect everything to be perfect.'

'Oh, come on,' the Asian man said – American, Michelle amended, from his accent. 'Machine guns? Grenade launchers?'

'I'm talking about a few robberies, not *narcos* killing each other.'

'This town depends on tourists and foreign residents. If crime gets out of control and people stop coming here, everyone is fucked. Right down to your favorite Babaloo on the beach selling shrimp on a stick.'

Michelle's head hurt. Probably from all the cheap rum and sugar. She really wanted to go back to the hotel and sleep, even though the sun had barely set.

'Gary, Vicky tells me you might have Danny's address,' she said.

'I might.'

Gary smiled, pushing his pillowy cheeks up to meet his puffy eyes. Like a debauched cherub, Michelle thought. 'You want to check up on him? See how he's doing?'

'No.' She pushed down the urge to snap off some hostile response. 'I mean yes, but mainly I have some of his things. His phone. And I think he has mine.'

423

'Ah.' From his little smirk, she wondered if he believed her. He appeared to consider. 'Well, I think I can help you out,' he finally said. 'Anybody have a pen?'

Vicky did.

He extracted a business card from his wallet and scribbled on its back. 'This isn't the exact address, but any cab driver will be able to find it.' He held it out to her, fingertips brushing hers when she took it. 'I wouldn't go there tonight, though. I don't think he's home right now. Try him tomorrow.' The smirk again. 'Not too early.'

She glanced at the front of the card. Plain black letters on white linen—nice design and good-quality paper.

Gary Wallace. Trinity Consulting. A cell-phone number. An e-mail address.

'Thanks.' She stood up, unsteady from the rum. 'I'd better get going,' she said. 'Thanks for the drinks.'

Vicky rose with her and gave her a hug. 'This is a good place,' she said in Michelle's ear. 'Don't let what happened spoil Vallarta for you.'

CHAPTER FOUR

'I think you will want to take a cab,' the woman at the front desk told her after looking at the address written on Gary's card. 'It is a ways from here, and up the hill.'

'But close enough to walk?'

'If you like walking.'

Between last night's drinks and the margarita she'd just had at lunch, she could use the walk. 'I do.'

'Maybe two miles.'

I could take some pictures, she thought. Like she'd set out to do yesterday, before Daniel's phone rang.

She went back to her room, grabbed the Che bag with Daniel's clothes, retrieved her Olympus E-3 from the hotel safe, and set off, heading south from the hotel, up a road that curved around the hill.

The heat made it hard to keep walking. It felt like being smothered in a steaming-hot blanket. Sweat dripped into her eyes, smeared her sunglasses when she pushed them onto her head. And trying to take pictures while juggling her purse and the Che bag was awkward. The camera, which usually fit so comfortably in her hand, slipped in her grip.

Nothing was going to go right today.

She tried. Shot a few images. Nothing very interesting. Wrought iron and bougainvillea. Superhero piñatas. She'd seen these photos before, she was certain, and seen them better executed.

Michelle put the camera back in its bag and slung it over her shoulder.

The road ahead was cobblestoned, the banks lining it tangled with browning vegetation that would not green until after the summer rains, with plastic bags and food wrappers caught up in the branches. A lot of the houses looked expensive. New construction clung tenuously to the hillside, as though the flesh of the land had wasted away, leaving skeletal frames stacked unsteadily on top of one another, foundations undermined before they'd even been laid. With enough rain saturating the hill, she could just see one of these buildings giving up, letting go, the cheap rebar popping out of the ground like a rotten tooth.

Halfway up the hill was a little street that branched off the main road at an impossibly steep angle. She followed it, as per Gary's directions. The street led to a cluster of small, multistory buildings – apartments or condominiums.

The one on the right, Gary's note said, light brown with a dark roof.

She looked. She thought the description fit, but blue tarps covered most of the roof, and there was other evidence of ongoing construction or repairs: a small cement mixer and a pile of gravel, a dug-up walkway, a boarded window. No workers. The place looked abandoned.

Daniel's unit was the one on the upper right, according to Gary's note. The tarps extended halfway across what would have been his roof.

Michelle stood there for a moment. She was absurdly sweaty, drenched; her blouse was actually wet, her hair separated into salty tendrils. Really, she wasn't in any condition to see Daniel if he *was* there.

Did she want to see him? She wasn't sure.

Stupid, she told herself. You need your phone. You've come all this way. Say hello, how are you, and good-bye.

She shifted the tote bag on her shoulder and approached the building.

An external staircase with a wrought-iron banister led up to Daniel's unit, crossing the side of the building and leading to a balcony facing the ocean, wide enough to accommodate two chairs and a small glass table.

When she reached the balcony, she could see only a sliver of water above the roof of the building below. Still a nice view, she supposed.

There was no name on the door, no number, no mailbox. She'd have to take Gary's word that this was the right unit. If it wasn't . . . well, this was a small building. Someone would have to know where Daniel lived.

If no one answers, she thought, I'll leave the bag by the door with a note. Take his phone back to the hotel, and he can pick it up there.

Heart pounding, she knocked on the door.

Which swung open. About six inches before the rusting hinges slowed it to a halt.

Michelle hesitated at the threshold.

'Daniel?' she called out.

She heard something from within. Not a person. She couldn't make it out at first. A sort of hum.

A fly flew out the door, bumping into her shoulder.

I have to look, she told herself. I have to look.

She pushed the door further open.

It was dim inside, the curtains drawn, and hot. The smell, the flies – for that was the hum she'd heard, the buzzing of flies – hit her at once, and she couldn't entirely sort out one thing from the other – the darkness, the closed heat, the smell: a sweetish rot. She fumbled for a light switch, thinking there must be one, but there wasn't, not by the door at least.

Her eyes adjusted. It wasn't really dark. There was enough light seeping through the curtains, from the open door.

The living room. This was the living room. It was simple, hardly anything in it. A couch. A chair. A television. A coffee table.

On the coffee table was something dark, an oval shape with protrusions she couldn't make out. The thing almost seemed to shimmer, as though its lines were mutable, fluid, shifting ever so slightly.

She approached the table, and a cloud of flies rose from the object.

A head.

She shrieked, batting away the flies, one of them hitting her lip, another, her eyelid, her ear. She thought she might have inhaled them, and she swatted at them and retched a little, then finally stood still. She looked again.

It was a pig's head. A pig's head, sitting on the coffee table. On top of a *Time* magazine, next to an empty beer bottle. Covered with flies. Maggots, too, little white filaments that pulsed and contracted as they burrowed into the rotting flesh.

For a moment she could only stand there. She felt nothing at first. How was one supposed to regard this? It didn't make sense.

Something prickled the skin of her forearm. She looked down.

A fly, rubbing its legs together.

Get out, she thought. Just get out.

She took a few steps back, toward the door, toward air and light, stumbling a bit, the back of her hand striking the doorknob. She clutched at it to steady herself. Leaned there against the wall, hand on doorknob, until her heart slowed and she could think again.

What did it mean? Why would someone do this?

Maybe she should call the police. She wondered how you did that here. Was it 911? Or something else?

But what would she tell them? That she'd found a pig's head in an empty apartment?

There was no one in the apartment. She was certain. How could you stand to be in there with a rotting carcass on the table? There was no movement, no sound other than the flies.

Then she thought maybe there *was* someone, unconscious or dead.

Don't be stupid, she told herself, but the idea burrowed itself into her head, and she had to be sure.

The apartment had a kitchenette, separated from the living room by a bar counter, and a short hall with three doors opening off it. A bathroom – blue tiles, plastic shower curtain. A toothbrush, some toothpaste, and a few sundries. Nothing much. Some curly dark hair in the sink.

The door next to that opened onto an odd little room – a bonus room, she supposed you'd call it – with a small barred window high up a whitewashed wall. You could put a daybed in here if you had guests, Michelle thought, but there was no furniture, just a workout bench, some barbells, a bag of golf clubs, and what looked like snorkeling equipment in a couple of crates beneath the window.

On the other side of the hall was the main bedroom.

No body on the bed. Michelle almost laughed. Of course there wouldn't be. The bed was big, a king. Well, Daniel probably had his share of overnight guests, judging from her encounter with him – though anyone who didn't know her well could say the same of her based on that night, and that wasn't how she was, not how she'd been for a long time, anyway.

Don't be so quick to judge, she told herself.

But it was hard not to wonder. The apartment – the condominium – was modest. Anonymous, almost. No paintings on the walls. Hardly any books. Nothing personal at all. Not much different from her room at the hotel.

This must just be a vacation home for Daniel, Michelle thought. Not the place where he actually *lived*.

Back in the living room, the flies had regrouped on the pig head.

Just leave, she told herself. It's not your problem, and you have a plane to catch tomorrow.

But if it was something criminal . . . People knew she planned to come here. Gary knew, and Vicky and Charlie. If she just left, would that implicate her somehow?

She felt the camera tucked against her side as the thought occurred to her.

I should take pictures.

Just to document it. She could decide later whether she needed to show the photos to anyone. But at least she'd have proof of what she saw. Just in case there were any questions.

She hadn't intended to get artsy, only snap off a few clear shots, but as she focused on the pig's snout, a part of her noted that it was a compelling image, with the flies around its eye sockets, the beer bottle next to it, the television in the background. As bland as the room was, the pig's head was the only thing that really drew your eye.

Still Life with Pig Head and Beer Bottle, Michelle thought, adjusting the depth of field, taking another shot, then the angle, shooting again. She almost laughed. All this time in Puerto Vallarta, and she'd finally found a good picture.

'What . . .?'

She dropped the camera against her chest.

'What the *fuck*?'

Daniel stood there in the doorway.

'I . . .'

In two strides he'd crossed to the coffee table. 'What the *fuck* is this?'

His fingers dug into her arm, just beneath her bicep. 'You . . . Who told you to do this?'

'What are you talking about?'

She stared at his face: rigid and white with anger.

'I have some of your things,' she said. 'I just came here and saw this. I thought . . .'

'Who told you where I live?'

'Gary,' she said. 'Please let go of me.'

'Gary?' He released her arm with a jerk. 'How do you know Gary?'

431

'I met him at the Tiburón,' Michelle said. 'I didn't know how to get a hold of you. Gary gave me your address.'

'Why didn't you just call?' The anger had not diminished, only retreated.

'I have your phone.' She started to reach into her purse, and instantly he tensed again, not with anger this time but something cold and predatory.

She froze. God, did he think she had a gun?

'Check yours,' she said. 'I think it's mine.'

He reached into the pocket of his cargo shorts and pulled out an iPhone. Black. He powered it up. 'Shit,' he said after a moment. 'It . . . it was off.'

'For two days?'

'I wanted to get some rest and not have people fucking calling me.'

'So can we trade phones now?' She felt a rush of anger. 'You're not going to . . . to attack me?'

'Sorry. I'm . . .' He lifted his hand to his forehead, winced. His head was shaved where he'd been cut, a patch between crown and temple covered with a square of gauze. 'Fucking Gary.' He attempted a smile. 'This is probably his idea of a joke.'

'A joke?' The buzzing of the flies, the smell of rot, the close, shut-in heat of the apartment made her suddenly dizzy. 'I need some air.'

She pushed past Daniel and sat down on one of the chairs on the balcony, let her head fall into her hands.

'You okay?'

'Fine.' She raised her head. 'What kind of joke is that?'

'A stupid one.' Daniel sat down in the chair next to her. 'He knew I checked into a hotel for a few days. Air conditioner's busted here, and I felt pretty lousy. Figured I'd let somebody bring me food and make my bed.'

There was something he wasn't saying, something that didn't fit, but Michelle couldn't think of what it was.

'You want a beer? I think there's a couple cold ones in the fridge.'

He sounded friendly enough, but the way he looked at her, studying her face – was that concern or something else?

'That's okay. I think I'd better go.'

'No, listen, stay a minute. You had a shock. Let me get you a beer.'

He got up before she could object.

By the time Daniel had returned with the beers, bottles already sweating in the heat, she'd figured it out. 'Why me?'

'Huh?' Daniel handed her a bottle. Bohemia. She'd had that a few times in Los Angeles.

'If he was playing a joke on you, why did he send *me* up here to find it?'

'He's an asshole.'

'He doesn't even know me.'

'Guess he thought it would be funny,' Daniel muttered.

The sun was striking the balcony now, the light glaring. He squinted for a moment and put on his sunglasses, which had been propped up on his head. Serengetis, she thought.

Michelle rested the beer on her cheek for a moment. The chill felt even better than drinking it.

'So, the pictures,' Daniel said. He was smiling, trying to keep his voice friendly. 'Why were you taking pictures of that thing?'

433

'I thought there should be a record of it. In case someone threw it away.'

'Are you a photographer or something?'

She shook her head. 'It's just a hobby.'

They sat in silence for a while. What else was there to say?

'I should go,' Michelle said. She reached into her purse and got out his phone. He retrieved hers from his pocket.

'Let me get you a cab.'

'You don't need to.'

'I want to.' He smiled again. Maybe it was genuine this time. 'Look, I'm really sorry about how I acted just now. It was just . . . kind of a shock, finding you and *that* in my place, and . . . I'm still a little jumpy over everything. You know?'

She supposed she did. 'Don't worry about it.'

He walked her through the apartment, past the pig's head.

'Let me buy you dinner,' he said suddenly. 'You went to a lot of trouble, and I didn't exactly thank you for it.'

'Thanks, but . . . I'm leaving tomorrow, and I need some time to pack.'

It was a lame excuse, and he had to know it, but he couldn't really want to have dinner with her after everything that had happened, could he? It was probably just a belated courtesy on his part, and she wasn't interested.

He was a nice-looking man, and maybe none of this was his fault, but she'd had enough. Enough of him, enough of his creepy friends and their sick jokes. Enough of this place.

It was time to go home.

434

'Well, if you change your mind . . .' He stared at her, eyes hidden by his sunglasses.

'I have your number,' she said.

She didn't, but he didn't need to know that.

He still looked pale, she thought. Behind him the pig's head pulsed with flies. 'Do you . . . need some help with that?' she asked reluctantly.

'Thanks. That's . . . Thanks.' He smiled again, a real one. 'If you could, maybe just hold the bag?'

Daniel put on a pair of rubber gloves he had stashed under the kitchen sink, and Michelle held the garbage bag. He picked up the pig's head, holding it as far away from his body as possible. Michelle did the same with the garbage bag.

Even after they twisted the bag shut, she could hear the buzzing of trapped flies.

Killer Reads.com

The one-stop shop for the best in crime and thriller fiction

Be the first to get your hands on the **latest releases, exclusive interviews** and **sneak previews** from your favourite authors.

Browse the site and sign up to the newsletter for our pick of the **hottest** articles as well as a chance to **win** our monthly competition!

Writing so good it's criminal